The Complete Lythande

D0760644

Marion Zimmer Bradley

Edited by Elisabeth Waters

ISBN: 1-938185-11-0
ISBN-13: 978-1-938185-11-3

Trade Paperback Edition

November 5, 2013

A Publication of
The Marion Zimmer Bradley Literary Works Trust
PO Box 193473
San Francisco, CA 94119-3473

www.mzbworks.com

TABLE OF CONTENTS

INTRODUCTION

You say this name is new to you? that you have not heard of this tall, mysterious figure whose forehead bears the Blue Star, who delights one and all with music and then terrifies with magic? Then pull up a bench and listen, and you shall be enlightened. But be prepared to travel, for Lythande is a powerful magician and is not confined to one world—or even one universe...

As with all things worth learning, one must start at the beginning. Secrets will be revealed, truths told and lies spun (and who can tell the one from the other?), promises fulfilled and hopes destroyed, lessons received and skills tested—all in their proper time. For now, hear of one who would be known as Lythande, who wished to learn the secrets of Creation and discovered, like all students throughout history, that if you truly want an education, you must pay the price.

THE SECRET OF THE BLUE STAR
Marion Zimmer Bradley

On a night in Sanctuary, when the streets bore a false glamour in the silver glow of fall moon, so that every ruin seemed an enchanted tower and every dark street and square an island of mystery, the mercenary-magician Lythande sallied forth to seek adventure.

Lythande had but recently returned—if the mysterious comings and goings of a magician can be called by so prosaic a name—from guarding a caravan across the Grey Wastes to Twarid. Somewhere in the Wastes, a gaggle of desert rats—two-legged rats with poisoned steel teeth—had set upon the caravan, not knowing it was guarded by magic, and had found themselves fighting skeletons that howled and fought with eyes of flame; and at their center a tall magician with a blue star between blazing eyes, a star that shot lightnings of a cold and paralyzing flame. So the desert rats ran, and never stopped running until they reached Aurvesh, and the tales they told did Lythande no harm except in the ears of the pious.

And so there was gold in the pockets of the long, dark magician's robe, or perhaps concealed in whatever dwelling sheltered Lythande.

For at the end, the caravan master had been almost more afraid of Lythande than he was of the bandits, a situation which added to the generosity with which he rewarded the magician, According to custom, Lythande neither smiled nor frowned, but remarked, days later, to Myrtis, the proprietor of the Aphrodisia House in the Street of Red Lanterns, that sorcery, while a useful skill and filled with many aesthetic delights for the contemplation of the philosopher, in itself puts no beans on the table.

A curious remark, that. Myrtis pondered, putting away the ounce of gold Lythande had bestowed upon her in consideration of a secret which lay many years behind them both. Curious that Lythande should speak of beans on the table, when no one but herself had ever seen a bite of food or a drop of drink pass the magician's lips since the blue star had adorned that high and narrow brow. Nor had any woman in the Quarter ever been able to boast that a great magician had paid for her favors, or been able to imagine how such a magician behaved in that situation when all men were alike reduced to flesh and blood.

Perhaps Myrtis could have told if she would; some of her girls thought so, when, as sometimes happened, Lythande came to the Aphrodisia House and was closeted long with its owner; even, on rare intervals, for an entire night. It was said, of Lythande, that the Aphrodisia House itself had been the magician's gift to Myrtis, after a famous adventure still whispered in the bazaar, involving an evil wizard, two horse-traders, a caravan master, and a few assorted toughs who had prided themselves upon never giving gold for any woman and thought it funny to cheat an honest working woman. None of them had ever showed their faces—what was left of them—in Sanctuary again, and Myrtis boasted that she need never again sweat to earn her living, and never again entertain a man, but would claim her Madam's privilege of a solitary bed.

And then, too, the girls thought, a magician of Lythande's stature could have claimed the most beautiful women from Sanctuary to the mountains beyond Ilsig; not courtesans alone, but princesses and noble women and priestesses would have been for Lythande's taking. Myrtis had doubtless been beautiful in her youth, and certainly she boasted enough of the princes and wizards and travelers who had paid great sums for her love. She was beautiful still (and of course there were those who said that Lythande did not pay her, but that, on the contrary, Myrtis paid the magician great sums to maintain her aging beauty with strong magic) but her hair had gone grey and she no longer troubled to dye it with henna or goldenwash from Tyrisis-beyond-the-sea.

But if Myrtis were not the woman who knew how Lythande behaved in that most elemental of situations, then there was no woman in Sanctuary who could say. Rumor said also that Lythande called up female demons from the Grey Wastes, to couple in lechery, and certainly Lythande was neither the first nor the last magician of whom that could be said.

But on this night Lythande sought neither food nor drink nor the delights of amorous entertainment; although Lythande was a great frequenter of taverns, no man had ever yet seen a drop of ale or mead or fire-drink pass the barrier of the magician's lips. Lythande walked along the far edge of the bazaar, skirting the old rim of the governor's palace, keeping to the shadows in defiance of footpads and cutpurses, that love for shadows which made the folk of the city say that Lythande could appear and disappear into thin air.

Tall and thin, Lythande, above the height of a tall man, lean to emaciation, with the blue star-shaped tattoo of the magician-adept above thin, arching eyebrows; wearing a long, hooded robe which melted into the shadows. Clean-shaven, the face of Lythande, or beardless—none had come close enough, in living memory, to say whether this was the whim of an effeminate or the hairlessness of a freak. The hair beneath the hood was as long and luxuriant as a woman's, but greying, as no woman in this city of harlots would have allowed it to do.

Striding quickly along a shadowed wall, Lythande stepped through an open door, over which the sandal of Thufir, god of pilgrims, had been nailed up for luck; but the footsteps were so soft, and the hooded robe blended so well into the shadows, that eyewitnesses would later swear, truthfully, that they had seen Lythande appear from the air, protected by sorceries, or by a cloak of invisibility.

Around the hearthfire, a group of men were banging their mugs together noisily to the sound of a rowdy drinking-song, strummed on a worn and tinny lute—Lythande knew it belonged to the tavern-keeper, and could be borrowed—by a young man, dressed in fragments of foppish finery, torn and slashed by the chances of the road. He was sitting lazily, with one knee crossed over the other; and when the rowdy song faded away, the young man drifted into another, a quiet love song from another time and another country. Lythande had known the song, more years ago than bore remembering, and in those days Lythande the magician had borne another name and had known little of sorcery. When the song died, Lythande had stepped from the shadow, visible, and the firelight glinted on the blue star, mocking at the center of the high forehead.

There was a little muttering in the tavern, but they were not unaccustomed to Lythande's invisible comings and goings. The young man raised eyes which were surprisingly blue beneath the black hair elaborately curled above his brow. He was slender and vague, and Lythande marked the rapier at his side, which looked well handled, and the amulet; in the form of a coiled snake, at his throat. The young man said, "Who are you, who has the habit of coming and going into thin air like that?"

"One who compliments your skill at song." Lythande flung a coin to the tapster's boy. "Will you drink?"

"A minstrel never refuses such an invitation. Singing is dry work." But when the drink was brought, he said, "Not drinking with me, then?"

"No man has ever seen Lythande eat or drink," muttered one of the men in the circle round them.

"Why, then, I hold that unfriendly," cried the young minstrel. "A friendly drink between comrades shared is one thing; but I am no servant to sing for pay or to drink except as a friendly gesture!"

Lythande shrugged, and the blue star above the high brow began to shimmer and give forth blue light The onlookers slowly edged backward, for when a wizard who wore the blue star was angered, bystanders did well to be out of the way. The minstrel set down the lute, so it would be well out of range if he must leap to his feet. Lythande knew, by the excruciating slowness of his movements and great care, that he had already shared a good many drinks with chance-met comrades. But the minstrel's hand did not go to his sword hilt but instead closed like a fist over the amulet in the form of a snake. "You are like no man I have ever met before," he

3

observed mildly, and Lythande, feeling inside the ripple, nerve-long, that told a magician he was in the presence of spellcasting, hazarded quickly that the amulet was one of those which would not protect its master unless the wearer first stated a set number of truths—usually three or five—about the owner's attacker or foe. Wary, but amused, Lythande said, "A true word. Nor am I like any man you will ever meet, live you never so long, minstrel."

The minstrel saw, beyond the angry blue glare of the star, a curl of friendly mockery in Lythande's mouth.

He said, letting the amulet go, "And I wish yon no ill and you wish me none, and those are true sayings too, wizard, hey? And there's an end of that. But although perhaps you are like to no other, you are not the only wizard I have seen in Sanctuary who bears a blue star about his forehead."

Now the blue star blazed rage, but not for the minstrel. They both knew it. The crowd around them had all mysteriously discovered that they had business elsewhere. The minstrel looked at the empty benches.

"I must go elsewhere to sing for my supper, it seems."

"I meant you no offense when I refused to share a drink." said Lythande. "A magician's vow is not as lightly overset as a lute. Yet I may guest-gift you with dinner and drink in plenty without loss of dignity, and in return ask a service of a friend, may I not?"

"Such is the custom of my country. Cappen Varra thanks you, magician."

"Tapster! Your best dinner for my guest, and all he can drink tonight!"

"For such liberal guesting I'll not haggle about the service," Cappen Varra said, and set to the smoking dishes brought before him. As he ate, Lythande drew from the folds of the mage-robe a small pouch containing a quantity of sweet-smelling herbs, rolled them into a blue-grey leaf, touched a ring to spark the roll alight, and drew on the smoke, which drifted up sweet and greyish.

"As for the service, it is nothing so great; tell me all you know of this other wizard who wears the blue star. I know of none other of my Order south of Azehur, and I would be certain you did not see me, nor my wraith."

Cappen Varra sucked at a marrow-bone and wiped his fingers fastidiously on the tray-cloth beneath tile meats. He bit into a ginger-fruit before replying.

"Not you, wizard, nor your fetch or doppelganger; this one had shoulders brawnier by half, and he wore no sword, but two daggers cross-girt astride his hips. His beard was black; and his left hand missing three fingers."

"Ils of the Thousand Eyes! Rabben the Half-Handed, here in Sanctuary! Where did you see him, minstrel?"

"I saw him crossing the bazaar; but he bought nothing that I saw. And I saw him in the Street of Red Lanterns, talking to a woman. What service am I to do for you, magician?"

"You have done it." Lythande gave silver to the tavernkeeper—so much that the surly man bade Shalpa's cloak cover him as he went—and laid another coin, gold this time, beside the borrowed lute.

"Redeem your harp; that one will do your voice no boon." But when the minstrel raised his head in thanks, the magician had gone unseen into the shadows.

Pocketing the gold, the minstrel asked, "How did he know that? And how did he go out?"

"Shalpa the swift alone knows," the tapster said. "Flew out by the smoke-hole in the chimney, for all I ken! That one needs not the night-dark cloak of Shalpa to cover him, for he has one of his own. He paid for your drinks, good sir; what will you have?" And Cappen Varra proceeded to get very drunk, that being the wisest thing to do when one becomes entangled unawares in the private affairs of a wizard.

Outside in the street, Lythande paused to consider. Rabben the Half-handed was no friend; yet there was no reason his presence in Sanctuary must deal with Lythande, or personal revenge. If it were business concerned with the Order of the Blue Star, if Lythande must lend Rabben aid, or the Half-handed had been sent to summon all the members of the Order, the star they both wore would have given warning.

Yet it would do no harm to make certain. Walking swiftly, the magician had reached a line of old stables behind the governor's palace. There was silence and secrecy for magic. Lythande stepped into one of the little side alleys, drawing up the magician's cloak until no light remained, slowly withdrawing farther and farther into the silence until nothing remained anywhere in the world—anywhere in the universe but the light of the blue star ever glowing in front. Lythande remembered how it had been set there, and at what cost—the price an adept paid for power.

The blue glow gathered, fulminated in many-colored patterns, pulsing and glowing, until Lythande stood *within* the light, and there, in the Place That Is Not, seated upon a throne carved apparently from sapphire, was the Master of the Star.

"Greetings to you, fellow star, star-born, *shyryu.*" The terms of endearment could mean fellow, companion, brother, sister, beloved, equal, pilgrim; its literal meaning was sharer of starlight. "What brings you into the Pilgrim Place this night from afar?"

"The need for knowledge, star-sharer. Have you sent one to seek me out in Sanctuary?"

"Not so, *shyryu.* All is well in the Temple of the Star-sharers; you have not yet been summoned; the hour is not yet come."

For every adept of the Blue Star knows; it is one of the prices of power. At the world's end, when all the doings of mankind and mortals are done, the last to fall under the assault of Chaos will be the Temple of the Star; and then, in the Place That Is Not, the Master of the Star will summon all of the Pilgrim Adepts from the farthest corners of the world, to fight with all their magic against Chaos; but until that day, they have such freedom as will best strengthen their powers. The Master of the Star repeated, reassuringly, "The hour has not come. You are free to walk as you will in the world."

The blue glow faded, and Lythande stood shivering. So Rabben had not been sent in that final summoning. Yet the end and Chaos might well be at hand for Lythande before the hour appointed, if Rabben the Half-handed had his way.

It was a fair test of strength, ordained by our master. Rabben should bear me no ill-will... Rabben's presence in Sanctuary need not have to do with Lythande. He might be here upon his lawful occasions—if anything of Rabben's could be said to be lawful; for it was only upon the last day of all that the Pilgrim Adepts were pledged to fight upon the side of Law against Chaos. And Rabben had not chosen to do so before then.

Caution would be needed, and yet Lythande knew that Rabben was near...

South and east of the governor's palace, there is a little triangular park, across from the Street of Temples. By day the graveled walks and turns of shrubbery are given over to predicants and priests who find not enough worship or offerings for their liking; by night the place is the haunt of women who worship no goddess except She of the filled purse and the empty womb. And for both reasons the place is called, in irony, the Promise of Heaven; in Sanctuary, as elsewhere, it is well known that those who promise do not always perform.

Lythande, who frequented neither women nor priests as a usual thing, did not often walk here. The park seemed deserted; the evil winds had begun to blow, whipping bushes and shrubbery into the shapes of strange beasts performing unnatural acts; and moaning weirdly around the walls and eaves of the Temples across the street, the wind that was said in Sanctuary to be the moaning of Azyuna in Vashanka's bed. Lythande moved swiftly, skirting the darkness of the paths. And then a woman's scream rent the air.

From the shadows Lythande could see the frail form of a young girl in a torn and ragged dress; she was barefoot and her ear was bleeding where one jeweled earring had been torn from the lobe. She was struggling in the iron grip of a huge burly black-bearded man, and the first thing Lythande saw was the hand gripped around the girl's thin, bony wrist, dragging her; two fingers missing and the other cut away to the first joint. Only then—when it was no longer needed—did Lythande see the Blue Star between the black bristling brows, the cat-yellow eyes of Rabben the Half-handed!

Lythande knew him of old, from the Temple of the Star. Even then Rabben had been a vicious man, his lecheries notorious. Why, Lythande wondered, had the Masters not demanded that he renounce them as the price of his power? Lythande's lips tightened in a mirthless grimace; so notorious had been Rabben's lecheries that if he renounced them, everyone would know the Secret of his Power.

For the powers of an Adept of the Blue Star depended upon a secret. As in the old legend of the giant who kept his heart in a secret place outside his body, and with it his immortality, so the adept of the Blue Star poured all his psychic force into a single Secret; and the one who discovered the Secret would acquire all of that adept's power. So Rabben's Secret must be something else... Lythande did not speculate on it.

The girl cried out pitifully as Rabben jerked at her wrist; as the burly magician's star began to glow, she thrust her free hand over her eyes to shield them from it. Without fully intending to intervene, Lythande stepped from the shadows, and the rich voice that had made the prentice-magicians in the outer court of the Blue Star call Lythande "minstrel" rather than "magician," rang out:

"By Shipri the All-Mother, release that woman!"

Rabben whirled. "By the nine-hundred-and-ninety-ninth eye of Ils! Lythande!

"Are there not enough women in the Street of Red Lanterns, that you must mishandle girl-children in the Street of Temples?" For Lythande could see how young she was, the thin arms and childish legs and ankles, the breasts not yet full-formed beneath the dirty, torn tunic.

Rabben turned on Lythande and sneered, "You were always squeamish, *shyryu*. No woman walks here unless she is for sale. Do you want her for yourself? Have you tired of your fat Madam in the Aphrodisia House?"

"You will not take her name into your mouth, *shyryu*!"

"So tender for the honor of a harlot?"

Lythande ignored that. "Let that girl go, or stand to my challenge."

Rabben's star shot lightnings; he shoved the girl to one side. She fell nerveless to the pavement and lay without moving. "She'll stay there until we've done. Did you think she could run away while we fought? Come to think of it, I never did see you with a woman, Lythande—is that your Secret, Lythande, that you've no use for women?"

Lythande maintained an impassive face; but whatever came, Rabben must not be allowed to pursue *that* line. "You may couple like an animal in the streets of Sanctuary, Rabben, but I do not. Will you yield her up, or fight?"

"Perhaps I should yield her to you, this is unheard of, that Lythande should fight in the streets over a woman! You see, I know your habits well,

Lythande!"

Damnation of Vashanka! Now indeed I shall have to fight for the girl!

Lythande's rapier snicked from its scabbard and thrust at Rabben as if of its own will.

"Ha! Do you think Rabben fights street-brawls with the sword like any mercenary?" Lythande's sword-tip exploded in the blue star-glow, and became a shimmering snake, twisting back in itself to climb past the hilt, fangs dripping venom as it sought to coil around Lythande's fist. Lythande's own star blazed. The sword was metal again but twisted and useless, in the shape of the snake it had been, coiling back toward the scabbard. Enraged, Lythande jerked free of the twisted metal, sent a spitting rain of fire in Rabben's direction. Quickly the huge adept covered himself in fog, and the fire-spray extinguished itself. Somewhere outside consciousness Lythande was aware of a crowd gathering; not twice in a lifetime did two Adepts of the Blue Star battle by sorcery in the streets of Sanctuary. The blaze of the stars, blazing from each magician's brow, raged lightnings in the square.

On a howling wind came little torches ravening, that flickered and whipped at Lythande; they touched the tall form of the magician and vanished. Then a wild whirlwind sent trees lashing, leaves swirling bare from branches, and battered Rabben to his knees. Lythande was bored; this must be finished quickly. Not one of the goggling onlookers in the crowd knew afterward what had been done, but Rabben bent, slowly, slowly, forced inch by inch down and down, to his knees, to all fours, prone, pressing and grinding his face farther and farther into the dust, rocking back and forth, pressing harder and harder into the sand...

Lythande turned and lifted the girl. She stared in disbelief at the burly sorcerer grinding his black beard frantically into the dirt.

"What did you—"

"Never mind—let's get out of here. The spell will not hold him long, and when he wakes from it he will be angry." Neutral mockery edged Lythande's voice, and the girl could see it, too, Rabben with beard and eyes and Blue Star covered with the dirt and dust—

She scurried along in the wake of the magician's robe; when they were well away from the Promise of Heaven, Lythande halted, so abruptly that the girl stumbled.

"Who are you, girl?"

"My name is Bercy. And yours?"

"A magician's name is not lightly given. In Sanctuary they call me Lythande." Looking down at the girl, the magician noted, with a pang, that beneath the dirt and dishevelment she was very beautiful, and very young.

"You can go, Bercy. He will not touch you again. I have bested him fairly upon challenge."

She flung herself on to Lythande's shoulder, clinging. "Don't send me away!" she begged, clutching, eyes filled with adoration. Lythande scowled.

Predictable, of course. Bercy believed, and who in Sanctuary would have disbelieved, that the duel had been fought for the girl as prize, and she was ready to give herself to the winner. Lythande made a gesture of protest.

"No—"

The girl narrowed her eyes in pity. "Is it then with you as Rabben said— that your secret is that you have been deprived of manhood?" But beyond the pity was a delicious flicker of amusement—what a tidbit of gossip! A juicy bit for the Streets of Women.

"Silence!" Lythande's glance was imperative. "Come."

She followed, along the twisting streets that led into the Street of Red Lanterns. Lythande strode with confidence, now, past the House of Mermaids, where, it was said, delights as exotic as the name promised were to be found; past the House of Whips, shunned by all except those who refused to go elsewhere; and at last, beneath the face of the Green Lady as she was worshiped far away and beyond Ranke, the Aphrodisia House.

Bercy looked around, eyes wide, at the pillared lobby, the brilliance of a hundred lanterns, the exquisitely dressed women lounging on cushions till they were summoned. They were finely dressed and bejeweled—Myrtis knew her trade, and how to present her wares—and Lythande guessed that the ragged Bercy's glance was one of envy; she had probably sold herself in the bazaars for a few coppers or for a loaf of bread, since she was old enough. Yet somehow, like flowers covering a dungheap, she had kept an exquisite fresh beauty, all gold and white, flowerlike. Even ragged and half-starved, she touched Lythande's heart.

"Bercy, have you eaten today?"

"No, master."

Lythande summoned the huge eunuch Jiro, whose business it was to conduct the favored customers to the chambers of their chosen women, and throw out the drunks and abusive customers into the street. He came— huge-bellied, naked except for a skimpy loincloth and a dozen rings in his ear—he had once had a lover who was an earring-seller and had used him to display her wares.

"How we may serve the magician Lythande?"

The women on the couches and cushions were twittering at one another in surprise and dismay, and Lythande could almost hear their thoughts.

None of us has been able to attract or seduce the great magician, and this ragged street wench has caught his eyes? And, being women, Lythande knew they could see the unclouded beauty that shone through the girl's rags.

"Is Madame Myrtis available, Jiro?"

"She's sleeping, O great wizard, but for you she's given orders she's to be waked at any hour. Is this—" no one alive can be quite so supercilious as the chief eunuch of a fashionable brothel—"yours, Lythande, or a gift for my Madame?"

"Both, perhaps. Give her something to eat and find her a place to spend the night."

"And a bath, magician? She has fleas enough to louse a floorful of cushions!"

"A bath, certainly, and a bath-woman with scents and oils," Lythande said, "and something in the nature of a whole garment."

"Leave it to me," said Jiro expansively, and Bercy looked at Lythande in dread, but went when the magician gestured to her to go. As Jiro took her away, Lythande saw Myrtis standing in the doorway; a heavy woman, no longer young, but with the frozen beauty of a spell. Through the perfect spelled features, her eyes were warm and welcoming as she smiled at Lythande.

"My dear, I had not expected to see you here. Is that yours?" She moved her head toward the door through which Jiro had conducted the frightened Bercy. "She'll probably run away, you know, once you take your eyes off her."

"I wish I thought so, Myrtis. But no such luck, I fear."

"You had better tell me the whole story," Myrtis said, and listened to Lythande's brief, succinct account of the affair.

"And if you laugh, Myrtis, I take back my spell and leave your grey hairs and wrinkles open to the mockery of everyone in Sanctuary!"

But Myrtis had known Lythande too long to take that threat very seriously. "So the maiden you rescued is all maddened with desire for the love of Lythande!" She chuckled. "It is like an old ballad, indeed!"

"But what am I to do, Myrtis? By the paps of Shipri the All-Mother, this is a dilemma!"

"Take her into your confidence and tell her why your love cannot be hers," Myrtis said.

Lythande frowned. "You hold my Secret, since I had no choice; you knew me before I was made magician, or bore the Blue Star—"

"And before I was a harlot," Myrtis agreed.

"But if I make this girl feel like a fool for loving me, she will hate me as much as she loves; and I cannot confide in anyone I cannot trust with my life and my power. All I have is yours, Myrtis, because of that past we shared. And that includes my power, if you ever should need it. But I cannot entrust it to this girl."

"Still she owes you something, for delivering her out of the hands of Rabben."

Lythande said, "I will think about it; and now make haste to bring me food, for I am hungry and athirst." Taken to a private room, Lythande ate and drank, served by Myrtis's own hands. And Myrtis said, "I could never have sworn your vow—to eat and drink in the sight of no man!"

"If you sought the power of a magician, you would keep it well enough," said Lythande. "I am seldom tempted now to break it; I fear only lest I break it unawares; I cannot drink in a tavern lest among the women there might be some one of those strange men who find diversion in putting on the garments of a female; even here I will not eat or drink among your women, for that reason. All power depends on the vows and the secret."

"Then I cannot aid you," Myrtis said, "but you are not bound to speak truth to her; tell her you have vowed to live without women."

"I may do that." Lythande said, and finished the food, scowling.

Later Bercy was brought in, wide-eyed, enthralled by her fine gown and her freshly washed hair, softly curling about her pink-and-white face and the sweet scent of bath oils and perfumes that hung about her.

"The girls here wear such pretty clothes, and one of them told me they could eat twice a day if they wished! Am I pretty enough, do you think, that Madame Myrtis would have me here?"

"If that is what you wish. You are more than beautiful."

Bercy said boldly, "I would rather belong to *you*, magician," and flung herself again on Lythande, her hands clutching and clinging, dragging the lean face down to hers. Lythande, who rarely touched anything living, held her gently, trying not to reveal consternation.

"Bercy, child, this is only a fancy. It will pass."

"No," she wept. "I love you, I want only you!"

And then, unmistakably, along the magician's nerves, Lythande felt that little ripple, that warning thrill of tension which said: *spellcasting is in use.* Not against Lythande. That could have been countered. But somewhere within the room.

Here, in the Aphrodisia House? Myrtis, Lythande knew, could be trusted with life, reputation, fortune, the magical power of the Blue Star itself; she had been tested before this. Had she altered enough to turn betrayer, it would have been apparent in her aura when Lythande came near.

That left only the girl, who was clinging and whimpering, "I will die if you do not love me! I will die! Tell me it is not true, Lythande, that you are unable to love! Tell me it is an evil lie that magicians are emasculated, incapable of loving woman..."

"That is certainly an evil lie," Lythande agreed gravely. "I give you my solemn assurance that I have never been emasculated." But Lythande's nerves tingled as the words were spoken. A magician might lie, and most of them did. Lythande would lie as readily as any other, in a good cause. But the law of the Blue Star was this: when questioned directly on a matter bearing directly on the Secret, the adept might not tell a direct lie. And Bercy, unknowing, was only one question away from the fatal one hiding the Secret.

With a mighty effort, Lythande's magic wrenched at the very fabric of Time itself; the girl stood motionless, aware of no lapse, as Lythande stepped away far enough to read her aura. And yes, there within the traces of that vibrating field, was the shadow of the Blue Star. Rabben's; overpowering her will.

Rabben. Rabben the Half-handed, who had set his will on the girl, who had staged and contrived the whole thing, including the encounter where the girl had needed rescue; put the girl under a spell to attract and bespell Lythande.

The law of the Blue Star forbade one adept of the Star to kill another; for all would be needed to fight side by side, on the last day, against Chaos. Yet if one adept could prise forth the secret of another's power... then the powerless one was not needed against Chaos and could be killed.

What could be done now? Kill the girl? Rabben would take that, too, as an answer. Bercy had been so bespelled as to be irresistible to any man; if Lythande sent her away untouched, Rabben would know that Lythande's secret lay in that area and would never rest in his attempts to uncover it. For if Lythande was untouched by this sex-spell to make Bercy irresistible, then Lythande was a eunuch, or a homosexual, or... sweating, Lythande dared not even think beyond that. The Secret was safe only if never questioned. It would not be read in the aura; but one simple question, and all was ended.

I should kill her, Lythande thought. *For now I am fighting, not for my magic alone, but for my secret and for my life. For surely, with my power gone, Rabben would lose no time in making an end of me, in revenge for the loss of half a hand.*

The girl was still motionless, entranced. How easily she could be killed! Then Lythande recalled an old fairy-tale, which might be used to save the Secret of the Star.

The light flickered as Time returned to the chamber. Bercy was still clinging and weeping, unaware of the lapse. Lythande had resolved what to do, and the girl felt Lythande's arms enfolding her, and the magician's kiss on her welcoming mouth.

"You must love me or I shall die!" Bercy wept.

Lythande said, "You shall be mine." The soft neutral voice was very gentle. "But even a magician is vulnerable in love, and I must protect myself. A place shall be made ready for us without light or sound save for what I provide with my magic; and you must swear that you will not seek to see or to touch me except by that magical light. Will you swear it by the All-Mother, Bercy? For if you swear this, I shall love you as no woman has ever been loved before."

Trembling, she whispered, "I swear." And Lythande's heart went out in pity, for Rabben had used her ruthlessly; so that she burned alive with her unslaked and bewitched love for the magician, that she was all caught up in her passion for Lythande. Painfully, Lythande thought; *if she had only loved me, without the spell; then I could have loved...*

Would that I could trust her with my secret! But she is only Rabben's tool; her love for me is his doing, and none of her own will... and not real... And so everything which would pass between them now must be only a drama staged for Rabben.

"I shall make all ready for you with my magic."

Lythande went and confided to Myrtis what was needed; the woman began to laugh, but a single glance at Lythande's bleak face stopped her cold. She had known Lythande since long before the Blue Star was set between those eyes; and she kept the Secret for love of Lythande. It wrung her heart to see one she loved in the grip of such suffering. So she said, "All will be prepared. Shall I give her a drug in her wine to weaken her will, that you may the more readily throw a glamour upon her?"

Lythande's voice held a terrible bitterness. "Rabben has done that already for us, when he put a spell upon her to love me."

"You would have it otherwise?" Myrtis asked, hesitating.

"All the gods of Sanctuary—they laugh at me! All-Mother, help me! But I would have it otherwise; I could love her, if she were not Rabben's tool."

When all was prepared, Lythande entered the darkened room. There was no light but the light of the Blue Star. The girl lay on a bed, stretching up her arms to the magician with exalted abandon.

"Come to me, come to me, my love!"

"Soon," said Lythande, sitting beside her, stroking her hair with a tenderness even Myrtis would never have guessed. "I will sing to you a love-song of my people, far away."

She writhed in erotic ecstasy. "All you do is good to me, my love, my magician!"

Lythande felt the blankness of utter despair. She was beautiful, and she was in love. She lay in a bed spread for the two of them, and they were separated by the breadth of the world. The magician could not endure it.

Lythande sang, in that rich and beautiful voice; a voice lovelier than any spell:

Half the night is spent; and the crown of moonlight
Fades, and now the crown of the stars is paling;
Yields the sky reluctant to coming morning;
Still I lie lonely.

Lythande could see tears on Bercy's cheeks.

I will love you as no woman has ever been loved.

Between the girl on the bed, and the motionless form of the magician, as the magician's robe fell heavily to the floor, a wraith-form grew, the very wraith and fetch, at first, of Lythande, tall and lean, with blazing eyes and a star between its brows and a body white and unscarred; the form of the magician, but this one triumphant in virility, advancing on the motionless woman, waiting. Her mind fluttered away in arousal; was caught, captured, bespelled. Lythande let her see the image for a moment; she could not see the true Lythande behind; then, as her eyes closed in ecstatic awareness of the touch, Lythande smoothed light fingers over her closed eyes.

"See—what I bid you to see!

"Hear—what I bid you hear!

"Feel—only what I bid you feel, Bercy!"

And now she was wholly under the spell of the wraith.

Unmoving, stony-eyed, Lythande watched as her lips closed on emptiness and she kissed invisible lips; and moment by moment Lythande knew what touched her, what caressed her. Rapt and ravished by illusion that brought her again and again to the heights of ecstasy, till she cried out in abandonment. Only to Lythande that cry was bitter; for she cried out not to Lythande but to the man-wraith who possessed her.

At last she lay all but unconscious, satiated; and Lythande watched in agony. When she opened her eyes again, Lythande was looking down at her, sorrowfully.

Bercy stretched up languid arms. "Truly, my beloved, you have loved me as no woman has ever been loved before."

For the first and last time, Lythande bent over her and pressed her lips in a long, infinitely tender kiss. "Sleep, my darling."

And as she sank into ecstatic, exhausted sleep, Lythande wept.

Long before the girl woke, Lythande stood, girt for travel, in the little room belonging to Myrtis.

"The spell will hold. She will make all haste to carry her tale to Rabben—the tale of Lythande, the incomparable lover! Of Lythande, of untiring virility, who can love a maiden into exhaustion!" The rich voice of Lythande was harsh with bitterness.

"And long before you return to Sanctuary, once freed of the spell, she will have forgotten you in many other lovers," Myrtis agreed. "It is better and safer that it should be so."

"True." But Lythande's voice broke. "Take care of her, Myrtis. Be kind to her."

"I swear it, Lythande."

"If only she could have loved *me*—" the magician broke and sobbed again for a moment; Myrtis looked away, wrung with pain, knowing not what comfort to offer.

"If only she could have loved me as I am, freed of Rabben's spell! Loved me without pretense! But I feared I could not master the spell Rabben had put on her... nor trust her not to betray me, knowing..."

Myrtis put her plump arms around Lythande, tenderly.

"Do you regret?"

The question was ambiguous. It might have meant: *Do you regret that you did not kill the girl?* or even: *Do you regret your oath and the secret you must bear to the last day?* Lythande chose to answer the latter.

"Regret? How can I regret? One day I shall fight against Chaos with all of my order; even at the side of Rabben, if he lives unmurdered as long as that. And that alone must justify my existence and my secret. But now I must leave Sanctuary, and who knows when the chances of the world will bring me this way again? Kiss me farewell, my sister."

Myrtis stood on tiptoe. Her lips met the lips of the magician.

"Until we meet again, Lythande. May She attend and guard you forever. Farewell, my beloved, my sister."

Then the magician Lythande girded on her sword, and went silently and by unseen ways out of the city of Sanctuary, just as the dawn was breaking. And on her forehead the glow of the Blue Star was dimmed by the rising sun. Never once did she look back.

THE INCOMPETENT MAGICIAN
Marion Zimmer Bradley

Throughout the length and breadth of the world of the Twin Suns, from the Great Salt Desert in the south to the Ice Mountains of the north, no one seeks out a mercenary-magician unless he wants something; and it's usually trouble. It's never the same thing twice, but whatever it is, it's always trouble.

Lythande the Magician looked out from under the hood of the dark, flowing mage-robe; and under the hood, the blue star that proclaimed Lythande to be Pilgrim Adept began to sparkle and give off blue flashes of fire as the magician studied the fat, wheezing little stranger, wondering what kind of trouble this client would be.

Like Lythande, the little stranger wore the cloak of a magician, the fashion of mage-robe worn in the cities at the edge of the Salt Desert. He seemed a little daunted as he looked up at the tall Lythande, and at the glowing blue star. Lythande, cross-belted with twin daggers, looked like a warrior, not a mage.

The fat man wheezed and fidgeted, and finally stammered "H-h-high and noble sor-sor-sorcerer, th-this is embaras—ass-assing—"

Lythande gave him no help, but looked down, with courteous attention, at the bald spot on the fussy little fellow's head. The stranger stammered on, "I must co-co-confess to you that one of my ri-ri-rivals has st-st-stolen my m-m-magic wa-wa-wa—" He exploded into a perfect storm of stammering, then abandoned "wand" and blurted out, "My p-p-powers are not suf-suf-su—not strong enough to get it ba-ba-back. What would you require as a f-f-fee, O great and noble ma-ma-ma—" he swallowed and managed to get out "sorcerer?"

Beneath the blue star Lythande's arched and colorless brows went up in amusement.

"Indeed? How did that come to pass? Had you not spelled the wand with such sorcery that none but you could touch it?"

The little man stared, fidgeting, at the belt-buckle of his mage-robe. "I t-t-t-told you this was embarrass-as-as— hard to say, O great and noble ma-ma-magician. I had imbi-bi-bi—"

"In short," Lythande said, cutting him off, "you were drunk. And somehow your spell must have failed. Well, do you know who has taken it, and why?"

"Roy—Roygan the Proud," said the little man, adding, "He wanted to be revenged upon m-m-me because he found me in be-be-be—"

"In bed with his wife?" Lythande asked, with perfect gravity, though one better acquainted with the Pilgrim Adept might have detected a faint glimmer of amusement at the corners of the narrow ascetic mouth. The fat little magician nodded miserably and stared at his shoes.

Lythande said at last, in that mellow, neutral voice which had won the mercenary-magician the name of minstrel even before the reputation for successful sorcery had grown, "This bears out the proverb I have always held true, that those who follow the profession of sorcery should have neither wife nor lover. Tell me, O mighty mage and most gallant of bedroom athletes, what do they call you?"

The little man drew himself up to his full height—he reached almost to Lythande's shoulder—and declared, "I am known far and wide in Gandrin as Rastafyre the Incom-comp-comp—"

"Incompetent?" suggested Lythande gravely.

He set his mouth with a hurt look and said with sonorous dignity, "Rastafyre the Incomparable."

"It would be amusing to know how you came by that name," Lythande said, and the eyes under the mage-hood twinkled, "but the telling of funny stories, although a diverting pastime while we await the final battle between Law and Chaos, puts no beans on the table. So you have lost your magic wand to the rival sorcery of Roygan the Proud, and you wish my services to get it back from him—have I understood you correctly?"

Rastafyre nodded, and Lythande asked, "What fee had you thought to offer me in return for the assistance of my sorcery, O Rastafyre the incom—" Lythande hesitated a moment and finished smoothly "incomparable."

"This jewel," Rastafyre said, drawing forth a great sparkling ruby which flashed blood tones in the narrow darkness of the hallway.

Lythande gestured him to put it away. "If you wave such things about here, you may attract predators before whom Roygan the Proud is but a kitten-cub. I wear no jewels but this," Lythande gestured briefly at the blue star that shone with pallid light from the midst of the high forehead, "nor have I lover nor wife nor sweetheart upon whom I might bestow it; I preach only what I myself practice. Keep your jewels for those who prize them." Lythande made a snatching gesture in the air and between the long, narrow fingers, three rubies appeared, each one superior in color and luster to the one in Rastafyre's hand. "As you see, I need them not."

"I but offered the customary fee lest you think me niggardly," said Rastafyre, blinking with surprise and faint covetousness at the rubies in

Lythande's hand, which blinked for a moment and disappeared. "As it may happen, I have that which may tempt you further."

The fussy little magician turned and snapped his fingers in the air. He intoned "Ca-Ca-Carrier!"

Out of thin air a great dark shape made itself seen, a dull lumpy outline; it fell and flopped ungracefully at his feet, resolving itself, with a bump, into a brown velveteen bag, embroidered with magical symbols in crimson and gold.

"Gently! Gently, Ca-Ca-Carrier," Rastafyre scolded, "or you will break my treasures within, and Lythande will have the right to call me Incom-comp-competent."

"Carrier is more competent than you, O Rastafyre; why scold your faithful creature?"

"Not Carrier, but Ca-Ca-Carrier," Rastafyre said, "for I knew myself likely to st-st-stam—that I did not talk very well, and I la-la-labeled it by the cogno-cogno—by the name which I knew I would fi-find myself calling it."

This time Lythande chuckled aloud. "Well done, O mighty and incomparable magician!"

But the laughter died as Rastafyre drew forth from the dark recesses of Ca-Ca-Carrier a thing of rare beauty.

It was a lute, formed of dark precious woods, set about with turquoise and mother-of-pearl, the strings shining with silver; and upon the body of the lute, in precious gemstones, was set a pallid blue star, like to the one which glowed between Lythande's brows.

"By the bloodshot eyes of Keth-Ketha!"

Lythande was suddenly looming over the little magician, and the blue star began to sparkle and flame with fury; but the voice was calm and neutral as ever.

"Where got you that, Rastafyre? That lute I know; I myself fashioned it for one I once loved, and now she plays a spirit lute in the Courts of Light. And the possessions of a Pilgrim Adept do not pass into the hands of others as readily as the wand of Rastafyre the Incompetent!"

Rastafyre cast down his tubby face, and muttered, unable to face the blue glare of the angry Lythande, that it was a secret of the trade.

"Which means, I suppose, that you stole it, fair and square, from some other thief," Lythande remarked, and the glare of anger vanished as quickly as it had come. "Well, so be it; you offer me this lute in return for the recovery of your wand?" The tall mage reached for the lute, but Rastafyre saw the hunger in the Pilgrim Adept's eyes and thrust it behind him.

"First the service for which I sought you out," he reminded Lythande.

Lythande seemed to grow even taller, looming over Rastafyre as if to fill the whole room. The magician's voice, though not loud, seemed to resonate like a great drum.

"Wretch, incompetent, do you dare to haggle with me over my own possession? Fool, it is no more yours than mine—less, for these hands brought the first music from it before you knew how to turn goat's milk sour on the dungheap where you were whelped! By what right do you demand a service of me?"

The bald little man raised his chin and said firmly. "All the world knows that Lythande is a servant of L-L-Law and not of Chaos, and no ma-ma-magician bound to the L-Law would demean hi-hi-himself to cheat an honest ma-ma-man. And what is more, noble Ly-Lythande, this instru—tru-tru—this lute has been cha-changed since it dwelt in your ha-ha-hands. Behold!"

Rastafyre struck a soft chord on the lute and began to play a soft, melancholy tune. Lythande scowled and demanded, "What do you—?"

Rastafyre gestured imperatively for silence. As the notes quivered in the air, there was a little stirring in the dark hallway, and suddenly, in the heavy air, a woman stood before them.

She was small and slender, with flowing fair hair, clad in the thinnest gown of spider-silk from the forests of Noidhan. Her eyes were blue, set deep under dark lashes in a lovely face; but the face was sorrowful and full of pain. She said in a lovely singing voice "Who thus disturbs the sleep of the enchanted?"

"Koira!" cried Lythande, and the neutral voice for once was high, athrob with agony. "Koira, how—what—?"

The fair-haired woman moved her hands in a spell-bound gesture. She murmured, "I know not—" and then, as if waking from deep sleep, she rubbed her eyes and cried out, "Ah, I thought I heard a voice that once I knew—Lythande, is it you? Was it you who enchanted me here, because I turned from you to the love of another? What would you? I was a woman—"

"Silence," said Lythande in a stifled voice, and Rastafyre saw the magician's mouth move as if in pain.

"As you see," said Rastafyre, "it is no longer the lute you knew."

The woman's face was fading into air, and Lythande's taut voice whispered, "Where did she go? Summon her back for me!"

"She is now the slave of the enchanted lute," said Rastafyre, chuckling with what seemed obscene enthusiasm, "I could have had her for any service—but to ease your fastidious soul, magician, I will confess that I prefer my women more—" his hands sketched robust curves in the air, "So I have asked other, only, that now and again she sing to the lute—knew you not this, Lythande? Was it not you who enchanted the woman thither, as she said?"

Within the hood Lythande's head moved in a negative shake, side to side. The face could not be seen, and Rastafyre wondered if he would, after all, be the first to see the mysterious Lythande weep. None had ever seen Lythande show the slightest emotion; never had Lythande been known to eat or to drink wine in company—perhaps, it was believed, the mage *could* not, though most people guessed that it was simply one of the strange vows which bound a Pilgrim Adept.

But from within the hood, Lythande said slowly, "And you offer me this lute, in return for my services in the recovery of your wand?"

"I do, O noble Lythande. For I can see that the enchanted la-la-lady of the lute is known to you from old, and that you would have her as slave, concubine—what have you. And it is this, not the mu-mu-music of the lute alone, that I offer you—when my wa-wa-wand is my own again."

The blaze of the blue star brightened for a moment, then dimmed to a passive glow, and Lythande s voice was flat and neutral again.

"Be it so. For this lute I would undertake to recover the scattered pearls of the necklace of the Fish-goddess should she lose them in the sea; but are you certain that your wand is in the hands of Roygan the Proud, O Rastafyre?"

"I ha-ha-have no other en-en-enem—there is no one else who hates me," said Rastafyre, and again the restrained mirth gleamed for a moment.

"Fortunate are you, O Incom—" the hesitation, and the faint smile, "Incomparable. Well, I shall recover your wand—and the lute shall be mine."

"The lute—and the woman," said Rastafyre, "but only wh-wh-when my wand is again in my own ha-ha-hands."

"If Roygan has it," Lythande said, "it should present no very great difficulties for any competent magician."

Rastafyre wrapped the lute into the thick protective covering and fumbled it again into Ca-Ca-Carriers capacious folds. Rastafyre gestured fussily with another spell.

"In the name of—" He mumbled something, then frowned. "It will not obey me so well without my wa-wa-wand," he mumbled. Again his hands twisted in the simple spell. "G-g-go, confound you, in the name of Indo-do-do in the name of Indo-do—"

The bag flopped just a little and a corner of it disappeared, but the rest remained, hovering uneasily to the air.

Lythande managed somehow not to shriek with laughter, but remarked, "Allow me, O Incomp—O Incomparable," and made the spell with swift narrow fingers. "In the name of Indovici the Silent, I command you. Carrier—"

"Ca-Ca-Carrier," corrected Rastafyre, and Lythande, lips twitching, repeated the spell.

"In the name of Indovici the Silent, Ca-Ca-Carrier, I command you, go!"

The bag began slowly to fade, winked in and out for a moment, rose heavily into the air, and by the time it reached eye level, was gone.

"Indeed, bargain or no," Lythande said, "I must recover your wand, O Incompetent, lest the profession of magician become a jest for small boys from the Salt Desert to the Cold Hills!"

Rastafyre glared, but thought better of answering; he turned and fussed away, trailed by a small, lumpy brown shadow where Ca-Ca-Carrier stubbornly refused to stay either visible or invisible. Lythande watched him out of sight, then drew from the mage-robe a small pouch, shook out a small quantity of herbs and thoughtfully rolled them into a narrow tube; snapped narrow fingers to make a light, and slowly inhaled the fragrant smoke, letting it trickle out narrow nostrils into the heavy air of the hallway.

Roygan the Proud should present no very great challenge. Lythande knew Roygan of old; when that thief among magicians had first appeared in Lythande's life, Lythande had been young in sorcery and not yet tried in vigilance, and several precious items had vanished without trace from the house where Lythande then dwelt. Rastafyre would have been so easy a target that Lythande marveled that Roygan had not stolen Ca-Ca-Carrier, the hood and mage-robe Rastafyre wore, and perhaps his back teeth as well; there was an old saying in Gandrin, *if Roygan the Proud, shakes your hand, count your fingers before he is out of sight.*

But Lythande had pursued Roygan through three cities and across the Great Salt Desert; and when Roygan had been trailed to his lair, Lythande had recovered wand, rings and magical dagger; and then had affixed one of the rings to Roygan's nose with a permanent binding-spell.

Wear this, Lythande had said, *in memory of your treachery, and that honest folk may know you and avoid you.* Now Lythande wondered idly if Roygan had ever found anyone to take the ring off his nose.

Roygan bears me a grudge, thought Lythande, and wondered if Rastafyre the Incompetent, lute and all, were a trap set for Lythande, to surprise the secret of the Pilgrim Adept's magic. For the strength of any Adept of the Blue Star lies in a certain concealed secret which must never be known; and the one who surprises the secret of a Pilgrim Adept can master all the magic of the Blue Star. And Roygan, with his grudge....

Roygan was not worth worrying about. *But,* Lythande thought, *I have enemies among the Pilgrim Adepts themselves. Roygan might well be a tool of one of these. And so might Rastafyre.*

No, Roygan had not the strength for that; he was a thief, not a true magician or an adept. As for Rastafyre—soundlessly, Lythande laughed. If anyone sought to use that incompetent, the very incompetence of the fat, fussy little magician would recoil upon the accomplice. *I wish no worse for my enemies than Rastafyre for their friend.*

And when I have succeeded—it never occurred to Lythande to say if—*I shall have Koira; and the lute. She would not love me; but now, whether or no, she shall be mine, to sing for me whenever I will.*

If it should become known to Lythande's enemies—and the magician knew that there were many of them, even here in Gandrin—that Roygan had somehow incurred the wrath of a Pilgrim Adept, they would be quick to sell the story to any other Pilgrim Adept they could find. Lythande, too, knew how to use that tactic; the knowledge of another Pilgrim Adept's Secret was the greatest protection known under the Two Suns.

Speaking of Suns—Lythande cast a glance into the sky—it was near to First-sunset; Keth, red and somber, glowed on the horizon, with Reth like a bloody burning eye, an hour or two behind. Curse it, it was one of those nights where there would be long darkness. Lythande frowned, considering; but the darkness, too, could serve.

First Lythande must determine where in Old Gandrin, what corner or alley of that city of rogues and impostors, Roygan might be hiding.

Was there any Adept of the Blue Star who knew of the quarrel with Roygan? Lythande thought not. They had been alone when the deed was done; and Roygan would hardly boast of it; no doubt, that wretch had declared the ring in his nose to be a new fashion in jewelry! Therefore, by the Great Law of Magic, the law of Resonance, Lythande still possessed a tie to Roygan; the ring which once had been Lythande's own, if it was still on Roygan's nose, would lead to Roygan just as inescapably as a homing pigeon flies to its own croft.

There was no time to lose; Lythande would rather not brave the hiding place of Roygan the thief in full darkness, and already red Keth had slipped below the edge of the world. Two measures, perhaps, on a time-candle; no more time than that, or darkness would help to hide Roygan beneath its cloak, in the somber moonless streets of Old Gandrin.

The Pilgrim Adept needs no wand to make magic. Lythande raised one narrow, fine hand, drew it down to a curious, covering movement. Darkness flowed down from the slender fingers behind that movement, covering the magician with its veil; but inside the spelled circle, Lythande sat cross-legged on the stones, flooded with a neutral shadowless light.

Holding one hand toward the circle, Lythande whispered, "Ring of Lythande, ring which once caressed my finger, be joined to your sister."

Slowly the ring remaining on Lythande's finger began to gleam with an inner radiance. Beside it in the curious light, a second ring appeared, hanging formless and weightless in midair. And around this second ghost-ring, a pallid face took outline, first the beaky and aquiline nose, then the mouthful of broken teeth which had been tipped like fangs with shining metal, then the close-set dark-lashed eyes of Roygan the Proud.

He was not here within the spelled light-circle, Lythande knew that. Rather, the circle, like a mirror, reflected Roygan's face, and at a commanding gesture, the focus of the vision moved out, to encompass a room piled high with treasure, where Roygan had come to hide the fruits of his theft. Magpie Roygan! He did not use his treasure to enrich himself—like Lythande, he could have manufactured jewels at will—but to gain power over other magicians! And so, the links retaining their hold on their owners, Roygan was vulnerable to Lythande's magic as well.

If Rastafyre had been even a halfway competent magician—even the thought of that tubby little bungler curved Lythande's thin lips in a mocking smile—Rastafyre would have known of that bond, and tracked Roygan the Proud himself. For the wand of a magician is a curious thing; in a very real sense it *is* the magician, for he must put into it one of his very real powers and senses. As the Blue Star, in a way, was Lythande's emotion—for it glowed with blue flame when Lythande was angry or excited—so a wand, to those magicians who must use them, often reflects the most cherished power of a male magician. Again Lythande smiled mockingly; no bedroom athletics, no seduction of magicians' wives or daughters, till Rastafyre's wand was in his hand again!

Perhaps I should become a public benefactor, and never restore what Rastafyre considers so important, that the women of my fellow mages may be safe from his wiles! Yet Lythande knew, even as the image lingered, and the amusement, that Rastafyre must have back his wand and with it his power to do good or evil.

For Law strives ever against Chaos, and every human soul must be free to take the part of one or another; this was the basic law that the Gods of Gandrin had established, and that all Gods everywhere stood as representative; that life itself, on the world of the Twin Suns as everywhere till the last star of Eternity is burnt out, is forever embodying that one Great Strife. And Lythande was sworn, through the Blue Star, servant to the Law. To deprive Rastafyre of one jot of his power to choose good or evil was to set that basic truth at naught, setting Lythande's oath to Law in the place of Rastafyre's own choices, and that in itself was to let in Chaos.

And the karma of Lythande should stand forever responsible for the choice of Rastafyre. Guardians of the Blue Star, stand witness I want no such power, I carry enough karma of my own! I have set enough causes in motion and must see all their effects... abiding even to the Last Battle!

The image of Roygan, ring in nose, still hung in the air, and around it the pattern of Roygan's treasure room. But try as Lythande would, the Pilgrim Adept could not focus the image sufficiently to see if the wand of Rastafyre was among his treasure. So Lythande, with a commanding gesture, expanded the circle of vision still further, to include a street outside whatever cellar or storeroom held Roygan and his treasures. The circle expanded farther and farther, till at last the magician saw a known landmark: the Fountain of Mermaids, in the Street of the Seven Sailmakers. From there, apparently, the treasure room of Roygan the Thief must be situated.

And Rastafyre had risked his wand for an affair with Roygan's wife. *Truly,* Lythande thought, *my maxim is well-chosen, that a mage should have neither sweetheart nor wife...* and bitterness flooded Lythande, making the Blue Star glimmer; *Look what I do. for Koira's mere image or shadow! But how did Rastafyre know?*

For in the days when Koira and Lythande played the lute in the courts of their faraway home, both were young, and no shadow of the Blue Star or Lythande's quest after magic, even into the hidden Place Which Is Not of the Pilgrim Adepts, had cast its shadow between them. And Lythande had borne another name.

Yet Koira, or her shade, knew me, and called me by the name Lythande bears now. Why called she not... and then, by an enormous effort, almost physical, which brought sweat bursting from the brow beneath the Blue Star, Lythande cut off that memory; with the trained discipline of an Adept, even the memory of the old name vanished.

I am Lythande. The one I was before I bore that name is dead, or wanders in the limbo of the forgotten. With another gesture, Lythande dissolved the spelled circle of light and stood again in the streets of Old Gandrin, where Keth, too, had begun dangerously to approach the horizon.

Lythande set off toward the Street of the Seven Sailmakers. Keeping ever to the shadows which hid the dark mage-robe, and moving as noiselessly as a breath of wind or a cat's ghost, the Pilgrim Adept traversed a dozen streets, paying little heed to all that inhabited them. Men brawled in taverns, and on the cobbled street merchants sold everything from knives to women; children, grubby and half-naked, played their own obscure games, vaulting over barrels and carts, screaming with all the joys and tantrums of innocence. Lythande, intent on the magical mission, hardly saw or heard them.

At the Fountain of Mermaids, half a dozen women, draped in the loose robes which made even an ugly woman mysterious and alluring, drew water from the bubbling spring, chirping and twittering like birds. Lythande watched them with a curious, aching sadness. It would have been better to await their going, for the comings and goings of a Pilgrim Adept are better not gossiped about; but Reth was perilously near the horizon and Lythande sensed, in the way a magician will always know a danger, that even a Pilgrim Adept should not attempt to invade the quarters of Roygan the Proud under cover of total night.

They dissolved away, clutching with murmurs at their children, as Lythande appeared noiselessly, as if from thin air, at the edge of the fountain square. One child clung, giggling, to one of the sculptured mermaids, and the mother, who seemed to Lythande little more than a child herself, came and snatched it up, covertly making the sign against the Evil Eye—but not covertly enough. Lythande stood directly barring her path back to the other women, and said "Do you believe, woman, that I would curse you or your child?"

The woman looked at the ground, scuffing her sandaled foot on the cobbles, but her hands, clutching the child to her breast, were white at the knuckles with fear, and Lythande sighed. *Why did I do that?* At the sound of the sigh, the woman looked up, a quick darting glance like a bird's, as quickly averted.

"The blinded eye of Keth witness that I mean no harm to you or your child, and I would bless you if I knew any blessings," Lythande said at last, and faded into shadow so that the woman could gather the courage to scamper away across the street, her child's grubby head clutched against her breast. The encounter had left a taste of bitterness in Lythande's mouth, but with iron discipline, the magician let it slide away into limbo, to be taken out and examined, perhaps, when the bitterness had been attenuated by Time.

"Ring, sister of Roygan's ring, show me where, in the nose of Roygan the thief, I must seek you!"

One of the shadowed buildings edging the square seemed to fade somewhat in the dying sunset; through the walls of the building, Lythande could see rooms, walls, shadows, the moving shadow of a woman unveiled, a saucy round-bodied little creature with ringlets tumbled over a low brow, and the mark of a dimple in her chin, and great dark-lashed eyes. So this was the woman for whom Rastafyre the Incompetent had risked wand and magic and the vengeance of Roygan?

Do I scorn his choice because that path is barred to me?

Still; madness, between the choice of love and power, to choose such counterfeit of love as such a woman could give. For, silently approaching the walls which were all but transparent to Lythande's spelled Sight, the Pilgrim Adept could see beneath the outer surface of artless coquetry, down to the very core of selfishness and greed within the woman, her grasping at treasures, not for their beauty, but for the power they gave her. Rastafyre had not seen so deep within. Was he blinded by lust, then, or was it only farther evidence of the name Lythande had given him, *Incompetent?*

With a gesture, Lythande banished the spelled Sight; there was no need of it now, but there was need of haste, for Keth's orange rim actually caressed the western rim of the world. *Yet I can be in, and out, unseen, before the light is wholly gone,* Lythande thought, and, gesturing darkness to rise like a more enveloping mage-robe, stepped through the stone wall. It felt grainy, like walking through maize-dough, but nothing worse. Nevertheless Lythande hastened, pulling against the resistance of the stone; there were tales, horror tales told in the outer courts of the Pilgrim Adepts where this art was taught, of an Adept of the Blue Star who had lost his courage halfway through the wall, and stuck there, half of his body still trapped within the stone, shrieking with pain until he died... Lythande hated to risk this walking through walls, and usually relied on silence, stealth and spells applied to locks. But there was no time even to find the locks, far less to sound them out by magic and press by magic upon the sensitive tumblers of the bolts. When all the magician's body was within the shadowy room, Lythande drew a breath of relief; even the smell of mold and cobwebs was preferable to the grainy feel of the wall, and now, whatever came, Lythande resolved to go out by the door.

And now, in the heavy darkness of Roygan's treasure room, the light of the Blue Star alone would serve; Lythande felt the curious prickling, half pain, as the Blue Star began to glow... a blue light stole through the darkness, and by that subtle illumination, the Pilgrim Adept made out the contours of great chests, carelessly heaped jewels, bolted boxes... where, in all this hodgepodge of stolen treasure, laid up magpie fashion by Roygan's greed, was Rastafyre's wand to be found? Lythande paused, thoughtful, by one great heap of jewels, rubies blazing like Keth's rays at sunrise, sapphires flung like dazzling reflections of the light of the Blue Star, a superb diamond necklace, loosely flung like a constellation blazing beneath the pole-star of a single great gem. Lythande had spoken truly to Rastafyre, jewels were no temptation, yet for a moment the magician thought almost sadly of the women whose throats and slender arms and fingers had once been adorned with these jewels; why should Roygan profit by their great losses, if they felt the need of these toys and trinkets to enhance their beauty? And Lythande hesitated, considering. There was a spell which, once spoken, would disperse all these jewels back to their rightful owners, by the Law of Resonances.

Yet why should Lythande take on the karma of these unknown women, women Lythande would never see or know? If it had not been their just fate to lose the jewels to the clever hands of a thief, no doubt Roygan would have sought in vain for the keys to their treasure chests.

By that same token, why should I interfere with my magic in the just karma of Rastafyre, who lost his wand because he could not contain his lust for the wife of Roygan? Would not the loss of wand and virility teach him a just respect for the discipline of continence? It would not be for long, only till he could take the trouble to fashion and consecrate another wand of Power....

But Lythande had given the word of a Pilgrim Adept; for the honor of the Blue Star, what was promised must be performed. Sworn to the Law, it was Lythande's sworn duty to punish a thief, and all the more because Roygan preyed, not on Lythande whose defenses were sufficient for revenge, but upon the harmless Rastafyre... and if Roygan's wife found him not sufficient, then that was Roygan's karma too. Shivering somewhat in the darkness of the storeroom, Lythande whispered the spell that would make the treasure boxes transparent to the Sight. By the witchlight, Lythande scanned box after box, seeing nothing which might, by the remotest chance, be the wand of Rastafyre.

And outside the light was fading fast, and in the darkness, all the things of magic would be loosed....

And as if the thought had summoned it, suddenly it was there, though Lythande had not seen any door by which it could have entered the treasure chamber, a great grey shape, leaping high at the mage's throat. Lythande whirled, whipping out the dagger on the right, and thrust, hard, at the bane-wolf's throat.

It went through the throat as if through air. Not a true beast, then, but a magical one.... Lythande dropped the right-hand dagger, and snatched, left-handed, at the other, the dagger intended for fighting the powers and beasts of magic; but the delay had been nearly fatal; the teeth of the bane-wolf met, like fiery needles, in Lythande's right arm, forcing a cry from the magician's lips. It went unheard; the magical beast fought in silence, without a snarl or a sound even of breathing; Lythande thrust with the left-hand dagger, but could not reach the heart; then the bane-wolf's uncanny weight bore Lythande, writhing, to the ground. Again the needle-teeth of the enchanted creature met like flame in Lythande's shoulder, then in the knee thrust up to ward the beast from the throat. Lythande knew; if the fiery teeth met but once in the throat, it would cut off breath and life. Slowly, painfully, fighting upward, thrusting again and again, Lythande managed to wrestle the beast back, at the cost of bite after bite from the cruel flame-teeth; the bane-wolfs blazing eyes flashed against the light of the Blue Star, which grew fainter and feebler as Lythande's struggles weakened.

Have I come this far to die in a dark cellar in the maw of a wolf, and not even a true wolf, but a thing created by the filthy misuse of sorcery at the hands of a thief?

The thought maddened the magician, with a fierce effort, Lythande thrust the magical dagger deeper into the shoulder of the were-beast, seeking for the heart. With the full thrust of the spell, backed by all Lythande's agony, the magician's very arm thrust through unnatural flesh and bone, striking inward to the lungs, into the very heart of the creature... the blazing breath of the wolf smoked and failed; Lythande withdrew arm and dagger, slimed with the magical blood, as the beast, to eerie silence, writhed and died on the floor, slowly curling and melting into wisps of smoke, until only a little heap of ember, like burnt blood, remained on to floor of the treasure room.

Lythande's breath came loud in the silence as the Pilgrim Adept wiped the slime from the magical dagger, thrust it back into one sheath, then sought on the floor for where the right-hand dagger had fallen. There was slime on the magician's left hand, too, and the Adept wiped it, viciously, on a bolt of precious velvet; Roygan's things to Roygan, then! When the right-hand dagger was safe again in the other sheath, Lythande turned to the frantic search again for Rastafyre's wand. It was not to be thought of, that there would be much more time. Even if Roygan toyed with the wife who was all his now Rastafyre's power was gone, he could not stay with her forever, and if his magical power had created the bane-wolf, surely the death of the creature, drawing as it did on Roygan's own vitality, would alert him to the intrusion into his treasure room.

Through the lid of one of the boxes, Lythande could see, in the magical witchlight which responded only to the things of magical Power, a long narrow shape, wrapped in silks but still glowing with the light that singled out the things of magic. Surely that must be Rastafyre's wand, unless Roygan the Thief had a collection of such things—and the kind of incompetence which had allowed Roygan to get the wand was uncommon among magicians... praise to Keth's all-seeing eye!

Lythande fumbled with the lock. Now that the excitement of the fight with the bane-wolf had subsided, shoulder and arm were aching like half-healed burns where the enchanted teeth had met in Lythande's flesh. Worse than burns, perhaps, Lythande thought, for they might not yield to ordinary burn remedies! The magician wanted to tear off the tattered tunic where the bane-wolf had torn, but there were reasons not to do this within an enemy's stronghold! Lythande drew the mage-robe's folds closer, bitten hands wrenching at the bolts. The Pilgrim Adept was very strong; unlike those magicians who relied always on magic and avoided exertion, Lythande had traveled afoot and alone over all the highroads and by-roads lighted by the Twin Suns, and the wiry arms, the elegant-looking hands, had the strength of the daggers they wielded. After a moment the first hinge of the chest yielded, with a sound as loud, in the darkening cellar, as the explosion of fireworks; Lythande flinched at the sound... surely even Roygan must hear that in his wife's very chamber! Now for the other hinge. The bitten hands were growing more painful by the moment; Lythande took the right-hand dagger, the one intended for objects which were natural and not magic, and tried to wedge it under the hinge, prying to grim silence without success. Was the damned thing spelled shut? No; for then Lythande's hands alone could not have budged the first bolt. Blood was dripping from the blistered hand before the second lock gave way, and Lythande reached into the chest, and recoiled as if from the very teeth of the bane-wolf. Howling with rage and pain and frustration, Lythande swept into the chest with the left-hand dagger; there was a small ghastly shrilling and something ugly, horrible and only half visible, writhed and died. But now Lythande held the wand of Rastafyre, triumphant.

Wincing at the pain, Lythande stripped the concealing cloths from the wand. A grimace of distaste came over the magician's narrow face as the phallic carvings and shape of the wand were revealed, but after all, this had been fairly obvious—that Rastafyre would arm his wand with his manhood. It was, after all, his own problem; it was not Lythande's karma to teach other magicians either discretion or manners. A bargain had been made and a service should be performed.

Hastily wadding the protective silks around the wand—it was easier to handle that way, and Lythande had no wish even to look upon the gross thing—Lythande turned to the business of getting out again. Not through the walls. Darkness had surely fallen by now; though in the windowless treasure-room it was hard to tell, but there must be a door somewhere.

Lythande had heard nothing; but abruptly, as the witchlight flared, Roygan the Proud stood directly in the center of the room.

"So, Lythande the Magician is Lythande the Thief! How like you the business of thievery, then, Magician?"

A trap, then. But Lythande's mellow, neutral voice was calm.

"It is written; from the thief all shall be stolen at last. By the ring in your nose, Roygan; you know the truth of what I say."

With an inarticulate howl of rage, Roygan hurled himself at Lythande. The magician stepped aside, and Roygan hurtled against a chest, giving a furious yelp of pain as his knees collided with the metalled edge of the chest. He whirled, but Lythande, dagger in hand, stood facing him.

"Ring of Lythande, ring of Roygan's shame, be welded to this," Lythande murmured, and the dagger flung itself against Roygan's face. Roygan grunted with pain as Lythande's dagger molded itself against the ring, curling around his face.

"Ai! Ai! Take it off, damn you by every god and godlet of Gandrin, or I—"

"You will what?" demanded Lythande, looking with an aloof grin at Roygan's face, the dagger curled around the end of his nose, and gripping, as if by a powerful magnet, at the metal tips of Roygan's teeth. Furious, howling, Roygan flung himself again at Lythande, his yell wordless now as the metal of the dagger fastened itself tighter to his teeth. Lythande laughed, stepping free easily from Roygan's clutching hands; but the thief's face was alight with sudden triumphant glee.

"Hoy," he mumbled through the edges of the dagger. "Now I have touched Lythande and I know your secret... Lythande, Pilgrim Adept, wearer of the Blue Star, you are—ai! *Ai-ya!*" With a fearful screech of pain, Roygan fell to the floor, wordless as the dagger curled deeper into his mouth; blood burst from his lip, and in the next moment, Lythande's other dagger thrust through his heart, in the merciful release from agony.

Lythande bent, retrieved the dagger which had thrust into Roygan's heart. Then, Blue Star blazing magic, Lythande reached for the other dagger, which had bitten through Roygan's lips, tongue, throat. A murmured spell restored it to the shape of a dagger, the metal slowly uncurling under the stroking hands of the owner's sorcery. Slowly, sighing, Lythande sheathed both daggers.

I meant not to kill him. But I knew too well what his next words would be; and the magic of a Pilgrim Adept is void if the Secret is spoken aloud. And, knowing, I could not let him live. Why was she so regretful? Roygan was not the first Lythande had killed to keep that Secret, the words actually on Roygan's mutilated tongue: *Lythande, you are a woman.*

A woman. A woman, who in her pride had penetrated the courts of the Pilgrim Adepts in disguise, and when the Blue Star was already between her brows, had been punished and rewarded with the Secret she had kept well enough to deceive even the Great Adept in the Temple of the Blue Star.

Your Secret, then, shall be forever, for on the day when any man save my self shall speak your secret aloud, your power is void. Be then forever doomed with the Secret you yourself have chosen, and be forever in the eyes of all men what you made us think you.

Bitterly, Lythande thrust the wand of Rastafyre under the folds of the mage-robe. Now she had leisure to find a way out by the doors. The locks yielded to the touch of magic; but before leaving the cellar, Lythande spoke the spell which would return Roygan's stolen jewels to their owners.

A small victory for the cause of Law. And Roygan the thief had met his just fate.

Stepping out into the fading sunlight, Lythande blinked. It had seemed to take hours, that silent struggle in the darkness of the Treasure-room. Yet the sun still lingered, and a little child played noiselessly, splashing her feet in the fountain, until a chubby young woman came to scold her merrily and tug her within-doors. Listening to the laughter, Lythande sighed. A thousand years, a thousand memories, cut her away from the woman and the child.

To love no man lest my Secret be known. To love no woman lest she be a target for my enemies in quest of the Secret.

And she risked exposure and powerlessness, again and again, for such as Rastafyre. *Why?*

Because I must. There was no answer other than that, a Pilgrim Adept's vow to Law against Chaos. Rastafyre should have his wand back. There was no law that all magicians should be competent.

She laid a narrow hand along the wand, trying not to flinch at the shape, and murmured, "Bring me to your master."

Lythande found Rastafyre in a tavern; and, having no wish for any public display of power, beckoned him outside. The tubby little magician stared up in awe at the blazing Blue Star.

"You have it? Already?"

Silently, Lythande held out the wrapped wand to Rastafyre. As he touched it, he seemed to grow taller, handsomer, less tubby; even his face fell into lines of strength, and virility.

"And now my fee," Lythande reminded him.

He said sullenly "How know I that Roygan the Proud will not come after me?"

"I knew not," said Lythande calmly, "that your magic had power to raise the dead, oh Rastafyre the Incomparable."

"You—you—k-k-k—he's dead?"

"He lies where his ill-gotten treasures rest, with the ring of Lythande still through his nose," Lythande said calmly. "Try, now, to keep your magic wand out of the power of other men's wives."

Rastafyre chuckled. He said "But wha-wha—what else would I do w-w-with my p-p-power?"

Lythande grimaced. "Koira's lute," she said, "or you will lie where Roygan lies."

Rastafyre the Incomparable raised his hand. "Ca-ca-Carrier," he intoned, and, flickering in and off in the dullness of the room, the velvet bag winked in, out again, came back, vanished again even as Rastafyre had his hand within it.

"Damn you, Ca-ca-Carrier! Come or go, but don't flicker like that! Stay! Stay, I said!" He sounded, Lythande thought, as if he were talking to a reluctant puppy dog.

Finally, when he got it entirely materialized, he drew forth the lute. With a grave bow, Lythande accepted it, tucking it out of sight under the mage-robe.

"Health and prosperity to you, O Lythande," he said—for once without stuttering; perhaps the wand did that for him too?

"Health and prosperity to you, O Rastafyre the Incom—" Lythande hesitated, laughed aloud and said, "Incomparable."

He took himself off then, and Lythande added silently, "And more luck to your adventures," as she watched Ca-ca-Carrier dimly lumping along like a small surly shadow at his heels, until at last it vanished entirely.

Alone, Lythande stepped into the dark street, under the cold and moonless sky. With a single gesture the magical circle blotted away all surroundings; there was neither time nor space. Then Lythande began to play the lute softly. There was a little stirring in the silence, and the figure of Koira, slender, delicate, her pale hair shimmering about her face and her body gleaming through wispy veils, appeared before her.

"Lythande—" she whispered. "It is you!"

"It is I, Koira. Sing to me," Lythande commanded. "Sing to me the song you sang when we sat together in the gardens of Hilarion."

Lythande's fingers moved on the lute, and Koira's soft contralto swelled out into an ancient song from a country half a world away and so many years Lythande feared to remember how many.

The years shall fall upon you, and the light

31

That dwelled in you, go into endless night;
As wine, poured out and sunk into the ground,
Even your song shall leave no breath of sound,
And as the leaves within the forest fall,
Your memory will not remain at all,
As a word said, a song sung, and be
Forever with the memories—

"Stop," Lythande said, strangled.

Koira fell silent, at last whispering, "I sang at your command and now I am still at your command."

When Lythande could look up without the agony of despair, Koira too was silent. Lythande said at last, "What binds you to the lute, Koira whom once I loved?"

"I know not," Koira said, and it seemed that the ghost or her voice was bitter, "I know only that while this lute survives, I am enslaved to it."

"And to my will?"

"Even so, Lythande."

Lythande set her mouth hard. She said, "You would not love me when you might; now shall I have you whether you will or no."

"Love—" Koira was silent. "We were maidens then and we loved after the fashion of young maidens; and then you went into a far country where I would not follow, my heart was a woman's heart, and you—"

"What do you know of my heart?" Lythande cried out in despair.

"I knew that my heart was a woman's heart and longed for a love other than yours," Koira said. "What would you, Lythande? You too are a woman; I call that no love..."

Lythande's eyes were closed. But at last the voice was stubborn. "Yet you are here and you shall sing forever at my will, and be forever silent about your desire for a man's love... for you there is none other than I, now!"

Koira bowed deeply, but it seemed to Lythande that there was mockery in the bow.

She said sharply "What enslaves you to the lute? Are you bound for a space, or forever?"

"I know not," Koira said, "Or if I know I cannot speak it."

So it was often with enchantments; Lythande knew... and now she would have all of time before her, and sooner or later, sooner or later, Koira would love her... Koira was her slave, she could bid her come and go with her hands on the lute as once they had sought for more than a shared song and a maiden's kiss...

But a slave's counterfeit of love is not love. Lythande raised the lute to her hands, poising her fingers on the strings; Koira's form began to waver a little, and then, acting swiftly before she could think better of it, Lythande raised the lute, brought it crashing down and broke it over her knee.

Koira's face wavered, between astonishment and sudden delirious happiness. "Free!" she cried, "Free at last—O, Lythande, now do I know you truly loved me..." and a whisper swirled and faded and was still, and there was only the empty bubble of magic, void, silent, without light or sound.

Lythande stood still, the broken lute in her hands. If Rastafyre could only see. She had risked life, sanity, magic, Secret itself and the Blue Star's power, for this lute, and within moments she had broken it and set free the one who could, over the years, been drawn to her, captive... unable to refuse, unable to break Lythande's pride further....

He would think me, too, an incompetent magician.

I wonder which of us two would be right?

With a long sigh, Lythande drew the mage-robe about her thin shoulders, made sure the two daggers were secure in their sheaths—for at this hour, in the moonless streets of Old Gandrin there were many dangers, real and magical—and went on her solitary way, stepping over the fragments of the broken lute.

SOMEBODY ELSE'S MAGIC
Marion Zimmer Bradley

In a place like the Thieves' Quarter of Old Gandrin, there is no survival skill more important than the ability to mind your own business. Come robbery, rape, arson, blood feud, or the strange doings of wizards, a carefully cultivated deaf ear for other people's problems—not to mention a blind eye, or better, two, for anything that is not your affair—is the best way, maybe the only way, to keep out of trouble.

It is no accident that everywhere in Old Gandrin, and everywhere else under the Twin Suns, they speak of the blinded eye of Keth-Ketha. A god knows better than to watch the doings of his creatures too carefully.

Lythande, the mercenary-magician, knew this perfectly well. When the first scream rang down the quarter, despite an involuntary shoulder twitch, Lythande knew that the proper thing was to look straight ahead and keep right on walking in the same direction. It was one of the reasons why Lythande had survived this long; through cultivating superb skill at own-business-minding in a place where there were a variety of strange businesses to be minded.

Yet there was a certain note to the screams—

Ordinary robbery or even rape might not have penetrated that carefully cultivated shell of blindness, deafness, looking straight into the thick of it. Lythande's hand gripped almost without thought at the hilt of the right-hand knife, the black-handled one that hung from the red girdle knotted over the mage-robe, flipped it out, and ran straight into trouble.

The woman was lying on the ground now, and there had been at least a dozen of them, long odds even for the Thieves Quarter. Somehow, before they had gotten her down, she had managed to kill at least four of them, but there were others, standing around and cheering the survivors on. The Blue Star between Lythande's brows, the mark of a Pilgrim Adept, had begun to glow and flicker with blue lightnings, in time with the in-and-out flicker of the blade. Two, then three went down before they knew what had hit them, and a fourth was spitted in the middle of his foul work, ejaculating and dying with a single cry. Two more fell, spouting blood, one from a headless neck, the other falling sidewise, unbalanced by an arm lopped away at the shoulder, bled out before he hit the ground. The rest took to their heels, shrieking. Lythande wiped the blade on the cloak of one of the dead men and bent over the dying woman.

She was small and frail to have done so much damage to her assailants; and they had made her pay for it. She wore the leather garments of a swordsman; they had been ripped off her, and she was bleeding everywhere, but she was not defeated—even now she made a feeble gesture toward her sword and snarled, her bitten lips drawn back over bared teeth, "Wait ten minutes, animal, and I will be beyond caring; then you may take your pleasure from my corpse and be damned to you!"

A swift look round showed Lythande that nothing human was alive within hearing. It was nowhere within the bounds of possibility that this woman could live and betray her. Lythande knelt, crushing the woman's head gently against her breast.

"Hush, hush, my sister. I will not harm you."

The woman looked up at her in wonder, and a smile spread over the dying face. She whispered, "I thought I had betrayed my last trust—I was sworn to die first; but there were too many for me. The Goddess does not forgive—those who submit—"

She was slipping away. Lythande whispered, "Be at peace, child. The Goddess does not condemn...." And thought: *I would not give a fart in sulphurous hell for a goddess who would.*

"My sword—" the woman groped; already she found it hard to see. Lythande put the hilt into her fingers.

"My sword—dishonored—" she whispered. "I am Larith. The sword must go—back to her shrine. Take it. Swear—"

Larithae! Lythande knew of the shrine of that hidden goddess and of the vow her women made. She could now understand, though never excuse, the thugs who had attacked and killed the woman. Larithae were fair game everywhere from the Southern Waste to Falthot in the Ice Hills. The shrine of the Goddess as Larith lay at the end of the longest and most dangerous road in the Forbidden Country, and it was a road Lythande had no reason nor wish to tread. A road, moreover, that by her own oath she was forbidden, for she might never reveal herself as a woman, at the cost of the Power that had set the Blue Star between her brows. And only women sought, or could come to, the shrine of Larith.

Firmly, denying, Lythande shook her head.

"My poor girl, I cannot; I am sworn elsewhere, and serve not your Goddess. Let her sword remain honorably in your hand. No," she repeated, putting away the woman's pleading hand, "I cannot. Sister. Let me bind up your wounds, and you shall take that road yourself another day."

She knew the woman was dying; but it would give her something,

Lythande thought, to occupy her thoughts in death. And if, in secret and in her own heart, she cursed the impetus that had prompted her to ignore that old survival law of minding her own business, no hint of it came into the hard but compassionate face she bent on the dying swordswoman.

The Laritha was silent, smiling faintly beneath Lythande's gentle ministrations; she let Lythande straighten her twisted limbs, try to stanch the blood that now had slowed to a trickle. But already her eyes were dulling and glazing. She caught at Lythande's fingers and whispered, in a voice so thready that only by Lythande's skill at magic could the words be distinguished, "Take the sword, Sister. Larith witness I give it to you freely without oath...."

With a mental shrug, Lythande whispered, "So be it, without oath... bear witness for me in that dark country. Sister, and hold me free of it."

Pain flitted over the dulled eyes for the last time.

"Go free—if you can—" the woman whispered, and with her last movement thrust the hilt of the larith sword into Lythande's palm. Lythande, startled, by pure reflex closed her hand on the hilt, then abruptly realized what she was doing—rumor had many tales of larith magic, and Lythande wanted none of their swords! She let it go and tried to push it back into the woman's hand. But the fingers had locked in death and would not receive it.

Lythande sighed and laid the woman gently down. Now what was to be done? She had made it clear that she would not take the sword; one of the few things that was really known about the Larithae was that their shrine was a shrine of women sword-priestesses, and that no man might touch their magic, on pain of penalties too dreadful to be imagined. Lythande, Pilgrim Adept, who had paid more highly for the Blue Star than any other Adept in the history of the Order, dared not be found anywhere in the light of Keth or her sister Reth with a sword of Larith in her possession. For the very life of Lythande's magic depended on this: that she never be known as a woman.

The doom had been just, of course. The shrine of the Blue Star had been forbidden to women for more centuries than can be counted upon the fingers of both hands. In all the history of the Pilgrim Adepts, no woman before Lythande had penetrated their secrets in disguise; and when at last she was exposed and discovered, she was so far into the secrets of the Order that she was covered by the dreadful oath that forbids one Pilgrim Adept to slay another—for all are sworn to fight, on the Last Day of All, for Law against Chaos. They could not kill her; and since already she bore all the secrets of their Order, she could not be bidden to depart.

But the doom laid on her had been what she had, unknowing, chosen when she came into the Temple of the Blue Star under concealment.

"As you have chosen to conceal your womanhood, so shall you forever conceal it," thus had fallen the doom, "for on that secret shall hang your power; on the day that any other Adept of the Blue Star shall proclaim forth your true sex, on that day is your power fallen, and ended with it the sanctity that protects you against vengeance upon one who stole our secrets. Be, then, what you have chosen to be, and be so throughout the eternity until the Last Battle of Law against Chaos."

And so, fenced about with all the other vows of a Pilgrim Adept, Lythande bore that doom of eternal concealment. Never might she reveal herself to any man; nor to any woman save one she could trust with power and life. Only three times had she dared confide in any, and of those three, two were dead. One had died by torture when a rival Adept of the Blue Star had sought to wring Lythande's secret from her; had died still faithful. And the other had died in her arms, minutes ago. Lythande smothered a curse; her weak admission to a dying woman might have saddled her with a curse, even though she had sworn nothing. If she were seen with a larith sword, she might as well proclaim her true sex aloud from the High Temple steps at midday in Old Gandrin!

Well, she would not be seen with it. The sword should lie in the grave of the Laritha who had honorably defended it.

Lythande stood up, drawing down the hood of the mage-robe over her face so that the Blue Star was in shadow. Nothing about her—tall, lean, angular—betrayed that she was other than any Pilgrim Adept; her smooth, hairless face might have been the hairlessness of a freak or an effeminate had there been any to question it—which there was not—and the pale hair, square-cut after an ancient fashion, the narrow hawk-features, were strong and sexless, the jawline too hard for most women. Never, for an instant, by action, word, mannerism, or inattention, had she ever betrayed that she was other than magician, mercenary. Under the mage-robe was the ordinary dress of a north-countryman—leather breeches; high, laceless boots; sleeveless leather jerkin—and the laced and ruffled under-tunic of a dandy. The ringless hands were calloused and square, ready to either of the swords that were girded at the narrow waist; the right-hand blade for material enemies, the left-hand blade against things of magic.

Lythande picked up the larith blade and held it distastefully at arm's length. Somehow she must see to having the woman buried, and the heap of corpses they had made between them. By fantastic luck, no one had entered the street till now, but a drunken snatch of song raised raucous echoes between the old buildings, and a drunken man reeled down the street, with two or three companions to hold him upright, and seeing Lythande standing over the heap of bodies, got the obvious impression.

"Murder!" he howled. "Here's murder and death! Ho, the watch, the guards—help, murder!"

"Stop howling," Lythande said, "the victim is dead, and all the rest of her assailants fled."

The man came to stare drunkenly down at the body.

"Pretty one, too," said the first man. "Did you get your turn before she died?"

"She was too far gone," Lythande said truthfully. "But she is a countrywoman of mine, and I promised her I would see her decently buried." A hand went into the mage-robe and came out with a glint of gold. "Where do I arrange for it?"

"I hear the watchmen," said one man, less drunk than his companions, and Lythande, too, could hear the ringing of boots on stone, the clash of pikes. "For that kind of gold, you could have half the city buried, and if there weren't enough corpses, I'd make you a few more myself."

Lythande flung the drunk some coins. "Get her buried, then, and that carrion with her."

"I'll see to it," said the least drunk, "and not even toss you a coin for that fine sword of hers; you can take it to her kinfolk."

Lythande stared at the sword in her hand. She would have sworn she had laid it properly across the dead woman's breast. Well, it had been a confusing half hour. She bent and laid it on the lifeless breast. "Touch it not; it is a larith sword; I dare not think what the Larithae would do to you, should they find you with that in your hand."

The drunken men shrank back. "May I defile virgin goats if I touch it," said one of them, with a superstitious gesture. "But do you not fear the curse?"

And now she was confused enough that she had picked up the larith blade again. This time she put it carefully down across the Laritha's body and spoke the words of an unbinding-spell in case the dying woman's gesture had somehow sought to bind that sword to her. Then she moved into the shadows of the street in that noiseless and unseen way that often caused people to swear, truthfully, that they had seen Lythande appearing or disappearing into thin air. She looked on from the shadows until the watchmen had come, cursing, and dragged away the bodies for burial. In this city, they knew little of the Goddess Larith and her worship, and Lythande thought, conscience-stricken, that she should have seen to it that the woman and her ravishers were not buried in the same grave. Well, and what if they were? They were all dead, and might await the Last Battle against Chaos together; they could have no further care for what befell their corpses, or if they did, they could tell it to whatever judges awaited them on the far side of death's gate.

This story is not concerned with the business that had brought Lythande to Old Gandrin, but when it was completed the next day, and the mercenary-magician emerged from a certain house in the Merchants' Quarter, stowing more coins into the convenient folds of the mage-robe, and ruefully remembering the depleted stocks of magical herbs and stones in the pouches and pockets stowed in odd places about that mage-robe, Lythande, with a most unpleasant start, found her fingers entangled with a strange object of metal tied about her waist. It was the larith sword; and it was, moreover, tied there with a strange knot that gave her fingers some little trouble to untie, and was certainly not her own work!

"Chaos and hellfire!" swore Lythande. "There is more to larith magic than I ever thought!"

That damnable impulse that had prompted her to meddle in somebody else's business had now, it seemed, saddled her with someone else's magic. Furthermore, her unbinding-spell had not worked. Now she must make strong magic that would not fail; and first she must find herself a safe place to do it.

In Old Gandrin she had no safe-house established, and the business that had brought her here, though important and well paid, was not of the kind that makes many friends or incurs much gratitude. She had been gifted past what she had asked for her services; but should Lythande present herself at that same door where she had worked spells to thrust out ghosts and haunts, she did not deceive herself that she would receive much welcome. What, then, to do? A Pilgrim Adept did not make magic in the street like a wandering juggler!

A common tavern? Some shelter, indeed, she must find before the burning eye of Reth sank below the horizon; she was carrying much gold, and had no wish to defend it in the night-streets of the Thieves' Quarter. She must also replenish her stocks of magical herbs, and also find a place to rest, and eat, and drink, before she set off northward to the shrine of the Goddess at Larith....

Lythande cursed aloud, so angrily that a passerby in the street turned and stared in protest. Northward to Larith? Was that forever-be-damned sorcerous sword beginning to work on her very thoughts? This was strong magic; but she would not go to Larith, no, by the Final Battle, she would not go northward, but south, and nowhere near that accursed shrine of the Larithae! *Not while there is magic left in the arsenal of a Pilgrim Adept, I will not!*

In the market, moving noiselessly in the concealment of the mage-robe, she found a stall where magical herbs were for sale, and bartered briefly for them; briefly, because the law of magic states that whatever is wanted for the making of magic must be bought without haggling, gold being no more than dross at the service of magical arts. Yet, Lythande mused darkly, that knowledge had evidently become common among herb-sellers and spell-

39

candlers of the Gandrin market, and as a result their prices had gone from the merely outrageous to the unthinkable. Lythande remonstrated briefly with a woman at one of these stalls.

"Come, come, four Thirds for a handful of darkleaf?"

"And how am I to know that when ye give me gold, ye havena' spelled it from copper or worse?" demanded the herb-seller. "Last moon I sold one of your Order a full quartern of dreamroot and bloodleaf, full cured by a fire o' hazel and spellroot, and that defiler of virgin goats paid me with two rounds of gold—he said. But when the moon changed, I looked at 'em, and it was no more than a handful of barley stuck together wi' spellroot and smelling worse than the devil's ferts! I take that risk into account when I set my prices, magician!"

"Such folk bring disrepute on the name of the magician," Lythande agreed gravely, but secretly wished she knew that spell. There were dishonest innkeepers who would be better paid in barley grains; in fact, the grain would be worth more than their services! The spell-candler was looking at Lythande as if she had more to say, and Lythande raised inquiring eyebrows.

"I'd give you the stuff for half if you'd show me a spell to tell true gold from false, magician."

Lythande looked round, and on a nearby stall saw the crystals she wanted. She picked up one of them.

"The crystal called blue zeth is a touchstone of magic," Lythande said. "False gold will not have a true gold shimmer; and other things spelled to look like gold will show what they are, but only if you blink thrice and look between the second and third blink. That bracelet on your arm, good woman—"

The woman slid the bracelet down over her plump hand; Lythande took it up and looked through the blue zeth crystal.

"As you can clearly see," she said, "this bracelet is—" and to her surprise, concluded—"false gold; pot-metal gilded."

The woman squinted, blinked at the bracelet. "Why, that defiler of virgin goats," she howled. "I will kick his arse from here to the river! Him and his tales of his uncle the goldsmith—"

Lythande restrained a smile, though the corners of her lips twitched. "Have I created trouble with husband or lover, O good woman?"

"Only that he'd like to be, I make no doubt," muttered the woman, throwing the cheap bracelet down with contempt.

"Look at something I know to be true gold, then," Lythande said, and picked up one of the coins she had given the woman. "True gold will look like this—" And at her wave, the woman bent to look at the golden shimmer of the coin. "What is not gold will take on the blue color of the zeth crystal, or"—she took up a copper, gestured, and the copper shone with a deceptive gold luster; she thrust it under the crystal—"if you blink three times and look between the second and third blink, you can tell what it is really made of."

Delighted, the stallkeeper bought a handful of blue zeth crystals at the neighboring stall. "Take the herbs, then, gift for gift," she said, then asked suspiciously, "What else will you ask me for this spell? For if is truly priceless—"

"Priceless, indeed," Lythande agreed. "I ask only that you tell the spell to three other persons, and exact a promise that each person to whom it is told tell three others. Dishonest magicians bring evil repute—and then it is hard for an honest one to make a living."

And, of course, what nine market women knew would soon be known everywhere in the city. The sellers of blue zeth would profit, but not beyond their merits.

"Yet the magicians of the Blue Star are honest, so far as I've had dealings with 'em," the woman said, putting away the blue zeth crystals into a capacious and not-very-clean pocket. "I got decent gold from the one who bought spellroot from me last New Moon."

Lythande froze and went very still, but the Blue Star on the browless forehead began to sparkle slightly and glow. "Know you his name? I knew not that a brother of my Order had been within Old Gandrin this season."

It meant nothing, of course. But, like all Pilgrim-Adepts, Lythande was a solitary, and would have preferred that what she did in Old Gandrin should not be spied on by another. And it lent urgency to her errand; above all, she must not be seen with the larith sword, lest the secret of her sex become known; it was not well known within Gandrin—for the Larithae seldom came so far south—but in the North it was known that only a woman might touch, handle, or wield a larith sword.

"Upon reflection," she said, "I have done you, as you say, a priceless service; do you one for me in return."

The woman hesitated for a moment, and Lythande for one did not blame her. It is not, as a general rule, wise to entangle oneself in the private affairs of wizards, and certainly not when that wizard glows with lightning flash of the Blue Star. The woman glowered at the false gold bracelet and muttered, "What is your need?"

"Direct me to a safe lodging place this night—one where I may make magic, and see to it that I do so unobserved."

The woman said at last, grudgingly, "I am no tavern, and have no public-room and no great kitchens for roasting meat. Yet now and again I let out my upper chamber, if the tenant is sober and respectable. And my son—he's nineteen and like a bull about the shoulders—he'll stand below wi' a cudgel and keep away anyone who would spy. I'll gi' you that room for a half o' gold."

A half? That was more outrageous than the price she had set on her bags of spellroot. But now, of all times, Lythande dared not haggle.

"Done, but I must have a decent meal served me in privacy."

The woman considered adding to the charge, but under the glare of the Blue Star, she said quickly, "I'll send out to the cookshop round the corner and get ye roast fowl and a honey-cake."

Lythande nodded, thinking of the sword of Larith tied under the mage-robe. In privacy, then, she could work her best unbinding-spell, then bury the sword by the riverbank and hasten southward.

"I shall be here at sunset," she said.

As the crimson face of Reth faded below the horizon, Lythande locked herself within the upper chamber. She was fiercely hungry and thirsty— among the dozen or more vows that fenced about the power of a Pilgrim Adept, it was forbidden to eat or drink within the sight of any man. The prohibition did not apply to women, but, ever conscious of the possibility of disguise like her own, she had fenced it with unending vigilance and discipline; she could not, now, have forced herself to swallow a morsel of food or drink except in the presence of one or two of her trusted confidantes, and only one of these knew Lythande to be a woman. But that woman was far away; in a city beyond the world's end, and Lythande had no trusted associate nearer than that.

She had managed, hours ago, a sip of water at a public fountain in a deserted square. She had eaten nothing for several days save for a few bites of dried fruit, taken under cover of darkness, from a small store she kept in pockets of the mage-robe. The rare luxury of a hot meal in assured privacy was almost enough to break her control, but before touching anything, she checked the locks and searched the walls for unseen spy-holes where she might be overlooked, unlikely, she knew, but Lythande's survival all these years had rested on just such unsparing vigilance.

Then she drank from the ewer of water, washed herself carefully, and setting a little water to heat by the good fire in the room, carefully shaved her eye-brows, a pretense she had kept up ever since she began to look too old to pass for a beardless boy. She left the razor and soap carefully by the hearth where they could be seen. She could, if she must, briefly create an illusion of beard, and sometimes smeared her face with dirt to add to it, but it was difficult and demanded close concentration, and she dared not rely on it; so she shaved her eyebrows close, with the thought that a man known to shave his eyebrows would probably have to shave his beard as well.

Hearing steps on the stair, she drew the mage-robe about her, and the herb-seller puffed up the last steps and into the opened door. She set the smoking tray on the table, murmured, "I'll empty that for ye," and took up the bowl of soapy water and the slop jar. "My son's at the stairway wi' his cudgel; none will disturb you here, magician."

Nevertheless, Lythande, alone again, made very sure the bolt was well-drawn and the room still free of spy-eyes or spells; who knew what the herb-seller might have brought with her? Some spell-candlers had pretensions to the arts of sorcery. Moreover, the woman had mentioned that she had seen another Adept of the Blue Star; and Lythande had enemies among them. Suppose the herb-seller were in the pay of Rabben the Half-handed, or Beccolo, or... Lythande dismissed this unprofitable speculation. The room appeared empty and harmless. The smell of roast fowl and the freshly baked loaf was dizzying in her famished condition, but magic could not be made on a full stomach, so she packed away the smell into a remote corner of her consciousness and drew out the Larith's sword.

It felt warm to the touch, and there was the small tingling that reminded Lythande that powerful magic resided in it.

She cast a pinch of a certain herb into the fire and, breathing the powerful scent, focused all her powers into one spell. Under her feet, the floor rocked as the Word of Power died, and there was a faint, faraway rumble as of falling walls and towers—or was it only distant summer thunder?

She passed her hand lightly above the sword, careful not to touch it. She was not really familiar with the magic of the Larithae; as Lythande the Pilgrim Adept, she could not be, and while she still lived as a woman, she had never come closer than to know what every passerby knew. But it seemed to her that whatever magic dwelt in the sword was gone; perhaps not banished, but sleeping.

From her pack she sacrificed one of the spare tunics she carried, and carefully wrapped the sword. The tunic was a good one, heavy white silk from the walled and ancient city of Jumathe, where the silkworms were tended by a special caste of women, blinded in childhood so that their fingers would have more sensitivity when the time came to strip the silk from the cocoons, Their songs were legendary, and Lythande had once gone there, dressed as a woman, a cloak hiding the Blue Star, grateful for the women's blindness so that she could speak in her own voice; she had sung them songs of her own north-country, and heard their songs in return, while they thought her only a wandering minstrel girl. The sighted overseer, however, had been suspicious, and had finally accused her of being a man in disguise—for a man to approach the blind women was a crime punishable by death in a particularly unpleasant fashion—and it had taken all of Lythande's magic to extricate herself. But that is another story.

Lythande wrapped the sword in the tunic. She regretted the necessity of giving it up—she had had it for a long time; she shrank from thinking how many years ago she had sung her songs within the house of the blind silkworm-tenders in Jumathe! But for such magic a real sacrifice was necessary, and she had nothing else to sacrifice that meant the least thing to her; so she wrapped the sword in it, and bound it with the cord she had passed through the herb-smoke, tying it with the magical ninefold knot.

Then she set it aside and sat down to eat up the roast fowl and the freshly baked bread with the sense of a task well done.

When the house was quiet, and the herb-seller's son had put his cudgel away and retired to rest, Lythande slipped down the stairs noiselessly as a shadow. She had to spell the lock so that it would not creak, and a somewhat smaller spell would make any passerby think that the drawn-back bolt, open padlock, and open door were firmly shut and bolted. Silken bundle under her arm, she slipped silently to the riverbank and, working by the dim light of the smaller moon, dug a hole and buried the bundle; then, speaking a final spell, strode away without looking back.

Returning to the herb-seller's house, she thought she saw something following in the street, and turned to look. No, it was only a shadow. She slipped in through the open door—which still looked charmed and locked—locked it tight from within, and regained her room with less sound than a mouse in the walls.

The fire had burned to coals. Lythande sat by the fire and took from her pack a small supply of sweet herbs with no magical properties whatever, rolled them into a narrow tube, and sparked it alight. So relaxed was she that she did not even use her fire-ring, but stooped to light the tube from the last coals of the fire. She leaned back, inhaling the fragrant smoke and letting it trickle out slowly from her nostrils. When she had smoked it down to a small stub, she took off her heavy boots, wrapped herself tightly in the mage-robe and then in the herb-seller's blanket, and lay down to sleep.

Before dawn she would arise and vanish as if by magic, leaving the door bolted behind her on the inside—there was no special reason for. this, but a magician must preserve some mystery, and if she left by the stairs in the ordinary way, perhaps the innkeeper would be left with the impression that perhaps magicians were not so extraordinary after all, since they ate good dinners and washed and shaved and filled slop jars like any ordinary mortal. So when Lythande had gone, the room would be set to rights without a wrinkle in the bed-clothes or an ash in the fireplace, the door still bolted on the inside as if no one had left the room at all. And besides, it was more amusing that way.

But for now, she would sleep for a few hours in peace, grateful that the clumsiness that had entangled her in somebody else's magic had come to a good end. No whisper disturbed her sleep to the effect that it hadn't really even started yet.

The last of the prowling thieves had slipped away to their holes and corners, and the red eye of Keth was still blinded by night when Lythande slipped out of Old Gandrin by the southern gate. She took the road south for two reasons: there was always work for mercenary or magician in the prosperous seaport of Gwennane, and also she wished to be certain in her own mind that after her drastic unbinding-spell, nothing called her northward to the Larith shrine.

The least of the moons had waned and set, and it was that black-dark hour when dawn is not even a promise in the sky. The gate was locked and barred, and the sleepy watchman, when Lythande asked quietly for the gate to be opened, growled that he wouldn't open the gate at that hour for the High-Autarch of Gandrin himself, far less for some ne'er-do-well prowling when honest folk and dishonest folk were all sleeping, or ought to be. He remembered afterward that the star between the ridges where Lythande's brows ought to have been had begun to sparkle and flare blue lightning, and he could never explain why he found himself meekly opening the gate and then doing it up again afterward. "Because," he said earnestly, "I never saw that fellow in the mage-robe go through the gate, not at all; he turned hisself invisible!" And because Lythande was not all that well known in Old Gandrin, no one ever told him it was merely Lythande's way.

Lythande breathed a sigh of relief when the gate was shut behind her, and began to walk swiftly in the dark, striding long and fall and silent. At that pace, the Pilgrim Adept covered several leagues before a faint flush in the sky told where the eye of Keth would stare through the dawn clouds. Reth would follow some hours later. Lythande continued, covering ground at a rate, then was vaguely troubled by something she could not quite identify. Yes, something was wrong....

It certainly was. Keth was rising, which was as it should be, but Keth was rising on her right hand, which was not as it should be; she had taken the southward road out of Old Gandrin, yet here she was, striding northward at a fast pace. To the north. Toward the shrine of Larith.

Yet she could not remember turning round for long enough to become confused and take the wrong direction in the darkness. She must have done so somehow. She stopped in mid-stride, whirled about, and put the sun where it should be, on her left, and began pacing steadily south.

But after a time she felt the prickle in her shins and buttocks and the cold-flame glow of the Blue Star between her brows, which told her that magic was being made somewhere about her. And the sun was shining on her right hand, and she was standing directly outside the gates of Old Gandrin.

Lythande said aloud, "No. Damnation and Chaos!" disturbing a little knot of milkwomen who were driving their cows to market. They stared at the tall, sexless figure and whispered, but Lythande cared nothing for their gossip. She started to turn round again and found herself actually walking through the gates of Old Gandrin again.

Through the south gate. Traveling north.

Now this is ridiculous, Lythande thought. *I buried the sword myself, locked there with my strongest unbinding spell!* Yet her pack bulged strangely; ripping out a gutter obscenity, Lythande unslung the pack and discovered what she had known she would discover the moment she felt that strange prickling cramp that told her there was magic in use—somebody else's magic! At the very top of the pack, wedged in awkwardly, was the white silk tunic, draggled with the soil of the riverbank, and thrusting through it—as if, Lythande thought with a shudder, it were trying to get out—was the larith sword.

Lythande had not survived this long under the Twin Suns without becoming oblivious to hysteria. The Adepts of the Blue Star held powerful magic; but every mage knew that sooner or later, everyone would encounter magic stronger yet. Now she felt rage rather than fear. Heartily, Lythande damned the momentary impulse of compassion for a dying woman that led her to reveal herself. Well, done was done. She had the larith sword and seemed likely—Lythande thought with a flicker of irony—to have it until she could devise a strong enough magic to get rid of it again.

Was she fit for a really prolonged magical duel? It would attract attention; and somewhere within the walls of Old Gandrin—or so the herb-seller had told her—there was another Adept of the Blue Star. If she began making really powerful magic—and the unbinding-spell itself had been a risk—sooner or later she would attract the attention of whichever Pilgrim Adept had come here. With the kind of luck that seemed to be dogging her, it would be one of her worst enemies within the Order: Rabben the Half-handed, or Beccolo, or....

Lythande grimaced. Bitter as it was to concede defeat, the safest course seemed to be to go north as the Larith sword wanted. Perhaps, then, when she arrived there, she could somehow contrive to return the sword to Larith's own shrine. She had resolved to leave Old Gandrin anyway, and one direction was no better than another.

So be it. She would take the damned thing north to the Forbidden Shrine, and there she would leave it. Somehow she would manage to plant it on someone who could enter the shrine where she could not enter... rather, the worst was that she could enter but dared not be known to do so. Northward, then, to Larith's shrine—

But within the hour, though Lythande had been in Old Gandrin for a score of sunrises and should have known her way, the Adept was hopelessly lost. Whatever path Lythande found through marketplace or square, thieves' market or red-lamp quarter, however she tried to keep the sun on her right hand, within minutes she was hopelessly turned round. Four separate times she inquired for the north gate, and once it was actually within sight, when it seemed as if the cobbled street would shake itself and give itself a little twist, and Lythande would discover she was lost in the labyrinthine old Streets again. Finally, exhausted, furiously hungry and thirsty, and without a chance of finding a moment to eat or drink in privacy now that the sun was high and the streets thronged, she dropped grimly on the edge of a fountain in a public square, maddened by the splashing of the water she dared not drink, and sat there to think it over.

What did the damned thing want, anyway? She was bound north to the Forbidden Shrine as she thought she was commanded to go, yet she was prevented by the sword, or by the magic in the sword, from finding the northern gate, as she had been prevented from taking the road south. Was she to stay in Old Gandrin indefinitely? That did not seem reasonable, but then, there was nothing reasonable about this business.

At least this will teach me to mind my own business in the future!

Grimly, Lythande considered what alternatives were open. To try and find the burial place of the ravished Laritha and bury the sword with a binding-spell stronger yet? Even if she could find the place, she had no assurance that the sword would stay buried, and all kinds of assurances that it would not. The chances now seemed that all the power of the Blue Star would be expended in vain, unless Lythande wished to expend that kind of power that would in turn leave her powerless for days.

To seek safety in the Place Which Is Not, outside the boundaries of the world, and there attempt to find out what the sword really wanted and why it would not allow her to leave the city? For that, the cover of darkness was needful; was she to spend this day aimlessly wandering the streets of Old Gandrin? The smell of food from a nearby cookshop tantalized her, but she was accustomed to that and resolutely ignored it. Later, in some deserted street or alley, some of the dried fruit in the pockets of the mage-robe might find their way into her mouth, but not, now.

At least she could enjoy a moment's rest here on the fountain. But even as that thought crossed her mind, she discovered she was on her feet and moving restlessly across the square, thrusting the little packet of smoking-herbs back into the pocket.

She wondered angrily where in the hells she was going now. Her hand was lightly on the hilt of the larith sword, and she could only hope that none of the bystanders in the street could see it or would know what it meant if they did. She bashed into someone who snarled at her and accused her in a surly tone of some perversion involving being a rapist of immature nanny goats. The profanity of Old Gandrin, she concluded, was no more imaginative, and just as repetitive, as it was anywhere beneath the blinded eye of Keth-Ketha.

Across the fountain square, then, and into a narrow, winding street that emerged, a good half hour's walk later, into another square, this one facing a long, narrow barracks. Lythande was in a curiously dreamy state that she recognized, later, as almost hypnotic; she watched herself from inside, walking purposefully across the square, quite as if she knew where she was going and why, feeling that at any time, if she wished, she could resist this eerie compulsion—but that was simply too much trouble; why not go along and see what the larith wanted?

Four men were sloshing their faces in the great water trough before the barracks, their riding animals snorting in the water beside them. The Larith's sword was in her hand, and one man's head was bobbing like an apple in the water trough before Lythande knew what she—or rather, the sword—was doing. A second went down, spitted, before the other two had their swords out. The larith sword had lost its compulsion and was slack in her hand as she heard their outraged shouts, thinking ironically that she was as bewildered by the whole thing as they were, or maybe more so. She scrambled to get control of the sword, for now she was fighting for her life. There was no way these men were going to let her escape, now that she had slain two of their companions unprovoked. She managed to disarm one man, but the second drove her back and back, holding her ground as best she could; thrust, parry, recover, lunge—her foot slipped in something slick on the ground, and she went down, staggering for the support of the wall; somehow got the sword up and saw it go into the man's breast; he groaned and fell across the bodies of his companions, two dead and one sorely wounded.

Lythande started to turn away, sickened and outraged—at least the fifth man need not be murdered in cold blood—then realized she had no choice. That survivor could testify to a magician with the Blue Star blazing between hairless brows, bearing the larith sword, and any Pilgrim Adept who might ever hear the story would know that Lythande had borne the larith unscathed. As only a woman could do. She whipped out the sword again. The man shouted, "Help! Murder! Don't kill me, I have no quarrel with you—" and took to his heels, but Lythande strode swiftly after him, like a relentless avenging angel, and ran him through, grimacing in sick self-disgust. Then she ran, seeing other men flooding out of the barracks at their comrades' death cries, losing herself in the tangle of streets again.

Eventually, she had to stop to recover her breath. Why had the sword demanded those deaths? Immediately the answer came, imprinting the faces of the first two men she had killed—or the sword had killed almost without her help or knowledge—on her mind; they had been in the jeering circle of men who had ravished the dying priestess-swordswoman. So among other powers, the larith sword was spelled to vengeance on its own.

But she, Lythande, had not even stopped with killing the men the sword wished to kill. She had killed the other two men in cold blood to protect the secret of her sex and her magic.

Now the damned thing has entangled me not only in someone else's magic but in someone else's revenge!

Had the sword drunk its fill, or was it one of those that would go on killing and killing until it was somehow, unthinkably, sated? But now it seemed quiet enough in her scabbard. And after all, when she had killed the two who had either witnessed or shared in the rape of the Laritha, the compulsion had departed; the others she had killed more or less of her own free will.

A picture flashed behind her eyes: a burly man with a hook nose and ginger whiskers. He had been in the crowd around the dying Laritha and had escaped. He was not in the barracks behind the fountain, or no doubt the sword would have dragged her inside to kill him, probably killing everyone that lay between them.

Now, perhaps, she could depart the city—she was not sure how far to the north lay the Forbidden Shrine, but she grudged every hour now before the larith sword was out of her hands.

And I swear, from this day forth, I will never interfere—come battle, arson, murder, rape, or death—in any of the 9,090 forms the blinded eye of Keth has seen. I have had enough of somebody else's magic!

Lythande turned and took a path toward the northern gate, striding with a long, competent pace that fairly ate up the distance, and that compelled young children playing in the streets or idlers lounging there to get out of the way, sometimes with most undignified haste. Still, it was late in the day and one of the pallid moons had appeared, like a shadowy corpse-face in the sky, before she sighted the northern gate. But she was no longer heading in its direction.

Damnation! Had the thing spotted another prey? Now it took all Lythande's concentration to keep from snatching out the larith and holding it in her hand. She tried, deliberately, to slow her pace. She *could* do it, when she concentrated, which relieved her a little; at least she was not completely helpless before the magic of the Larithae. But it took fierce effort, and whenever her concentration slipped even a little, she was hurrying, pushed on by the infernal thing that nagged at her. If only it would let her know where it was going!

No doubt the dead and ravished Laritha, the priestess who owned the sword or was owned by it, *she* was in the sword's confidence. Would Lythande really want that, to be symbiote, sharing consciousness and purpose with some damned enchanted sword? Or was the sword enchanted only by the death of its owner, and did the Larithae normally carry it only for the purposes of an ordinary weapon?

She wished the wretched sword would make up its mind. Again the face renewed itself in her mind, a man with ginger whiskers and a hook nose, but the chin of a rabbit with protruding buck teeth. Of course. Most men who would stoop to rape were ugly and near to impotence, anyhow; anything recognizably male could get a woman without resorting to force.

Damn it, must she track down and kill everyone even in the crowd who had seen? If all who had witnessed the violation were dead, was the disgrace then canceled, or did it run so in the philosophy of the Larithae and their swords? She didn't want to know any more about it than she knew already. She wanted only to be rid of the thing.

"Have a care where you step, ravisher of virgin goats," snarled a passerby, and Lythande realized she had stumbled again in her haste. She forced herself to stammer an apology, glad that the mage-robe was drawn about her face so that the Blue Star was invisible. Damn it, this had gone far enough. It was beginning to infringe on her very personality—she was Lythande, the core of whose reputation was for appearing and disappearing as if made of shadow. Her best spells could not rid her of it. She must now contrive to give it what it wanted, and be done with it, and swiftly. It would be just as bad if the marketplace gossiped about an Adept of the Blue Star bearing Larith magic, as if she should encounter her worst enemy so; only less swift.

It would be easier if she knew where she was going. There was the continual temptation to fall into the dreamy hypnotic state, dragged on by the larith sword; but Lythande fought to remain alert. Once again she was lost in the tangled streets of a quarter in the city where she had never been. And then, crossing the square in front of a wineshop, one of those where the customs and drinkers all came spilling out into the street, she saw him: Ginger Whiskers.

She wanted to stop and get a good look at the man she was fated to kill. It was against her principles to kill, for unknown reasons, men whose names she did not know.

Yet she knew enough about him; he had violated, or attempted to violate, or witnessed the violation of a Laritha. In general, if rape were a capital crime in Old Gandrin, the city would be depopulated, thought Lythande; or inhabited only by women and those virgin goats who formed such a part in the profanity of that city. She supposed that was why there were not many unaccompanied women walking the streets in Old Gandrin.

The Laritha and I. And she did not escape; and I only because my womanhood is unknown. The women of Old Gandrin seem to submit to that unwritten law, that the woman who walks alone can expect no more than ravishment. The Laritha sought to challenge it, and died.

But she will be avenged.... And Lythande swore under her breath. She was acting as if it mattered a damn to her if every woman who had not the sense of wisdom to stay out of a ravisher's hands paid the penalty of that foolishness or incaution. She had had her fill of taking upon herself someone else's curse and someone else's magic.

Was the sword of larith, then, which might never be borne by a man, beginning to work its accursed magic upon her? Lythande stopped dead in the middle of the square, trying not to stare across the intervening space at Ginger Whiskers. If she fought the sword's magic, could she let him live and turn and go on her way? Let someone else right the wrongs of the Larithae!

What, after all, have I to do with women? If they do not wish for the common fate of women, let them do as I have done, renounce skirts and silks and the arts of the women's quarters, and put on sword and breeches or a mage-robe and dare the risks I have dared to leave all that behind me. I paid dear for my immunity.

She suspected the Laritha had paid no less a price. But that was, after all, none of her concern. She took a deep breath, summoned her strongest spell, and by a great effort turned her back on Ginger Whiskers, walking in the opposite direction.

Just in time, too. The hood of Lythande's mage-robe was drawn over her head, concealing the Blue Star; but beneath the heavy folds she could feel the small stinging that meant the star was flaming, sparkling, and could see the blue lightnings above her eyes. *Magic....*

It was not the larith sword. That was quiet in her belt... no, somehow she had it in her hands. Lythande stood quietly, trying to fight back, and dared a peep beneath the mage-robe.

It was not the flare of the Blue Star between her brows. Somehow she had seen, had seen... where was it, what had she seen? The man's back was turned to her, she could see the brown folds of a mage-robe not too unlike her own; but though she could not see forehead or star, she felt the Blue Star resonate in time with her own.

He would feel it, too. *I had better get out of here as fast as I can.* Which settled it. Ginger Whiskers would not pay for his part in the ravishment of the Laritha. She, Lythande, had had enough of someone else's magic; she would take the larith sword northward to its shrine, but she was not, by Chaos and the Last Battle, going to be seen here in the presence of another other Order, doing battle—or call it by its right name, murder—with a larith sword.

51

The sword was quiet in her hand and made no apparent struggle when she slid it back into the scabbard, though at the last moment it seemed to Lythande that it squirmed a little, reluctant to be forced into the sheath. Too bad, she would give it no choice. Lythande muttered the words of a bonding-spell to keep it there, carefully slipped behind a pillar in the square, and cautiously, moving like a breath of wind or a northland ghost, circled about until she could see, unseen, the man in the mage-robe. On her forehead, the Blue Star throbbed, and she could see by tiny movements of the man's hood that he, too, was trying to look about him unseen to know if another Pilgrim Adept was truly within the crowd in the square. Well, that was her greatest skill, to see without being seen.

The man's hands, long-fingered and muscular, swordsman's hands, were clasped over the staff he bore. Not Rabben the Half-handed, then. He was tall and burly; if it was Ruhaven, he was one of her few friends in the Order, and he was not a north-country man, he would not know the technicalities of a Larith curse, would not, probably, know that a larith could be borne only by a woman. Lythande toyed briefly with the notion, if it was Ruhaven, of making some part of her predicament known to him. No more than she must, only that she had become saddled with an enchanted sword, perhaps ask his help in formulating a stronger unbinding-spell.

The Pilgrim Adept turned with a slight twitch of his shoulders, and Lythande caught a glimpse of dark hair under the hood. Not Ruhaven, then—Ruhaven's gray hair was already turning white—and he was the only one in the Order to whom she felt she might have turned, at least before the Last Battle between Law and Chaos.

And then the Pilgrim Adept made a gesture she recognized, and Lythande ducked her head farther within the mage-robe's folds and tried to slither into the crowd, to reach its edge and drift unseen into the alley beyond the square and the tavern. Beccolo! It could hardly be worse. Yes, he thought Lythande a man. But they had once been pitted, within the Temple of the Star, in a magical duel, and it had not been Lythande who had lost face that day.

Beccolo might not know the details of Larith magic. He probably did not. But if he once recognized her, and especially if he should guess that she was hag-ridden by a curse, he would be in a hurry to have his revenge.

And then with horror Lythande realized that while she was thinking about Beccolo and her consternation that it should be one of her worst enemies within the Pilgrim Adepts, she had lost her fierce concentration, by which alone she had kept control of the larith sword; it was out of the scabbard, naked now in her hand, and she was striking straight through the crowd, men and women shrinking back from her purposeful stride. Ginger Whiskers saw her and shrank back in consternation. Yesterday he had stood and cheered on the violation of a Larith—at least, of a woman rendered helpless by fearful odds. And he had been among those who took to their heels as a tall, lean fighter in a mage-robe with a Blue Star blazing lightning had cut down four men within as many seconds.

His bench went over and he kicked away the man who went down with it, making for the far end of the square. Lythande thought, wrathfully: Go on, get the hell out of here; I don't want to kill you any more than you want to be killed. And she knew Beccolo's eyes were on her, and on the Blue Star now blazing between her brows. And Beccolo would have known her without that. Known her for the fellow Pilgrim Adept who had humiliated him in the outer courts of the Temple of the Star, when they were both novices and before the blazing star was set between either of their brows.

She almost thought for a moment that he would get away. Then she kicked the fallen bench aside and leaped on him, the sword out to run him through. This one was not so easy; he had jerked out his own sword and warded her off with no small skill. Men and women and children surged back to leave them a clear space for fighting, and Lythande, angry because she did not really want to kill him at all, nevertheless knew it was a fight for life, a fight she dared not lose. She crashed down backward, stumbling as she backed away; and then the world went into slow motion. It seemed a minute, an hour that Ginger Whiskers bent over her, sword in hand, coming at her naked throat slowly, slowly. And then Lythande's foot was in his belly, he grunted in pain, and then she had scrambled to her feet and her sword went through his throat. She backed away from the jetting blood. Her only feeling was rage, not against Ginger Whiskers, but against the larith. She slammed it back into the scabbard and strode away without stopping to look back. Fortunately, the larith did not resist this time, and she made off toward the northern gate. Maybe she could make it there before Beccolo could get through the crowd to trail her. Within mere minutes, Lythande was out of the city and striding north, and behind her— as yet—there was no sign of Beccolo. Of course not. How could he know to which quarter of the compass she was making her course?

All that day, and into much of the night that followed, Lythande strode northward at a steady pace that ate up the leagues. She was weary and would have welcomed rest, but the nagging compulsion of the larith at her belt allowed her no halt. At least this way—she thought dimly—there was less likelihood that Beccolo would trail her out of the city and northward.

Shortly after Keth sank into the darkness, in the dim half-twilight of Reth's darkened eye, she paused for a time on the bank of a river, but she could not rest; she only cleaned, with meticulous care, the blade of the larith and secured it in the scabbard. Dim humps and hillocks on the riverbank showed where travelers slept, and she surveyed them with vague envy, but soon she strode on, walking swiftly with apparent purpose. But in reality she moved within a dark dream, hardly aware when the last dim light of Reth's setting beams died away altogether. After a time, the blotched and leprous face of the larger moon cast a little light on the pathway, but it made no difference to Lythande's pace.

She did not know where she was going. The sword knew, and that seemed to be enough.

Some hidden part of Lythande knew what was happening to her and was infuriated. It was her work as magician to act, not to remain passive and be acted upon. That was for women, and again she felt the revulsion to this kind of women's sorcery where the priestess became passive tool in the hands of her sword... that was no better than being slave to a man! But perhaps the Larithae themselves were not so bound; she had been put under compulsion by the ravished Laritha and had no choice.

The Laritha requited the impulse that caused me to stop, in the vain hope of saving her life or delivering her from her ravishers—by binding me with this curse! And when that came to her mind, Lythande would curse softly and vow revenge on the Larithae. But most of that night she walked in that same waking dream, her mind empty of thought.

Under cover of the darkness, on her solitary road, she munched dried fruit, her mind as empty as a cow chewing its cud. Toward morning she slept for a little, in the shelter of a thicket of trees, careful to set a watch-spell that would waken her if anyone came within thirty paces. She wondered at herself; in man's garb, she had wandered everywhere beneath the Twin Suns, and now she was behaving like a fearful woman afraid of ravishment; was it the larith, accustomed to being borne by women who did not conceal their sex, but walked abroad defending it as they must, that had put this woman's watchfulness again on her? How many years had it been since Lythande had even considered the possibility that she might be surprised alone, stripped, discovered as a woman?

She felt rage—and worse, revulsion—at herself that she could still think in these woman's ways. *As if I were a woman in truth, not a magician,* she thought furiously, and for a moment the rage she felt congested in her forehead and brought tears to her eyes, and she forced them back with an effort that sent pain lancing through her head.

But I am a woman, she thought, and then in a furious backlash: *No! I am a magician, not a woman! The wizard is neither male nor female, but a being apart!* She resolved to take off the watch-spell and sleep in her customary uncaring peace, but when she tried it, her heart pounded, and finally she set the watch-spell again to guard her and fell asleep. Was it the sword itself that was fearful, guarding the slumbers of the woman who bore it?

When she woke, Keth was divided in half at the eastern horizon, and she moved on, her jaw grim and set as she covered the ground with the long, even-striding paces that ate up the distance under her feet. She was growing accustomed to the weight of the larith at her waist; absently, now and again, her hand caressed it. A light sword, an admirable sword for the hand of a woman.

Children were playing at the second river; they scattered back to their mothers as Lythande approached the ferry, flinging coins at the ferryman in a silent rage. *Children. I might have had children, had my life gone otherwise, and that is a deeper magic than my own.* She could not tell whence that alien thought had come. Even as a young maiden, she had never felt anything but revulsion at the thought of subjecting herself to the desire of a man, and when her maiden companions giggled and whispered together about that eventuality, Lythande had stood apart, scornful, shrugging with contempt. Her name had not been Lythande then. She had been called... and Lythande started with horror, knowing that in the ripples of the lapping water she had almost heard the sound of her old name, a name she had sworn never again to speak when once she put on men's garb, a name she had vowed to forget, no, a name she had forgotten... altogether forgotten.

"Are you fearful, traveler?" asked a gentle voice beside her. "The ferry rocks about, it is true, but never in human memory has it capsized nor has a passenger fallen into the water, and this ferry has run here since before the Goddess came northward to establish her shrine as Larith. You are quite safe."

Lythande muttered ungracious thanks, refusing to look round. She could sense the form of the young girl at her shoulder, smiling up expectantly at her. It would be noted if she did not speak, if she simply moved northward like the accursed, hell-driven thing she was. She cast about for some innocuous thing to say.

"Have you traveled this road often?" she asked.

"Often, yes, but never so far," said the gentle girlish voice. "Now I travel north to the Forbidden Shrine, where the Goddess reigns as Larith. Know you the shrine?"

Lythande mumbled that she had heard of it. She thought the words would choke her.

"If I am accepted," the young voice went on, "I shall serve the Goddess as one of her priestesses, a Laritha."

Lythande turned slowly to look at the speaker. She was very young, with that boyish look some young girls keep until they are in their twenties or more. The magician asked quietly, "Why, child? Know you not that every man's hand will be against you?" and stopped herself. She had been on the point of telling the story of the woman who had been ravished and killed in the streets of Old Gandrin.

The young girl's smile was luminous. "But if every man's hand is against me, still, I shall have all those who serve the Goddess at my side."

Lythande found herself opening her lips for something cynical. That had not been her experience, that women could stand together. Yet why should she spoil this girl's illusion? Let her find it out herself, in bitterness. This girl still cherished a dream that women could be sisters. Why should Lythande foul and embitter that dream before she must? She turned pointedly away and stared at the muddy water under the prow of the ferry.

The girl did not move away from her side. From under the mage-hood, Lythande surveyed her without seeming to do so: the ripples of sunny hair, the unlined forehead, the small snub nose still indefinite, the lips and earlobes so soft that they looked babyish, the soft little fingers, the boyish freckles she did not trouble to paint.

If she goes to the Larith shrine, perhaps then I might prevail upon her to take the sword of Larith thither. Yet if she knows that I, an apparent male, bear such a sword— if she goes to petition the shrine—surely she must know that no man may lay a hand upon one of the larith swords without such penalty as were better imagined than spoken.

And since I bear that sword unscathed, then am I either accused of blasphemy—or revealed as a woman, naked to my enemies. And now, close to her destination, Lythande realized her dilemma. Neither as a man nor as a woman could she step inside the shrine of the Goddess as Larith. What, then, could she do with the sword?

The sword didn't care. So long as the damned thing got home in one piece, she supposed, it mattered not what the carrier was—swordswoman, a girl like that one, or one of those virgin goats who played such a part in the profanity of Gandrin. If she simply asked the girl to take it to the shrine, she revealed either her blasphemy or her true sex.

She might plant the sword upon her, spelled or enchanted into something else; a loaf of bread, perhaps, as the herb-seller had been given barley grains spelled to look like gold. It was not, after all, as if she were sending anything into the Larith shrine to do them harm, only something of its own, and something, moreover, that had played hell with Lythande's life and given her four—no, five; no, there were all the ones she had killed over the body of the Laritha—had given her eleven or a dozen lives to fight among the legions of the dead at the Last Battle where Law shall fight at last against Chaos and conquer or die once and for all. And something that had dragged Lythande all this weary way to get back where it was going.

She seriously considered that. Give the girl the sword, enchanted to look like something other than what it was. A gift for the shrine of the Goddess as Larith.

The girl was still standing at her side. Lythande knew her voice was abrupt and harsh. "Well, will you take a gift to the shrine, then, from me?"

The girl's guileless smile seemed to mock her. "I cannot. This Goddess accepts no gifts save from her own."

Lythande said with a cynical smile, "You say so? The key to every shrine is forged of gold, and the more gold, the nearer the heart of the shrine, or the god."

The girl looked as if Lythande had slapped her. But after a moment, she said quietly, "Then I am sorry you have known such shrines and such gods, traveler. No man may know our Goddess, or I would try to show you better," and looked down at the deck. Rebuked, Lythande stood silent as the ferry bumped gently against the land. The passengers on the ferry began to stream onto the shore. Lythande awaited the subsidence of the crowd, the larith sword for once quiet inside the mage-robe.

The town was small, a straggle of houses, farms outside the gates, and, high on the hill above a sprawling market, the shrine of Larith. One thing, at least, the girl spoke true: there was nothing of gold about this shrine, at least where the passerby could see; it was a massive fortress of unpretentious gray stone.

Lythande noticed that the girl was still at her side as she stepped onshore. "One gift at least your Goddess has accepted from the sex she affects to despise," Lythande said. "No women's hands built that keep, which is more fortress than shrine to my eyes!"

"No, you are mistaken," the girl said. "Do you not believe, stranger, that a woman could be as strong as you yourself?"

"No," Lythande said, "I do not. One woman in a hundred—a thousand, perhaps. The others are weak."

"But if we are weak," said the girl, "still our hands are many." She spoke a formal farewell, and Lythande, repeating it, jaws clenched, stood and watched her walk away.

Why am I so angry? Why did I wish to hurt her?

And the answer rushed over her in a flood. *Because she goes where I can never go, goes freely. There was a time when I would willingly have pawned my soul, had there been a place where a woman might go to learn the arts of sorcery and the skills of the sword. Yet there was no place, no place. I pawned my soul and my sex to seek the secrets of the Blue Star, and this, this soft-handed child, with her patter of sisterhood... where were my sisters on that day when I knew despair and renounced the truth of my self? I stood alone; it was not enough that every man's hand was against me on that day, every woman's hand was against me as well!*

Pain beat furiously in her head, pain that made her clench her teeth and scowl and tighten her fists on the hilts of her own twin swords. One would think, she said to herself, deliberately distancing herself from the pain, that I were about to weep. *But I forgot how to weep more than a century ago,* and no doubt there will be more cause than this for weeping before I stand at the Last Battle and fight against Chaos. But I shall not live to that battle unless somehow I can contrive to enter where no man may enter and return the cursed larith where it belongs!

For already she felt, streaming from the larith, the same intense, nagging compulsion, to plunge up the hill, walk into the shrine, and throw down the sword before the Goddess who had dragged it here and Lythande with it.

Within the shrine, all women are welcomed as sisters... did the whisper come from the girl who had spoken of the shrine? Or did it come from the sword itself, eager to tempt her on with someone else's magic? *Not I. It is too late for me.* Through the pain in her head, Lythande's old watchfulness suddenly asserted itself. The ferry had moved from the shore again, and at the far shore, passengers again were streaming on its deck. Among them, among them—no, it was too far to see, but with the magical sight of the Blue Star throbbing between her brows, Lythande knew a form in a mage-robe not unlike her own. Somehow Beccolo had trailed her here.

He did not necessarily know the laws of the shrine. All of the north-country was scattered with shrines to every god from the God of Smiths to the Goddess of Light Love. *And her shrine, too, is forbidden to me, as all is forbidden save the magical arts for which I renounced all.* Forbidden to men lest they know my Secret; to women, lest some man attempt to wrest it from them... Beccolo probably did not know the peculiarities of the Larithae. If she could lead him into the shrine itself somehow, then would the priestesses work on him the wrath they were reputed to work on every man who found his way inside there, and then would Lythande be free of his meddling. What, indeed, would the Goddess as Larith do to any man who penetrated her shrine as Lythande had done to the Temple of the Blue Star, in disguise, wearing the garb and the guise of a sex that was not her own?

She fought to resist the magical compulsion in her mind. The larith that had brought her all this way, almost sleepwalking, was now awake and screaming to be returned to its home, and Lythande could hear that screaming in her mind, even as her own rage and confusion fought to silence it. She could not enter the Larith's shrine as Lythande, nor as the Adept of the Blue Star, though at least if she did, Beccolo could not follow her there—or if he tried, would meet swift vengeance.

She saw the ferry approaching the shore, and now could see with her own tired eyes, not with the magical sight, the narrow form of the Pilgrim Adept who had trailed her all this long way. The Twin Suns stood high in the sky, Keth racing Reth for the zenith, dazzling the water into brilliant swords of light that blinded Lythande's eyes with painful flame. She stepped into the market, trying to summon around herself the magical stillness, so that everywhere beneath the Twin Suns those who knew Lythande spoke of the magician's ability to appear or disappear before their very eyes.

Most women seek to attract all men's eyes. Even before I came to the Temple of the Blue Star, I sought to turn their eyes away. Magic cannot give to any magician the thing not desired.

And as that thought came within her mind, Lythande stood perfectly still. All the long road here, she had cursed the mischance that had led her into somebody else's magic. Yet nothing had forced her to turn aside from her path to save the Laritha from violation; she could never have been entangled in the magic of the larith sword had something within her not consented to it. Had she turned aside from a woman's ravishment, then would Lythande have been supporting Chaos in the place of Law.

Nonsense. What is a stranger woman to me? And, pain splitting her head asunder, Lythande fought the answer that came, without her consent and against her will.

She is myself. She walks where I dare not, a woman for all to see.

In a rage, Lythande turned aside and sought darkness between the stalls of a market. Early as it was in the day, men brawled in the shadow of a wineshop. Market women milked their goats and sold the fresh milk. A caravan master loaded protesting pack animals. In Lythande's mind, the larith sword nagged, knowing its home was not far.

Could she send it now by some unwitting traveler bound for the shrine? She could not enter. She need not. Perhaps now she could seek a binding-spell that would return it home, or an unbinding-spell, now that the larith was in its own country, to free her of its curse, as she had freed herself of the curse of being no more than woman when the Blue Star was set between her brows. She had performed the most massive unbinding-spell of all, culminating in that day when she had been doom-set to live forever as what she had pretended to be. This lesser unbinding-spell should be simple by comparison with that.

From here she could survey, unseen, the upward road to the shrine of the Larithae. Women went upward, seeking whatever mysterious comfort they could have from that Goddess; they led goats to the shrine, whether for sacrifice or to sell milk Lythande neither knew or cared. She fancied that among them she could see the young girl of the ferry, who had come to offer herself to the Goddess, and Lythande found herself following, in her mind, that young girl whose name she would never know.

Never could I have been entangled in the magic of the Larithae, or in anyone else's magic, unless something within me claimed it as mine, Lythande thought. It was not a comfortable thought. *Was I perhaps secretly longing for the womanhood I had renounced and for which the Laritha died?*

Was it a will to death that brought me here?

Rage and the pain in her head, flaring like the lightnings of the Blue Star, burst in revulsion. *What folly is it that dragged me here, questioning all that I am and all that I have done? I am Lythande! Who dares challenge me, man or woman or goddess?*

One would think I had come here to die as a woman among my own kind! And what would these sworn priestesses, sworn to the sword and to magic, think then of a woman who had renounced her self—?

But I did not renounce my self! Only my vulnerability to the hazards of being woman and bearing sword and magic....

Which they bear with such courage as they can, her mind reminded her, and again the dying eyes of the ravished Laritha, smiling as she pressed the sword into Lythande's fingers, haunted her. Well. So she died for walking abroad as a woman. That was *her* choice. This is mine, Lythande said to herself, and clutched the mage-robe about her, setting her hand on her two swords—the right-handed knife for the enemies of this world, the knife on the left for the evils and terrors of magic. And the larith sword, tucked uncomfortably between them. *Still, I am Lythande!*

The shrine is forbidden to me, as the silk-woman of Jumathe were forbidden to me. And into that shrine I went, among the blind silk-weavers. But the Larithae are not so conveniently devoid of sight. If I walk among them as an Adept of the Blue Star, they will believe—as the overseer of the blind silk-women believed—that I am a man come among them to despoil or conquer. The very best that could befall is that I should be stripped and revealed a woman. And soon or late, the ripples stirred by that stone would reach my enemies, and Lythande be proclaimed abroad what no man may know.

She was walking now between two stalls where articles of women's clothing were displayed in brilliant folds, colorfully woven skirts of the thick cotton of the Salt Deserts, long scarves and shawls, all the soft and colored things women doted on and for which they pawned their lives and their souls, pretty trash! Lythande curled her lip with scorn and contempt, then stood completely motionless.

It is forbidden that any man may know me for a woman. For on that day when any man shall speak it aloud or hear that I am a woman, then is my Power forfeit to him and I may be slain like a beast. Yet within the walls of the Larith shrine, no man may come, so no man may see. The idea flamed in her mind with the brilliance of Keth-Ketha at zenith; she would penetrate the shrine of the Larithae *disguised as a woman!*

It is truly a disguise, she thought with a curl of her lip. She had no idea how many years it had been since she had worn women's garb, and by now it would be pure pretense to put it on. It was no longer her self.

Nor could she, a man, purchase such things openly. If an apparent man should vanish after purchasing women's garments, and a strange woman, suddenly appear at the shrine—well, one could not hope that all the

Larithae would be so conveniently stupid, nor all who kept their gates and brought them gifts.

She must, then, manage to steal the garments unseen. No very great trick, after all, for one whose teasing nickname in the outer courts of the Blue Star had been "Lythande, the Shadow." To appear and disappear unseen was her special gift. She had begun to move stealthily, a shadow against the darkness of the tents of the sellers, out of sight of Keth and Reth. Later that day, a skirt-seller would discover that only six skirts hung in their colorful bands where seven had hung before; a seller of fards and cosmetics discovered that three little pots of paint had vanished before his very eyes, and although he remembered a lanky stranger in a mage-robe lounging nearby, he would swear he had not taken his eyes for a minute from the stranger's hands; and a woolen shawl and a veil likewise found their way out of a tangled pile of castoffs and were never missed at all.

Keth was declining again when a lean and angular woman, with an awkward bundle on her back, striding like a man, made her way up the hill toward the shrine. Her forehead appeared strangely scarred, and her eyebrows and cheeks were painted, her eyes deeply underlined with kohl. She stumbled against a woman leading pack animals, who cursed her as a despoiler of virgin goats. So they had that oath here, too. Lythande was ready to assure the woman, in that mellow and cynical voice, that her maiden beasts were perfectly safe, but it seemed not worth the trouble. Wearing the unfamiliar garments of a woman was penance enough. At least she could bear the larith openly, tied awkwardly about her waist as a woman not accustomed to the handling of a sword would do. And she knew she moved so clumsily in the skirts she had not had about her knees in a century, that at any moment she might be accused of being a man in disguise. Which would, she thought grimly, be the ultimate irony.

I have worn a mask for more years than most of this crowd has been alive. Against her will, she remembered an old horror tale that a nurse, decades since dust and ashes, had told to frighten a girl whose name Lythande now honestly could not remember, of a mask worn so long that it had frozen to the face and become the face. *I have become what I pretended. And that is all my reward or my punishment.*

There is no woman, now, under these skirts, and it would be just, she thought, if I were exposed as a man. Yet she had considered and refused a glamouring-spell that might make her more visibly a woman. She would go into the Larith shrine with such resources as were her own, without magic. Yet the Blue Star beneath the paint throbbed as if with unshed tears.

Between a woman leading goats and a woman bearing a sick child, Lythande stepped between the pillars of the shrine of the Goddess as Larith, built at some time by the hands of women. She did not know or care when she had begun to believe that. But obscurely it comforted her that women could build such an edifice.

Against her will, a curious question nagged at her, like the voice of the larith tied clumsily with a rope at her waist:

If I had not forsaken or forsworn myself for the Blue Star, if I had joined my hands to the weak and despised hands of my sisters, would this temple have risen the sooner? She dismissed the thought with an effort that made her eyes throb, asking herself in scornful wrath, *If the stone lions of Khoumari had kittens, would the Khoumari shepherds guard their lambs more safely of nights?*

She stood on a great floor, mosaicked in black and white stone in a pentagram pattern. Above her rose a great blue dome, and before her stood the great figure of the Goddess as Larith, fashioned of stone and without any trace of gold. The girl had spoken truth, then. And at the far end, where a little band of priestesses stood, accepting the gifts of the pilgrims in that outer court, she fancied she could see the slender and boyish form of the girl among them. It was only fancy! No doubt they had whisked her away into their inner courts, there to await that mysterious transition into a Laritha, under the eyes of their stone Goddess. A pregnant warrior! Lythande heard herself make a small inner sound of contempt, but she was in their territory and she knew she dared not draw attention to herself. She must behave like a woman and be meek and silent here. Well, she was skilled at disguise; it was no more than a challenge to her.

I would like to take the girl with me, rather than letting her go to these women-sorceresses and their flimsy magic! (Not so flimsy, after all; it had dragged her here!) *I would teach her the arts of the sword and the laws of magic. I would be alone no longer....*

Daydream. Fantasy. Yet it persisted. Outsiders might think her no more than a mercenary-magician who traveled with an apprentice, as many did; and even if any of them suspected her apprentice to be a maiden, they would think her only the more manly. And the girl would know her secret, but it would not matter, for Lythande would be teacher, master, lover....

The woman ahead of her, bearing a sick child, was standing now before the priestess of the Larith who accepted gifts for the shrine. The woman tried to hand her a golden bracelet, but the priestess shook her head.

"The Goddess accepts gifts only from her own, my sister. Larith the Compassionate bestows gifts upon the children of men, but does not accept them. You would have healing for your son? Go through yonder door into the outer court, and one of the healers there shall give you a brew for his fever; the Goddess is merciful."

The woman murmured thanks and knelt for a blessing, and Lythande was looking into the eyes of the priestess.

"I bring you—your own," said Lythande, and fumbled at the strings that bore the larith sword. For the first time, she looked at it clearly and found she was cradling it in her fingers as if reluctant to let it go. The priestess said, in her gentle voice, "How have you come by this?"

"One of your own lay violated and dying; she spelled this sword to me that I should return it here."

The priestess—she was old, Lythande thought; not as old as Lythande, but no magical immunity gave her the appearance of youth—said gently, "Then you have our thanks, my sister." Her eyes rested on the reluctance with which Lythande's fingers released the blade. Her voice was even more gentle.

"You may remain here if you will, my sister. You may be trained in the ways of the sword and of magic, and will wander the world no more alone."

Here? Within walls? Among women? Lythande felt her lip curling again with scorn, and yet her eyes ached. *If I had not forgotten how, I would think I were about to weep.*

"I thank you," she forced herself to say thickly, "but I cannot. I am pledged elsewhere."

"Then I honor what oath keeps you, Sister," the priestess said, and Lythande knew she should turn from the shrine. Yet she made no move to go, and the priestess asked her softly, "What would you have from the Goddess in return for this great gift?"

"It is no gift," said Lythande bluntly. "I had no choice, or I would not have come; surely you must know that your larith swords do not await a freely given pilgrimage. I came at the larith's will, not my own. And you have no gifts I seek."

"Gifts are not always asked," said the priestess, almost inaudibly, and laid her hands in blessing on Lythande's brow. "May you be healed of the pain you cannot speak, my sister."

I am no sister of yours! But Lythande did not speak the words aloud; she pressed her lips tight against them, and saw blue lights glare against the priestess's fingers. Would the woman expose her, recognizing the Blue Star? But the woman only made a gesture of blessing, and Lythande turned away.

At least it was over. Her venture into the Larith shrine was ended, and now she must get out safely. She held her breath as she recrossed the great mosaic floor with the pattern of stars. She passed beneath the doorway and out of the shrine. Now, standing again in the free light of Keth, trailed down the sky by the eye of Reth, she had come safe and free from this adventure of someone else's magic.

And then a cynical voice cut through her sense of sudden peace.

"By all the gods, Lythande! So the Shadow is at his old trick of thievery and silence? And you have forced yourself into this alien shrine? How much of their gold did you cozen from their shrine, O Lythande?"

The voice of Beccolo! So even with her women's garments, he had recognized her! But of course he would think it only the most clever and subtle of disguises.

"There is no gold in the shrine of the Larithae," she said in her most mellow tones. "But if you doubt me, Beccolo, seek for yourself within that shrine; freely I grant you my share of any Larith gold."

"Generous Lythande!" Beccolo taunted, while Lythande stood silent, angry because in this alien guise, skirts about her body, Blue Star hidden behind paint, she knew herself at his mercy. She longed for the comfort of her knives at her waist, the familiar breeches and mage-robe. Even the larith sword would have been comforting at this moment.

"And you make a pretty woman indeed," Beccolo taunted. "Perhaps the gold within the shrine is only the bodies other priestesses; did you find, then, that gold?"

She turned a little, her hands fumbling swiftly within her pack. The sword was in her hand. But she could tell by the feel that it was the wrong sword, the one that killed only the creatures of magic, the bane-wolf or werewolf, the ghoul and the ghost would fall before it; but against Beccolo she was helpless, and that sword of no avail. Her hands buried in her pack, she fumbled in the folds of the bundled-up mage-robe and the hard leather of her own breeches to find the hilt of the sword that was effective against an enemy as unpleasantly corporeal as Beccolo. The Blue Star between his brows mocked her with its flare; she swept one hand over her forehead and wiped the cosmetic from her own.

"Ah, don't do that," Beccolo mocked. "Shame to spoil a pretty woman with your scrawny hawk-face. And here you are where perhaps I can make Lythande as much of a fool as you made me in yonder courts of the Temple of the Star! Suppose, now, I shouted to all men to come and see Lythande the Magician, Lythande the Shadow, here disguised as a woman, primed for some mischief in their shrine—what then, Lythande?"

It is only his malice. He does not know the law of Larith. Yet if he should carry out his threat, there were those in this town who would know—or believe—that Lythande, a man, an Adept of the Blue Star, had cheated her way into the shrine where no man might set his foot. There was no safety here for Lythande either as a man or a woman; and now she had her hand on the hilt of her right-hand blade but could not extricate it from the tangled belongings of her pack.

It would serve her right, she thought, if for this womanish folly she was entrapped here in a duel with Beccolo cumbered with skirts and disarmed by her own precautions. She had hidden her swords too well, thinking she would have leisure and the cover of night to shed the disguise!

"Yet before Lythande is Lythande again," Beccolo's hateful, mocking voice snarled, "perhaps I should try whether or not it is not more fitting to Lythande to put skirts about his knees... how good a woman do you make, then, O fellow Pilgrim?" His hand dragged Lythande to him; his free hand sought to ruffle the fair hair. Lythande wrenched away, snarling a gutter obscenity of Old Gandrin, and Beccolo, snatching back a blackened hand that smoked with fire, howled in anguish.

I should have stood still and let him have his fun until I could get my sword in my hand....

Lightning flared from the Blue Star, and Lythande brought her own hand up in a warding-spell, furiously rummaging for her right-hand sword. The smell of magic crackled in the air, but Beccolo plunged at Lythande, yelling in fury.

If he touches me, he will know I am a woman. And if the secret of any Adept is spoken aloud, then is his Power forfeit. He has only to say, Lythande, you are a woman, and he is revenged for all time for that foolishness in the outer court of the Blue Star.

"Damn you, Lythande, no one makes a fool of Beccolo twice—"

"No," said Lythande, with calm contempt, "you do so admirably yourself." Desperately she wrenched at the trapped sword. He yelled again, and a spell sizzled in the air between them.

"Thief! Hedgerow-sorcerer," Lythande shouted at him, delaying as the sword sawed at the leather holding it in the pack, "Defiler of virgin goats!"

Only for a moment Beccolo paused; but she caught the flash of despair in his eyes. Somehow, in the careless profanity of Old Gandrin, had Beccolo delivered himself into her hands? Had the spirit of the larith prompted her to a curse Lythande had never used before and would never use again?

What, after all, had she now to lose, without even a sword in her hand? "Beccolo," she repeated, slowly and deliberately, "you are a despoiler of virgin goats!"

He stood motionless as the words echoed in the square around them. She could feel the voiding of Power from the Blue Star. Truly she had stumbled upon his Secret; he stood silent, unmoving, as she got the sword in her hand and ran him through with it.

A crowd was gathering; Lythande picked up her skirts without dignity, the sword in her hand along with the fold other skirt, and ran, disappearing around a market-stall and there enfolding herself in a magical sphere of silence. The shouts and yells of the crowd were cut off in a thick, quenched, *clogged* silence, as the utter stillness of the Place Which Is Not enfolded her, a sphere of nothingness, like colorless water or dazzling fire. Lythande drew a long breath and began to shuck her borrowed skirts. Now for the unbinding-spell that would return these things to the stalls of their owners, somewhat the worse of wear. As she spoke the spell, she began to chuckle at the picture of Beccolo engaged in the Secret on which he had gambled his life—for the secret spoken in careless abuse, hidden out in the open, was harmless; only when Lythande spoke it openly to his face did it acquire the magical Power of an Adept's Secret.

But not even in secret may I be a woman....

Setting her lips tight, she waved her hand and dispelled the sorcerous sphere. Once again Lythande had appeared in a strange street from thin air, and that would do her reputation no harm either, nor the reputation of the Pilgrim Adepts.

Glancing at the sky, she noticed that the time-annihilating magical sphere had cost her a day and more; Keth again stood at the zenith. She wondered what they had done with Beccolo's body. She did not care. A stream of pilgrims was winding its way upward still to the shrine of the Goddess as Larith, and Lythande stood watching for a moment, remembering the face of the young girl and the soft-spoken blessing of a priestess. Her hand felt empty without the larith sword.

Then she turned her back on the shrine and strode toward the ferry.

"Watch where you step, you swaggering defiler of virgin goats," a man snarled as the Adept passed in the swirling mage-robe.

Lythande laughed. She said, "Not I," and stepped on board the ferry, turning her back on the shrine of women's magic.

SEA WRACK
Marion Zimmer Bradley

The crimson eye of Keth hovered near the horizon, with the smaller sun of Reth less than an hour behind. At this hour the fishing fleet should have been sailing into the harbor. But there was no sign of any fleet; only a single boat, far out, struggling against the tide.

Lythande had walked far that day along the shore, enjoying the solitude and singing old, soft sea-songs to the sounds of the surf. Tonight, surely, the Pilgrim-Adept thought, supper must be earned by singing to the lute, for in a simple place like this there would be none to need the services of a mercenary magician, no need for spells or magics, only simple folk, living simply to the rhythms of sea and tides.

Perhaps it was a holiday; all the boats lay drawn up along the shore. But there was no holiday feel in the single street: angry knots of men sat clumped together scowling and talking in low voices, while a little group of women were staring out to sea, watching the single boat struggling against the tide.

"Women! By the blinded eyes of Keth-Ketha, how are women to handle a boat?" one of the men snarled. "How are they to handle fishing nets? Curse that—"

"Keep your voice down," admonished a second, "That-that thing might hear, and wake!"

Lythande looked out into the bay and saw what had not been apparent before; the approaching boat was crewed, not by men, but by four hearty half-grown girls in their teens. Their muscular arms were bare to the shoulder, skirts tucked up to the knee, their feet clumsy in sea-boots. They seemed to be handling the nets competently enough; and were evidently enormously strong, the kind of women who, if they had been milking a cow, could sling the beast over their shoulder and fetch it home out of a bog. But the men were watching with a jealous fury poorly concealed.

"Tomorrow I take my own boat out, and the lasses stay home and bake bread where they belong!"

"That's what Leukas did, and you know what happened to him—his whole crew wrecked on the rocks, and—and something, some *thing* out there ate boat and all! All they ever found was his hat, and his fishing net chewed half-through! An' seven sons for the village to feed till they're big enough to go out to the fishing—that's supposing we ever have any more fishing around here, and that whatever-it-is out there ever goes away again!"

Lythande raised a questioning eyebrow. Some menace, to the mercenary magician. Though Lythande bore two swords, girdled at the narrow waist of the mage-robe, the right-hand sword for the everyday menace of threatening humankind or natural beast, the left-hand sword to slay ghost or ghast or ghoul or any manner of supernatural menace, the Adept had no intention of here joining battle against some sea-monster. For that the village must await some hero or fighting man. Lythande was magician and minstrel, and though the sword was for hire where there was need, the Adept had no love for ordinary warfare, and less for fighting some menacing thing needing only brute strength and not craft.

There was but one inn in the village; Lythande made for it, ordered a pot of ale, and sat in the corner, not touching it—one of the vows fencing the power of an Adept of the Blue Star was that they might never be seen to eat or drink before men—but the price of a drink gave the mage a seat at the center of the action, where all the news of the village could be heard. They were still grousing about the fear that kept them out of the water. One man complained that already the ribs of his boat were cracking and drying and would need mending before he could put it back into the water.

"If there's ever to be any fishing here again..."

"Ye could send the wife and daughters out in the boat like Lubert—"

"Better we all starve or eat porridge for all our lives!"

"If we ha' no fish to trade for bread or porridge, what then?"

"Forgive my curiosity," Lythande said in the mellow, neutral voice that marked a trained minstrel, "but if a sea-monster is threatening the shore, why should women be safe in a boat when men are not?"

It was the wife of the innkeeper who answered her. "If it was a sea monster, we could go out there, all of us, even with fish-spears, and kill it, like the plainsmen do with the tusk-beasts. It's a mermaid, an' she sits and sings and lures our menfolk to the rocks—look yonder at my goodman," she said in a lowered voice, pointing to a man who sat apart before the fire, back turned to the company, clothing all unkempt, shirt half-buttoned, staring into the fire. His fingers fiddled nervously with the lacings of his clothing, snarling them into loops.

"He heard her," she said in a tone of such horror that hearing, the little hairs rose and tingled on Lythande's arms and the Blue Star between the magician's brows began to crackle and send forth lightnings. "He heard her, and his men dragged him away from the rocks. And there he sits from that day to this—him that was the jolliest man in all this town, staring and weeping and I have to feed him like a little child, and never take my eyes off him for half a minute or he'll walk out into the sea and drown, and there are times"—her voice sank in despair—"I'm minded to let him go, for he'll never have his wits again—I even have to guide him out to the privy, for he's forgotten even that!" And indeed, Lythande could see a moist spreading stain on the man's trousers, while the woman hastened, embarrassed, to lead her husband outside.

Lythande had seen the man's eyes; empty, lost, not seeing his wife, staring at something beyond the room.

Far from the sea, Lythande had heard tales of mermaids, of their enchantments and their songs. The minstrel in Lythande had half-desired to hear those songs, to walk on the rocks and listen to the singing that could, it was said, make the hearer forget all the troubles and joys of the world. But after seeing the man's empty eyes, Lythande decided to forgo the experience.

"And that is why some of the women have gone in the boats?"

"Not women," said the innkeeper's potboy, stopping with a tray of tankards to speak to the stranger, "girls too young for men. For they say that to women, it calls in the voice of their lover—Natzer's wife went out last fall moon, swearing she'd bring in fish for her children at least, and no one ever saw her again; but a hank of her hair, all torn and bloody, came in on the tide."

"I never heard that a mermaid was a flesh-eater," Lythande observed.

"Nor I. But I think she sings, and lures 'im on the rocks, where the fishes eat them...."

"There is the old stratagem," Lythande suggested. "Put cotton or wax plugs in your ears—"

"Say, stranger," said a man belligerently, "you think we're all fools out here? We tried that; but she sits on the rocks and she's so beautiful... the men went mad, just seeing her, threw me overboard—you can't blind-fold yourself, not on the sea with the rocks and all—there's never been a blind fisherman and never will. I swam ashore, and they drove the boat on the rocks, and only the blinded eyes of Keth-Ketha know where they've gone, but no doubt somewhere in the Sea-God's lockup." Lythande turned to face the man, he saw the Blue Star shining out from under the mage-robe and demanded, "Are you a spell-speaker?"

"I am a Pilgrim-Adept of the Blue Star," Lythande said gravely, "and while mankind awaits the Final Battle of Law and Chaos, I wander the world seeking what may come."

"I heard of the Temple of the Blue Star," said one woman fearfully. "Could you free us of this mermaid wi' your magic?"

"I do not know. I have never seen a mermaid," said Lythande, "and I have no great desire for the experience."

Yet why not? Under the world of the Twin Suns, in a life lasting more than most people's imaginations could believe, the Pilgrim-Adept had seen most things, and the mermaid was new. Lythande pondered how one would attack a creature whose only harm seemed to be that it gave forth with beautiful music—so beautiful that the hearer forgot home and family, loved ones, wife or child; and if the hearer escaped—Lythande shuddered. It was not a fate to be desired—sitting day after day staring into the fire, longing only to hear again that song.

Yet whatever magic could make, could be unmade again by magic. And Lythande held all the magic of the Temple of the Blue Star, having paid a price more terrifying than any other Adept in the history of the Pilgrim-Adepts. Should that magic now be tried against the unfamiliar magic of a mermaid?

"We are dying and hungering," said the woman. "Isn't that enough? I believed wizards were sworn to free the world from evil—"

"How many wizards have you known?" asked Lythande.

"None, though my mother said her granny told her, once a wizard came and done away wi' a sea-monster on them same rocks."

"Time is a great artificer," said Lythande, "for even wizards must live, my good woman; the pride of magic, while a suitable diversion while we all await the burning out of the Twin Suns and the Final Battle between Law and Chaos, puts no beans on the table. I have no great desire to test my powers against your mermaid, and I'll wager you anything you like that yonder old wizard charged your town a pretty penny for ridding the world of that sea-monster."

"We have nothing to give," said the innkeeper's wife, "but if you can restore my man, I'll give you my gold ring that he gave me when we were wedded. And since he's been enchanted, what kind of man are you if you can't take away one magic with another?" She tugged at her fat finger, and held out the ring, thin and worn, in the palm other hand. Her fingers clung to it, and there were tears in her eyes, but she held it out valiantly.

"What kind of man am I?" Lythande asked with an ironic smile. "Like none you will ever see. I have no need of gold, but give me tonight's lodging, and I will do what I can."

The woman slid the ring back on her hand with shaking fingers. "My best chamber. But, oh, restore him! Or would ye have some supper first?"

"Work first, then pay," said Lythande. The man was sitting again in the corner by the fire. staring into the flames, and from his lips came a small, tuneless humming. Lythande unslung the lute in its bag, and took it out, bending over the strings. Long, thin fingers strayed over the keys, head bent close as Lythande listened for the sound, tuning and twisting the pegs that held the strings.

At last, touching the strings, Lythande began to play. As the sound of the lute stole through the big common room, it was as if the chinks letting in the late sun had widened, and the light spread in the room; Lythande played sunlight and the happy breeze on the shore. Softly, on tiptoe, not wanting to let any random sound interrupt the music, the people in the inn stole nearer to listen to the soft notes. Sunlight, the shore winds, the sounds of the soft, splashing waves. Then Lythande began to sing.

Afterward—and for years, all those who heard often spoke of it—no one could remember what song was sung, though to everyone it sounded familiar, so that every hearer was sure it was a song they had heard at their mother's knee. To everyone it called, in the voice of husband or lover or child or wife, the voice of the one most loved. One old man said, with tears in his eyes, that he had heard his mother singing him to sleep with an old lullaby he had not heard in more than half a century. And at last, even the man who sat by the fire, clothes unkempt and stinking, hair rough and tangled, and his eyes lost in another world, slowly raised his head and turned to listen to the voice of Lythande, soft contralto or tenor; neutral, sexless, yet holding all the sweetness of either sex. Lythande sang of the simple things of the world, of sunlight and rain and wind, of the voices of children, of grass and wind and harvest and the silences of dawn and twilight. Then, the tempo quickening a little, she sang of home and fireside, where the children gathered in the evening, calling to their fathers to come home from the sea. And at last, the soft voice deepening and growing quieter so that the listeners had to lean forward to hear it, yet every whispered note clearly audible even to the rafters of the inn, Lythande sang of love.

And the eyes of every man widened, and the cheek of every woman reddened to a blush, yet to the innocent children there, every word was innocent as a mother's kiss on their cheek.

And when the song fell silent, the man by the fireside raised his head and brushed the tears from his eyes.

"Mhari, lass," he said hoarsely, "where are ye—ye and the babes—why, ha' I been sitting here the day-long and not out to the fishing? Why, lass, ye're crying, what ails the girl?" And he drew her to his knee and kissed her, and his face changed, and he shook his head, bewildered.

"Why, I dreamed— I dreamed—" His face contorted, but the woman drew his head down on her breast, and she, too, was weeping.

"Don't think of it, goodman, ye' were enchanted, but by the mercy of the gods and this good wizard here, ye're safe home and yourself again...."

He rose, his hands straying to his uncombed hair and unshaven chin. "How long? Aye, what devil's magic kept me here? And"—he looked around, seeing Lythande laying the lute in the case—"what brought me back? I owe ye gratitude, Lord Wizard," he said. "All my poor house may offer is at your command." His voice held the dignity of a poor workingman, and Lythande bent graciously to acknowledge it.

"I will take a lodging for the night, and a meal served in private in my room, no more." And though both the fisherman and his wife pressed Lythande to accept the ring and other gifts, even to the profits of a year's fishing, the wizard would accept nothing more.

But the others in the room crowded near, clamoring.

"No such magic has ever been seen in these parts! Surely you can free us, with your magic, from this evil wizardry! We beg you, we are at your mercy—we have nothing worthy of you, but such as we can, we will give...."

Lythande listened, impassive, to the pleading. It was to be expected; magic had been demonstrated, and knowing what it could do, they were greedy for more. Yet it was not greed alone, their lives and their livelihoods were at stake. These poor folk could not continue to live by the fishing if the mermaid continued to lure them onto the rocks, to be wrecked or eaten by sea-monsters, or, if they came safe and alive to their homes, to live on rapt away by the memory.

Yet what reason could this mermaid have for her evildoing? Lythande was well acquainted with the laws of magic, and magical things did not exercise their powers only out of a desire to make mischief among men. Why, after all, had this mermaid come to sing and enchant these simple shore folk? What could her purpose be?

"I will have a meal served in private, that I may consider this," the magician said, "and tomorrow I will speak with everyone in the village who has heard this creature's song or looked upon her. And then I will decide whether my magic can do anything for you. Further than that I will not go."

When the woman had departed, leaving the tray of food, Lythande locked and double-locked the door of the room behind her. A fine baked fish lay on a clean white napkin—Lythande suspected it was the best of the meager catch brought in by the young girls, which alone kept the village from starving. The fish was seasoned with fragrant herbs, and there was a hot, coarse loaf of maize-bread, with butter and cream, and a dish of sweet boiled seaweed on the tray.

First Lythande cast about the room, the Blue Star blazing between the narrow brows, seeking hidden spy-holes or magical traps. Eternal vigilance was the price of safety for any Adept of the Blue Star, even in a village as isolated as this one. It was not likely that some enemy had trailed Lythande here, nor pre-arranged a trap, but stranger things had happened in the Adept's long life.

But the room was nowhere overlooked and seemed impregnable, so that at last Lythande was free to take off the voluminous mage-robe and even to ungird the belt with the two swords, and draw off the soft dyed-leather boots. So revealed, Lythande presented still the outward appearance of a slender, beardless man, tall and strongly framed and sexless; yet, free of observation, Lythande was revealed as what she was; a woman. Yet a woman who might never be known to be so in the sight of any living man.

A masquerade that had become truth; for into the Temple of the Pilgrim-Adepts, Lythande alone in all their long history had successfully penetrated in male disguise. Not till the Blue Star already shone between her brows, symbol and sign of Adepthood, had she been discovered and exposed; and by then she was sacrosanct, bearing their innermost secrets. And then the Master of the Pilgrim-Adepts had laid on her the doom she still bore.

"So be it; be then in truth what you have chosen to seem. Till Law and Chaos meet in that Final Battle where all things must die, be what you have pretended; for on that day when any Pilgrim-Adept save myself shall proclaim your true sex, on that day is your power forfeit and you may be slain."

So together with all the vows that fenced about the power of a Pilgrim-Adept, Lythande bore this burden as well; that of concealing her true sex to the end of the world.

She was not, of course, the only Adept heavily burdened with a *geas*; every Adept of the Blue Star bore Some such Secret in whose concealment, even from other Adepts of the Order, lay all his magic and all his strength. Lythande might even have a woman confidante, if she could find one she could trust with her life and her powers.

The minstrel-Adept ate the fish, and nibbled at the boiled seaweed, which was not to her taste. The maize bread, well-wrapped against grease, found its way into the pockets of the mage-robe, against some time when she might not be able to manage privacy for a meal and must snatch a concealed bite as she traveled.

This done, she drew from a small pouch at her waist a quantity of herbs that had no magical properties whatever (unless the property of bringing relaxation and peace to the weary can be counted magical), rolled them into a narrow tube, and set them alight with a spark blazing from the ring she bore. She inhaled deeply, leaned back with her narrow feet stretched out to the fire, for the sea-wind was damp and cold, and considered.

Did she wish, for the prestige of the Order, and the pride of a Pilgrim-Adept, to go out against a mermaid?

Powerful as was the magic of the Blue Star, Lythande knew that somewhere beneath the world of the Twin Suns, a magic might lie next to which a Pilgrim-Adept's powers were mere hearth-magic and trumperies. There were moments when she wearied, indeed, of her long life of concealment and felt she would welcome death, more especially if it came in honorable battle. But these were brief moods of the night, and always when day came, she wakened with renewed curiosity about all the new adventures that might lie around the next bend in the road. She had no wish to cut it short in futile striving against an unknown enemy.

Her music had indeed recalled the enchanted man to himself. Did this mean her magic was stronger than that of the mermaid? Probably not; she had needed only to break through the magical focus of the man's attention, to remind him of the beauty of the world he had forgotten. Then, hearing again, his mind had chosen that real beauty over the false beauty of the enchantment, for beneath the magic that held him entranced, the mind of the man must have been already in despair, struggling to break free. A simple magic and nothing to give overconfidence in her strength against the unknown magic of mermaids.

She wrapped herself in the mage-robe and laid herself down to sleep, halfway inclined to rise before dawn and be far away before anyone in the village was astir. What were the troubles of a fishing village to her? Already she had given them a gift of magic, restoring the innkeeper's husband to himself; what else did she owe them?

Yet, a few minutes before the rising of the pale face of Keth, she woke knowing she would remain. Was it only the challenge of testing an unknown magic against her own? Or had the helplessness of these people touched her heart?

Most likely, Lythande thought with a cynical smile, it was her own wish to see a new magic. In the years she had wandered under the eyes of Keth and Reth, she had seen many magics, and most were simple and almost mechanical, set once in motion and kept going by something not much better than inertia. Once, she remembered, she had encountered a haunted oak grove, with a legend of a dryad spirit who seduced all male passersby. It had proved to be no more than an echo of a dryad's wrath when spurned by a man she had tried and failed to seduce; her rage and counterspell had persisted more than forty seasons, even when the dryad's tree had fallen, lightning-struck, and withered. The remnants of the spell had lingered till it was no more than an empty grove where women took their reluctant lovers, that the leftover powers of the angry dryad might arouse at least a little lust. Lythande, despite the pleas of the women fearing to lose their husbands to the power of the spell, had not chosen to meddle; the last she heard, the place had acquired a pleasant reputation for restoring potency, at least for a night, to any man who slept there.

The village was already astir. Lythande went out into the reddening sunrise, where the fishermen gathered from habit, though they were not dragging down their boats to the edge of the tide. Seeing Lythande, they left the boats and crowded around.

"Say, wizard, will you help us or no?"

"I have not yet decided," said Lythande. "First I must speak with everyone in the village who has encountered the creature."

"Ye can't do that," said one old man with a fierce grin, "'less ye can walk down into the Sea-God's lockup an' question them down there! Or maybe wizards can do that, too?"

Rebuked, Lythande wondered if she were taking their predicament too lightly. To her, perhaps, it was challenge and curiosity; to these folk it was their lives and their livelihood, their very survival at stake.

"I am sorry; I should have said, of course, those who have encountered the creature and lived." There were not, she supposed, too many of those.

She spoke first to the fisherman she had recalled with her magic. He spoke with a certain, self-consciousness, his eyes fixed on the ground away from her.

"I heard her singing, that's all I can remember, and it seemed there was nothing in the world but only that song. Mad, it is, I don't care all that much for music—savin' your presence, minstrel," he added sheepishly. "Only I heard that song, somehow it was different, I wanted no more than just to listen to it forever...." He stood silent, thoughtful. "For all that, I wish I could remember...." And his eyes sought the distant horizon.

"Be grateful you cannot," Lythande said crisply, "or you would still be sitting by your fire without wit to feed or clean yourself. If you wish my advice, never let yourself think of it again for more than a moment."

"Oh, ye're right, I know that, but still an' all, it was beautiful—" He sighed, shook himself like a great dog, and looked up at Lythande. "I suppose my mates must ha' dragged me away an' back to the shore; next I knew I was sitting by my fireplace listening to your music, minstrel, an' Mhari cryin' and all."

She turned away; from him she had learned no more than she had known before. "Is there anyone else who met the beast, the mermaid, and survived the meeting?"

It seemed there were none; for the young girls who had taken out the boat either had not encountered the mermaid or it had not chosen to show itself to them. At last one of the women of the village said hesitantly, "When first it came, and the men were hearin' it and never coming back, there was Lulie—she went out with some of the women—she didna' hear anything, they say; she can't hear anything, she's been deaf these thirty years. And she says she saw it, but she wouldna' talk about it. Maybe, knowin' what you're intending to do, she'll tell you, magician."

A deaf woman. Surely there was logic to this, as there was logic to all the things of magic if you could only find out the underlying pattern to it. The deaf woman had survived the mermaid because she could not hear the song. Then why had the men of the village been unable to conquer it by the old ruse of plugging their ears with wax?

It attacked the eyes, too, apparently, for one of the men had spoken of it as "so beautiful." This man said he had leaped from the boat and tried to swim ashore. Ashore—or on the rocks toward the creature? She should try to speak with him, too, if she could find him. Why was he not here among the men? Well, first, Lythande decided, she would speak with the deaf woman.

She found her in the village bake shop, supervising a single crooked-bodied apprentice in unloading two or three limp-looking sacks of poor-quality flour, mixed with husks and straw. The village's business, then, was so much with the fishing that only those who were physically unable to go into the boats found it permissible to follow any other trade.

The deaf woman glowered at Lythande, set her lips tight, and gestured to the cripple to go on with what he was doing, bustling about her ovens. The doings of a magician, said her every truculent look, were no business of hers and she wanted nothing to do with them.

She went to the apprentice and stood over him. Lythande was a very tall woman, and he was a wee small withered fellow; as he looked up, he had to tilt his head back. The deaf woman scowled, but Lythande deliberately ignored her.

"I will talk with you," she said deliberately, "since your mistress is too deaf and perhaps too stupid to hear what I have to say."

The little apprentice was shaking in his shoes.

"Oh, no, Lord Magician... I can't.... She knows every word we say, she reads lips; and I swear she knows what I say even before I say it...."

"Does she indeed?" Lythande said. "So now I know." She went and stood over the deaf woman until she raised her sullen face. "You are Lulie, and they tell me that you met the seabeast, the mermaid, whatever it is, and that it did not kill you. Why?"

"How should I know?" The woman's voice was rusty as if from long disuse; it grated on Lythande's musical ear.

It was unfair to think ill of a woman because of her misfortune; yet Lythande found herself disliking this woman very much. Distaste made her voice harsh.

"You have heard that I have committed myself to rid the village of this creature that is preying on it." Lythande did not realize that she had, in fact, committed herself until she heard herself say so. "In order to do this, I must know what it is that I face. Tell me all you know of this thing, whatever it may be."

"Why do you think I know anything at all?"

"You survived." And, thought Lythande, I would like to know why, for when I know why it spared this very unprepossessing woman, perhaps I will know what I must do to kill it—if it must be killed, after all. Or would it be enough to drive it away from here?

Lulie stared at the floor. Lythande knew she was at an impasse; the woman could not hear, and she, Lythande, could not command her with her eyes and presence, or even with her magic, as long as the woman would not meet her eyes. Anger flared in her; she could feel, between her brows, the crackling blaze of the Blue Star; her anger and the blaze of magic reached the baker woman and she looked up. Lythande said angrily, "Tell me what you know of this creature! How did you survive the mermaid?"

"How am I to know that? I survived. Why? You are the magician, not I; let you tell me that, wizard."

With an effort Lythande moderated her anger. "Yet I implore you, for the safety of all these people, tell me what you know, however little."

"What do I care for the folk of this village?" Lythande wondered what her grudge was that her voice should be so filled with wrath and contempt. It was probably useless to try and find out. Grudges were often quite irrational; perhaps she blamed them for her loss of hearing, perhaps for the isolation that had descended on her when, as with many deaf people, she had withdrawn into a world of her own, cut off from friends and kin.

"Nevertheless, you are the only one who has survived a meeting with this thing," Lythande said, "and if you will tell me your secret, I will not tell them."

After a long time the woman said, "It—called to me. It called in the last voice I heard; my child, him that died o' the same fever that lost me my hearing; crying and calling out to me. And so for a time I thought they'd lied to me when they said my boy was dead of the fever, that somehow he lived, out there on the wild shores. I spent the night seeking him. And when the morning came, I came to my senses, and knew if he had lived, he wouldna' call me in that baby voice—he died thirty years ago, by now he'd be a man grown, and how could he have lived all this tame alone?" She stared at the floor again, stubbornly.

There was nothing Lythande could say. She could hardly thank the woman for a story Lythande had wrenched from her, if not by force, so near it as not to matter.

So I was on the wrong track, Lythande thought. The deaf woman had not been keeping from Lythande some secret that could have helped to deal with the menace to this village. She was only concealing what would have made her feel a fool.

And who am I to judge her, I who hold a secret deeper and darker than hers?

She had been wrong and must begin again. But the time had not been wasted, not quite, for now she knew that whereas it called to men in the voices of the ones they loved, it was not wholly a sexual enticement, as she had heard some mermaids were. It called to men in the voice of a loved woman; to at least one woman, it had called in the voice of her dead child. Was it, then, that it called to everyone in the voice of what they loved best?

This, then, would explain why the young girls were at least partly immune. Before the power of love came into a life, a young boy or girl loved his parents, yes, but because of the lack of experience, the parents were still seen as someone who could protect and care for the child, not to be selflessly cared for.

Love alone could create that selflessness.

Then—thought Lythande—*it will be safe for me to go out against the monster. For there is, now, no one and nothing I love. Never have I loved any man. Such women as I have loved are separated from me by more than a lifetime, and I know enough to be wary if any should call to me in the voice of the heart's desire, then I am safe from it. For I love no one, and my heart, if indeed I still have a heart, desires nothing.*

I will go and tell them that I am ready to rid the village of their curse.

They gave her their best boat, and would have given her one of the half-grown girls to row it out for her, but Lythande declined. How could she be sure the girl was too young to have loved, and thus become vulnerable to the call of the sea-creature? Also, for safety, Lythande left her lute on the shore, partly because she wished to show them that she trusted them with it, but mostly because she feared what the damp in the boat might do to the fragile and cherished instrument. More, if it came to a fight, she might step on it or break it in the boat's crowded conditions.

It was a clear and brilliant day, and Lythande, who was physically stronger than most men, sculled the boat briskly into the strong offshore wind. Small clouds scudded along the edge of the horizon, and each breaking wave folded over and collapsed with a soft, musical splashing. The noise of the breakers was strong in her ear, and it seemed to Lythande that under the sound of the waves, there was a faraway song; like the song of a shell held to the ear. For a few minutes she sang to herself in an undertone, listening to the sound of her own voice against the voice of the sea's breaking; an illusion, she knew, but one she found pleasurable. She thought, if only she had her lute, she would enjoy improvising harmonies to this curious blending. The words she sang against the waves were nonsense syllables, but they seemed to take on an obscure and magical meaning as she sang.

She was never sure, afterward, how long this lasted. After a time, though she believed at first that it was simply another pleasant illusion like the shell held to the ear, she heard a soft voice inserting itself into the harmonies she was creating with the wave-song and her own voice; somewhere there was a third voice, wordless and incredibly sweet. Lythande went on singing, but something inside her pricked up its ears—or was it the tingling of the Blue Star that sensed the working of magic somewhere close to her?

The song, then, of the mermaid. Sweet as it was, there were no words. *As I thought, then. The creature works upon the heart's desire. I am desireless, therefore immune to the call. It cannot harm me.*

She raised her eyes. For a moment she saw only the great mass of rocks of which they had warned her, and against its mass a dark and featureless shadow. As she looked at the shadow, the Blue Star on her brow tingling, she willed to see more clearly. Then she saw—

What was it? Mermaid, they had said. Creature. Could they possibly call it evil?

In form, it was no more than a young girl, naked but for a necklace of small, rare, glimmering shells; the shells that had a crease running down the center, so that they looked like a woman's private parts. Her hair was dark, with the glisten of water on the smooth globes of bladder wrack lying on the sand at high tide. The face was smooth and young, with regular features. And the eyes....

Lythande could never remember anything about the eyes, though at the time she must have had some impression about the color. Perhaps they were that same color of the sea where it rolled and rippled smooth beyond the white breakers. She had no attention to spare for the eyes, for she was listening to the voice. Yet she knew she must be cautious; if she were vulnerable at all to this thing, it would be through the voice, she to whom music had been friend and lover and solace for more than a lifetime.

Now she was close enough to see. How like a young girl the mermaid looked, young and vulnerable, with a soft, childish mouth. One of the small teeth, teeth like irregular pearls, was chipped out of line, and it made her look very childish. A soft mouth. A mouth too young for kissing, Lythande thought, and wondered what she had meant by it.

Once I, even I was as young as that, Lythande thought, her mind straying among perilous ways of memory; a time—how many lifetimes ago?—when she had been a young girl already restless at the life of the women's quarters, dreaming of magic and adventure; a time when she had borne another name, a name she had vowed never to remember. But already, though she had not yet glimpsed the steep road that was to lead her at last to the Temple of the Blue Star and to the great renunciations that lay ahead of her as a Pilgrim-Adept, she knew her path did not lie among young girls like these—with soft, vulnerable mouths and soft, vulnerable dreams, lovers and husbands and babies clinging around their necks as the necklace of little female shells clung to the neck of the mermaid. Her world was already too wide to be narrowed so far.

Never vulnerable like that, so that this creature should call to me in the voice of a dead and beloved child....

And as if in answer, suddenly there were words in the mermaid's song, and a voice Lythande had not remembered for a lifetime. She had forgotten his face and his name; but her memory was the memory of a trained minstrel, a musician's memory. A man, a name, a life might be forgotten; a song or a voice—no, never.

My princess and my beloved, forget these dreams of magic and adventure, together we will sing such songs of love that life need hold no more for either of us.

A swift glance at the rocks told her he sat there, the face she had forgotten, in another moment she would remember his name.... *No! this was illusion; he was dead, he had been dead for more years than she could imagine....* *Go away*, she said to the illusion. *You are dead, and I am not to be deceived that way, not yet.*

They had told her the vision could call in the voice of the dead. But it could not trick her, not that way; as the illusion vanished, Lythande sensed a little ripple of laughter, like the breaking of a tiny wave against the rocks where the mermaid sat. Her laugh was delicious. Was that illusion, too?

To a woman, then, it calls in the voice of a lover. But never had Lythande been vulnerable to that call. He had not been the only one; only the one to whom Lythande had come the closest to yielding. She had almost remembered his name; for a moment her mind lingered, floating, seeking a name, a name... then, deliberately, but almost with merriment turned her mind willfully away from the tensed fascination of the search.

She need not try to remember. That had been long, long ago, in a country so far from here that no living man within a ten-day's journey knew so much as the name of that country. So why remember? She knew the answer to that; this sea-creature, this mermaid, defended itself this way, reaching into her mind and memory, as it had reached into the mind and memory of the fishermen who sought to pass by it, losing them in a labyrinth of the past, of old loves, heart's desires. Lythande repressed a shudder, remembering the man seated by the fire, lost in his endless dream. How narrowly had she escaped that? And there would have been none to rescue her.

But a Pilgrim-Adept was not to be caught so simply. The creature was simple, using on her its only defense, forcing the mind and memory: and she had escaped. Desireless, Lythande was immune to that call of desire.

Young girl as she looked, that at least must be illusion, the mermaid was an ageless creature... like herself, Lythande thought.

For the creature had tried for a moment to show herself to Lythande in that illusory form of a past lover—no, he had never been Lythande's lover, but in the form of an old memory to trap her in the illusory country of heart's desire. But Lythande had never been vulnerable in that way to the heart's desire.

Never?

Never, creature of dreams. Not even when I was younger than you appear now to be.

But was this the mermaid's true form, or something like it? The momentary illusion vanished, the mermaid had returned to the semblance of the young girl, touchingly young; there must then be some truth to the appearance of the childish mouth, the eyes that were full of dreams, the vulnerable smile. The mermaiden was protecting itself in the best way it could, for certainly a sea-maiden so frail and defenseless, seeming so young and fair, would be at the mercy of the men of the fisherfolk, men who would see only a maiden to be preyed upon.

There were many such tales along these shores, still told around the hearthfires, of mermaids and of men who had loved them. Men who had taken them home as wives, bringing a free sea-maiden to live in the smoke of the hearthfire, to cook and spin, servant to man, a mockery of the free creature she should be. Often the story ended when the imprisoned sea-maiden found her dress of fish scales and seaweed and plunged into the sea again to find her freedom, leaving the fisherman to mourn his lost love.

Or the loss of his prisoner...? In this case, Lythande's sympathy was with the mermaid.

Yet she had pledged herself to free the village of this danger. And surely it was a danger, if only of a beauty more terrible than they dared to know and understand, a fragile and fleeting beauty like the echo of a song, or like the sea wrack in the ebb and flow of the tide. For with illusion gone, the mermaid was only this frail-looking creature, ageless but with the eternal illusion of youth. *We are alike*, thought Lythande; *in that sense, we are sisters, but I am freer than she is.*

She was beginning to be aware of the mermaid's song again, and knew it was dangerous to listen. She sang to herself to try and block it away from her awareness. But she felt an enormous sympathy for the creature, here at the mercy of a crude fishing village, protecting herself as best she could, and cursed for her beauty.

She looked so like one of the young girls Lythande had known in that faraway country. They had made music together on the harp and the lute and the bamboo flute. Her name had been... Lythande found the name in her mind without a search... her name had been Riella, and it seemed to her that the mermaid sang in Riella's voice.

Not of love, for already at that time Lythande had known that such love as the other young girls dreamed of was not for her, but there had been an awareness between them. Never acknowledged; but Lythande had begun to know that even for a woman who cared nothing for man's desire, life need not be altogether empty. There were dreams and desires that had nothing to do with those simpler dreams of the other women, dreams of husband or lover or child.

And then Lythande heard the first syllable of a name, a name she had vowed to forget, a name once her own, a name she would not—no. No. A name she *could* not remember. Sweating, the Blue Star blazing with her anger, she looked at the rocks. Riella's form there wavered and was gone.

Again the creature had attempted to call to her in the voice of the dead. There was no longer the least trace of amusement in Lythande's mind. Once again she had almost fatally underestimated the sea-creature because it looked so young and childlike, because it reminded her of Riella and of the other young girls she had loved in a world, and a life, long lost to her. She would not be caught that way again. Lythande gripped the hilt of the left-hand dagger, warder against magic, as she felt the boat beneath her scrape on the rocks.

She stepped out onto the surface of the small, rocky holt, wrinkling her nose at the rankness of dead fish and sea wrack left by the tide, a carrion smell—how could so young and fair a creature live in this stench?

The mermaid said in the small voice of a very young girl, "Did they send you to kill me, Lythande?"

Lythande gripped the handle of her left-hand dagger. She had no wish to engage in conversation with the creature; she had vowed to rid the village of this thing, and rid it she would. Yet even as she raised the dagger, she hesitated.

The mermaid, still in that timid little-girl voice, said, "I admit that I tried to ensnare you. You must be a great magician to escape from me so easily. My poor magic could not hold you at all!"

Lythande said, "I am an Adept of the Blue Star."

"I do not know of the Blue Star. Yet I can feel its power," said the sea-maiden. "Your magic is very great—"

"And yours is to flatter me," said Lythande carefully, and the mermaid gave a delicious, childish giggle.

"You see what I mean? I can't deceive you at all. can I, Lythande? But why did you come here to kill me, when I can't harm you in any way? And why are you holding that horrible dagger?"

Why, indeed? Lythande wondered, and slid it back into its sheath. This creature could not hurt her. Yet surely she had come here for some reason, and she groped for it. She said at last, "The folk of the village cannot fish for their livelihood and they will all starve. Why do you want to do this?"

"Why not?" asked the mermaid innocently.

That made Lythande think a little. She had listened to the villagers and their story; she had not stopped to consider the mermaid's side of the business. The sea did not belong, after all, to the fishermen; it belonged to the fish and to the creatures of the sea—birds and fish and waves, shellfish of the deep, eels and dolphins and great whales who had nothing to do with human-kind at all—and, yes, to the mermaids and stranger sea creatures as well.

Yet Lythande was vowed to fight on the side of Law against Chaos till the Final Battle should come. And if humankind could not get its living as did the other creatures inhabiting the world, what would become of them?

"Why should they live by killing the fish in the sea?" the mermaid asked. "Have they any better right to survive than the fish?"

That was a question not all that easily answered. Yet as she glanced about the shore, smelling the rankness of the tide, Lythande knew what she should say next.

"You live upon the fish, do you not? There are enough fish in the sea for all the people of the shore, as well as for your kind. And if the fishermen do not kill the fish and eat them, the fish will only be eaten by other fish. Why not leave the fisherfolk in peace, to take what they need?"

"Well, perhaps I will," said the mermaid, giggling again, so that Lythande was again astonished; what a childish creature this was, after all. Did she even know what harm she had done?

"Perhaps I can find another place to go. Perhaps you could help me?" She raised her large and luminous eyes to Lythande. "I heard you singing. Do you know any new songs, magician? And will you sing them to me?"

Why, the poor creature is like a child; lonely, and even restless, all alone here on the rocks. How like a child she was when she said it.... Do you know any new songs? Lythande wished for a moment that she had not left her lute on the shore.

"Do you want me to sing to you?"

"I heard you singing, and it sounded so sweet across the water, my sister. I am sure we have songs and magics to teach one another."

Lythande said gently, "I will sing to you."

First she sang, letting her mind stray in the mists of time past, a song she had sung to the sound of the bamboo reed-flute, more than a lifetime ago. It seemed for a moment that Riella sat beside her on the rocks. Only an illusion created by the mermaid, of course. But surely a harmless one! Still, perhaps it was not wise to allow the illusion to continue; Lythande wrenched her mind from the past, and sang the sea-song that she had composed yesterday, as she walked along the shore to this village.

"Beautiful, my sister," murmured the mermaid, smiling so that the charming little gap in her pearly teeth showed. "Such a musician I have never heard. Do all the people who live on land sing so beautifully?"

"Very few of them," said Lythande. "Not for many years have I heard such sweet music as yours."

"Sing again. Sister," said the mermaid, smiling. "Come close to me and sing again. And then I shall sing to you."

"And you will come away and let the fisherfolk live in peace?" Lythande asked craftily.

"Of course I will, if you ask it, Sister," the mermaid said. It had been so many years since anyone had spoken to Lythande, woman to woman, without fear. It was death for her to allow any man to know that she was a woman, and the women in whom she dared confide were so few. It was soothing balm to her heart.

Why, after all, should she go back to the land again? Why not stay here in the quiet peace of the sea, sharing songs and magical spells with her sister, the mermaid? There were greater magics here than she had ever known, yes, and sweeter music, too.

She sang, hearing her voice ring out across the water. The mermaid sat quietly, her head a little turned to the side, listening as if in utter enchantment, and Lythande felt she had never sung so sweetly. For a moment she wondered if, hearing her song echoing from the ocean, any passerby would think that he heard the true song of a mermaid. For surely she, too, Lythande, could enchant with her song. Should she stay here, cease denying her true sex, where, she could be at once woman and magician and minstrel? She, too, could sit on the rocks, enchanting with her music, letting time and sea roll over her, forgetting the struggle of her life as Pilgrim-Adept, being only what she was in herself. She was a great magician; she could feel the very tingle of her magic in the Blue Star on her brow, crackling lightings....

"Come nearer to me, Sister, that I can hear the sweetness of your song," murmured the mermaid. "Truly, it is you who have enchanted me, magician—"

As if in a dream, Lythande took a step farther up the beach. A shell crunched hard under her foot. Or was it a bone? She never knew what made her look down, to see that her foot had turned on a skull.

Lythande felt ice run through her veins. This was no illusion. Quickly she gripped the left-hand dagger and whispered a spell that would clear the air of illusion and void all magic, including her own. She should have done it before.

The mermaid gave a despairing cry. "No, no, my sister, my sister musician, stay with me... now you will hate me too..." But even as the words died out, like the fading sound of a lute's broken string, the mermaid was gone, and Lythande stared in horror at what sat on the rocks.

It was not remotely human in form. It was three or four times the size of the largest sea-beast she had ever seen, crouching huge and greenish, the color of sea-weed and sea wrack. All she could see of the head was rows and rows of teeth, huge teeth gaping before her. And the true horror was that one of the great fangs had a chip knocked from it.

Little pearly teeth with a little chip....

Gods of Chaos! I almost walked down that thing's throat!

Retching, Lythande swung the dagger; almost at once she whipped out the right-hand knife, which was effective against material menace; struck toward the heart of the thing. An eerie howl went up as blackish green blood, smelling of sea wrack and carrion, spurted over the Pilgrim-Adept. Lythande, shuddering, struck again and again until the cries were silent. She looked down at the dead thing, the rows of teeth, the tentacles and squirming suckers. Before her eyes was a childish face, a voice whose memory would never leave her.

And I called the thing "Sister"....

It had even been easy to kill. It had no weapons, no defenses except its song and its illusions. Lythande had been so proud of her ability to escape the illusions, proud that she was not vulnerable to the call of lover or of memory.

Yet it had called, after all, to the heart's desire... for music. For magic. For the illusion of a moment where something that never existed, never could exist, had called her "Sister," speaking to a womanhood renounced forever. She looked at the dead thing on the beach, and knew she was weeping as she had not wept for three ordinary lifetimes.

The mermaid had called her "Sister," and she had killed it.

She told herself, even as her body shook with sobs, that her tears were mad. If she had not killed it, she would have died in those great and dreadful rows of teeth, and it would not have been a pleasant death.

Yet for that illusion, I would have been ready to die....

She was crying for something that had never existed.

She was crying because it had never existed, and because, for her, it would never exist, not even in memory. After a long time, she stooped down and, from the mass that was melting like decaying seaweed, she picked up a fang with a chip out of it. She stood looking at it for a long time. Then, her lips tightening grimly, she flung it out to sea, and clambered back into the boat. As she sculled back to shore, she found she was listening to the sound in the waves, like a shell held to the ear. And when she realized that she was listening again for another voice, she began to sing the rowdiest drinking song she knew.

THE WANDERING LUTE
Marion Zimmer Bradley

In the glass bowl the salamander hissed blue fire. Lythande bent over the bowl, extending numbed white fingers; the morning chill at Old Gandrin nipped nose and fingers. At a warning hiss from the bowl, the magician stepped back, looking questioningly at the young candlemaker.

"Does he bite?"

"Her name is Alnath," Eirthe said. "She usually doesn't need to."

"Allow me to beg her pardon," Lythande said. "Essence of Fire, may I borrow your warmth?"

Fire streamed upward; Lythande bent gratefully over the bowl; Alnath coiled within, a miniature dragon, flames streaming upward from the fire elemental's substance.

"She likes you," said Eirthe. "When Prince Tashgan came here, she hissed at him and the silk covering of his lute began to smolder; he went out faster than he came in."

The hood of the mage-robe was thrown back, and by the light of the fire streaming upward, the Blue Star could be clearly seen on Lythande's high, narrow forehead.

Tashgan? I know him only by reputation," Lythande said, "Will you enjoy living in a palace, Eirthe? Will Her Brilliance adapt kindly to a bowl of jewels and diamonds?"

Eirthe giggled, for Prince Tashgan was known throughout Old Gandrin as a womanizer. "He was looking for you, Lythande. How do you feel about life in a palace?"

"For me? What need could the prince have of a mercenary-magician?"

"Perhaps." Eirthe said, "he wishes to take music lessons." She nodded at the lute slung across the magician's shoulder. "I have heard Tashgan play at three summer-festivals, and he plays not half so well as you. The lute is not his best instrument." She giggled, with a suggestive roll of her eyes.

Lythande enjoyed a raunchy joke as well as anyone; the magician's mellow chuckle filled the room. "It is frequently so with those who take up the lute for pleasure. As for those who wear a crown, who can tell them their playing could be bettered, whatever the instrument? Flattery ruins much talent."

"Tashgan wears no crown, nor ever will," Eirthe said. "The High-lord of Tschardain had three sons—know you not the story?"

"Is he the third son of Tschardain? I had heard he was in exile," Lythande said, "but I have only passed briefly through Tschardain."

"The old King had a stroke, seven years ago; while he lingered, paralyzed and unable to speak, his older son assumed the power; his second son became his brother's adviser and marshal of his armies. Tashgan was, they said, weak, absentminded, and a womanizer; I daresay it was only that the young Lord wanted few claimants to challenge his position."

She bent to rummage briefly under her worktable and pulled out a silk-wrapped bundle. "Here are the candles you ordered. Remember that they're spelled not to burn unless they're in one of Cadmon's glasses—though you can probably find a counter-spell easily enough."

"One of Cadmon's glasses I have already." Lythande took the candles, but lingered, close to the salamander's heat. Eirthe glanced at the lute on an embroidered leather band across Lythande's shoulder.

She asked, "Were you magician first or minstrel? It seems a strange combination."

"I was musician from childhood," Lythande said, "and when I took up magic I deserted my first love. But the lute is a forgiving mistress." The magician bestowed the packet of candles in one of the concealed pockets in the dark mage-robe, bowed in courtly fashion to Eirthe, and murmured to the salamander, "Essence of Fire, my thanks for your warmth."

A streamer of cobalt fire surged upward out of the bowl; leaped to Lythande's outstretched hand. Lythande did not flinch as the salamander perched for a moment on the slender wrist, though it left a red mark. Eirthe whistled faintly in surprise.

"She never does that to strangers!" The girl glanced at the callus on her own wrist where the salamander habitually rested.

"She is like a were-dragon made small in appearance." Hearing that, Alnath hissed again, stretching out her long fiery neck, and as Eirthe watched in astonishment, Lythande stroked the flaming scales. "Perhaps she knows we are kindred spirits; she is not the first fire-elemental I have known," said the magician. "A good part of the business of an adept is playing with fire. There, fair Essence of the purest of all Elements, go to your true Mistress." Lythande raised an arm in a graceful gesture; streamers of fire seared the air as Alnath flashed toward Eirthe's wrist and came to rest there. "Should Tashgan seek me again, tell him I lodge at the Blue Dragon."

But Lythande saw Prince Tashgan before Eirthe did.

The Adept was seated in the common-room of the Blue Dragon, a pot of ale untouched on the table—for one of the many vows fencing the powers of an Adept of the Blue Star was that they might never be seen to eat or drink before strangers. Nevertheless, the pot of ale was the magician's unquestioned passport to sit among the townsfolk and listen to whatever might be happening among them.

"Will you favor us with a song, High-born?" asked the innkeeper. The Pilgrim Adept uncovered the lute and began to play a ballad of the countryside. As the soft notes stole into the room, the drinkers fell silent, listening to the mellow sound of Lythande's voice, soft, neutral, and sexless.

As the last note died away, a tall, richly clad man, standing at the back of the room, came forward. "Master Minstrel, I salute you," he said. "I had heard from afar of your skill with the lute and came here a little before my proper season, to hear you play and—other things. You lodge here? Might I buy you a drink in privacy, Magician? I have heard that your services are for hire; I have need of them."

"I am a mercenary magician," Lythande said, "I give no instruction on the lute."

"Nevertheless let us discuss in private whether if would be worth your while to give me lessons," said the man. "I am Tashgan, son of Idriash of Tschardain."

Some of the watchers in the room had the uneasy sense that the Blue Star on Lythande's brow shrugged itself and focused to look at Tashgan. Lythande said, "So be it. Before the final battle of Law and Chaos many unusual things may come to pass, and for all I know this may well be one of them."

"Will it please you to speak in your chamber, or in mine?"

"Let it be in yours," said Lythande. The items with which any person chose to surround himself could often give the magician an important clue to character; if this prince was to be a client—for the services of magician or minstrel—such clues might prove valuable.

Tashgan had commanded the most luxurious chamber at the Blue Dragon; its original character had almost been obscured by silken hangings and cushions. Elegant small musical instruments—a tambour adorned with silk ribbons, a bodhran, a pair of serpent rattles, and a gilded sistrum—hung on the wall. As the door opened, a slight girl in a chemise, arms bare and hair loosened and falling in a disheveled cloud over her bared young breasts, rolled from the bed and scurried away behind the hangings. Lythande's face drew together into a frown of distaste.

"Charming, is she not?" asked Tashgan negligently. "A local maiden; I want no permanent ties in this town. Indeed, it is of ties of this sort—undesired ties, and involuntary—that I would speak. Lissini, bring wine from my private stock."

The girl poured wine; Lythande formally lifted the cup without, however, tasting it, and bowed to Tashgan.

"How may I serve your Excellency?"

"It is a long story." Tashgan unfastened the strap of the lute across his shoulder. "What think you of this lute?" His weak, watery blue eyes followed the instrument as he undid the case and displayed it.

Lythande studied the instrument briefly; smaller than Lythande's own lute, exquisitely crafted of fruitwood inlaid with mother-of-pearl.

"I remember not one so fairly crafted since I came into this country."

"Appearances are deceiving," said Tashgan. "This instrument, magician, is at once my curse and my blessing."

"May I?" Lythande put forth a slender hand and touched the delicately fretted neck. The blue star blazed suddenly, and Lythande frowned.

"This lute is under enchantment. This is the long story of which you spoke. The night is young; long live the night. Tell on."

Tashgan signaled to the girl to pour more of the fragrant wine. "Know you what it is to be a third son in a royal line, magician?"

Lythande only smiled enigmatically. Royal birth in a faraway country was a claim made by many rogues and wandering magicians; Lythande never made such a claim. "It is your story, Highness."

"A second son insures the succession and may serve as counselor to the first, but after my elder brothers were safely past childhood ailments, my royal parents knew not what to do with this inconvenient third prince. Had I been a daughter, they could have schooled me for a good marriage, but a third son? Only a possible pretender for factions or a rebel against his brethren. So they cast about to give my life some semblance of purpose, and had me instructed in music."

"There are worse fates," murmured Lythande. "In many lands a minstrel holds honor higher than a prince."

"It is not so in Tschardain," Tashgan gestured for more wine. Lythande lifted the glass and inhaled the delicate bouquet of the wine, without, however, touching or tasting it.

Tashgan went on: "It is not so in Tschardain; therefore I came to Old Gandrin where a minstrel has his own honor. For many years my life has assumed its regular character; guested in the spring on the borders of Tschardain, then northward into Old Gandrin for fair time, and northerly through the summer, to Northwander. Then at the summer's height I turn southward again, through Old Gandrin, retracing my steps, guested and welcomed as a minstrel in castle and manor and at last, for Yule-feast, to Tschardain. There I am welcomed for a hand-span of days by father and brothers. So it has been for twelve years, since I was only a little lad; it changed nothing when my father the High-lord was laid low by a stroke and my brother Rasthan assumed his powers. It seemed that it would go on for a lifetime, till I grew too old to threaten my brother's throne or the throne of his sons."

"It sounds not too ill a life," Lythande observed neutrally.

"Not so ill indeed," said Tashgan, with a lascivious roll of his eyes. "Here in Old Gandrin, a musician is highly favored, as indeed you did say, and when I am guested in castle and manor—well, I suppose ladies tire of queendom, and a musician who can give them lessons on his instrument—" another suggestive wink and roll of his eyes—"Well, master magician and minstrel, you too bear a lute, I dare say you too could tell tales, if you would, of how women give hospitality to a minstrel."

The blue star on Lythande's brow furrowed again with hidden distaste; the magician said only, "Is there, then, some reason why it cannot go on as you willed it?"

"Say rather as my father and my brother Rasthan willed it," said Tashgan. "They took no chances that I would choose to stay more than my appointed hand of days every year in Tschardain. My father's court magician made for me this lute, and set it about with enchantments, so that my wanderings with the lute would bring me never, for instance, into the country of any noble who might be plotting against Tschardain's throne, or allow me to linger long enough anywhere to make alliances. Day by day, season by season and year by year, my rounds are as duly set as the rising of sun and moon or the procession of solstice following equinox and back again to solstice; a week here, ten days there, three days in this place and a fortnight in that... I cannot tarry in any place beyond my allotted span, for the compulsion in the lute sets me to wandering again."

"And so?"

"And so for many years it was not unwelcome," said Tashgan, "among other things—well, it freed me from the fear that any of those women—" yet once more the suggestive roll of the watery eyes—"would entrap me for more than a little—dalliance. But three moons ago, a messenger from Tschardain reached me. A were-dragon came from the south, and both my brothers perished in his flame. So that I, with no training or inclination to rule, am suddenly the High-lord's only heir—and my father may die at any moment, or linger for another hand of years as a paralyzed figurehead. My father's vizier has bidden me return at once to Tschardain and claim my heritage."

Tashgan slammed his hand with rage on the table, making the lute rattle and the ribbons tremble.

"And I cannot! The enchantment of this accursed lute compels me northward, even to Northwander! If I set out southward to my kingdom, I am racked with queasiness and pain, I can stomach neither food nor wine, nor can I even look on a woman with pleasure till I have set off in the appointed direction for the time of year. I can go nowhere save upon my appointed rounds, for this damnable enchanted lute compels me!"

Lythande's tall narrow body shook with laughter, and Tashgan's ill-natured scowl fixed itself upon the Adept.

"You laugh at my curse, magician?"

"Everything under the sun has a funny side," Lythande said, and struggled to control unseemly laughter. "Bethink yourself, my prince; had this happened to another, would you not find it funny?"

Tashgan's eyes narrowed to slits, but finally he grinned weakly and said, "I fear so. But if it was your predicament, magician, would you laugh?"

Lythande laughed again. "I fear not, highness. And that says much about what folk call amusement. So now tell me; how can I serve you?"

"Is it not obvious from my tale? Take this enchantment off the lute!" Lythande was silent, and Tashgan leaned forward in his chair, demanding aggressively, "Can you take off such a binding-spell, magician?"

"Perhaps I can, if the price is right, highness," Lythande said slowly. "But why put yourself at the mercy of a stranger, a mercenary magician? Surely the court magician who obliged your father would be more than happy to ingratiate himself with his new monarch by freeing you from this singularly inconvenient spell."

"Surely," Tashgan said glumly, "but there is one great difficulty in that. The wizard whom I have to thank—" he weighted the word with another of his ill-natured scowls—"was Ellifanwy."

"Oh." Ellifanwy's messy end in the lair of a were-dragon was known from Northwander to the Southron Sea. Lythande said, "I knew Ellifanwy of old. I told Ellifanwy that she could not handle any were-dragon and proffered my services for a small fee, but she begrudged the gold. And now she lies charred in the caves of the dragonswamp."

"I am not surprised," said Tashgan, "I am sure you will agree with me that women have no business with the High Magic. Small magics, yes, like love charms—and I must say Ellifanwy's love charms were superb," he added, preening himself like a peacock. "But for dragons and such, I think, you will agree with me, seeing Ellifanwy's fate, that female wizards should mind their cauldrons and spin love charms."

Lythande did not answer, leaning forward to take up the lute. Again the lightning from the Blue Star on the magician's brow glared in the room.

"So you would have me undo Ellifanwy's spell? That should present no trouble," Lythande said, caressing the lute; slender fingers strayed for a moment over the strings. "What fee will you give?"

"Ah, there lies the problem," said Tashgan, "I have but little gold; the messenger who brought news of the deaths of my brothers expected to be richly rewarded, and I have lived mostly as guest for these many years; given all I could desire, rich food and rich clothing, wine and women, but little in the way of ready money.

But if you will unbind this spell, I shall reward you well when you come to Tschardain—"

Lythande smiled enigmatically. "I am well acquainted with the gratitude of kings, highness." Tashgan would hardly wish Lythande's presence in Tschardain, able to tell his future subjects of their new high-lord's former ridiculous plight. "Some other way must be found."

The magician's hands lingered for a moment on Tashgan's lute. "I have taken a fancy to your lute, highness, binding-spell and all. I have long desired to travel to Northwander. But I do not know the way. Do I assume correctly that this lute will keep its bearer on the direct path?"

Tashgan said sourly, "No native guide could do better. Should I ever stray from the path, as I have done once or twice after too much hospitality, the lute would bring me back within a few dozen paces. It is like being a child again, clinging to a nanny's hand!"

"If sounds intriguing," Lythande murmured. "I lost the only lute which meant anything to me in—shall we say, a magical encounter—and had little ready money with which to replace it; but the one I bear now has a fine tone. Exchange lutes with me, noble Tashgan, and I shall travel to Northwander, and deal with the unbinding-spell at my leisure."

Tashgan hesitated only a moment. "Done," he said, and picked up Lythande's plain lute, leaving the magician to put the elaborate inlaid one, with its interlaced designs of mother-of-pearl, into its leather case. "I leave for Tschardain at dawn. May I offer you another cup of wine, magician?"

Lythande politely declined, and bowed to Tashgan for leave to withdraw.

"So you will travel to Northwander on my circuit of castle and court? They will welcome you, magician. Good fortune." Tashgan chuckled, with a suggestive roll of his eyes. "There are many ladies bored with ladylike accomplishments. Give my love to Beauty."

"Beauty?"

"You will meet her—and many others—if you follow my lute very far," said Tashgan, licking his lips. "I almost envy you, Lythande; you have not had time to become wearied of their—friendly devices. But," he added, this time with a frank leer, "no doubt there are many new adventures awaiting me in my fathers courts."

"I wish you joy of them," said Lythande, bowing gravely. On the stairs, the magician resolved that when the sun rose Old Gandrin would be far behind. Tashgan might not wish anyone surviving who could tell this tale. True, he had seemed grateful; but Lythande had reason to distrust the gratitude of kings.

Northward from Old Gandrin the hills were steeper; on some of them snow was still lying. Lightly burdened only with pack and lute, Lythande traveled with a long athletic stride that ate up the miles.

Three days north of Old Gandrin, the road forked, and Lythande surveyed the paths ahead. One led down toward a city, dominated by a tall castle; the other led upward, farther into the hills. After a moment's thought, Lythande took the upward road.

For a time, nothing happened. The brilliant sunlight had given Lythande a headache; the magician's eyes narrowed against the sun. After a few more paces, the headache was joined with a roiling queasiness. Lythande scowled, wondering if the bread eaten for breakfast had become tainted. But under the hood of the mage-robe Lythande could feel the burning prickle of the Blue Star.

Magic. Strong magic....

The lute. The enchantment. Of course. Experimentally, Lythande took a few more steps up the forest road. The sickness increased, and the pressure of the Blue Star was painful.

"So," Lythande said aloud, and turned back, retracing the path; then took the road leading down to city and castle. At once the headache diminished, the queasiness subsided, even the air seemed to smell fresher. The Blue Star was again quiescent on Lythande's brow.

"So." Tashgan had not exaggerated the enchantment of the lute. Shrugging slightly, Lythande took the road down into the city, feeling an enthusiasm and haste which was quite alien to the magician's own attitude. Magic. But Lythande was no stranger to magic.

Lythande could almost feel the lute's pleasure like a gigantic cat purring. Then the spell was silent and Lythande was standing in the courtyard of the castle.

A liveried servant bowed.

"I welcome you, stranger. May I serve you?"

With a mental shrug, Lythande resolved to test Tashgan's truth. "I bear the lute of Prince Tashgan of Tschardain, who has returned to his own country. I come in the peace of a minstrel."

The servant bowed, if possible, even lower. "In the name of my lady, I welcome you. All minstrels are welcome here, and my lady is a lover of music. Come with me, minstrel, rest and refresh yourself, and I will conduct you to my lady."

So Tashgan had not exaggerated the tales of hospitality. Lythande was conducted to a guest chamber, brought elegant food and wine and offered a luxurious bath in a marble bathroom with water spouting from golden spigots in the shape of dolphins. Guest-garments of silk and velvet were readied by servants.

Alone, unspied-upon (Adepts of the Blue Star have ways of knowing whether they are being watched), Lythande ate modestly of the fine foods, and drank a little of the wine, but resumed the dark mage-robe. Waiting in the elaborate guest quarters, Lythande took the elegant lute from its ease, tuned it carefully, and awaited the summons.

It was not long in coming. A pair of deferential servants led Lythande along paneled corridors and into a great salon, where a handsome, richly dressed lady awaited the musician. She extended a slender, perfumed hand.

"Any friend and colleague of Tashgan is my friend as well, minstrel; I bid you a hundred thousand welcomes. Come here." She patted the side of her elegant seat as if—Lythande thought—she was inviting one of the little lapdogs in the salon to jump up into her lap. Lythande went closer and bowed, but an Adept of the Blue Star knelt to no mortal.

"Lady, my lute and I are here to serve you."

"I am *so* fond of music," she murmured gushingly, and patted Lythande's hand. "Play for me, my dear."

With a mental shrug, Lythande decided that rumor had not exaggerated Tashgan's accomplishments. Lythande unslung the lute and sang a number of simple ballads, judging accurately the level of the lady's taste, She listened with a faintly bored smile, tapping her fingers restlessly and not even, Lythande noticed, in time to the music. Well, it was shelter for the night.

"Tashgan, dear fellow, always gave me lessons on the lute and on the clavier," the lady murmured. "I understand that you have come to—take over his lessons? How kind of the dear man; I am so bored here, and so alone, I spend all my time with my music. But now the palace servants will be escorting us to dinner, and my husband, the Count, is so jealous. Please do play for dinner in the Great Hall? And you will stay for a few days, will you not, to give me—private lessons?"

Lythande said, of course, that such talents as the gods had given were all entirely at the lady's service.

At dinner in the great hall, the Count, a huge, bluff, and not unkindly man whom Lythande liked at once, called in all his servants, nobles, housefolk, and even allowed the waiters and cooks to come in from the kitchens that they might hear the minstrel's music. Lythande was glad to play a succession of ballads and songs, to give the news of Tashgan's succession to the High-lordship of Tschardain, and to tell whatever news had been making the rounds of the fair at Old Gandrin.

The pretty Countess listened to music and news with the same bored expression. But when the party was about to break up for the night, she murmured to Lythande, "Tomorrow the Count will hunt. Perhaps then we could meet for my—lessons?" Lythande noted that the Countess's hands were literally trembling with eagerness.

I should have known, Lythande thought. *With Tashgan's reputation as a womanizer, with all that he said about Ellifanwy's love charms. Now what am I to do?* Lythande stared morosely at the enchanted lute, cursing Tashgan and the curiosity which had impelled the exchange of instruments.

To attempt an unbinding-spell, even if it destroyed the lute? Lythande was not quite ready for that yet. It was a beautiful lute. And no matter how lascivious the Countess, however eager for illicit adventure, there would be, there always were, servants and witnesses.

Who ever thought I would think of a fat chamberlain and a couple of inept ladies-in-waiting as chaperones?

All the next morning, and all the three mornings after that, Lythande, under the eyes of the servants, deferentially placed and replaced the Countess's fingers on the strings of her lute, the keyboard of her clavier, murmuring of new songs, of chords and harmonies, of fingering and practice. By the end of the third morning the Countess was huffy and sniffing, and had ceased trying to touch Lythande's hand surreptitiously on the keyboard.

"On the morrow, Lady, I must depart," Lythande said. That morning the curious pull of the enchanted lute had begun to make itself felt, and the magician knew it would grow stronger with every hour.

"Courtesy bids us welcome the guest who comes and speed the guest who departs," said the Countess, and for a final time she sought Lythande's slender fingers.

"Perhaps next year—when we know one another better, dear boy," she murmured.

"It shall be my pleasure to know my lady better," Lythande lied, bowing. A random thought crossed the magician's mind.

"Are you—*Beauty*? If so, Tashgan bade me give you his love."

The Countess simpered. "Well, he called me his lovely spirit of music," she said coyly, "but who knows, he might have called me Beauty when he spoke of me to someone else. The dear, dear boy. Is it true he will not be coming back?"

"I fear not, madam. His duties are many in his own country now."

The Countess sighed.

"What a loss to music! I tell you, Lythande, he was a minstrel of minstrels; I shall never know his like again," she said, and posed sentimentally with her hand over her heart.

"Very likely not," said Lythande, bowing to take leave.

Lythande moved northward, drawn by curiosity and by the spell of the wandering lute. It was a new experience for the Pilgrim Adept, to travel without knowing where each day would lead, and the magician savored it with curiosity unbounded. Lythande had attempted a few simple unbinding-spells, so far without success; all the simpler spells had proved insufficient, and unlike Tashgan, Lythande did not make the mistake of underestimating Ellifanwy's spells, when the wizardess had been operating within the sphere of her own competence.

Ellifanwy might not have been able to cope with a were-dragon. But for binding-spells and enchantments, she had had no peer. Every night

Lythande attempted a new unbinding-spell, at the conclusion of which the lute remained enchanted and Lythande was racking a brain which had lived three ordinary lifetimes for yet more unbinding spells.

Summer lay on the land north of Old Gandrin, and every night Lythande was welcomed to inn or castle, manor or Great House, where news and songs were welcomed with eagerness. Now and again a wistful matron or pretty housewife, innkeeper's daughter or merchant's consort, would linger at Lythande's side, with a lovesick word or two about Tashgan; Lythande's apparent absorption in the music, the cool sexless voice and the elegantly correct manner, left them sighing, but not offended. Once, indeed, in an isolated farmstead where Lythande had sung ancient rowdy ballads, when the farmer snored the farmer's wife crept to the straw pallet and murmured, but Lythande pretended to be asleep and the farm wife crept away without a touch.

But when she had crawled back to the farmer's side, Lythande lay awake, troubled. Damn Tashgan and his womanizing. He might have spread joy among neglected wives and lonely ladies from Tschardain to Northwander, for so many years that even his successor was welcomed and cosseted and seduced; and for a time it had been amusing. But Lythande was experienced enough to know that this playing with fire could not continue.

And it was playing with fire, indeed. Lythande knew something of fire, and fire elementals—the Pilgrim Adept was familiar with fire, even the fire of were-dragons. But no were-dragon alive could rival the rage of a scorned woman, and sooner or later one of them would turn nasty. The Countess had simply believed Lythande was shy, and put her hopes in another year. (By then, Lythande thought, surely one of the spells would prove adequate to take off the enchantment.) It had been a close call with the farmer's wife; suppose she had tried fumbling about the mage-robe when Lythande slept?

That would have been disaster.

For, like all adepts of the Blue Star, Lythande cherished a secret which might never be known; and on it all the magician's power depended. And Lythande's secret was doubly dangerous; Lythande was a woman, the only woman ever to bear the Blue Star.

In disguise, she had penetrated the secret Temple and the Place Which Is Not, and not till she already bore the blue star between her brows had she been exposed and discovered.

Too late, then, for death, for she was sacrosanct to the final battle of Law and Chaos at the end of the world. Too late to be sent forth from them. But not too late for the curse.

Be then what you have chosen to seem, so had run the doom. *Until the end of the world, on that day when you are proclaimed a woman before any man but myself...* thus had spoken the ancient Master of the Star... *on that day you are stripped of power and on that day you may be slain.*

Traveling northward at the lute's call, Lythande sat on the side of a hill, the lute stripped of its wrappings and laid before her. If for a time this had been amusing, it was so no longer. Besides, if she was not free of the spell by Yule, she would be guesting in Tashgan's own castle—and that she had no wish to do.

Now it was time for strong remedies. At first it had been mildly amusing to work her way through the simpler spells, beginning with, "Be ye unbound and opened, let no magic remain save what I myself place there," which was the sort of spell a farmer's wife might speak over her churn if she fancied some neighboring herb-wife or witch had soured her milk, and working her way up through degrees of complexity to the ancient charm beginning, "Asmigo; Asmagd..." which can be spoken only in the dark of the moon in the presence of three gray mice.

None of them had worked. It was evident that, knowing of Ellifanwy's incompetence with her last were-dragon, and her success with love-charms (to Lythande, the last refuge of incompetent sorcery) Lythande had seriously underestimated Ellifanwy's spell.

And so it was time to bypass all the simpler lore of spells to bind and unbind, and proceed to the strongest unbinding-spell she knew. Unbinding-spells were not Lythande's specialty—she seldom had cause to use them. But once she had inadvertently taken upon herself a sword spell-bonded to the shrine of Larith, and had never managed to unbind it, but had been forced to make a journey of many days to return the sword whence it had come; after which, Lythande had made a special study of a few strong spells of that kind, lest her curiosity, or desire for unusual experiences, lead her again into such trouble. She had held this one in reserve; she had never known it to fail.

First she removed from her waist the twin daggers she bore. They had been spell-bonded to her in the Temple of the Blue Star, so that they might never be stolen or carelessly touched by the profane; the right-hand dagger for the dangers of a lonely road in dangerous country, whether wild beast or lawless men; the left-hand dagger for menaces less material, ghost or ghast, werewolf or ghoul. She did not wish to undo that spell by accident. She carried them out of range, or what she hoped would be out of range, set her pack with them, then returned to the lute and began the circlings and preliminary invocations of her spell. At last she reached the powerful phrases which could not be spoken save at the exact moment of high noon or midnight, ending with;

"Uthriel, Mastrakal, Ithragal, Ruvaghiel, angels and archangels of the Abyss, be what is bound together undone and freed, so may it be as it was commanded at the beginning of the world; So it was, so it is, so shall it be and no otherwise!"

Blue lightnings flamed from an empty sky; the Blue Star on Lythande's forehead crackled with icy force that was almost pain. Lythande could see the lines of light about the lute, pale against the noonday glare. One by one, the strings of the lute uncoiled from the pegs and slithered to the ground. The lace holding Lythande's tunic slowly unlaced itself, and the strip wriggled to the ground. The bootlaces, like twin serpents, crawled down the boots through the holes in reverse order, and writhed like live things to the ground. The intricate knot in her belt untied itself and the belt slithered away and fell..

Then, slowly, the threads sewing her tunic at sides and shoulders unraveled, coming free stitch by stitch, and the tunic, two pieces of cloth, fell to the ground, but the process did not stop there; the embroidered braid with which the tunic was trimmed came unsewed and uncoiled bit by bit till it was mere scraps of thread lying on the grass. The side seams unstitched themselves, a little at a time, in the breeches she wore; and finally the sewn stitches of the boots crawled down the leather so that the boots lay in pieces on the ground, while Lythande still stood on the bootsoles. Only the mage-robe, woven without seam and spelled into its final form, maintained its original shape, although the pin came undone, the metal bending itself to slip free of its clasp, and clinked on the hard stones.

Ruefully, Lythande gathered up the remains of clothing and boots. The boots could be resewn in the next town that boasted a cobbler's shop, and there were spare clothes in the pack she had fortunately thought to carry out of reach. Meanwhile it would not be the first time a Pilgrim Adept had gone barefoot, and it was worth the wreck of the clothing to be freed of the accursed, the disgusting, the fantastic enchantment laid on that lute.

It lay harmless and silent before the minstrel magician; a lute, Lythande hoped, like any other, bearing no magic but its own music. Lythande found a spare tunic and breeches in the pack, girded on the twin daggers once more (marveling at any spell that could untie the mage-knot her fingers had tied, by habit, on the belt) and sat down to re-string the lute. Then she went southward, whistling.

At first Lythande thought the fierce pain between her brows was the glare of the noonday sunlight, and readjusted the deep cowl of the mage-robe so that her brow was shadowed. Then it occurred to her that perhaps the strong magic had wearied her, so she sat on a flat rock beside the trail and ate dried fruits and journey-bread from her pack, looking about to be sure she was unobserved except by a curious bird or two.

She fed the crumbs to the birds, and re-slung her pack and the lute. Only when she had traveled half a mile or so did she realize that the sun was no longer glaring in her eyes and that she was traveling northward again.

Well, this was unfamiliar country; she might well have mistaken her way. She stopped, reversed her bearings and began to retrace her steps.

An hour later, she found herself traveling northward again, and when she tried to turn toward Old Gandrin and the southlands the racking queasiness and pain were more than she could bear.

Damn the hedge-wizard who gave me that spell! Wryly, Lythande reflected that the curse was probably redundant. Turning northward, and feeling, with relief, the slackening of the pain of the binding-spell, Lythande resigned herself. She had always wanted to see the city of Northwander: there was a college of wizards there who were said to keep records of every spell which had ever wrought its magic upon the world. Now, at least, Lythande had the best of reasons for seeking them out.

But her steps lagged resentfully on the northward road.

There was no sign of city, village or castle. In even a small village she could have her boots resewn—she must think up some good story to explain how they had come undone—and in a larger city she might find a spell-candler who might sell her an unbinding-spell.

Though, if the powerful spell she had already used did not work, she was unlikely to find a workable spell this side of Northwander and the college of wizards.

She had come down from the mountain and was traversing a woody region, damp from the spring rains, which gradually grew wetter and wetter underfoot till Lythande's second-best boots squelched and let in water at every step. At the edges of the muck-dabbed trail were soggy trees and drooping shagroots covered in hanging moss.

I cannot believe that the lute means to lead me into this dismal bog, thought Lythande, but when, experimentally, she tried to reverse direction, the queasiness and pain returned. Indeed, the lute was leading her into the bog, farther and farther until it was all but impossible to distinguish between the soggy path and the mire to either side.

Where can the accursed thing be taking me? There was no sign of human habitation anywhere, nor any dwellers but the frogs who croaked off-key in dismal minor thirds. Was she indeed to sup tonight with the frogs and crocodiles who might inhabit this dreadful place? To make matters worse, it began to drizzle—though it was already so wet underfoot that it made little difference to the supersaturated ground—and then to rain in good earnest.

The mage-robe was impervious to the damp, but Lythande's feet were soaked in the mud, her legs covered with mud and water halfway to the knees, and still the lute continued to lead her farther into the mire. It was dark now; even the mage's sharp eyes could no longer discern the path, and once she measured her length on the ground, soaking what garments remained dry under the mage-robe. She paused; intending, first to make a spell of light, and then to find some sort of shelter, even if only under a dry bush, to wait for light and sunshine and, perhaps, dry weather.

I cannot believe, she thought crossly, *that the lute has in sober truth led me into this impassable marsh! What sort of enchantment is that?*

She had come to a standstill, and was searching in her mind for the most effective light-spell, wishing that she, like Eirthe, had access to a friendly fire-elemental to supply not only light but heat, when a glimmer showed through the murky darkness, and strengthened momentarily. A hunter's campfire? The cottage of a mushroom-farmer or a seller of frogskins or some such trade which could be carried on in this infernal sloshing wilderness?

Perhaps she could beg shelter there for the night. *If this infernal lute will permit.* The thought was grim. But as she turned her steps toward the light, there was the smallest of sounds from the lute, Satisfaction? Pleasure? Was this, then, some part of Tashgan's appointed rounds? She did not admire Ellifanwy's taste, if the old sorceress had indeed set this as a part of the lute's wandering.

She plodded on through the mire at such a speed as the sucking bog underfoot would allow, and after a time came to what looked like a cottage, with light spilling through the window. Inside the firelight was almost like the light of a fire-elemental, which came near to searing Lythande's eyes; but when she covered them and looked again, the light came from a perfectly ordinary fire in an ordinary fireplace, and by its glow Lythande saw a little old lady, in a gown of bottle-green, after the fashion of a few generations ago, with a white linen mutch covering her hair, pottering about the fire.

Lythande raised her hand to knock, but the door swung slowly open, and a soft sweet voice called but, "Come in, my dear; I have been expecting you."

The star on Lythande's brow prickled blue fire. Magic, then, nearby, and the little old lady was a hearth-witch or a wise-woman, which could explain why she made her home in this howling wilderness. Many women with magical powers were neither liked nor welcomed among mankind. Lythande, in her male disguise, had not been subjected to this, but she had seen it all too often during her long life.

She stepped inside, wiping the moisture from her eyes. Where had the little old lady gone? Facing her was a tall, imposing, beautiful woman, in a gown of green brocade and satin with a jeweled circlet in the satiny dark curls. Her eyes were fixed, in dismay and disbelief, on the lute and on Lythande. Her deep voice had almost the undertone of a beast's snarl.

"Tashgan's lute! But where is Tashgan? How did you come by his instrument?"

"Lady, it is a long story," Lythande said, through the burning of the Blue

Star which told her that she was surrounded by alien magic, "and I have been wandering half the night in this accursed bog, and I am soaked to the very skin. I beg of you, allow me to warm myself at your fire, and you shall be told everything; there is time for the telling of many long tales before the final battle between Law and Chaos."

"And why should you curse my chosen home, this splendid marsh?" the lady said, with a scowl coming between her fine-arched brows, and Lythande drew a long breath.

"Only that in this—this blessed expanse of bog and marsh and frogs I have becomes drenched, muddied, and lost," she said, and the lady gestured her to the fire.

"For the sake of Tashgan's lute I make you welcome, but I warn you, if you have harmed him, slain him or taken his lute by force, stranger, this is your last hour; make, therefore, the best of it."

Lythande went to the fire, pulled off the mage-robe and disposed it on the hearth where the surface water and mud would dry; removed the sodden boots and stockings, the outer tunic and trousers, standing in a linen under-tunic and drawers to dry them in the fire-heat. She was not too sure of customs this near to Northwander, but she surmised that the man she appeared to be would not, for modesty's sake, strip to the skin before a strange woman, and that custom of modesty safeguarded her disguise.

Lythande could—briefly, when she must—cast over herself the glamour of a naked man; but she hated doing it, and the illusion was dangerous, for it could not hold long, and not at all, she suspected, in the presence of this alien magic.

The lady, meanwhile, busied herself about the fire—in a way, Lythande thought as she watched her out of the corner of her eye, better fitted to the little old lady she had first appeared to be. When Lythande's under-tunic stopped steaming, she hung the outer clothing to dry over a rack, and dipped up soup from a kettle, cut bread from a crusty loaf, and set it on a bench before the fire.

"I beg of you, share my poor supper; it is hardly worthy of a great magician, as you seem to be, but I heartily make you welcome to it."

The vows of an Adept of the Blue Star forbade Lythande to eat or drink in the sight of any man; however, women did not fall under the prohibition, and whether this was the little old hearth-witch she had first surmised, or whether the beautiful lady put on the hearth-witch disguise that she might not be easy prey for such robbers or beggarly men as might make their way into the bog, she was at least woman. So Lythande ate and drank the food, which was delicious; the bread had the very texture and scent she remembered from her half-forgotten home country.

"My compliments to your cook, lady; this soup is like to what my old nanny, in a far country, made for me when I was a child." And even as she spoke, she wondered; *is it some enchantment laid on the food?*

The lady smiled and came to sit on the bench beside Lythande. She had Tashgan's enchanted lute in her arms, and her fingers strayed over it lovingly, bringing small kindly sounds. "You see in me both cook and feaster, servant and lady; none dwells here but I. Now tell me, stranger with the Blue Star, how came you by Tashgan's lute? For if you took it from him by force, be assured I shall know; no lie can dwell in my presence."

"Tashgan made me a free gift of the lute," Lythande said, "and to my best knowledge he is well, and lord of Tschardain; his brothers perished, and he returned to his home. But first he must free himself of the enchantment of the lute, which had other ideas as to how he should spend his time. And this is the whole of the tale, lady."

The lady sniffed, a small disdainful sniff. She said, "And for that, being a little lord in a little palace, he gave up the lute? Freely, you say, and unforced? A minstrel gave up a lute enchanted to his measure? Stranger, I never thought Tashgan a fool!"

"The tale is true as I have told it," said Lythande. "Nor is the lute such a blessing as you might think, lady, for in that world out there beyond the— the blessed confines of this very marsh, minstrels are given less honor than lords or even magicians. And freedom to wander whither one wills is perhaps even more to be desired than being at the mercy of a wandering lute."

"Do you speak with bitterness, minstrel?"

"Aye," said Lythande with heartfelt truth, "I have spent but one summer wandering at the behest of this particular lute, and I would willingly render it to anyone who would take its curse! Tashgan had twelve years of that curse."

"Curse, you say?"

The lady sprang up from the bench; her eyes glared like coals of fire at Lythande, fire that curled and melted about her with sizzling heat; fire that glowed and flared and streamed upward like the wings of a fire-elemental.

"Curse, you say, when it brought Tashgan yearly to my dwelling?"

Lythande stood very still. The heat of the blue star was painful between her brows. *I do not know who this lady may be, or what,* she thought, *but she is no simple hearth-witch.*

She had laid aside her belt and twin daggers; she stood unprotected before the anger and the streaming fire, and could not reach the dagger which was effective against the creatures of enchantment. Nor, she thought, had it come yet to that.

"Madam, I speak for myself; Tashgan spoke not of curse but of enchantment. I am a Pilgrim Adept, and cannot live except when I am free to wander where I will. And when Tashgan could not linger as long beneath your gracious roof and accept your hospitality as long as his heart might desire; and I doubt not he found that a kind of curse."

Slowly the fire faded, the streamers of blue dimming out and dying, and the lady shrank to a normal size and looked at Lythande with a smile that was still arrogant but had a kind of pleased simper to it.

In the name of all the probably nonexistent Gods of Old Gandrin, what is this woman? For woman she is, and like all women vain and greedy for praise, Lythande thought with scorn.

"Be seated, stranger, and tell me your name."

"I am Lythande, a Pilgrim Adept of the Blue Star, and Tashgan gave me this lute that he might return to become Lord of Tschardain. I am not to blame for his folly, that he willingly forwent the chance of beholding again your great loveliness." And even as she spoke Lythande had misgivings, could any woman actually swallow such incredible flattery? But the woman—or was she a powerful sorceress?—was all but purring.

"Well, his loss is his own choice, and it has brought you here to me, my dear. Have you then Tashgan's skill with the lute?"

That would not take much doing, thought Lythande, but said modestly that of this, only the Lady must be the judge. "Is it your desire that I play for you, Madam?"

"Please. But shall I bring you wine? Tashgan, dear boy, loved the wine I serve."

"No, no wine," Lythande said. She wanted her wits fully about her. "I have dined so well, I would not spoil that taste in memory. Rather I would enjoy your presence with my mind undimmed by the fumes of wine," she added, and the lady beamed.

"Play, my dear."

Lythande set her fingers to the lute, and sang, a love-song from the distant hills of her homeland.

A single sweet apple clings
to the top of the branch;
The pickers did not forget
But could not reach;
Like the apple, you are not forgotten,
But only too high and far from my hands.
I long to taste that forbidden sweetness.

Lythande looked up at last at the woman by the fire. Well, she had done a foolish thing; she should have sung a comic ballad or a tale of knightly and heroic deeds. This was not the first time she had seen a woman eager for more than flirtation, thinking Lythande a handsome young man. Was that one of the qualities of the enchantment of the lute, that it inspired woman hearers with desire for the player? Judging by what had happened on this journey, she would not be at all surprised.

It grows late," said the Lady softly, "time for a night of love such as I often shared with Tashgan, dear lad." And she reached out to touch Lythande lightly on the shoulder; Lythande remembered the farmer's wife. A woman rejected could be dangerous.

Lythande mumbled "I could not presume so high; I am no Lord but a poor minstrel."

"In my domain,' said the lady, "minstrels are honored above princes or lords."

This was too ridiculous, Lythande thought. She had loved women; but if this woman had been Tashgan's mistress, she would not seek among women for a lover. Besides, Lythande was not happy with the thought of Tashgan's leavings.

The *geas* she was under was literal; she might reveal herself to no man. *I am not sure this harpy is a woman,* Lythande thought, *but I am certain she is no man.*

"Do you mock at me, minstrel?" the woman demanded. "Do you think yourself too good for my favors?" Once again it seemed that fire streamed from her hair, from the spread wings of her sleeves. And at that moment Lythande knew what she saw.

"Alnath," she whispered, and held out her hand. Yet this was nothing so simple as a fire-elemental; this was a were-dragon in full strength, and she remembered the fate of Ellifanwy.

"Lady," she said, "you do me too much honor, for I am not Tashgan, nor even a man. I am but a humble minstrel woman."

She bowed her head before the flames suddenly surrounding her. Were-dragons were always of uncertain temper; but this one chose to be amused; flames licked around Lythande with the gusting laughter, but Lythande knew that if she showed the slightest fear, she was doomed.

Calling up the memory of the fire-elemental, Lythande made a clear picture in her mind of Alnath perched on her wrist, flames sweeping gracefully upward. She felt again the sense of kinship she had experienced with the little fire-elemental, and it enabled her to look up and smile at the were-dragon confronting her.

The gusts of laughter subsided to a chuckle, and once again it was woman not dragon confronting Lythande: the little hearth-witch. "And did Tashgan know your sex—or did he expect you to take over his round in all things?"

Lythande said ruefully "The latter, judging by the instructions he gave me," and the lady was laughing again.

"You must have had a most *interesting* journey here, my dear!"

Lythande's mind suddenly started working furiously, recalling quite clearly the instructions Tashgan had given her. He had definitely been amused about something: yet Lythande was sure he had not known her secret. No, what amused him had been... "Beauty!" The lady was regarding her attentively. "By any chance, Lady, was he given to calling you—Beauty?"

"The dear boy! He remembered!" The lady was positively simpering.

He certainly did, Lythande thought grimly. *And boyish is a mild description of his sense of humor! Perhaps he thought me as vulnerable to playing with fire as Ellifanwy?* It would have amused Tashgan to send her to share Ellifanwy's fate. Aloud she said, "He asked me to give you his love." Her hostess looked pleased, but Lythande decided that a bit more flattery would probably help. "Of all the sacrifices he made for his throne, you were the one he regretted most. His duty called him to Tschardain." She hesitated slightly, remembering the look in the dragon-woman's eyes at the sight of the lute. "If you would not object, I think this affair would make a splendid romantic ballad." By now the were-dragon was virtually purring.

"Nothing would delight me more, my dear, than to serve as inspiration to art."

"And," Lythande continued, "I would be honored—and I know it would give Tashgan the greatest pleasure—if you would accept this lute as a small token of the devotion we feel toward you."

Flame flared almost to the ceiling; but the were-dragon's face was wreathed in joyous smiles as she gently took up the lute and caressed the strings.

Early the next morning, Lythande took cordial leave of her hostess. As she picked a careful way through the bog she could hear the strumming of the lute behind her. The were-dragon had more musical ability than Prince Tashgan, that was certain, but the ballad that formed in Lythande's mind was not of love bravely sacrificed to duty, but of a wandering were-dragon minstrel and an unexpected guest at the Yule-feast in Tschardain. Making a mental note to spend Yule in Northwander—if not even farther north—Lythande left the bog behind her and went laughing up the northward road.

BITCH
Marion Zimmer Bradley

Darkness was falling in Old Gandrin, in an unfamiliar quarter of the city. Lythande, the Pilgrim Adept of the Blue Star, was alone, isolated and abandoned, far from her usual haunts—insofar as she had usual haunts, or could count on anything to recur and be ordinary in her far from ordinary life. To add to the general dismalness of the night, a light rain was falling, not heavily but with drizzling persistence, not enough to soak anything, but enough to banish dryness, warmth or comfort and imbue everything with a miserable and pervasive dampness throughout.

Although the streets of Old Gandrin were perhaps safer for an Adept of the Blue Star than for an average citizen, they could hardly be said to be altogether safe for anyone after dark, and Lythande had no desire to be attacked or robbed in the deserted fields of the graveyard district. She had come there considerably earlier in the day, in search of certain herbs and ingredients for the making of spells; it was said to add to the efficacy of such ingredients that they grew or had been gathered in the shadow of the gallows.

Lythande was not altogether certain that she believed this, but if her clients believed it, she could hardly afford the luxury of flouting this belief; after all, belief was a major ingredient which must be liberally stirred into every spell before it could work at all.

Around her stretched a series of barren open fields which had perhaps been last cultivated before the city walls were built; here and there she could see the dim lights of occasional scattered dwellings. Even if the night had been clear there would have been little moon; it was her business to know such things. The aforesaid gallows cast a long and wavering shadow almost to Lythande's very feet, but there was no sign anywhere of light such as might have marked out an inn or any such place where one might find lodging. Beyond the gallows a broken field stretched, lumpy and barren with the uneven shapes of old and fallen gravestones. A deserted place, good perhaps for ghosts but less salubrious for mortals; and Lythande, in spite of a life prolonged by magic to the span of three ordinary lifetimes, still counted herself among the living and mortal.

At this moment a shadow crossed her path and a not unfamiliar voice spoke. "Who goes there? Speak!"

"I am a minstrel and magician by the name of Lythande," she said, and in answer came the most unexpected of words.

"Greetings, fellow Pilgrim; what do you on this lonely road at this god-forgotten hour?"

"If indeed there are gods, a question about which I entertain certain doubts," Lythande observed calmly, "I would think it unlucky to call any place god-forgotten in the fear that they might in fact forget it."

"Even if there be no gods," replied the newcomer, a dark shadow on the path, "I should consider it unlucky to say so, for fear that if they do in fact exist and I show bad manners by refusing to believe in them, they might retaliate by refusing to believe in me."

Lythande found the sound of that paradox sufficiently familiar to say "Do I speak then to a fellow Pilgrim?"

"You do," replied the voice, "I am your fellow minstrel Rajene; we have debated these questions before this time in the courts of the Blue Star to the sound of the lute. Do I guess rightly that we should together seek shelter, if only against damp and ghosts, for the exchange of songs?"

"I am unfamiliar with these quarters," Lythande said. "And while I have not yet encountered a ghost here or elsewhere, I observe somewhat similar precautions about ghosts as you against gods touching their existence or nonexistence, in case I should have good reason for abandoning my disbelief."

Now in the darkness Lythande could make out the lines of a voluminous mage-robe cut like her own, deeply hooded; and in the folds of the mage-robe's hood, the pale blue burning outline of a star like the one that glowed between her own brows. She said, "If you know of any shelter against this possibly god-infested and ghost-harboring quarter, I will follow you to it."

Rajene's voice was a strong and resonant baritone; far deeper than the mellow and sexless contralto of Lythande's own, though perhaps equally musical. Across the back where Lythande's lute was strung, Lythande could make out the outline of a chitarrone, an archaic but tuneful instrument almost as tall as the man who bore it. In fact, of all her fellow Adepts of the Blue Star, there were few Lythande would have rather met on a dark night; for as far as she knew, she had no quarrel with Rajene, and when they were fellow apprentices in the Temple of the Star, they had been friends—or as near to friends as any magician could come to friendship. Which is to say that at the least they were not enemies.

Lythande had had no true friends there; had dared have none; for alone among all the Pilgrim Adepts from one end of Time to the other, Lythande was a woman; alone and in disguise she had penetrated the secrets of the temple, and only after she bore the Blue Star between her brows had her disguise been exposed. She had paid the highest price ever for the power of a Pilgrim Adept; for when the truth was known, the Master of the Star had laid a doom upon her, thus: "Be then, forever, what you have chosen to be," he said. "For on that day when your true sex shall be proclaimed aloud by any man save myself, on that day is your power at an end, and your immunity from your fellows."

So it had been since that day: a life of perpetual concealment, without relief; an eternal solitude, with none but brief and superficial companionship, such as she might now find for a time with Rajene.

And now, as if to add to the general bleakness of the deserted and ghost-haunted quarter, the faint mizzling rain began to come down harder into the darkness, blotting out even the semblance of any ordinary night.

Lythande was not altogether sorry; the drizzle of the past hours would create discomfort, but added nothing to the safety of the darkness; this sudden downpour would send any enterprising footpad or cutpurse back to shelter, or if a thief or assassin were desperate, would make it less likely that an assailant would identify the victim as a Pilgrim Adept. No sane thief would attempt to rob a magician of that stature; but in this darkness and rain they might make the mistake of trying it.

Rajene tugged the hood of his mage-robe tighter over his head, trying to rearrange the folds to protect the musical instrument.

"Let us seek shelter," he said urgently. "I have not visited these parts for many years—I forget quite how many, but if my memory still serves me at all, there was once an old dame who kept a kind of ale-house, and when her public room was not too full, she would allow me to sleep on her floor by the fire. It was not the best shelter, but it was an inestimable improvement over the rain, and this is not such a night as I would willingly sleep under the stars—even if there were any stars to sleep under, which there are not."

"Lead on," Lythande said briefly, "I follow."

This was better than she had hoped. She had little fear of women, and she had dwelt among the Adepts of the Blue Star for seven years of her apprenticeship without her true sex being even once suspected or exposed. A large public inn filled with men would have meant a night of endless vigilance; in the company of one fellow Pilgrim Adept and an old woman— and if Rajene's old acquaintance had been elderly in Rajene's early days as a magician, she must be truly venerable now—she would have little to fear.

She followed Rajene's shadowy form before her, with little light except the pallid glimmer of the Blue Star which shone faintly between her brows, and a similar gleam escaping from beneath Rajene's concealing hood.

She tried to protect her lute from the worst of the rain; not easy to do because the spell which kept it dry was a taxing one, and when she concentrated on keeping up with Rajene in the darkness, she tended to lose sight of the spell. At worst it was more important that the lute be kept dry than that her own feet and body be sheltered from rain; they would dry without harm, and the lute would not.

After what seemed a long time of darkness and rain, stumbling on uneven ground broken with what might have been old sunken gravestones, Lythande made out the dim lights of a cottage; an old and tumbledown building with sagging stone walls and a door of planks so old, split and broken that the firelight streamed out between them. Sheltering out of the wind (which came around the corner of the building with howling violence) Lythande hugged her mage-robe close to her shoulders and thought that even if this place was deserted and the haunt of ghosts or even ghouls, she would have shelter this night from the rain.

From inside came the sound of a cracked and quavering voice; then the door was pulled open from inside and a stooped old woman stood in the firelight. She was dressed in faded rags and tatters, a much-patched shawl over her bent shoulders being almost more patch than shawl, her face so wrinkled and drawn that Lythande, who was herself immensely old, could not even begin to guess her age.

"Dame Lura," cried Rajene, "I am rejoiced to see that you still dwell in this world! I have brought a friend to beg shelter at your fire this night. Had you no longer dwelled here, I was prepared to spend this wild night begging shelter of some poor ghost in his tomb!"

Dame Lura chuckled, a sound which seemed to Lythande so wild and humorless that it was hardly human.

"Ah, Rajene, my friend, there is better shelter than that for you here; even if this were no better than a tomb, I would deny shelter neither to the living nor the dead on such a night as this. Come inside, dry yourselves by the fire there." She gestured them to the hearth where a large rug covered the cold stone, and stretched out on the stone lay two large dogs; hairy and shaggy, sound asleep with their noses to the fire.

Rajene shoved the nearer dog, black and shaggy, with his foot, and the animal made a sleepy grumbling sound without waking, and scooted a little to one side to make room for Rajene to shed the mage-robe and hang it over a rickety stool which stood at the edge of the hearth-rug. After a moment Lythande did the same, boosting another stool to the fireside and hauling off her own drenched robe. Rajene sat between the dogs, stretching his stockinged feet to the fire and drew the chitarrone to himself, tuning the instrument to make certain it had taken no harm. Lythande pulled off her boots, stretching her narrow feet to the fire. The smaller of the two dogs, a tan and shaggy long-haired bitch, crowded against her, but the animal was warm and friendly and after all it had a better right to the fire than she did.

Dame Lura pulled a huge cauldron from its crane over the fire and asked, "May I offer ye some supper? And will ye play me a tune on yer lutes?"

"My pleasure," muttered Rajene, and began to play an old ballad of the countryside. Lythande discovered that the strings of her lute were soaked with the rain; but she had spare lengths of gut stowed in the many pockets of the mage-robe; she fumbled in them and set about mending and replacing the strings.

The old woman scooped a ladleful of stew into each of a couple of coarsely carved wood bowls and held one bowl out to Lythande. It smelled delicious, and Lythande, seeing that Rajene was looking into the fire and not at her, ventured a couple of bites. One of the many vows fencing the power of a Pilgrim Adept was that she might neither be seen to eat nor drink in the sight of any man; but the vows did not apply to women and Rajene was not looking at her. She chose to apply the prohibition quite literally, and hastily. While Rajene was bent over his lute and tuning it, she managed to get down a good part of the stew; though when he raised his eyes and asked her to play she at once left off eating.

"No, you play; I am not familiar with the sound of the chitarrone," she asked. He seemed gratified by the request, and again bent his face over the lute so that Lythande managed to finish the stew. After that Lythande played and sang but soon began to feel sleepy close to the fire; she covered herself with the mage-robe—which also covered the dogs—and tumbled quickly into sleep. Her last awareness was of the strong smell of wet dog-hair and of Rajene snoring on the rug beside her.

When she woke she was aware of firelight and silence; she looked up and saw no sign of Rajene, but only of the large dog stretched out on the hearth. Then, about to stretch out, she looked at her hand and her hand was not there; only a hairy tan paw extended toward the fire. Something was wrong with her perspective; she seemed closer to the fire than before. She sprang up, trying to cry out, and heard only a long lugubrious howl. At the sound the other dog sprang up, barking wildly; and above the dog's low hairy forehead she saw a pale gleam of blue in the shape of a star. She *recognized* the other dog; it was Rajene, and she herself had somehow been transformed into the bitch lying beside her on the rug.

Dame Lura still crouched over her cauldron muttering in some unknown language—or was it only that Lythande could no longer understand human speech? Lythande rushed for the door, on all fours, followed by the other dog who was Rajene.

Outside it had stopped raining; and by a curious distorted moonlight she raced through the deserted lands, stumbling over gravestones, Rajene racing after her.

Transformed by sorcery; and since I have become a bitch, Rajene will know I am a woman, she thought, and wondered why she was thinking about that; trapped in animal form she could not even speak a spell to break the enchantment. Or was this the kind of spell which lasted only until sunrise or moonset? But why had nothing warned her of magic in action? The blue star should have warned her of the presence of sorcery. Yet in all justice she realized that the unaccustomed warmth after a cold soaking, the hot food, and her attempt to eat unobserved, had taken her mind from any thought of hostile magic.

She wondered for a moment if Rajene had betrayed her. No, he himself was victim of the same magic; they had blundered together into the spell.

Rajene was still racing away in panic; Lythande tried to call out to him but heard only a curious whining growl and desisted almost at once.

Can this be only a dream? Can it be that I am still lying before the fire in the witch's cottage, dreaming this? she wondered; but the chill of the graveyard was penetrating the pads on her paws, and there was no change in the dream-surroundings; so this was no dream, but some vicious sorcerous reality, and she—and Rajene—were trapped inside it.

Rajene—or rather the dog in whose consciousness Rajene now dwelt—stopped his headlong rush, and turned back toward her, whining pitifully and circling around, barking softly. Then he stopped and whimpered, stretching himself out as if he were trying to crawl into the very ground.

Lythande's thoughts were now wholly concerned with the spell into which she had blundered and how she could get out of it. There were magical herbs which grew in the shadow of the gallows; perhaps she could find one which would break the spell. The problem was that she had no particular belief in the efficacy of that kind of spell. Nevertheless under these circumstances she found her disbelief eroding away; it evidently made a difference which side of the spell you were on.

She looked round, trying to orient herself from the peculiar perspective of a dog's vision; her eyesight was excellent but everything seemed very high up and she was afraid of stumbling over the fallen gravestones. The long shadow of the gallows still dominated the wasteland, and she went closer; she smelled the faint bitterness and found the herb for which she was looking, the threefold shiny leaf and pale berry, colorless by moonlight—although by normal day and in normal sight it might have been pale green. She bent to nibble the herb; she knew from experience that it was faintly bitter, like most herbs; but when her sharp dog's teeth bruised the leaf, it was intense, nauseating, releasing a harsh violent oil which flooded her with such sickness that she reflexively spat it out.

So much for that. Dogs didn't eat herbs—she should have remembered that. They sometimes ate grass when they were sick, but evidently sorcery did not qualify as an illness.

She tried to bite at the ordinary grass to take the taste of the herb out of her mouth; the grass tasted bland and coarse, like tasteless lettuce. What next? She recalled an ancient superstition; if she circled seven times clockwise round the gallows... or was it counterclockwise? Well, she would try it seven times clockwise, and if that had no effect she would try it seven times counter-clockwise; and if *that* had no effect—well, she would have to think of something else.

But Rajene—to her amazement she saw that the larger dog was bounding around the gallows and actually frisking his tail—he had already thought of that. She followed, but nothing happened; as she began her eighth circumambulation of the gallows, she stopped and reversed the direction.

But nothing happened. *We could keep this up all night; dogs probably would.* She scowled—it distorted her vision oddly because her hairy forehead was at such an odd angle to her eyes—and flung herself down on the grass to think of any other possibility.

There must be something else that they could try. She turned about to look for Dame Lura's cottage. If she went back and confronted the hag, threatened to tear out her throat, the damnable hag would probably consent to take off her spell.

But she could see not the smallest glimmer of light from the witch's fire; she thought (but was not sure) that she could see the outline of the cottage, but it was entirely dark; the hag must have doused her fires and gone to bed, as if the enchanting of two wizards were just part of a good night's work. In a rage, Lythande thought, *Let me get my hands—my paws—on her and if I don't make it the worst night's work she ever did, my name is not Lythande.*

Reversing her direction she went bounding over uneven grass and gravestones toward the faraway dark outline of the cottage. Then she stopped; her acutely keen hearing in dog form sensed a movement on the grass not too far away; she stopped to allow Rajene to come up with her; she could hear him panting with his tongue hanging out.

The movement advanced and a shadow loomed over her, a robed figure: a wizard? No, some kind of priest. His sacred staff was extended; Rajene jumped up and gripped the staff between his teeth; the priest cried out in surprise as it clattered to the gravestones. As Lythande touched it she felt a shudder run through her limbs and stretching, rose easily to her feet. The priest was gaping, reaching for his staff.

"A thousand pardons," Rajene said easily. "And as many thanks, for you have released us from an evil enchantment."

The priest gathered up his staff, with an exclamation of astonishment. Rajene was wearing a loose whitish pajama-like garment; Lythande was dressed in leather tunic and breeches, and her feet were bare and cut on the loose stones and gravestones. Limping, she bowed to the priest, saying gravely, "Lythande thanks you, priest."

"Er—my pleasure to be of service," said the priest uneasily. "But tell me, how and when did all this happen? I did not know that this deserted quarter was subject to enchantments."

"Obviously we did not either," said Lythande.

Rajene added "I thought I was visiting an old friend; I think now it must have been a ghost or evil fiend in her shape."

"An old friend living hereabouts?" asked the priest. "But my good man, no one dwells in this quarter."

"Dame Lura's cottage," Rajene said, "And I must return there—"

"But, my good fellow," the priest began to argue, then, at Rajene's grim stare, subsided and followed him as he set out toward the outline of the cottage. "It is fortunate I came along; I was going out to greet the sun from that hill yonder. I visit this necropolis only once in a year, on the anniversary of the death of my old great-aunt; I come to say a prayer for her, for she was good to me in her own way, though I fear she was a wicked woman. This was that self-same Dame Lura your companion claims to have seen—"

"*Claims* be damned," said Lythande, "Dame Lura sheltered us by her fire last night, and fed us with a stew which led to this enchantment."

"But my good man, that is simply impossible," said the priest, and followed them as they approached the dark line of the cottage. It was beginning to get light now, and she could clearly make out the familiar line of the odd peaked roof, though no light showed through the dilapidated planks of the door.

Rajene banged on the door, then shouted; silence. Then he shoved the door open.

Inside by the growing light they could clearly see; the cabin was empty. No fire, no dogs, no rug where the dogs had lain; only bare stone flooring, and lying on the floor, two mage-robes, Lythande's lute and the broken-stringed chitarrone.

"I suppose we should be glad for this," said Lythande, picking up the lute; she shrugged the mage-robe around her shoulders and felt less vulnerable, though the priest no more than any other man could have identified her lean, breastless figure as that of a woman. The spare strings of the lute were untouched in her pocket, the packet still sealed, yet she remembered mending and re-stringing the lute while she sat between the dogs on the hearth-rug.

Rajene, dressing slowly in his own mage-robe, looked angry, the blue star gleaming between his scowling brows. He went to the hearth where the great cauldron still hung on its crane; inside the cauldron was cold and empty; yet Lythande could still in memory taste the stew she had eaten.

"I told you so," said the priest with a smug injured air. "Dame Lura died on yonder gallows fifty years ago this night."

Lythande turned her back on the empty cottage and began to walk swiftly away; she could clearly see now in the frost the footprints of two dogs, running this way, then abruptly her own human footprints and

Rajene's coming to the cottage. After a moment Rajene caught up with her.

"I gave the priest two silver pieces," he said, "Even though he disenchanted us by accident, I am grateful."

Lythande fumbled in her pockets and handed him a silver coin. "I will share the fee," she said.

"Even so, we were lucky," Rajene said. "We encountered no bitches. I have no sons, and if I did they might well be sons-of-bitches; but I would prefer that they be so metaphorically rather than literally, if you take my meaning."

So he had not even noticed—or if he did, had thought Lythande assumed the other dog's shape out of default.

"If I had had a son," Lythande said, trying to make her voice casual, "I would prefer that he be not a cur. Nevertheless, Rajene, I knew when we dwelt in the Temple of the Blue Star that you were a real son-of-a-bitch. And now I can prove it."

The sun was coming up; Rajene looked at her and laughed. He said "Let's find a tavern—and a pot of ale. I wish I knew what was in that stew."

Lythande said, "I'm sure we're better off not knowing."

"Let's go," said Rajene. "Last one to the city gates is a dirty dog."

"Right," said Lythande, thinking, *That's one expression I'll never use again.*

THE WALKER BEHIND
Marion Zimmer Bradley

As one who on a lonesome road
Doth walk in fear and dread
And turns but once to look around
And turns no more his head
Because he knows a frightful fiend
Doth close behind him tread....

Lythande heard the following footsteps that night on the road: a little pause so that if she chose she could have believed it merely the echo of her own light footfall, step-pause-step, and then after a little hesitation, step-pause-step, step-pause-step.

And at first she did think it an echo, but when she stopped for a moment to assess the quality of the echo, it went on for at least three steps into the silence.

Step-pause-step-pause-step.

Not an echo then; but someone, or some *thing*, following her. In the world of the Twin Suns, where encountering magic was rather more likely than not, magic was more often than not of the evil kind. In a lifetime spanning at least three ordinary lifetimes, Lythande had encountered a great deal of magic; she was by necessity a mercenary-magician, and Adept of the Blue Star, and by choice a minstrel; and she had discovered early in her extended life that good magic was the rarest of all encounters and seldom came her way. She had lived this long by developing good instincts; and her best instincts told her that this footfall following her was not benevolent.

She had no notion of what it might be. The simplest solution was that someone in the last town she had passed through had developed a purely material grudge against her and was following her on mischief bent, for some reason or no reason at all; perhaps a mere moral distrust of magicians, or of magic (a condition not at all rare in Old Gandrin), and had chosen to take the law into his or her own hands and dispose of the unwelcome procurer of said magic. This was not at all rare, and Lythande had dealt with plenty of would-be assassins who wished to stop magic by putting and effective stop to the magician; however powerful and Adept's magic, it could seldom survive and knife in the back. On the other hand, that could be handled with equal simplicity; after three ordinary lifetimes, Lythande's back had not yet become a sheath for knives.

So Lythande stepped off the road, loosening the first of her two knives in its scabbard; the simple white-handled knife, who purposed was to handle purely material dangers of the road: footpads, assassins, thieves. She enveloped herself in the grey cloudy folds of the hooded mage-robe, which made her look like a piece of the night itself, or a shadow, and stood waiting for the owner of the footsteps to come up with her.

But it was not that simple. Step-pause-step, and the footfalls died; the mysterious follower was pacing her and it was not that simple. Lythande had hardly thought it would be so simple. She sheathed the white-handled knife again, and stood motionless, reaching out with all her specially trained senses to focus on the follower.

What she felt first was a faint electric tingle in the blue star which was between her brows and a small, not quite painful crackle in her head. *The smell of magic*, she translated to herself; whatever was following her, it was neither as simple, nor as easily disposed of, as an assassin with a knife.

She loosened the black-handled knife in the left-hand scabbard, and, stepping herself like a ghost or a shadow, retraced her steps at the side of the road. This knife was especially fashioned for supernatural menaces, to kill ghosts and anything else from spectres to werewolves; no knife but this one could have taken her own life had she wearied of it.

A shadow with an irregular step glided toward her, and Lythande raised the black-handled knife. It came plunging down, and the glimmer of the enchanted blade was lost in the shadow. There was a far-off, eerie cry which seemed to come, not from the shadow facing her on the dark road, but from some incredibly distant ghostly realm, to curdle the very blood in her veins, to wrench pain and lightnings from the Blue Star between her brows. Then, as that cry trembled into silence, Lythande felt the black handle of the knife come back into her hand, but a faint glimmer of moonlight showed her the handle alone; the blade had vanished, except for some stray drops of molten metal which fell slowly to the earth and vanished.

So the blade was gone; the black-handled knife which had slain unnumbered ghosts and other supernatural beings. Judging by the terrifying cry, Lythande had wounded her follower; but had she killed the thing which had eaten her magical blade? Anything that powerful would certainly be tenacious of life.

And if her black-handled knife would not kill it, it was unlikely it could be killed by any spell, protection or magic she could command at the moment. It had been driven away, perhaps, but she could not be certain she had freed herself from it. No doubt, if she went on, it would continue to follow her, and one day it would catch up with her on some other lonesome road.

But for the moment she had exhausted her protection. And... Lythande glowered angrily at the black knife-handle and the ruined blade... she had deprived herself needlessly of a protection which had never failed her before. Somehow she must manage to replace her enchanted knife before she again dared the roads of Old Gandrin by night.

For the moment—although she had traveled too far and for too long to fear anything she was *likely* to encounter on any ordinary night—she would be wiser to remove herself from the road. Such encounters as a mercenary-magician, particularly one such as Lythande, could expect, were seldom of the likely kind.

So she went on in the darkness, listening for the hesitating step of the follower behind. There was only the vaguest and most distant of sounds; that blow, and that screech, indicated that while she had probably not destroyed her follower, she had driven it at least for a while into some other place. Whether it was dead, or had chosen to go and follow someone safer, for the moment Lythande neither knew or cared.

The important thing at the moment was shelter. Lythande had been travelling these roads for many years, and remembered that many years ago there had been an inn somewhere hereabout. She had never chosen, before this, to shelter there—unpleasant rumors circulated about travelers who spent a night at that inn and were never seen again, or seen in dreadfully altered form. Lythande had chosen to stay away; the rumors were none of her business, and Lythande had not survived this long in Old Gandrin without knowing the first rule of survival, which was to ignore everything but your *own* survival. On the rare occasions when curiosity or compassion had prompted her to involve herself in anyone else's fate, she had had all kinds of reason to regret it.

Perhaps her obscure destiny had guided her on this occasion to investigate these rumors. She looked down the black expanse of the road—without even moonlight—and saw a distant glimmer of light. Whether it was the inn of uncanny rumor, or whether it was the light of a hunter's campfire, or the lair of a were-dragon, there, Lythande resolved, she would seek shelter for the night. The last client to avail himself of her services as a mercenary magician—a man who had paid her well to dehaunt his ancestral mansion—had left her with more than enough coin for a night at even the most luxurious inns; and if she could not pick up a commission to offset the cost of a night's shelter, she was no worse off. Besides, with the lute at her back, she could usually earn a supper and a bed as a minstrel; they were not common in these parts.

A few minutes of brisk walking strengthened the vague light into a brilliantly shining lantern hung over a painted sign which portrayed the figure of an old woman driving a pig; the inn sign read the Hag and Swine.

Lythande chuckled under her breath... the sign was comical enough, but it startled her that for such a cheerful sign there was no sound of music or jollity from inside; all was quiet as the very demon-haunted road itself. It made her remember again the very unsavory rumors about this very inn.

There was a very old story about a hag who had indeed attempted to transform random travelers into swine, and other forms, but Lythande could not remember where she had heard that story. Well, if she, an Adept of the Blue Star, was no match for any roadside hag, whatever her propensity for increasing her herd of swine—or perhaps furnishing her table with pork—at the expense of travelers, she deserved whatever happened to her. Shouldering her lute and concealing the handle of the ruined knife in one of the copious pockets of the mage-robe, Lythande strode through the half-open door.

Inside it was light, but only by contrast with the moonless darkness of the outdoors. The only light was firelight, from a hearth where a pale fire flickered with a dim and unpleasant flame. Gathered around the hearth were a collection of people, mere shapes in the dim room; but as Lythande's eyes adapted to the darkness, she began to make out forms, perhaps half a dozen men and women and a couple of shabby children; all had pinched faces, pushed-in noses which were somehow porcine. From the dimness arose the tall, heavy form of a woman, clad in shapeless garments which seemed to hang on her anyhow, much patched and botched.

Ah, thought Lythande, *This innkeeper must be the Hag. And those wretched children might very well be the swine.* Even secretly the jest pleased her.

In an unpleasant snuffling voice the tall hag demanded, "Who are you, sir, going about on the road where there be nowt but hants an' ghosts at this season?"

Lythande's first impulse was to gasp out, "I was *driven* here by evil magic; there is a monstrous Thing out there, prowling about this place!" But she managed to say instead, peacefully, "Neither hant nor ghost, but a wandering minstrel frightened like yourselves by the dangers of the road, and in need of supper and a night's lodging."

"At once, sir," said the hag, suddenly turning deferential. "Come to the fire and warm thyself."

Lythande came through the jostling crowd of small figures—yes, they were children, and at close range even more unpleasantly pig-like; their sounds and snuffles made them even more animal. She felt a distinct revulsion for having them crowding against her. She was resigned to the "sir" with which the hag-innkeeper had greeted her; Lythande was the only woman ever to penetrate the mysteries of the Order of the Blue Star, and when (already sworn as an Adept, the Blue Star already blazing between her brows) she had been exposed as a woman, she was already protected against the worst they could have done. And so her punishment had been only this:

Be forever, then, had decreed the Master of the Star, *what you have chosen to seem; for on that day when any man save myself proclaims you a woman, then shall your magic be void and you may be slain and die.*

So for more than three ordinary lifetimes had Lythande wandered the roads as a mercenary magician, doomed to eternal solitude; for she might reveal her true sex to no man, and while she might have a woman confidante if she could find one she could trust with her life, this exposed her chosen confidante to pressure from the many enemies of an Adept of the Blue Star; her a first such confidante had been captured and tortured, and although she had died without revealing Lythande's secret, Lythande had been reluctant ever to expose another to that danger.

What had begun as a conscious masquerade was now her life; not a single gesture or motion revealed her as anything but the man she seemed—a tall clean-shaven man with luxuriant fair hair, the blazing blue star between the high-arched shaven eyebrows, clad beneath the mage-robe in thigh-high boots, breeches and a leather jerkin laced to reveal a figure muscular and broad-shouldered as an athlete, and apparently altogether masculine.

The innkeeper-hag brought a pot of ale and set it down before Lythande. It smelled savory and steamed hot; evidently a mulled wine with spices, a specialty of the house. Lythande lifted it to her lips, only pretending to sip; one of the many vows fencing about the powers of an Adept of the Blue Star was that they might never be seen to eat or drink in the presence of any man. The drink smelled good—as did the food she could smell cooking somewhere—and Lythande resented, not for the first time, the law which had often condemned her to long periods of thirst and hunger; but she was long accustomed to it, and recalling the singular name and reputation of this establishment, and the old story about the hag and swine, perhaps it was just as well to shun such food or drink as might be found in this place; it was by their greed, if she remembered the tale rightly, that the travelers had found themselves transformed into pigs.

The greedy snuffling of the hog-like children, if that was what they were, served as a reminder, and listening to it, she felt neither thirsty nor hungry. It was her custom at such inns to order a meal served in the privacy of her chamber, but she decided that in this place she would not indulge it; in the pockets of her mage-robe she kept a small store of dried fruit and bread, and long habit had accustomed her to snatching a hurried bite whenever she could do so unobserved.

She took a seat at one of the rough tables near the fireplace, the pot of ale before her, and, now and again pretending to take a sip from it, asked, "What news, friends?"

Her encounter fresh in her mind, she half expected to be told of some monster haunting the roadway. But nothing was volunteered. Instead, a rough-looking man seated on the opposite bench from hers, on the other side of the fireplace, raised his pot of ale and said, "Your health, sir; it's a bad night to be out. Storm coming on, unless I'm mistaken. And I've been travelling these roads man and boy for forty years."

"Oh?" inquired Lythande courteously, "I am new to these parts. Are the roads generally safe?"

"Safe enough," he grunted, "unless the folks get the idea you're a jewel carrier or some such." He needed to add no more; there were always thieves who might take the notion that some person was not so poor as he sought to appear (so as to seem to have nothing worth stealing) and cut him open looking for his jewels.

"And you?"

"I travel the roads as my old father did; I am a dog-barber." He spoke the words truculently, "Anyone who has a dog to show or to sell knows I can make the beast look to its best advantage." Someone behind his back snickered, and he drew himself up to his full height and proclaimed, "It's a respectable profession."

"One of your kind," said a man before the fire, "sold my old father an old dog with rickets and the mange, for a healthy watchdog; the old critter hardly had the strength to bark."

"I don't sell dogs," said the man haughtily, "I only prepare them for show—"

"And o'course you'd never stoop to faking a mongrel up to look like a purebred, or fixing up an old dog with the mange to look like a young one with glossy topknots and long hair," said the heckler ironically. "Everybody in this county knows that when you have some bad old stock to get rid of, stolen horses to paint with false marks, there's old Gimlet the dog-faker, worse than any gypsy for tricks—"

"Hey, there, don't go insulting honest gypsies with your comparisons," said a dark man seated on a box on the floor by the fire and industriously eating stew from a wooden bowl; he had a gold earring in his ear like one of that maligned race. "We trade horses all up and down this country from here to Northwander, and I defy any man to say he ever got a bad horse from any of our tribe."

"Gimlet the dog-barber, are ye?" asked another of the locals, a shabby squint-eyed man, "I been looking for you; don't you remember me?"

The dog-barber put on a defiant face. "Afraid not, friend."

"I had a bitch last year had thirteen pups," said the newcomer, scowling, "Good bitch, been the pride and joy in my family since she was a pup. You said you'd fix her up a brew so she'd get her milk in and be able to feed them all—"

"Every dog-handler learns something of the veterinary art," said Gimlet, "I can bring in a cow's milk too, and—"

"Oh, I make no doubt you can shoe a goose, too, to hear you tell it," the man said.

"What's your complaint, friend? Wasn't she able to feed her litter?"

"Oh, aye, she was," said the complainer, "And for a couple of days it felt good watching every little pup sucking away at her tits; then it occurred to me to count 'em, and there were no more than eight pups."

Lythande restrained a smile.

"I said only that I would arrange matters so the bitch could feed all her brood; if I disposed of the runts who would have been unprofitable, without you having to harrow yourself by drowning them—" Gimlet began.

"Don't you go weaseling out of it," the man said, clenching his fists, "any way you slice it, you owe me for at least five good pups."

Gimlet looked round. "Well, that's as may be," he said. "Maybe tomorrow we can arrange something. It never occurred to me you'd get chesty about the runts in the litter, more than any bitch could raise. Not unless you've a childless wife or a young daughter who wants to cosset something and hankers to feed 'em with an eyedropper and dress 'em in doll's clothes; more trouble than it's worth, most folk say. But hunt me up tomorrow before I leave and we'll fix something. And here's my hand on it." He stuck out his hand with such a friendly open smile of good faith that Lythande was enormously entertained; between the rogue and the yokel, Lythande, after years spent travelling the roads, was invariably on the side of the rogue. The disgruntled dog-owner hesitated a moment but finally shook his hand and called for another pot of beer for all the company.

Meanwhile the hag-innkeeper, hovering to see if it would come to some kind of fight, and looking just a little disappointed that it had not, stopped at Lythande's side.

"You, sir, will you be wanting a room for the night?"

Lythande considered. She did not particularly like the look of the place, and if she spent the night, resolved she would not feel safe in closing her eyes. On the other hand, the dark road outside was less attractive than ever, now that she had tasted the warmth of the fireside. Furthermore, she had lost her magical knife, and would be unprotected on the dark road with something following.

"Yes," she said, "I will have a room for the night."

The price was arranged—neither cheap nor outrageous—and the innkeeper asked, "Can I find you a woman for the night?"

This was always the troublesome part of travelling in male disguise. Lythande, whatever her romantic desires, had no wish for the kind of women kept in country inns for travelling customers, without choice; they were usually sold into this business as soon as their breasts grew, if not before. Yet it was a singularity to refuse this kind of accommodation, and one which could endanger the long masquerade on which her power depended.

Tonight she did not feel like elaborate excuses.

"No, thank you; I am weary from the road and will sleep." She dug in her robe for a couple of spare coins. "Give the girl this for her trouble."

The hag bowed. "As you will, sir. Frennet! Show the gentleman to the South room."

A handsome girl, tall and straight and slender, with silky hair looped up into elaborate curls, rose from the fireside and gestured with a shapely arm half concealed by silken draperies. "This way, if ye please," she said, and Lythande rose, edging between Gimlet and the dog-owner. In a pleasant mellow voice she wished the company good night.

The stairs were old and rickety stretching up several flights, but had once been stately—about four owners ago, Lythande calculated. Now they were hung with cobwebs and the higher flights looked as if they might be the haunt of bats, too. From one of the posts at a corner landing, a dark form ascended, flapping its wings, and cried out in a hoarse croaking sound, "Good evening, ladies! Good evening, ladies!"

The girl Frennet raised an arm to warn off the bird.

"That accursed jackdaw! Madame's pet, sir; pay no attention," she said good-naturedly, and Lythande was glad of the darkness. It was beneath the dignity of an Adept of the Blue Star to take notice of a trained bird, however articulate.

"Is that all it says?"

"Oh, no, sir; quite a vocabulary the creature has, but then, you see, you never know what it's going to say, and sometimes it can rarely startle you if you ain't expecting it," said Frennet, opening the door to a large dark chamber. She went inside and lighted a candelabrum standing by the huge draped four-poster. The jackdaw flapped in the doorway and croaked hoarsely, "Don't go in there, Madame! Don't go in there, Madame!"

"Just let me get rid of her for you, sir," said Frennet, took up a broom and made several passes with it, attempting to drive the jackdaw back down the staircase. Then she noticed that Lythande was still standing in the doorway of the room.

"It's all right, sir, you can go right in; you don't want to let her scare you. She's just a stupid bird."

Lythande had stopped cold, however, not so much because of the bird as because of the sharp pricking of the Blue Star between her brows. *The smell of magic*, she thought, wishing she were a hundred leagues from the Hag and Swine; without her magical knife she was unwilling to spend a minute, let alone a night, in a room which smelled evilly of magic as that one did.

She said pleasantly, "I am averse to the omens, child. Could you perhaps show me to another chamber where I might sleep? After all, the inn is far from full, so find me another room, there's a good girl?"

"Well, I dunno what the Mistress would say," began Frennet dubiously, while the bird shrieked, "There's a good girl! There's a clever girl!" Then she smiled and said "but what she dunna know won't hurt her, I reckon. This way."

Up another flight of stairs, and Lythande felt the numbing prickling of the Blue Star, *the smell of magic*, recede and drop away. The rooms on this floor were lighted and smaller, and Frennet turned into one of them.

"Me own room, sir; yer welcome to the half of my bed if ye wish it, an' no obligation. I mean—I heard ye say ye didn't want a woman, but you sent a tip for me, and—" she stopped, swallowed and said determinedly, her face flushing, "I dunno why yer travelling like a man, ma'am. But I reckon ye have yer reasons an' they's none of me business. But ye came here in good faith for a night's lodgin' and I think ye've a right to that and nothin' else." The girl's face was red and embarrassed. "I swore no oath to keep my mouth shut about what's goin' on here, and I don't want yer death on my hands, so there."

"My death?" Lythande said, "What do you mean, child?"

"Well, I'm in for it now," Frennet said, "but ye've a right to know, ma'am— sir— noble stranger. Folk who sleep here don't come back no more human; did ye see those little children down yonder? They're only half-way changed; the potions don't work all that well on children. I saw you didn't drink yer wine; so when they came to drive you out to the sty, you'd still be human and they'd kill you—or drive you out in the dark where the Walker Behind can have ye."

Shivering, Lythande recalled the entity which had destroyed her magical knife. That, then, had been the Walker Behind?

"What is this—this Walker Behind?" she asked.

"I dunno, ma'am. Only it *follows*, and draws folk into the other world; thass all I know. And nobody ever came back to tell what it is. Only I heard 'em scream when it starts followin' them."

Lythande stared about the small mean chamber. Then she asked, "How did you know that I was a woman?"

"I dunno, ma'am. I always knows, that's all. I always knows, no matter what. I won't tell the Missus, I promise."

Lythande sighed. Perhaps the girl was somewhat psychic; she had accepted a long time ago that while her disguise was usually opaque to men, there would always be a few women who for one reason or another would see through it. Well, there was nothing to be done about it, unless she was willing to murder the girl, which she was not.

"See that you do not; my life depends on it," she said. "But perhaps you need not give up your bed to me either; can you guide me unseen out of this place?"

"That I can, ma'am, but it's a wretched night to be out, and the Walker Behind in the dark out there. I'd hate to hear you screamin' when it comes to take you away."

Lythande chuckled, but mirthlessly. "Perhaps instead you would hear *it* screaming when I came to take *it*," she said. "I think that is what I encountered before I came here."

"Yes'm. It drives folk in here because it wants 'em, and then it takes their souls. I mean when they's turned into pigs, I guess they don't need their souls no more, see? And the Walker Behind takes them."

"Well, it will not take me," Lythande said briefly, "nor you, if I can manage it. I encountered this thing before I came here; it took my knife, so I must somehow get another."

"They's plenty of knives in the kitchen, ma'am," Frennet said. "I can take ye out through there."

Together they stole down the stairs, Lythande moving like a ghost in that silence which had caused many people to swear that they had seen Lythande appear or disappear into thin air. In the parlor, most of the guests had gone to rest; she heard a strange grunting sound. Upstairs there were curious grunting noises; on the morrow, Lythande supposed, they would be driven out to the sty, their souls left for the Walker Behind and their bodies to reappear as sausages or roast pork. In the kitchen, as they passed, Lythande saw the innkeeper—the hag. She was chopping herbs; the pungent scent made Lythande think of the drink she had fortunately not tasted.

So why had this evil come to infest this country? Her extended magical senses could now hear the step in the dark, prowling outside: the Walker Behind. She could sense and feel its evil circling in the dark, awaiting its monstrous feast of souls. But how—and why?—had anything human, even that hag, come to join hands with such a ghastly thing of damnation?

There had been a saying in the Temple of the Star; that there was no fathoming the depths either of Law or of Chaos. And surely the Walker Behind was a thing from the very depths of Chaos; and Lythande, as a Pilgrim Adept, was solemnly sworn to uphold forever and defend Law against Chaos even at the final battle at the end of the world.

"There are some things," she observed to the girl Frennet, "which I would prefer not to encounter until the final battle where Law will defeat Chaos at world's end. And of those things the Walker Behind is first among them; but the ways of Chaos do not await my convenience; and if I encounter it now, and not at the end of the world, I have no choice." She stepped quietly into the kitchen, and the hag jerked up her head.

"You? I thought you was sleeping by now, magician. I even sent you the girl—"

"Don't blame the girl, she did as you bade her," Lythande said, "I came hither to the Hag and the Hog, though I knew it not, to rid the world of a pigsty of Chaos. Now you shall feed your own evil servant."

She gestured, muttering the words of a spell; the hag flopped forward on all fours, grunting and snuffling. Outside in the dark she sensed the approach of the great evil Thing, and motioned to Frennet.

"Open the door, child."

Frennet flung the door open; Lythande shoved the grunting thing outside over the threshold. There was a despairing scream, half animal, but dreadfully half human, from somewhere; then only the body of a pig remained grunting in the foggy darkness of the innyard. From the shadowy Walker outside there was a satisfied croon which made Lythande shudder. Well, so much for the Hag and Swine; she had deserved it.

"There's nothing left of her, ma'am."

"She deserves to be served up as sausages for breakfast, dressed with her own herbs," Lythande remarked, looking at what was left, and Frennet shook her head.

"I'd have no stomach for her meself, ma'am."

The jackdaw flapped out into the kitchen crying "Clever girl! Clever girl! There's a good girl!"

Lythande said, "I think if I had my way I'd wring that bird's neck. There's still the Walker to deal with; she was surely not enough to satisfy the appetite of—that thing."

"Maybe not, ma'am," Frennet said, "but you could deal with her; can you deal with it? It'll want your soul more than hers, mighty magician as you must be."

Lythande felt serious qualms; the innkeeper hag, after all, had been but a small evil, but in her day, Lythande had dealt with a few large evils, though seldom any as great and terrifying as the Walker. And this one had already taken her magical knife. Had the spells weakened it any?

A long row of knives was hanging on the wall; Frennet took down the longest and most formidable, proffering it to her, but Lythande shook her head, passing her hand carefully along the row of knives. Some knives were forged for material dangers alone and she did not think any of them would be much use against this great magic out of Chaos.

The Blue Star between her brows tingled and she stopped, trying to identify the source of the magical warning. Was it only that she could hear, out in the darkness of the innyard, the characteristic step of the Walker Behind?

Step-pause-step.

Step-pause-step.

No, the source was closer than that. It lay—moving her head cautiously, Lythande identified the source—the cutting board which lay on the table;

the hag had been cutting her magical herbs, the ones to transform the unwary into swine. Slowly, Lythande took up the knife; a common kitchen one with a long sharp blade. All along the blade was the greenish mark of the juices. From the pocket of her mage-robe Lythande took the ruined handle—the elaborately carved hilt with magical runes—of her ruined knife, looked at it with a sigh—she had always been proud of the elegance of her magical equipment, and this was hearthwitch or kitchen magic at best—but it would have to do. She returned the remains of her magical knife to her pocket, gripped the hag's knife firmly, and headed towards the door.

Frennet clutched at her. "Oh, don't go out there, ma'am! It's still out there a'waiting for you."

And the jackdaw, fluttering near the hearth, shrieked; "Don't go out there! Oh, don't go out there!"

Gently, Lythande disengaged the girl's arms. "You stay here," she said. "You have no magical protection, and I can give you none." She drew the mage-robe's hood closely about her head, and stepped into the foggy inn-yard.

It was there; she could feel it waiting, circling, prowling, its hunger a vast evil maw to be filled. She knew it hungered for her, to take in her body, her soul, her magic. If she spoke, she might find herself in its power. The knife firmly gripped in her hand, she traced out a pattern of circling steps, sunwise in spite of the darkness. If she could hold the thing of darkness in combat till sunrise, the very light might destroy it; but it could be not be much after midnight. She had no wish to hold this dreadful Thing at bay till sunrise, even if her powers should prove equal to it.

So it must be dispatched at once... and hopefully, since she had lost her own magical knife, with the knife she had taken from the monstrous thing's own accomplice. Alone in the fog, despite the bulky warmth of the mage-robe, Lythande felt her body dripping with ice—or was it only terror? Her knees wobbled, and the icy drips seemed to course down between her shoulders, which spasmed as if expecting a knife driven between them. Frennet, shivering in the light of the doorway, was watching her with a smile, as if she had not the slightest doubt.

Is this what men feel when their women are watching them?

Certainly, if she should call the thing to her and fail to destroy it, it would turn next on the girl, and for all she knew, on the jackdaw, too; and neither of them deserved death, far less soul-destruction. The girl was innocent, and the jackdaw only a dumb creature... well, a harmless creature; dumb it wasn't; it was still crying out gibberish.

"Oh, my soul, it's coming! It's coming! Don't go out there!"

It was coming; the blue star between her brow was pricking like live coals, the blue light burning through her brain from the inside out. Why, in the name of all the Gods there ever were or weren't, had she ever thought she wanted to be a magician? She clenched her hand on the rough wooden handle of the kitchen knife of the kitchen hag, and thrust up roughly into the greater darkness that was the Walker, looming over her and shadowing the whole of the innyard.

She was not sure whether the great scream that enveloped the world was her own scream of terror, or whether it came from the vast dark vortex which whirled around the Walker; she was enveloped in a monstrous whirlwind which swept her off her feet and into dark fog and dampness. She had time for a ghostly moment of dread—suppose the herbs on the blade should transform the Walker into a great Hog of Chaos? And how could she meet it if it did? But this was the blade of the Walker's own accomplice in his own magic of Chaos; she thrust into the thing's heart and, buffeted and battered by the whirlwinds of Chaos, grimly hung on.

Then there was a sighing sound and something unreeled and was gone. She was standing in the innyard, and Frennet's arms were hugging her hard.

The jackdaw shrieked, "It's gone! It's gone! Oh, good girl, good girl!"

It was gone. The innyard was empty of magic, only fog on the moldering stones. There was a shadow in the kitchen behind Frennet; Lythande went inside and saw, wrapped in his cloak and ready to depart, the pudgy face and form of Gimlet, the dog-faker.

"I was looking for the inn-keeper," he said truculently, "This place is too noisy for me; too much going on in the halls; and there's the girl. You," he said crossly to Frennet, "Where's your mistress? And I thought you were to join me."

Frennet said sturdily, "I'm me own mistress now, sir. And I ain't for sale. As for the Mistress, I dunno where she is; you can go an' ask for her at the gates of Heaven, an' if you don't find her there—well, you know where you can go."

It took a minute for that to penetrate his dull understanding; but when it did he advanced on her with a clenched fist.

"Then I been robbed of your price!"

Lythande reached into the pockets of the mage-robe. She handed him a coin.

"Here; you've made a profit on the deal, no doubt—as you always do. Frennet is coming with me."

Gimlet stared and finally pocketed the coin, which—Lythande could tell from his astonished eyes—was the biggest he had ever seen.

"Well, good sir, if you say so. I got to be off about my dogs. I wonder if I could get some breakfast first."

Lythande gestured to the joints of meat hanging along the wall of the kitchen. "There's plenty of ham, at least."

He looked up, gulped, and shuddered. "No, thanks." He slouched out into the darkness, and Lythande gestured to the girl.

"Let's be on our way."

"Can I really come with you?"

"For a while at least," Lythande said. The girl deserved that. "Go quickly, and fetch anything you want to take."

"Nothing from here," she said, "But the other customers—"

"They'll turn human again now the hag's dead, such of 'em as havn't been served up for roast pork," Lythande said. "Look there." And indeed the joints of ham hanging along the wall had taken on a horrible and familiar look, not porcine at all. "Let's get out of here."

They strode down the road toward the rising sun, side by side, the jackdaw fluttering after, crying out "Good morning, ladies! Good morning, ladies."

"Before the sun rises," Lythande said, "I shall wring that bird's neck."

"Oh, aye," Frennet said, "Or dumb it wi' your magic. May I ask why you travel in men's clothes, Lady?"

Lythande smiled and shrugged.

"Wouldn't you?"

THE MALICE OF THE DEMON
Marion Zimmer Bradley

The life of a mercenary magician is fraught with adventure... always remembering that, in the old definition, adventure is what happens when things go wrong, especially in the field of magic.

This adventure befell, then, early in Lythande's career—time is irrelevant in the career of a magician (for Lythande has lived at least three ordinary lifetimes)—but let us say it took place in her first lifetime, soon after the Blue Star had appeared between her brows.

Lythande, at the time of this adventure, was in the city of Old Gandrin, and to her lodging, by night, there came, then, a lady, wrapped in a dark cloak, who looked upon the magician and said, with an air of hostility which Lythande did not understand, "Are you the great magician Lythande?"

"I am Lythande," said the magician.

This befell soon after Lythande had assumed her male disguise, and she was still lacking in some of its refinements, so the woman's look of scorn worked on her sorely when she said, "I came here without my bodyguards."

"You have no need to fear me, Lady," Lythande said.

"I wish this visit to remain forever secret," she said.

"It will not be told by me, Lady," Lythande said.

"Still," said the lady, "you will swear an oath never to reveal this visit; you will swear an oath to be silent even though I myself should implore you to speak."

"If you wish, I will swear," said Lythande. "Yet your majesty should consider well; for even I have wished that time should run backward and my words be unspoken."

"Be silent," commanded the Queen, for it was she. "Do you dare to compare your resolve with my own? I have thought long and carefully before seeking you out. I need your services because, though much magic is known to me, I have not the art of summoning demons. But first you shall swear."

"I will swear it if you wish," Lythande repeated. "But, as I said, there are many evil chances in the world, and it may well be that your majesty has not reckoned upon the malice of the demon kind, for they will use your own words to destroy you."

"Be silent," repeated the Queen, an aging woman with the remains of really remarkable beauty. "I know of you, Lythande; you too have secrets which you do not wish spoken aloud; for instance...."

"If you wish, I will swear," said Lythande; and then and there she bound herself with a great oath that while time ran and the twin suns stood in the heavens, she would not speak, no matter who, even the Queen herself, should bid her to do so. Nor would she reveal, by glance or by hint or by any other means whatever, that she had so much as looked upon the Queen's face. "So be it; it is done," said Lythande. "But I implore your majesty—for there are many evil chances in the world, and it may come that you should wish that time should run backward and your request be unspoken—not to ask this. I cannot make time to run backward, or your majesty—"

"You quibble with me, Lythande, and that I will not have; summon now the demon, for I would that time should indeed run backward and restore to me that beauty I have lost, for I would once again have all men at my feet."

"I feared that," Lythande said, "and I implore your majesty not to ask this; for your majesty has not reckoned with the malice of the demon kind indeed; they will twist your words, and use your own request to destroy you.

"Do you think you know more of magic than I?" the Queen asked haughtily. "Or can you restore to me my lost beauty?"

"Lady, I cannot; the gods themselves have seen fit to deprive you of youth and of that beauty which comes from youth alone. Yet, there is a beauty which comes of age and wisdom, and to that end I may serve you." She was still too unpracticed in the ways of a courtier to say that time had in no way affected the lady's beauty, and the Queen scowled. Lythande found it politic to say, "You are beautiful indeed, my lady. Yet, if you will be guided by me, that beauty alone which comes of age and wisdom is fit for a woman to desire..."

"Be silent," repeated the Queen, "lest I lose patience and when I am done, bid the demon to rid me of you. For I do indeed desire my lost youth and beauty."

"Be it so," said Lythande. "Never name that well from which you will not drink. And now..."

Lythande thereupon lighted a certain incense, inscribed a magical circle and desired the Queen to disrobe and take her place within it. Then she performed the required chants and circumambulations, the air in the room first clouded, then swirled and grew opaque, and within the circle there materialized a singularly ugly demon.

It is done," said Lythande. "The demon is here to serve you. Yet I implore your majesty to beware of what words you use to ask your boon."

"Not a word," commanded the Queen, making a certain gesture; at which the demon said, wincing, "I am here to serve you."

"I have pondered this long and well," said the Queen. "Bid time to return; make me as beautiful as I ever was, place me at the moment of my greatest beauty, with all of my life before me."

"So be it," said the demon and gestured, and the elderly frame of the Queen began to waver a little; then there was a great blaze of light, and where the body of the old woman had been a beautiful girl baby lay unswaddled upon the hearth.

Lythande said, "That is not what she asked."

"How can you say so?" growled the demon. "The moment of her greatest beauty is, after all, a matter of opinion, and she cannot say she has not all her life before her."

"True," said Lythande.

"Dismiss me," said the demon. Lythande gestured; the demon vanished in a blaze of light.

The Queen was venting her rage and frustration in screams, but as she had not yet learned to talk; she could only cry, as babies do. Lythande, in whose life there was no room for an infant, swathed her in a cloak, and carried her to one of the pious sisterhoods whose business it was to care for the unwanted babes of the city.

Gandrin was all agog with the disappearance of the Queen, but when they inquired of Lythande whether she knew anything of it, Lythande was of course forced by the oath she had sworn to say nothing. Yet she found it politic to leave Old Gandrin and did not return there for many years.

As for the Queen, she had not forgotten her powers and as soon as she learned to talk, she tried to claim them; but it is well known that babes sometimes say such things and that unregarded orphans claim to be queens; so no one paid any attention to her.

And in time she forgot all about it, as children do.

THE FOOTSTEPS OF RETRIBUTION
Marion Zimmer Bradley

Although, among the vows of an Adept of the Blue Star, is that he or she may never be seen to eat or drink by living men, no such vow prevents sleeping in their presence.

The inn at the edge of the Great Moor was lonely and quiet, and yet, for its location, crowded; when Lythande sought shelter from a sudden downpour, it was all too evident that many a traveler had done the same. The best that the innkeeper could do was to offer Lythande the half of a bed in a chamber already occupied.

I have no gold," Lythande remarked, but I will sing to your company, in return for even a dry corner, if it must be so."

"Now the heavens forbid any beneath my roof should sleep so," said the innkeeper. "I am well acquainted with magicians; if you will show my guests some of your magic, I will throw in a hearty meal."

"Be it so," said Lythande, although the meal would do her no good in the inn's crowded state. "Yet I call to your attention that I have no gold, but only this small copper coin."

"So be it," said the innkeeper. "At least all men know that Lythande the magician will not stoop to setting a spell by which copper may appear to be gold."

"No," said Lythande, regretting her integrity—for at an inn such as this a gold piece would command not a corner by the fire, but the best room in the house, but as she had spoken, so she must do.

So it was that upon the evening, the guests at an otherwise unremarkable inn sat before the fire and heard a tall magician, who looked like any other tall and fair haired man save for the mage-robe and the Blue Star upon her brow—for her vows commanded Lythande to travel forever in the guise of a man, concealing the woman within—with a lute on her shoulder, singing of fields of roses blossoming in the sun, of garlands and crowns of honor to be won by the brave in contests of valor or strength, songs of milking the cattle, of wandering on the moors, and the sorrow of the sea.

And when Lythande had sung all the songs she knew, a fair young girl said to her, "Surely your songs would steal one's soul."

"Alas, no," said Lythande, remembering when another fair young girl, in another life, had said to her much the same, "I am no stealer of souls."

"No, forsooth," said a dark man wrapped in a dark traveling mantle, seated near the fire, "Yonder magician is no soul-stealer, that is plain to see."

"I am not," Lythande said, "nor, if that art were known to me, would I so defile a lute."

"Nor is that art known to any man beneath the Twin Suns," said the man.

But Lythande sensed by that prickling of the blue star between her brows that some magic other than her own was nearby. She said, gazing at the dark man with all the power of which she was capable, "Tell me, are you yourself a soul-stealer?"

"If I were," said the man, "should I be likely to proclaim it here, in your presence, magician?"

"Most likely not," said Lythande. *But I notice you did not deny it either*, she added to herself, resolving that she would not sleep that night; if there were any soul-stealer about, whether this man were he or a perfectly innocent bystander, he would have no chance in Lythande's presence.

"Tell me," said the pretty girl, "Such things may have happened—I have heard my grand-dame speak of them. Although they do not befall now, do they? For it would be sad indeed if anyone must go all her days in fear of evil magic."

"Indeed they do not," said Lythande, "nor is magic evil, as you shall see."

"A careless boast," said the dark traveler. "Who are you, Lythande, that you seek to appear before us as a great magician and lead my Mary to be speaking of soul-stealing and the like?"

"Are you, sir, a magician?"

"I make no claims," said the man. "And you?"

"Judge for yourself," said Lythande, for the last thing she wanted was a display of her powers in this company where she felt alien magic was to be found. "Call me but a poor minstrel and juggler. Would it please you, Mary, to see such powers as I have?"

"Indeed it would please me," said Mary, her blue eyes shining. "Though the thought of magic frightens me."

"What you shall see is but juggling and trickery," Lythande reassured her. And then she called the witchfire, showing flames that roared to the roof and became dragons which sang in the voice of a tenor; then she called up a fishbowl of golden fish, who prophesied in the voices of children, and finally flew away like birds; and finally called forth a head, robed and crowned, who told every guest what he wanted most to know, if it was pleasant, and finally forecast the weather; rain for many days to come. The guests begged like children to see more marvels, but Lythande knew the secret of pleasing audiences was to leave them hungry for more, never satiated; so she pleaded weariness, and watched the company go to their beds. She would willingly have slept before the fire—she had slept in many worse places—but the innkeeper would not have it.

"If there were a chamber free you should have my best," said he, "but as it is—you shall share with only two late comers," and he conducted Lythande into a room with only the dark traveler and his pretty traveling companion.

And at last—since the only alternative was to stalk haughtily into the rain—which now was falling more heavily than ever, Lythande let herself be persuaded to spread out her cloak in their room, although nothing would persuade her to take a share of either bed.

"No," she said, "Truly, the fire will do as well—"

"What, lord magician! Surely you do not believe that I—or my companion here—will steal your soul! I have the greatest respect for Adepts of the Blue Star, and not for worlds would I engage in sorcery in their presence." And all the time the pricking of the Star between her brows told her of the action of strange magic.

So she might have turned to young Mary—it would not be the first time one had seemed innocent and been magical—but Mary whispered to her, "Remain, I beg you; in your presence, at least, he cannot force himself upon me."

"I though him your father, my dear; how come you, then, to be traveling in his company?"

"Father I have none for many years; I dwell with my grand-dame upon the moor—and would I were back there—and when he passed by—I know not how—he said 'come', and I could not help but come, leaving behind my grand-dame and all that I love."

"I shall remain," said Lythande, grateful at least that this girl was not one to whom Lythande's disguise was transparent, but who had appealed to her gallantry.

So, thought Lythande, *the girl is spelled; and I thought rightly that this is a great sorcerer.* Aloud she asked, "Has he offered you any insult?"

"No, lord magician; I have not seen so much as his fingertip beyond that great dark mantle he wears," said Mary.

Lythande was almost sorry; for if he had done so, her vows, which bade her always fight law against chaos, would force a confrontation; but the girl had made no complaint and she could not interfere—nor from the experience of several lifetimes, would she have done so. She was not the first girl, and Lythande did not suppose she would be the last, despite a pretty face and innocence, to be lured away.

And so at last—telling herself that in her presence at least, the girl would suffer no insult from her companion—Lythande stretched out on the floor between the beds, refusing an offered share of the dark man's bed. She removed no garment but her boots; nor did the dark man, still wrapped in his enormous cloak. And so she composed herself for sleep.

But she did not sleep. All the night, conscious of the prickling of the star, and of unknown magic as stealthy as the mice in the walls, she did not sleep, but lay wakeful, conscious of the turning earth and of the snores of at least one of her companions, the soft breaths of the other. At last, toward dawn when pale light began to steal into the room, all fell silent, and Lythande fell into a fitful doze; and though her distrust of her companions was at highest pitch, she did sleep a little.

And from this sleep she was wakened by an almighty clamor, on the steps of the inn. A peasant woman, rough-handed, all soaked with the rain, her hair dripping wetly round her shoulders, was pounding at the door.

"Open! Open!" she cried, "wretch, monster, what have you done with my grand-daughter!"

So saying, she rushed past the protesting inn-keeper, who with sleepy astonishment made not much move to prevent her, and to the bed-chambers on the second floor. One by one she examined the sleepers, passing over Lythande and coming to the dark traveler; where she cried, "So! Rascal, devil—this is the man who lured away the child by magic—"

"I? My good woman, your grand-daughter, if such she be, followed me of her own free will," said the man. "Has she said otherwise?"

"No; but she shall make complaint when she is free—for Mary is a good girl—"

"So says every grandmother, and rightly so," said the dark man. "Ask of her, or of this stranger, if I have stirred this night from my bed; nor would I be capable of harming her."

Thus appealed to, Lythande agreed that he had never stirred from his bed, but toward morning, owing to a disturbed night, Lythande's sleep might have been too heavy to hear what took place. Then the grandmother, rushing to Mary's side, drew back the covers, demanding of her unstirring form that she answer, but Mary lay still, unmoving, and at last the grandmother howled that she was dead. And so indeed, she proved to be, without a mark upon her, nor any apparent cause of death.

"It was you nevertheless who slew her with your magic," insisted the grandmother. "Or how did she meet her death?"

"My dear lady, am I to blame if the girl was taken by a vampire, or a restless spirit?" he demanded. "I did not go near her—"

"I slept; I cannot attest to that," said Lythande.

"No; but these can," said the man, dragging off the traveling cloak and betraying two legs withered and like pipe stems, "For many years my legs have not borne me a single step without two walking sticks; and even I could not rise and cross the room upon them without awakening the magician here—not unless I were more nimble than any acrobat. How am I capable of doing harm to living man or beast? And you cannot prove I slew her by magic—no more than you could make that claim of the magician himself."

And Lythande realized she had been very neatly mouse-trapped; all the guests of the inn had seen Lythande do magic, and if inquiry were made about murder by magic, inquiry might as well turn to Lythande herself, and her identity would soon be exposed. Yet the prickling of her star told her very clearly that some form of magic was in use; he must have slain the girl by the same magic by which he had lured her from her home.

But in that case would he have made jokes about soul-stealers?

Yes; such was his arrogance; he had not said, either, that he had not killed the girl, but only that he was not capable of motion.

So be it; then Lythande would devote herself to proving that he could not, in her very presence, commit a magical murder with impunity.

While the bereaved grandmother—having thoroughly disrupted the entire inn—was being consoled and offered wine in the main room, Lythande stopped the man, who was readying himself for departure, and made a dreadful wry face at the old woman's lamentations, echoing through the breakfasting room, "What, no breakfast then? Or has the death spoilt your appetite?"

"I have fed well," said the man. "What a cacophony! As a musician, you will join me in regretting it."

"What I regret," said Lythande fiercely—was the soul-stealer actually boasting of his deed?—"is only the pure soul who has gone."

"Is it so?" asked the man lightly. "By now, I dare say, she regrets only her purity."

Lythande made an involuntary grimace, and the man, as if aware he had angered the magician, laughed a little. "You are shocked? But of course her death had nothing to do with me."

"Nor with me," said Lythande. "But I would see justice done."

"Why should I care for justice if it comes to that?"

"It is the obligation of every civilized being—" said Lythande, fastening her mage-robe about her throat.

"But I care not a fig for justice, as you call it," said the cripple, taking up his great traveling-cloak and preparing to leave the room.

"Then, since you have no interest in the girl, for life or death," said Lythande, "you will, of course, have no objection to calling down divine retribution on her killer?"

"Oh, no, no," he said, and as he prepared to leave the room, discovered that Lythande was standing directly in his way so he could not pass.

"As will I," said Lythande, "since I have no other way to prove I did not slay her by my magic. So I swear willingly; may the footsteps of divine retribution follow me forever, waking and sleeping, if I had art, part or knowledge of the death of this innocent soul. Now swear you the same." She made a mystical gesture, and the crippled man flinched.

"How know you her soul was innocent?"

"That has nothing to do with her death," said Lythande. "That is between her and whatever God may make it his business. Do you then refuse—before these witnesses—to swear to innocence of her death?" She gestured at the other guests at the inn, who began to look very ugly indeed.

"I fear no soul, innocent or otherwise," said the man. But I would have no chance against such footsteps, being a cripple."

"Then you refuse?"

"I so swear," he muttered.

"That the footsteps of divine retribution may follow you forever till her death is avenged?"

White as death itself he nodded. "I so swear," he growled at last. And Lythande stepped away and permitted him to leave the room.

Yet Lythande believed he would somehow manage to repudiate his oath; she beheld him preparing to depart.

"You go?"

"I go. Or are you preparing to follow me like the footsteps of—what was it—retribution?"

"Do you then fear those Footsteps? I would, if I were you."

"I fear no footsteps, divine or human. And by the same token, you may follow me to the end of the world, if you have nothing better to do, and much good may it do you."

"I will take my chances on that," commented Lythande, resolving at that moment that she would see the footsteps.

All that day the rain continued to fall, and when the night came, the dark man sought shelter, with Lythande at his very side, so that they were shown into the same chamber, for it was the only one vacant. Lythande, who had slept little the previous night, slept well, until she was wakened. It was full daylight, and her companion had cried out with alarm; for round and round the bed, in a ceaseless crossing and re-crossing of steps, were footprints upon footprints.

"That poor girl," said Lythande. "Do you suppose they have buried her in the rain?"

"How the devil should I know—or care?" snarled the man; but Lythande noticed that as he took his walking sticks and dragged himself from the room, he turned aside to avoid treading on the prints.

Still the rain continued to fall, and as they traveled through it, Lythande noticed that the other kept turning his head to the rear, as if against some sound. He asked at last, "What is that sound?"

"What sound? I heard nothing," said Lythande truthfully. "What sort of sound is it? Footsteps, perhaps?"

"How should I know?" snarled the man with a curse, but Lythande noticed that he still kept turning his head to the rear, as if to listen.

That night, when Lythande and her involuntary companion were shown to their room, Lythande woke again to find the room all but filled; her companion stared at the muddy marks on the rug, murmuring in horror, "Footsteps...."

"...of retribution," said Lythande curiously, but the man replied only with another curse.

"Mud," she said, "They must have buried her in the rain after all." He made no answer, but then she was not expecting any answer.

Magician," he said, "Can you rid me of a haunting?"

"I can."

"Name your fee, and do so."

"I can," said Lythande. "What sort of haunting?"

The man gestured at the muddy footsteps and hung his head. "You know," he said.

"Swear, then, your innocence in the matter, and I will do so at once," she said; "I take no commission from a man under a curse. But if you can swear there is nothing upon your conscience; then—"

There was no answer; the man left the room, turning again aside so that his foot would not cross the now-caked mud. His face was drawn with horror. When Lythande came up with him in the courtyard, he said truculently, "I forbid you to follow me further, Lythande."

"How do you propose to prevent me? I have not heard yet that you own all the roads hereabout," she said. "I go where I will, and if I choose to travel in the same direction as you—"

"Follow me then, since I cannot prevent you," he snarled, and went on his way. Lythande, traveling almost out of his sight, at the far range of his vision, saw that now and again he would turn and look backward; she did not think he was looking for her.

All the same she made certain to arrive at the inn with him at the end of the day, when the host led them to the top of the building, up flight after flight of stairs, again to the same chamber, one with a two beds, one of which was against a window, looking out on a stone flagged court below. On this bed the other traveler, without so much as a gesture at asking Lythande which she preferred, flung his pack and turned to Lythande with his hand resting on his knife.

"You will stop following me," he said, "or I will kill you."

"I would not advise that," Lythande said in her mellow neutral voice. "That would not prevent me from following you, but then I could walk through walls, or float in at windows like that one—oh, do take care, the landlord should at least have put a railing there!"

"Damn you," he burst out.

"If that be ordained," said Lythande calmly, "I assure you I have adequately seen to my own damnation and have no need of yours. However, if I were dead, I could, as I say, follow you—"

He flung out of the room with a curse. That night the man sat late in the tavern portion of the inn, swallowing pot after pot of ale. Lythande, on the contrary, went to bed directly she had finished singing, and slept the sleep of the proverbial just, being wakened near dawn by the entrance of her travelling companion, very drunk, stumbling in the dark. He lit the lamp and surveyed the unmarked carpet.

"You see?" he demanded, "There is nothing there."

"The night is not yet over," said Lythande. "Do take care you do not fall from that window."

With a savage snarl, he extinguished the lamp, went stumbling to his bed and fell into a restless snoring sleep.

Lythande slept again, being wakened by a cry from the cripple, who was staring in horror at the footprints, this time encircling his bed round and round.

Seeing Lythande awake, he said contemptuously, "Mud again; the footsteps of retribution are lacking in imagination."

"That is not mud," said Lythande, bending to pick up a crumbling fragment. "It's graveyard mould. What will be next, I wonder? Blood? Bone dust? Ectoplasm? Oh, take care—"

She was interrupted by a cry; the man staggered and fell headlong from the high window, with a shriek which was abruptly cut short. Lythande stepped to the window, looking down at the corpse below.

"I guess he didn't want to know what came next," she mused. "I never will understand mortals who have no curiosity."

Then she called for the innkeeper to tell him he had a corpse in his courtyard; and while she waited she noted that the footprints had vanished.

"Mud," she mused, fingering the fragment still in her hands. "I wonder what graveyard mould does look like?"

But of course there was no answer.

THE WUZZLES
Marion Zimmer Bradley

Lythande looked at her traveling companion and wondered if she would have to kill her. The law under which the Adept lived was rigid; she might never be known to any man as a woman; she knew that the law was perfectly literal and did not apply to a woman confidante, but the first such confidante Lythande had chosen had been tortured in the attempt to force from her the secrets of Lythande, and Lythande did not wish to expose her new companion to such a contingency. Yet she could not simply kill the girl out of hand, so the question was one which occupied Lythande's mind at the moment, without gravely troubling it as yet, for the country through which they passed was deserted, and for several days they had met no other travelers.

Now they appeared to be coming into a little village, and she must come to some conclusion about the girl. Frennet was not her lover—hardly, indeed, her friend, but she owed the girl something. Frennet had in fact saved her at the adventure of the inn at The Hag and Swine, and she did not want her to be killed, or tortured, to force her secret from her. So sooner or later the problem of her traveling companion must be faced, and if they were again coming to inhabited parts, sooner rather than later.

Fortunately, Lythande thought, Frennet had no inkling of the life and death problem which occupied the mind of the magician-minstrel. She yawned, stretched, and said "We seem to be coming to a town up there. I do hope it's a good one, an' we can get somethin' to eat."

"You don't know? I imagined this was your part of the world and you would be more familiar with it than I," Lythande said.

The girl laughed and replied, "Not I; that old hag I worked for wouldn't let me outen the house even at high festivals, far less any other time. I never been here—or anyplace else, not since'n I was a baby."

"Which, I dare say, you hardly remember," Lythande said. "As for an inn, I hardly know; but there is no charge for hoping, at least. If all else fails, I suppose once again I may sing for my supper; little country towns are fine for that and welcome minstrels, if not always magicians."

"Will you teach me the magician's art, lady?"

"I will not," said Lythande. "It has been little more than a liability to me.

140

Heaven forbid I should lay that curse on any other."

"Thass easy said," fretted the girl, "but you're long-lived, I see; an' I'd like makin' me own choice in that, ma'am."

"You might find out—as I did—when it was too late, just what a heavy burden it is," Lythande said. "But the day may come when I can apprentice you in a decent inn, as cook or house-maid, and leave you there. This town may be too small for that, but would you not like to be apprenticed to a sewing-woman or some such respectable trade?"

"But I don't want to leave you," the girl stated, and Lythande sighed.

"Don't make me regret I saved you at that inn, after all. There was no obligation upon me to do so," she said with some harshness. "If you traveled with me you would have much reason to know just how hard a life this pursuit of magic can be and how poor a trade it truly is. Just because you have picked up a little kitchen-magic does not make you a mage."

"No ma'am—"

"And you must not to call me *ma'am* where you can be heard—remember that I travel in disguise, and if I am recognized as a woman I may be in grave trouble," Lythande reminded her sternly. Thus chastised, Frennet fell silent, and they went on.

They were now passing through the little village, and as if it were in answer to Lythande's unspoken wishes, they passed an open square where something like a hiring-fair was in progress. Many men and women of the peasant-kind were lined up there: servant-maids with brooms or mops over their shoulders, farm hands with rakes or pitchforks, dairy-women each with a pail, and so forth. One of the more prosperous looking of the farmers saw Lythande with her companion, and came toward them.

Here, be you a magician for hire?"

"I am that," said Lythande, "but it is for my companion I seek work. And—"

"If ye're lawfully for hire—"

Lythande sighed; it was her own fault for showing herself at a hiring fair. "What can I do for you?"

"I got wuzzles in me barn, Magician."

Lythande stared; this was a new one.

"I beg your pardon," she said, "but I have never encountered... what sort of creature may a wuzzle be?"

"What? Don't ye have wuzzles where ye come from?"

"Indeed we do not, unless I know them by some other name."

"Oh well—they's grey an' fuzzy an' they gets in my barn an' they eats the grain—"

"My dear fellow," Lythande interrupted, "do you mistake me for an exterminator? Wouldn't it be simpler—and cheaper—to get yourself a cat?"

The farmer looked cross, but resigned, as if Lythande had made a mistake many times made before.

"I didn't say I had *mice*," he said resignedly, "I said I had *wuzzles*. Don't ye know the difference? They's grey an fuzzy—an' ten feet across—an' they eats the grain an' ye canna hardly see 'em."

Lythande sighed.

"I beg your pardon, sir; I have never encountered a—what is it—a wuzzle—they are unknown in my country. I presume they are creatures of magic, then?"

"I don' know what they are," said the farmer. "But I got 'em, an' I wants them out'n me barn, see? An' I'll pay ye well to get rid of 'em."

Lythande sighed.

"The fates have spoken," she declared. "I had no intention of hiring myself out here as a magician; but where there is need I must give my services. Tell me, since I know nothing of *wuzzles*, how does one get rid of the creatures?"

"Ye're the magician, not me," said the farmer truculently. "I thought sure ye'd know how to get rid o' the things. I ain't never had wuzzles before an' I dun'na know nothin 'bout gettin' rid o' them."

Lythande reflected that she knew no more of getting rid of—what was it, wuzzles—than did the farmer; rather less, for at least he had known what they were. But he had spoken truly; Lythande was the magician, and she should know how to get rid of them.

"I have never before encountered a wuzzle," she stated, "nevertheless there may still be many surprises for me before the Last Day, and I can do no more than to attempt it."

If they were creatures which infested a farmer's barn, she supposed a banishing-spell might be what was wanted. Following the farmer to his barn, she spoke a simple all-purpose banishing-spell which, she supposed, would rid the place of mice or of—what was it—wuzzles.

That had been simple enough; but the farmer scowled.

"Them wuzzles don't like your spell, magician; I see they's still here. I thought sure a great magician like to you could get rid of 'em for me."

"As I said before," remarked Lythande, "I have never before encountered wuzzles. They are not known in my country; but I have engaged myself to rid your barn of wuzzles, and I will do so. But I must first consult my masters, and my books of magic."

This was easy enough to say; but if wuzzles would not yield to a banishing spell, she had really no idea how she would get rid of them. She had with her, in lieu of books of magic, only a small all-purpose spell guide; she was sure wuzzles were not listed, but at last, under *infestation*, she did find a listing for wuzzles as a common infestation. She was quite, quite sure the listing had never been there before, but that was the way it tended to be with magical books; they tended not to have a thing listed until the magician needed it.

The remedy was listed as herbal banishing; and Lythande's knowledge of herbal spells was not as great as that of some other remedies. She said, "Is there in this village a seller of herbs?"

She would consult with him as to the remedy for wuzzles, if indeed such things were known hereabouts.

"There is an herb-seller," said the farmer warily. "I quarreled with him last winter; d'ye think it's *him* set this thing on me?"

"I do not know; I trust not," said Lythande. "You know your neighbors better than I; I am a newcomer to these parts." She thought to herself that the farmer looked not like one who would be on overly good terms with his neighbors; he looked a little too prosperous for that. And his truculent manner of speech was not such as to make him liked well. In fact, so Lythande thought, she did not like him at all, and did not blame his neighbors. Still, as she had promised, she must get rid of—what did he call them, wuzzles?—for the farmer, and it did not matter too much whether his personality pleased her, or not; she did not have to live with him.

She adjourned then to the inn she had seen in the village and sent out Frennet to speak to the herb-seller for her. After a time the girl came back with her eyes aglow.

"Well?"

"Oh, yes. There is an herb-seller," the girl enthused, "such a nice young men, too; tall an' handsome—an' he knows all about wuzzles. They used to be all over the place in his grandfer's time. An', an' he says that old farmer isn't liked by anyone, an' it serves him right if he got wuzzles, or worse things—if so be there is worse things. He's an' old skinflint, he is; he's known to keep back his grain till there's famine, an', an' he sells it at cut-throat prices when folk go hungry, an' sells it cheap so as to put folk out o' business when there's plenty. The herb-seller became a herb-seller because he couldn' make a livin' at the farming wi' that old fellow around."

Then he may have set the wuzzles on him, Lythande thought, but she did not say so; short of recommending that the farmer find a way to live at peace with his neighbors, she had no part in local disputes. "Bid the herb-seller to come and see me," she said.

It was late in the day and the first sun, Reth, was just beginning to touch the horizon, when the herb-seller came to the inn. He came into Lythande's presence, grinning and bowing, asking, "How may I serve my lord magician?"

At least Frennet had not revealed her secret.

"You know, then, how to rid the barn of wuzzles?"

"Oh, aya, sir; ye burn candles made o' herbs, an' they goes elsewhere. They canna' stand the smell o' me magical herbs.

She felt like asking him if he had set the wuzzles on his neighbor. But she supposed it did not matter. The last thing she wished for was to become entangled in the internal affairs of the village. Frennet was regarding the man with as much delight as if she had invented him. Lythande bought several packets of his magical herbs and paid him well for them, (though they made her sneeze, and she realized with dismay that she was allergic to either the magical herbs, or the wuzzles, or perhaps both). *A sneezing magician is not much better than a stuttering one*, she thought, and began grimly preparing to make the herbs into candles. This was a long affair; long before she finished, Frennet had gone to sleep peacefully on the floor, and Lythande, her nose dripping, resolved never again to entangle herself with an herb-seller, even if it meant she must learn a whole new method of magic.

Frennet woke cheerfully, and admired the candles.

"How pretty they are! I'll go an' tell the herb-seller what good use ye made of his herbs, shall I?"

"Do what you please; but let's get on with it, and get out of this accursed—ka-choo—town," Lythande said grimly.

"You caught a cold, ma'am—sir?" Frennet amended hastily, at Lythande's glare. "Shall I get you a remedy from the herb-seller?"

"No need," growled Lythande. "Let's just finish this up and get out of this town." Frennet's face fell; she obviously wanted to see the herb-seller again.

Soon they sent a message to the farmer, asking him to join them in the infested barn.

"I can clear your barn of the infestation of wuzzles," she remarked. "But I cannot insure that it will stay free—ka-choo—and I admonish you that you should learn to live at peace with your neighbors."

Another explosive sneeze perforated her remarks and the farmer regarded Lythande without enthusiasm.

"I'll let 'em alone if they lets me alone," he said.

"That may not—ka-choo—be good enough," Lythande warned. "I admonish you, forgive and forget, or something worse than wuzzles may come upon you." The effect of these exhortations was a little diminished by another enormous sneeze. The farmer looked frankly skeptical now. However, as admonished by Lythande, he began to set out the candles in a ring around the inside of the barn, while Lythande busied herself inscribing a pentagram on the wooden floor.

At last the herbal candles were set out in every point and valley of the pentagram, and Lythande, sneezing again, lighted the candles. The burning herbs, penetrating her offended nose, set off another paroxysm of sneezes, but she instructed the farmer to chase the wuzzles into the pentagram and proceeded to recite a banishing-spell.

Pop! A wuzzle, as she recited the spell, winked out of existence, then another. With a series of little pops, each followed by a sneeze, one by one the wuzzles faded into another dimension, or into somewhere, not here.

Soon they were all gone, and Lythande made haste to extinguish the candles.

"They are gone," she said, "now, I admonish you, find a way to live at peace with your neighbors, and every month, burn one of these candles." She taught him a banishing spell, and when the old man was done growling about the fee, ("I could ha' done that," he grumbled) she returned to the inn for Frennet.

"Are you ready to go?"

Frennet looked sad. Abruptly Lythande knew what ailed her.

"You wish to stay with this herb-seller."

"Well, an' I do. He says he'll teach me his herb-magic," Frennet replied, and Lythande, sneezing again, realized that this was a perfect solution.

"So be it," she said, and Frennet babbled with delight.

"If so be ye'd leave yer apprentice wi' me," the herb-seller said, "I can teach her all me herb-lore."

"So—" a vast sneeze punctuated Lythande's words, "So be it."

"Ye better let me make you up a remedy for that—" Frennet sneezed, "that cold."

"I do not think it necessary," Lythande said. "Only let me get out of this town" (*and its herbs, and its wuzzles*) "and all shall be well."

It was not nearly as easy as that; but by noon, Lythande turned her back on the little town, bidding goodbye to an ecstatic Frennet, burbling about having her own house and her own kitchen, once she was wedded to the herb seller.

Lythande bade her an affectionate farewell, genuinely pleased that she had found a solution for the girl, who sneezed as she said farewell, and Lythande remembered she had sneezed as she said "so be it," thus wishing sneezes upon her former traveling companion. Magic could be far too unpleasantly literal sometimes.

Well, at least she had gotten rid of the wuzzles, and her own sneezing would stop soon; and the herb-seller could make his wife up a remedy her sneezing, for all the good it would do. He was not much of a magician.

But for now she would put this town, and the wuzzles, as far behind her as possible.

She went down the road, sneezing.

THE VIRGIN AND THE VOLCANO
Marion Zimmer Bradley & Elisabeth Waters

The mercenary-magician Lythande was sitting by the fire in the common room of the village's only inn, playing the lute and singing in a clear light tenor voice for the assembled company—and also for supper. Between her love for music and her proximity to the fire, she didn't notice when the fire elemental arrived.

It was not until she stopped to rest her fingers and voice that she noticed the new additions to the inn's company, when the innkeeper came to her and pointed out a woman seated at a table in a quiet corner. "Sir, the lady would like to buy you a drink." His smirk made it obvious that he thought the "lady" was interested more in the man than the musician, but Lythande strongly suspected that it was neither. Eirthe Candlemaker was an old acquaintance, and, if she wanted Lythande for something, it was probably Lythande the magician that she was looking for.

Lythande didn't eat or drink in public, but she knew how to sit over a full tankard of ale for quite a long time, giving every impression of enjoying it. She joined Eirthe at the corner table, nodded thanks to the innkeeper for the ale, and waited until he was out of hearing. The fire elemental, a salamander named Alnath who had been with Eirthe as long as Lythande had known her, was concealed discreetly on Eirthe's wrist, under her cloak,

"Greetings, Eirthe," Lythande said, as if they had last met yesterday, instead of nearly six years ago. "And Alnath," as Alnath scrabbled along the bench to greet the magician, who was one of the very few people she would agree to touch. "Greetings, Essence of Fire." Lythande. said, stroking the salamander with a callused fingertip, while Alnath's fire blazed cobalt blue with pleasure. "And how is Cadmon these days?"

"He's dead, Lythande," Eirthe replied.

"I see," said Lythande quietly. "A most grievous loss for you indeed." Cadmon, a glassblower, had been Eirthe's partner, and Lythande was one of the few people who knew that Eirthe and Cadmon had become partners because each of them was under a curse, and their curses had canceled each other out. Cadmon made wonderful glassware, but anything put in it burned to vapor almost instantaneously. Eirthe made beautiful elegant tapers, as well as sculpted candles almost too real to burn, but the curse put on her was a cold spell; her fire wouldn't burn and neither would her candles—unless they were put in one of Cadmon's glasses. Together their products made a very safe lamp; if it was tipped over, the candle promptly went out. They had met each other eight years ago at a major trade fair, within hours of the time their respective curses were imposed, and had been good friends and partners ever since.

Now, with Cadmon gone, Eirthe was discovering for the first time just how bad the curse on her was. "It isn't that I'm about to starve," she told Lythande. "Cadmon and I always knew that one of us might be alone some day, so we were very careful to save money. I don't need to work for the rest of my life as far as finances go, but what else am I to do? It's not in my nature to sit around being useless! Without Cadmon to make glasses for the candles, there's no point in my making candles, even when I can build a fire to melt the wax over. I can still get a fire to burn," she explained, "but only in the fire pit Cadmon made me—which certainly isn't much help on a cold night on the trail. I don't even dare get too close to the fire here, for fear I'll put it out! I'm cold all the time now, and it's miserable!"

"I can certainly see that it would be," Lythande agreed. "So what brought you here?"

"It was Alnath's idea," Eirthe explained. "She said that going to Heart of Fire—the volcano here—would help me."

"Did she say how?" Lythande inquired curiously.

"Well, no," Eirthe replied, "but who should know fire better than a fire elemental?"

"There is a certain logic to that view," the magician acknowledged. "You certainly have my sympathy, but I gather you require some more tangible assistance. What is it you want from me?"

"I want to hire you to get me to the volcano's cone. There's some sort of barrier part way up the side of the mountain; I bumped into it this afternoon."

The blue star between Lythande's brows furrowed with thought as the magician come to a decision. "There are many things to do while awaiting the Last Battle of Law and Chaos, and this may well be one of them. We'll go have a look at this barrier first thing in the morning."

So the next morning Eirthe stood again in front of the barrier, with Alnath perched on her shoulder, and watched Lythande run a hand over its surface, then poke a fingertip through it. "I can't say that I think much of this barrier, Eirthe," Lythande remarked; "it's the kind of thing I'd put up to keep sheep from wandering over a cliff."

"Thank you very much!" Eirthe retorted.

Lythande chuckled. "I'm not calling you a sheep; I'm just saying that whoever put up this barrier either wasn't much of a magician or wasn't putting much effort into it." Half the magician's body followed the finger through the barrier, while the other hand reached out and grabbed Eirthe's wrist. "Come along, Eirthe," Lythande said, pulling her through.

The barrier felt a bit like the surface of the water when one dove into a lake—no, more like coming out of the water, for the air was hotter and drier on this side of the barrier. The heat increased as they continued up the slope toward the cone, and the air became more sulphurous and more difficult to breathe. They were about ten feet from the edge of the crater when the lava started to bubble out.

Lythande jumped quickly aside from the channel the lava was flowing down, dragging Eirthe, whose reaction to heat had apparently diminished greatly over the years. And a voice spoke from within the volcano.

"You are well come," it said in pure soprano tones. "It's been a long time since anyone sacrificed a virgin to me."

Eirthe gasped, and promptly choked on the sulphur in the air. In the time it took her to stop coughing, Lythande had mentally run though about half the curse words she knew. *I should have realized that barrier was too simple!*

"What makes you think any of us is a virgin?" Eirthe asked, when she got her voice back. "Or that we came here to sacrifice one?"

"A sacrificial procession, including a virgin, is the only thing that can pass through the barrier I put up," the volcano explained patiently. "I should think you'd know that, but then, it has been a long time."

"You put up the barrier?" she asked the volcano. "Why?"

"I was tired of being the garbage dump for the entire district," the volcano replied. "Anything—or anybody—they didn't want down the hill they brought up here and threw into me. Diseased animals, unwanted babies, murder victims—and then they had that plague. The fools didn't seem to realize that plague victims can give a volcano heartburn!"

"I can see how that might happen," Lythande said, forcing her voice to remain calm. "So you put up a barrier—"

"And the only thing that can get through it is a virgin in the company of someone who wants something," the volcano finished the sentence. "So tell me," it asked Eirthe, "what is it you want?"

"Do I have to say right now?" Eirthe asked. "Can I have some time to think about it, and, uh, put my request into the proper words?"

"I should have thought you would have done that before you came here," the volcano said. "But no matter, take all the time you need. You have until sunset."

"What happens at sunset?" Lythande asked.

"If a virgin hasn't been sacrificed by then," the volcano said simply, "I erupt."

"Oh." Eirthe appeared to have been rendered almost speechless by their current situation. Lythande reached out, grabbed her arm, and towed her along as she retreated a little way downhill and sat on a boulder to consider their options.

"I'm sorry to have dragged you into this mess, Lythande—"

"It isn't your fault," Lythande said fairly. "I should have checked the barrier spell more carefully."

"Then you are a virgin?" Eirthe asked. "I'm not, and I know that Alnath isn't—assuming the volcano cares about the virginity of a salamander. Do you have to be one for your magic to work, or is it just that while you're pretending to be a man it's hard to find an opportunity to change that condition?"

Lythande looked grim. "And how do you know I'm not a man?"

Eirthe shrugged. "I don't know how; I've just known ever since I first saw you that you were a woman. You didn't seem to want it known, so I kept quiet about it."

Lythande scowled. The fact that she was a woman was her greatest secret. Each Adept of the Blue Star had a Secret upon which all his power—and life—depended, and this was Lythande's. Some women, unfortunately, could take one look at her and tell she was female, and apparently Eirthe was one of them. She had, however, managed not to tell anyone, including Lythande, for almost a decade, so she was at least discreet.

"Kindly continue to keep it quiet. In answer to your question, while virginity per se is not strictly necessary to my magic, the day any man finds out I'm a woman is the day I lose my power—so I remain a virgin."

"Well, that answers that question," Eirthe said. "Now for the next one: have you any ideas on how to get us out of here?"

"I gather," Lythande said, slightly amused, "that you do not consider sacrificing me to the volcano to be a viable option?"

"Of course not!" Eirthe said indignantly. "I don't kill—I got the curse in the first place when I refused to make candles for a wizard who wanted to use them to kill people, and I'm certainly not going to kill you to get the curse lifted. I'd rather be accursed than a murderess."

Lythande regarded her from under raised eyebrows. "It's a refreshing change to see someone who is willing to suffer for her principles. I'd like to see you free of the curse, but I really have no intention of diving into a volcano to do it." She frowned thoughtfully. "I don't suppose the proximity to the volcano has weakened the curse any?"

Eirthe walked over to the lava flow, scooped up a handful, and began to mold it into a statuette as it cooled in her hands. "It doesn't look like it."

Lythande looked intently at the figure taking shape and said suddenly, "Tell me exactly what it was the wizard who cursed you wanted you to do."

Eirthe paused to collect her memories of the event into reasonable order. "Garak wanted me to make candles in the likenesses of all the rich merchants at the Fair—I was at an annual trade fair that spring; my father had died during the winter, and I was continuing with his business. But when Garak asked me, I remembered that Father had made a candle of one of the goldsmiths the previous year, which vanished after one of his drinking bouts with Garak, and then the goldsmith burned to death in his bed and they said the blankets weren't even charred—and Garak had a lot more money after that..."

"The Law of Similarity," Lythande murmured. "Was he running a protection racket?"

"That's what I thought at the time," Eirthe said, "but I couldn't prove it. Anyway, I refused to have anything to do with him—and he wasn't that good a magician, so I was pretty sure he couldn't pull it off without me. Unfortunately, he had gotten caught up in the worship of one of the proscribed gods, which was where he got the power for the curse."

Lythande sat quietly for several minutes, deep in thought. Eirthe continued to refine the statuette into the likeness of a young girl.

"So what you're saying is that your candles held enough magic to be Similar to the people they were modeled after."

"Yes, I guess so," Eirthe said uncertainly. "I never really thought of it in those terms..." Her voice trailed off as she looked at the figure in her hands. "Lythande? Do you think the volcano would consider this to be a virgin?"

"Its substance certainly is," Lythande said promptly. "You can't get a substance much more virgin than lava newly poured from a volcano." She reached over and took the figure from Eirthe, handling it gingerly by the edges. "And there's quite a bit of life in it, both from its essence and from your work on it." She handed the figure back to Eirthe and shrugged. "It's worth a try, I suppose. Formulate your request into words, and do it carefully. While the volcano is probably not as difficult and malicious as the average demon, it's always best to be very precise with your words."

"Be careful what you pray for, because you might get it?" Eirthe said lightly.

"You will almost certainly get it," Lythande corrected her.

Eirthe nodded. "I'll be careful," she promised. "At least this is one virgin that won't give the volcano heartburn!"

Together they went back to stand at the volcano's edge, with Alnath still perched on Eirthe's shoulder.

"Have you decided on your wish?" it asked.

"Yes," Eirthe said, choosing her words carefully. "I am a candlemaker under a curse so that I can't use fire and the candles I make will not burn. I want to be released from the curse, but not as if it had never been; I want the release to apply only from this moment forth and not to change the condition of any candles I have made in the past."

"Very well," the volcano said. "Give me the virgin and you shall have your will."

Eirthe dropped the lava figure she had fashioned into the volcano, closed her eyes, held her breath. Lythande was holding her breath as well; close proximity to the volcano did not encourage deep breathing, but she kept both eyes—and her magical senses as well—open. The figure fell from Eirthe's hands and disappeared into the lava, which promptly subsided to a calm lake. But Alnath was shrieking, and Eirthe's knees were buckling under her.

Lythande grabbed Eirthe before she fell into the volcano, tossed her over one shoulder, and sprinted downhill. Then there was the sensation of pushing through the barrier again, and Alnath stopped screaming. The air was breathable again too.

Lythande laid Eirthe gently on the ground and dropped to kneel beside her. "What happened?" she asked.

"I'm not sure," Eirthe said shakily. "The volcano didn't erupt, did it?" She cast a nervous glance uphill.

"No, it didn't," Lythande assured her. "It took the sacrifice and the lava subsided, but Alnath started screaming and you suddenly collapsed. So I grabbed you and got out of there."

Eirthe shuddered. "It felt as if I'd been thrown in there instead of the sacrifice." She turned her head to look at Alnath. "Alnath, are you all right?"

Yes, came the salamander's prompt reply, *but it really did feel as though we were in the volcano!*

Eirthe nodded. "Either there was too much of me in that figurine, or it was part of lifting the curse—I hope!" She struggled to sit up. "Where's my belt pouch? Oh, here it is." She pulled out a flint and steel with shaking hands and struck them together. Sparks flew, landing on the edge of her cloak, and she hastily beat at them, then pulled her hand back with a cry. "Ouch!" She looked at the slight burn on her hand. "Well, it appears the curse is lifted—now I'll have to get used the handling fire again."

Lythande smiled. "Be careful what you pray for—"

Together they finished the sentence, "—for you will certainly get it."

CHALICE OF TEARS
or, I Didn't Want That Damned Grail Anyway
Marion Zimmer Bradley

A long time ago, Lythande had had a sharp lesson in the fact that the first law in Magic is to mind your own business, in a world where the penalty for entangling yourself in someone else's magic can be severe. But that didn't occur to her when she saw the old man lying in the road. He looked as if he were choking to death; and with her Healer's instincts, which could always override common sense, she could not have kept herself from kneeling at his side and asking what ailed him.

"Nothing," the old man murmured weakly. "My day is done. I have lived too many years." And indeed it seemed that he might well be the age of Lythande's grandsire—and yet Lythande had lived the span of four or five ordinary lifetimes.

"You should not say so," rebuked Lythande, whose training led her always to deny death in her patient's thoughts. But secretly she thought he might very well be right. Never had she seen any man—not even the immortal magicians of her own Order—quite so bent and stooped with age.

Lythande lifted his head gently. "The first thing is to get you out of the very middle of the road; night has begun to fall, and there will be rain before morning."

"No." The old man struggled away from her hands when Lythande would have raised him up. "I must make disposition of what I bear; I am sworn." He fumbled among his ancient and tattered robes, grey more with age than with dirt.

What he brought out was a thing of beauty. At first it seemed to be a chalice of silver; but as Lythande looked more carefully, she could see that it was fashioned of birchwood, pale grey, and beautifully turned, and set into a silver frame. The wood was so pale and smooth that the whole thing looked as if it were fashioned of silver.

Lythande drew back. "I beg you, grandfather, do not bestow it upon me."

"I cannot, and I would not if I could," replied the old man, testily. "The Grail chooses its own Guardian. It is for you to seek out that Guardian, under the geas I now lay upon you."

Lythande jerked back in alarm; but before she could set the spell which would render the air around her void of magic, there was a brief flash like lightning.

"Behold the Chalice of Tears," whispered the old man. Under his ancient, grey gaze, the Grail seemed to shimmer with a strange luminescence, a sort of underwater radiance. Lythande did not want to behold, much less touch, the magical object; but almost of their own volition—or was it the spell laid upon the chalice?—her fingers closed about it. Resigned, she looked down again at the old man to ask him where she should seek the ordained Guardian of this Grail; but his face had gone slack and he had ceased to breathe.

Lythande sighed and drew the tattered grey robes over the old Guardian's dead face. She would have spoken a spell to rid herself of the outworn shell of his body, but the spell died unspoken. The chalice seemed to cast a faint shimmer in the air about her, and Lythande guessed that it was the sort of magical artifact that could endure the presence of no magic but its own. As she knelt in the road holding the chalice, the worn form of the Guardian began to vibrate, then to fade. Soon nothing remained but a little greyish dust stirred by invisible winds; and then it vanished.

"So," Lythande said aloud, "At least the Guardian of the Grail has saved me the trouble of burying him. Now what must I do? Guide me, I pray, ancient father."

Shorn for the moment of her magic, Lythande felt as helpless and vulnerable as a declawed cat. Goblet in hand, she withdrew to a hollow in the trees, aware that she must rely on her skill in divination to determine what she should do next.

She rummaged in her pack for the worn cards she kept there, took them out of their frayed silk shielding, and spread them before her. She had no especial faith in the cards, but with none of her own spells at her command, their wisdom was all she had to guide her. Her own magic would not serve to give her some hint of where she should seek this guardian.

She looked carefully at the cards spread before her, fascinated as always by their mysterious designs. These cards had been a gift from an ancient wisewoman, who had said that any given reading would be relevant only to Lythande's own immediate situation. As she might have suspected, the first card was the Ace of cups; immediately at its right lay the shrouded and enthroned form of the Priestess.

"Bother," thought Lythande. "That is the selfsame chalice which has been bestowed upon me, which tells me nothing." Again she cast the cards, and again the Grail—the Ace of Cups, not even a significator. This time she shuffled the cards for a long time before she set them out; and once again she beheld the Grail. One of the laws by which such as Lythande lived was 'Seek for that which repeats.' So she knew that somehow the cards had laid themselves out to guide her—if not by their own magic, then perchance that of the Grail itself.

Next to the Grail she beheld the form of the Hermit, seeking forever a light which burned like a star within his own lantern.

That is the Guardian of the Grail," said Lythande aloud. "Tell me something I don't know, oh cards, I entreat you."

Again she cast the cards; but this time she made very sure to thrust the ace of cups well within the pack. But, when she turned the first card, behold! There again was the ace of cups, and next to it, again the High Priestess. Lythande could not help smiling to herself.

"So," Lythande thought. "The Guardian of the Grail is a woman? Tell me now, oh cards, where dwells this sorceress, since the old man made it clear that this quest is not for me." Nor did she want it, though she felt a little miffed that she should be thought unfit. But then, perhaps the sorceress card kept coming up because the chalice was in fact in the hands of a woman, though Lythande might never be known by any man to be a woman—the destiny placed upon her by the master of the Order of Adepts of the Blue Star.

Lythande continued to cast the cards; but cast as she would, nothing came up but disasters—flood, fire and earthquake. And at last she thrust the cards back within their silk wrappings, thinking that if all these disasters were meant for the possessor of the Grail, she must make haste to get the thing into the hands of its ordained Guardian. But like the old man, the cards had given her no clue about where to begin looking.

Lythande wrapped herself in her grey mage-robe, placed the Grail carefully within her sack, and laid herself down to sleep. Perhaps she could find a clue in her dreams...

Her sleep was restless, and when she woke, a thin fine rain was drizzling down from a grey, occluded sky.

"So," Lythande said to herself, "the Chalice of Tears begins to make its influence felt; even the sky weeps. Guide me, I pray, Master."

When she had eaten a little of the bread and fruit she kept within her pack, she settled down to wait. Since the Grail had assumed mastery of her steps, she would await its guidance. If the Grail would choose its own Guardian, then it must give direction to her steps.

As she waited, letting her thoughts wander, she heard from afar the sound of a choric hymn. The singing grew gradually louder, and soon a group of pilgrims emerged from the trees, singing as they walked. At their head was a woman, tall and strong, swathed in a grey veil somewhat like Lythande's own mage-robe.

"I greet you, master musician," she called out cheerfully at sight of the lute strung over Lythande's shoulder. "Whither away?"

Lythande drew herself to her feet. "I am a minstrel," she said. "I have a quest which has been laid upon me."

"Will you tell me of your quest?" asked the woman gaily. "Perhaps one of us can lighten your load?"

"I think not," said Lythande arrogantly. She had never had a very high opinion of women, and did not believe that the magical thing she carried would bestow itself upon this coarse, jolly woman, red-handed and vulgar. Surely this could be only some fortuitous guidance on the steps of her quest, to indicate the direction she should take—no more. "Yet, if you will have it so, I will travel in your company."

"Be it so," said the woman. "All are welcome to share our road; and it may be that the Gods have sent us your way. Who knows? We may even have some part in your quest. Nothing is accidental, brother of magic."

"Indeed," Lythande said politely; but secretly she was not pleased to think that she had anything much in common with this sorceress. Those great red hands could hardly be given to the uses of the High magic; they were only fit to such hedge-magics as souring a farm wife's milk within the churn. Such a one to put herself on a footing with an Adept of the Blue Star? Lythande gave a secret shudder and resolved that she would stay in the company of these pilgrims not an instant longer than necessary.

"Let us be off, then," she said. It might be that in their holy city, they would encounter a great Sorceress fit to become the custodian of the Chalice of Tears—which after all had chosen Lythande herself as its temporary Guardian. Surely she must not bestow it upon any lesser than herself.

The fine misting rain had turned into a steady downpour. Lythande was not too much troubled, for the grey mage-robe was almost impervious to weather; but the women in the procession looked like so many wet cats. The woman leading the pilgrims grunted dolefully.

"You bring us ill fortune, magician. Will you not tell us of your quest?"

"I think not, at least not at present," said Lythande, thinking that this downpour might be the element of water telling her she was on the right track—surely no more than that. "Let us press on. For my quest has to do with the very elements themselves."

"So be it, my brother, if you say so," answered the woman, looking wistfully at the shape of lute beneath Lythande's robes. "While this weather continues, we can have no music; for the rain would damage your instrument."

"That it might," said Lythande, wondering crossly how long she would be marooned in this company. "Let us onward."

They slogged through rain for most of the day. Dusk had fallen when at last they came to an inn. Its sign bore the device of a bush of painted thistles and the words, 'The House of Necessity'.

This is surely a sign to me, Lythande thought, *for I am driven by necessity*.

"I think we must halt here," said the woman at the head of the pilgrims, "for our company numbers three dozen or more, and there is no other shelter for many miles on this rain-blighted moor. And its name is a sign to us, for surely we have been brought here by necessity."

"Quite," thought Lythande, certain that the sign had been for her. Indeed, how could it be otherwise? She gladly entered the welcoming inn, and took off her robes. She ate a hearty meal, for there were only women within the company; the *geas* which forbade Lythande to eat or drink in sight of any living man was completely literal, and did not forbid her to satisfy her hunger and thirst in the sight of any number of women. After her meal, and weary with walking, she began to prepare herself for sleep; but before she settled into her mage-robe, the women's leader asked, "Will you not give us a song, minstrel?"

"Gladly," replied Lythande, not sorry to have a good excuse for displaying her talents in this company. She sang a song of sorrowing Quest which sounded like the wild and stormy sea off her native coast.

"Such a song of woe," commented the group's leader. "If there is such sadness in your heart, minstrel, may I, Manuela, not share your burden? For I can see that it is heavy, Minstrel, and it has been laid on us that we should share one another's burdens and sorrows."

"It is not the time," said Lythande. She did not think this commoner sorceress could be of any help to her in much of anything, let alone her Quest; nor had she any love for being called 'brother' and so put upon an equal footing with this hedge-witch Manuela. But she said nothing more, and went to sleep in one of the smaller rooms, for she would not share a common chamber with the pilgrims.

When she woke, the sun was streaming through the windows, but that was not what had wakened her. It was a cry of consternation from the room in which the pilgrims had slept.

"Alas! We are marooned!"

Lythande sprang to the window. During the night, a dam had burst, and the inn was completely surrounded by water. Fortunately, the inn was on a small rise, or they might have been washed away and drowned.

Bother, thought Lythande. *Now I can neither pursue my Quest nor rid myself of these women; for good or ill, the Fates have cast me into their company.*

Manuela echoed her thoughts as she came into the room. "Alas, my brother," she cried, "the Fates have abandoned you, for how can you fulfill your Quest now? It is worse for you than for us; since we are pilgrims through life, our Quest may be fulfilled wherever the Fates choose to send us, but I can tell it is not so with you."

"It is not," said Lythande. "But as the Fates send me, so I must abide."

Manuela said hesitantly, "Are you sure I cannot be of any aid in your quest, brother magician? For it seems to me that there is something more than coincidence in our meeting. You are, I am sure, a great and powerful magician; but if I can serve you in anything—"

"I think not," said Lythande. "Yet I thank you for your good will, Manuela."

The water did not go down that day. Just before evening, the women were gathered in the main room of the inn, where Lythande was diverting herself by playing on the lute. Suddenly, there was a great rumbling noise, and the floor seemed to shake itself and rock. The women clung together in fright, crying out.

"What was that? Brother magician, what was that?"

"Only an earthquake," murmured Lythande, shaken. Again the ground shook, and then settled; floods, and then earthquake! She must make haste; for if this were the Grail ruling the elements, first the element of water, signifying flood, and then the earthquake—the element of earth—what could have gone so amiss? She must make haste with her quest, or worse might follow. Yet marooned in this inn, alone with these women, how could she continue the search for the Guardian of the Grail?

She could not cross the barrier of waters unless they went down substantially. Could it be that the Guardian was here—either among the pilgrims, or perhaps the keeper of the inn herself?

Lythande sought out the Innkeeper. She was a big woman, and looked like any of a hundred other women, wrapped in her great apron. Lythande's heart sank, but she felt compelled to ask.

"Mistress Innkeeper, are there other guests at the Inn? Other magicians, mayhap, who did not join with us in the common room last night? Those, perhaps, who bade you keep their presence secret?"

"No, my lord Magician. Only yourselves, and the pilgrim women. But did you not know that the leader of your company, one Manuela, is a great magician? Perhaps it is of her that you speak."

"I am sure it is not," said Lythande. "I am only by chance in her company." It vexed her that the Innkeeper should compare these hedge-witches with an Adept of the Blue Star. But for the moment she was marooned in their company; she must even bide with them until the Keeper of the Grail should see fit to come to her.

Dismissing her worries, Lythande went to her room and lay down. Soon she fell asleep, just before sunrise, she was jolted out of sleep by an earthquake, this one considerably more violent than the others.

"Look for that which repeats" thought Lythande. And suddenly, a look of utter consternation filled her face. "What a donkey I am, to be sure! Perhaps her goddess thought I needed a lesson in humility."

She sought out the common room where the pilgrims, clustered about Manuela, were kneeling and praying that the elements might turn away their wrath. Far out in the water surrounding them, Lythande could see an ominous bubble of fire—a volcano! The element of fire was about to join its fellow elements. Lythande knelt hastily beside Manuela, who broke off in her prayers.

"Yes, my brother magician?"

Lythande knelt and drew forth from the mage-robe the silks concealing the Grail. "I think I am guided to bear this to you," said Lythande. "It may be that the gods who own this thing think I need a lesson in humility." And suddenly Lythande felt long unaccustomed tears blurring her eyes.

Manuela rose to her feet. Her round, good-natured face seemed to glow; she held out her hand and said, "My brother—no, my sister—I wondered how long it would take you to get around to telling me about it. For when the waters rose, I guessed; and when the earthquakes shook us, I was nearly certain.

Her drably-draped form seemed to take on height and power; she raised the grail above her, in a ritual gesture older than time.

Beyond the window, the waters were receding in the dim light of early dawn. "You can be on your way, magician, " said Manuela, smiling. "I will care for the grail. And you, be not too quick to judge your fellow man—or woman. Oh, and forget not to break your fast before you go," she added, with homely sternness.

"So it is ordained," Lythande replied, and went to speak to the innkeeper about breakfast. Having surrendered the Chalice of Tears, she no longer felt like weeping. In fact, Manuela was right; she was hungry.

TO KILL THE UNDEAD
Marion Zimmer Bradley

Almost the first thing which Lythande had learned to do when first she came into any village was to look about for a wineshop or an inn. Because although one of the laws by which such an Adept lived was that she might never be seen to eat or drink by any man, yet for the price of a bowl of soup or a cup of wine, she could sit and listen as long as she liked to the gossip of the village and find out whether anyone in the area was in need of the services of a mercenary magician—and put her in the way of earning her bread.

On this particular evening she had walked a long time and was very weary, so she did not immediately make herself known, but sat for some time listening to the quiet rumor of voices about her.

At first, she was so tired that the voices rose and fell over her head almost without making an impression. Then she heard one voice saying aloud, "But what is this creature? It prowls by night, and tears out the throats of its victims; yet with the light it vanishes away, and lies in hiding all the day? Is that any natural beast, or some evil thing out of legend?"

"A wolf?" suggested another voice.

"Not by any means," replied the first voice. "A wolf is not unlike a big dog; and every wolf I have known is gentler and more timid than any dog. I have reared many wolves taken from the wild as pups, and never did I know any wild wolf but hunted in a pack. This killer hunts alone."

"Wolves are like other beasts," the first argued, "and no beast so tame but it can turn rogue. It might well be such a wolf turned rogue—but I say this is no natural beast."

"A werewolf, maybe?" sneered the first.

"As likely a werewolf as anything else," said the first gloomily. "But then perhaps it is only a matter of finding what shape it wears by day—and hunting it down in that shape."

At this point, Lythande straightened up. Her long aristocratic-looking feet were stretched out to the fire. She slowly lowered them to the stone floor and said, in that carefully neutral voice, "I know something of werewolves. How do you know this thing which preys upon your people is a werewolf?"

159

"What else could it be?" demanded the first speaker truculently. "To hunt by night and tear out the throat of its victims?"

"I can think of many things," Lythande answered carefully. "For all you say, it could still be some form of wild animal: a wolverine, perhaps; or an escaped lion from a menagerie. A captive tiger, or some other predator escaped its owner. Or, if you are speaking of supernatural creatures, why a werewolf, rather than a vampire or night-ghast or some similar creature?"

"Why not indeed?" demanded the first speaker.

"Tell me," Lythande asked, "does it hunt by night? Is there any way to see something it has attacked?"

A sturdy farmer spoke up, "In my barn, magician, is a sheep it has killed. You are welcome to see it—any of you."

Lythande slid her battered sandals on her feet, and several of the others rose and followed the farmer into a nearby barn. There, by the light of a lantern hanging from a rafter, lay a dead sheep, lacerated and much torn.

Lythande knelt down by the dead animal. From the tingling of the blue star on her forehead she could tell she was in the presence of some powerful magic. "It might well be victim of a werewolf or vampire at that. So what then can we do about it?"

"Can you kill this thing? This—vampire or whatever?"

"No," said Lythande. "By definition, a vampire is already dead. There is no way to kill the dead. I can do many things but to kill the dead is not among them."

That silenced them all for a moment. Then the innkeeper said tentatively, "Then can you—do away with this thing, dead or alive? If it is—for instance—a werewolf?"

"Be the Gods willing, I can," Lythande said.

The innkeeper said, "I know something of magicians, I dassay you will charge this village a pretty price for getting rid of this thing."

"Alas," Lythande said, "even a magician must somehow get a living. Is the presence of this thing not losing you much in the way of profit that you can gain if I rid you of it?"

"Thass true," said one of the farmers. "We can't even sell the dead sheep at market—an' if this thing gets much worse, we'll all lose all our sheep an' go broke. I'd say hire the magician now to get rid of this thing—an' pay him a decent wage afore we all of us loses our living."

"Thass true," said another farmer. "I suggest every farmer in this village gives half a silver piece. That way no one of us has to pay the whole thing."

Lythande looked around the room. Even at a quarter silver apiece she would make a good fee, for there were thirty men or so in the room. She checked both the scabbards hanging at her belt; the right-hand sword of steel, for footpad or villain, the left-hand sword for ghost or supernatural monster or any creature from the realms of magic. Then she bent to the floor and again slipped her battered shoes on her feet, tying them securely round her ankles. If she survived this battle, she thought, she must find out if there was a sandal-maker or shoe-cobbler in this village, and spend a piece or two of her silver to have new shoes made or the old ones botched together. These were as filled with holes as if they had been left out in the winter rains. For the moment, she murmured a spell which would give the road-worn bits of leather some semblance of wholeness; she did not wish the locals to see how battered they were, but this spell could last only a certain length of time.

There was no sense in delaying. Lythande went out into the star-sprinkled night and took up her station in the corral where the town's animals were kept. She had hoped to spend most of this evening with feet to the fire, but the chance of earning such a fee should not be put off. Wrapping herself in the warm folds of her mage-robe, Lythande took up a station by the fence and settled down to wait and watch.

The night dragged; it was damp and cold, and Lythande wished she had had leisure to have a cup of hot soup unobserved. As always, she had in the pockets of her mage-robe some pieces of dried fruit, and she chewed glumly on a handful of raisins without enthusiasm as she waited. The moon had set when she heard a soft padding sound and saw in the darkness two green and luminescent points of light at the very edge of the sheepfold. Lythande swallowed a raisin and in the darkness made certain her swords were loose in their sheaths.

And then she remembered. Months ago, in being pursued by the Walker Behind, she had struck with her magical dagger—and it had been destroyed—melted away, disappeared. In effect, then, she was unarmed against this thing if it were any form of magical creature. Her regular steel dagger was unharmed, not that a regular dagger of ordinary steel would be that much good against a werewolf or vampire. In the faint greenish light of ambient magic, Lythande examined what was left of the blade of the magical spelled one.

Not much: beyond the hilt only some three inches of twisted, melted metal remained. It shone faintly in the dimness with its own eerie light. Would it then be any defense against the uncanny green eyes still visible at the edge of the field?

Lythande could only try. The strength of the enchanted blade was not in its metal—of that there might be little left—but then, it might well have been drained of its magic too, in her confrontation with the Walker Behind. Lythande had no idea whether the faint tingle she now felt in the Blue Star was from the broken magical dagger, from the magical beast she could faintly see and sense approaching, from her own ambient magical senses and the Blue Star itself, or from something else unseen in the darkness.

It was near her now. She whispered a spell which would temporarily void the air of all magic near her, even including her own. This way she would be able to diagnose whether the thing approaching her were any natural creature or a thing of magic. The fact that for a few seconds of the spell she would also be at the mercy of the thing, whatever it might be, was not important; she had to know.

Sure enough, the green eyes vanished, but Lythande knew perfectly well that the terrible creature had not gone away, it was only that without magic she could no longer perceive it. The chance that it was not magical had always been very small, but she had to examine it.

She pulled the broken magical dagger from its sheath. Broken or no, it was all she had to face the creature. With the broken remnant she struck out at the gleaming green eyes, and at the same time she murmured the strongest banishing-spell in her repertoire. She did not think it was strong enough, not for this creature, but it was all she had.

The green sparks of the eyes went out. Hardly believing in her good fortune, Lythande sheathed the broken dagger. Well, she thought, while I am having my sandals cobbled, I must also find some weapons-maker who can attempt to replace the magical dagger. And while she was at it she must somehow find herself a spell-candler who could fashion some stronger spells. There was an old adage—and Lythande had never yet known it to be wrong, but there was a first time for everything—that for every magical danger there was somewhere a spell to conquer it. But, thought Lythande pessimistically, it did not follow that she could find that spell.

She took a careful backward look. No, there was nothing—as yet—following her.

But then—would she know?

A short time later she entered the common room of the inn, and when she was greeted with many questions, told them briefly that the beast was gone, "so far as I know; bearing in mind that I am neither a God, nor yet infallible."

They would have loaded her with their best, and Lythande was tempted. But she had learned it was not well to let commoners, no matter how grateful, diminish her mystery, so she thanked them courteously and went out into the rain, finding a little way down the road a snug barn where she slept warm, dry, and unseen. When she emerged, after breakfasting on an egg she found in a deserted nest and ate raw—no hardship this, for she liked it better that way—and taking a cup of milk from a complaisant cow, who reacted better than most to her soothing-spells, she turned her steps toward the village in search of a cobbler for her broken shoes and a spell-wright for the remnants of her magical dagger and the renewal of her arsenal of spells. This was not an unpleasant task, for it gave her a chance to speak freely with her only true peers, who were other magicians. She slept that night in the home of a local hearth-witch, who thought of it as an honor to entertain an Adept of Lythande's rank, but when, emerging well-pleased, for the bargaining for the mending of her shoes had gone well, and returning to the inn to hear the local gossip, she heard with dismay and consternation that the thing was back, more virulent than ever.

"And it seems to have thrived on your banishing-spells," said the innkeeper maliciously, "for this time it has not only taken sheep, but two of the shepherd's dogs and the shepherd as well."

After the first shock of dismay, for it was rare indeed that her spells should fail, Lythande managed to collect herself, saying with apparent insouciance that she had promised results and she would therefore certainly deliver them. And then, as soon as she was unobserved, she sat down to think it over.

This vampire was dead. Well, of course, all vampires were dead by definition, and whatever she had done, she had told them she could not kill the dead—and in truth she had failed to do so. How could she then make good on her promise to rid them of the creature—or whatever it was?

She took out her small book of spells and opened it at random. She had often noticed that any particular spell she wanted would not be in the book till she was most in need of it. It did not disappoint her; the first spell on which her eyes fell was one to bring the dead back to life. At first Lythande was dismayed; the last thing she wanted to do was to bring this thing to life again. Then she stopped to think. She had said she could not kill the dead and thus—by the curious laws of magic—had defined the grounds on which this battle was to be fought. Her attempts to do away with the dead had failed. Was it then required of her that she should bring it to life so she could kill it?

There was nothing for it but to try. The magician went out again into the darkening fields, awaiting the coming of the magical creature. As soon as its wicked green eyes appeared at the edge of the field, only a little fainter than they had been before, Lythande began to repeat the spell which would bring the dead to life.

As soon as she began the eyes were arrested, held motionless in the thick darkness. Like twin green torches they glared at Lythande, and from somewhere—perhaps between the worlds—came the sound of a despairing whine. Then all was silent and in the magical greenish glow Lythande could see the form of a man stretched on the ground. She should have known; if this spell awakened the dead to life, it would of course restore him in the form he had worn in life.

She had her magical dagger—the new one, not the old broken one—in her hand ready. She struck, then—a fraction of a second too late—remembered that this was, at the moment, no longer a magical creature.

Swiftly she spoke a spell rendering the air void of all magic. The last thing she wanted was to strike with her dagger of ordinary steel, and find that she was again facing a werewolf or vampire. The creature shimmered. It was already attempting shape-shifting, but Lythande's spell had trapped it in human form.

It gave a despairing—a human—cry as Lythande whipped up the dagger which was effective against mundane menaces. To a creature whose essence had been so long purely of magic, Lythande thought swiftly, how could anything be more humiliating than being killed in ordinary human form?

It lay dead before her, and she spoke—not unwillingly—a spell which would keep it from coming back to life. Everywhere in the village now, people were coming out of doors, and one of them bent over the pathetic corpse.

"Ah, Haymil," he said. "He was a suicide last year and buried in unhallowed ground."

"And therefore came back to an unnatural life," said Lythande. "And so you see that even a priest should err on the side of mercy. Had your priest allowed him to rest in sanctified ground, you could have saved many silvers."

They were all eager to buy her a drink, to shake her hand, but as for Lythande she could not too quickly shake the dust of the town off her shoes. At least, she reflected as the town vanished behind her in the distance, they were newly mended.

TO DRIVE THE COLD WINTER AWAY
Marion Zimmer Bradley

It was very dark, and needles of sleet pierced the greyish- black sky as Lythande fought her way through the still, freezing cold. The only light was that fitful radiance which came from the snow itself, and, at a distance, there was a faint glimmer as if a single candle sent a stray gleam of light. Hell, and the abode of lost souls—if there was one, Lythande thought— must be very like this: silent, cold and dark.

She struggled through the dark silence, toward the faraway light, her lute on her back in its ornately decorated woolen case, hoping the damp cold would not damage it. It seemed that the very idea of song had died out of the cold silence. Lythande would have struck up a song, but she was half frozen; neither her fingers nor her throat could have made the slightest sound. Even the idea of sound seemed to have died in the dark.

The single candle shone through the encompassing dark like a metaphor for Light against Darkness: symbol of the great struggle of humankind. It seemed to grow even more still as she struggled up the stone, snow-covered steps outside the inn.

She thrust the door open, her steps sounding loud in the silence. Indoors it was nearly as cold as outside, A fitful and inadequate fire barely showed her the faces of the few scattered men and women in the gloom. Lythande would gladly have gone out even faster than she had come in, so gloomy the place looked.

A scant half dozen men and women were seated around the inadequate fire, and a man in an innkeeper's leather apron turned to look at the minstrel.

"Here, you don't want to bring that lute in here," he said glumly. "Our duke's forbidden music in this town."

"Forbidden music?" Lythande had never heard of such a thing. "Then how are minstrels to get their living?"

It was a ridiculous question, and Lythande knew it when the innkeeper said morosely, "Duke says it would be better if none of 'em got a living at all; rogues and vagabonds all of 'em, he says."

"Now I resent that," Lythande said. "For while I am a vagabond and wanderer, having no home, no man can call me a rogue. Nor any woman neither."

For, while the laws of the Adepts of the Blue Star forbade her to be known as a woman, she must travel in disguise. Still, she did no harm to anyone.

"And why have you no home?" asked the glum landlord. "In weather like this, a man should stay by his own fire."

"But alas, I have neither home nor fire," Lythande said, "nor chick nor child nor wife. And I wander because it is a *geas* laid on me, that I roam the world till the last day of Chaos shall come, in the great battle of Good and Evil. I am sworn to fight against Evil, and I must say your ban on music strikes me as great evil. For what save music distinguishes men from beast? The birds may sing better but they have no lore of ballads. Any dog may bark louder, but none of their noises sings, or makes sense. And but for music, what is it that distinguishes the work of man from that of any beast? What else is there that men can do, that some beast cannot do better?"

"Why, you argue as good as t' Duke's preacher" said the innkeeper gloomily,

"Give me a pot of beer," Lythande said, not willing to continue the argument, and knowing that whatever was said or not said, she had won her argument and defended her way of life. That was enough.

"No beer in this town," said the innkeeper. "Duke says wine is a great evil, and beer worse. Ain't there no men in your town beat their wives and children when they been drinking?"

Once again, Lythande had never heard such a thing. "You might as well say that my lute should be outlawed, because I could use it to beat someone over the head till he is dead. Some men use knives to kill. By that logic, if you call it so, should I tear my meat with my teeth like a dog? Because some men are beasts, should all men suffer, and none use reason? Coffee, then?"

"No coffee, neither," said the innkeeper, "coffee contains wicked stimulants."

"Whatever folk drink in your town against bad weather, then," said Lythande, sick of the argument and only wanting to be warm. The innkeeper set before her a cup of steaming straw-colored fluid.

"Herb tea's good for you; contains none o' them wicked stimulants," the innkeeper remarked. Lythande, touching the colorless stuff to her lips, could well believe it. It tasted almost as flavorless as it looked.

At least it was warm; not very, but even so, Lythande could not drink it. She made no comment on that, lest they should suddenly discover warmth or savor was evil too, because it was so much sought after.

"A bowl of soup then, served in your warmest bedchamber," Lythande commanded. "And a fire, if that is allowed."

The servant conducted her to a cheerless bedroom, but at least a small fire was burning, though fitfully. Lythande sat down by the fire, wondering what would happen. The maid went to fetch the soup, and Lythande sat down by the sluggishly burning fire, and thought about the ban on music in this town. She had never heard of anything like it, in all her long travels.

"But is it laid on me that, because I think the ban on music evil, I must be required to fight it?" she wondered. She was afraid that it did mean just that. The very fact that she could formulate the question, by the peculiar laws of magic, probably did mean just that.

But how, then, was she to fight it? She had not done enough by protesting it? No, for it was still going on. She groaned, knowing that she must do something more.

But how? This at least Lythande knew she need not concern herself about. The very fact that the question had been raised in her mind meant it would soon appear in her life. Lythande resolved to sleep while she could. If the problem was to come to her, it would come, but there was nothing she could do to bring it nearer or to delay it.

When the maid brought a small bowl of thin and not too tasty soup, Lythande ate only a few spoonfuls before rolling herself in the clammy blankets, and after a while, she fell asleep.

When she woke, the pale light in the room told her it was still snowing. She thought it was late in the year for that; spring should have come at least ten days ago.

Surely the ban on music could not delay the coming of spring! Or could it? The very fact that she could put the question that way, meant it was very probable that the ban on music—and the ban on joy in men's hearts, which was what the ban on music was really all about—was something she might well be expected to remedy.

Lythande rose, and looked out of the window so that she could see what there was to be seen. Only a dreary grey landscape greeted her eyes, a hard pelting of snow whipping up into drifts like a great bowl of whipped cream. She smiled at the innocence of the simile and drew on her boots, wrapping herself in the mage-robe which had dried overnight. The tight windows reduced the noise of the storm to a faint distant roaring; the snowdrifts seemed to move noiselessly, with a curious effect. Lythande unslung her lute from her shoulder, and hoping to raise her own spirits before facing the hostility downstairs, began to play a song of many years ago, unheard since she was young. It had been the first song she had learned to play as a young girl, many years before the Blue Star was inscribed between her brows. At that time her name had still been—she slammed the thought shut, unwilling to let the forgotten name cross the barrier of her memory for the first time in—how many years? Could music then comfort her for the loss of a woman's name and identity? When nothing else in all these years had done so? Perhaps not; but it was, perhaps the only thing that could possibly have done so.

As the last notes of the song died into silence, Lythande prepared once again to take up the burden of her minstrel's identity and of this town. A random glance out the window showed her that the hard-driving snow had died down and its hiss was replaced by a dull roaring of the wind. Dim stretches of damp dismal-looking browned grass showed through the soggy-looking runnels of melted snow.

So, she thought, music's power has already shown itself. She hoisted the lute, and went down the inn stairs. In the common room, many of the people were staring out into the grey and silver lines of rain. As the gloomy innkeeper of last night set a cup of the colorless herb tea before her, he actually smiled.

"The bread this morning is fresh-baked," he said, and as she lifted it to her lips, she caught a whiff of cinnamon. The bread—which she could smell in the kitchen—was fresh and smelled delicious. "Would you like some, minstrel?"

"I would indeed," Lythande said, heart-felt; for the first time, perhaps, in a century, she resented the prohibition on eating or drinking in the sight of any man under which every Adept of the Blue Star must live.

The glum innkeeper said "I heard you playin' that there lute upstairs! That ain't allowed, minstrel. Like I told you, t' Duke won't have it in this town.

The bread smelled so good she wished she dared to snatch a bite, but she had not tried to break her *geas* in many years and did not know what would happen if she did.

She looked out the window instead. The view from the window encouraged her to come back to the innkeeper, and to say "You can see the results of my playing; should I not go on?"

"Looks like there's been a spring thaw," he said, "You trying to tell me you did that, minstrel?"

"Not I," Lythande said, "but the power of song."

And, since he did nothing, she looked defiantly back into the room which was filling up with travelers, and then lifted the lute to her fingers and began to play again. No one protested, not even the morose innkeeper; but something suspiciously like a smile cracked the frozen dignity of his face.

"I'll get you some o' the hot fresh bread," was all he said, and withdrew from the room.

One man said gloomily, "Well, I don' know what t' Duke'll say," and glared at Lythande.

The innkeeper came back into the room, and snarled, "If what Duke'll say matters so much, Giles, let 'im come himself an' stop this weather! Or do you want to try it?" He laid the hot fresh bread atop Lythande's pack, and said "Take it with you, an' eat it on the road, minstrel."

Lythande put the roll of bread into her pack and thanked the innkeeper, sincerely; then hoisted her pack and prepared to leave. She stopped to pay her reckoning.

Outside the window they could all see where stray spikes of green poked their way through the soggy lawn. Encouraged by the innkeeper's lack of protest Lythande began to sing.

Surely the time of singing has come
The voices of birds and springing of grass
With every living thing rejoicing;
Loving and nesting
Robins springing and warbling everywhere
Yes, everywhere around us,
Birds are singing, and waters flowing
And the first blossoms of the spring
And summer can be seen.

Beyond the window, the dead grey of the sky had begun to show stretches of blue, strewn with puffy clouds, and on the wide lawns pale and delicate flower buds were replacing the hills of snow. From somewhere beyond the window came the delicate sound of a little pipe. The travelers were all outside by now, in the spring morning.

Lythande was moved to go on singing as the innkeeper set before her a mug of what proved to be a particularly nutty blend of beer and went away without a word. Since she was now alone in the room, Lythande drained the mug, and left the cup of herb tea, which, she thought might make a good eyewash—from its smell, that was about all it was good for.

And Lythande sang again;

Birdsong drenches the land;
The birds, every one.
are building nests;
Even the worms, from their holes
Seeks each one his mate.

From the corner of her eye, Lythande saw a pair of rabbits enjoying themselves in the way rabbits always did. Quietly, still singing, she went out of the inn, and down the steps. Far away, the shepherd's pipe was still playing, and beyond clear view, she could see where two shadows merged into one.

And when she was out of sight of the inn, she began the last verse of her song:

Yes, all things seek a mate,
And only I languish in loneliness...

Well, she had restored joy and song to the blighted village; wasn't that supposed to be the next best thing to a love of one's own? As Lythande turned her back on the village and unobserved bit into her bread, she took up the road where patches of melting snow still lingered. She saw the world through a rainbow of tears, and her song remembered past love songs.

Yes, and I too, like every star, am alone.

But, she thought, *there is still beer and hot bread. And the spring has come.*

FOOL'S FIRE

Marion Zimmer Bradley

"If I owned Hell and Texas, I'd rent out Texas and live in Hell."
(Source unknown, but he was a wise man.)

Lythande saw in the distance the lights of a village. As she came closer she focused on one in particular, the lantern in the window of an inn.

The magician shifted the heavy pack slung over her mage-robe, and prepared to enter the inn to find out whether anyone in that village had need of the services of a magician. The life of a mercenary who was also a magician was hardly an easy one. Magic, as Lythande was fond of saying, while truly a fine art and of great aesthetic value, in itself put no beans on the table. And no Adept of Lythande's rank would practice her art for crass cash alone. Lythande was an Adept of the Blue Star, and such magicians could not stoop to the arts of the hedge-wizard or herb-wife. But at least those were assured of a living, while the Adept, who would not sell her magical arts lightly, must often rely on her minstrel's skills for her supper.

She went into the inn and took a seat, intending to begin by listening to the gossip. A frowsy waitress shambled toward her, and Lythande asked her for a bowl of wine. Not to drink—for the vows under which such Adepts lived forbade that she might ever be seen to eat or drink in the sight of any man. But at such an inn, at the center of village affairs, she could, for the price of a bowl of wine, sit as long as she wished, listen to all the gossip and perhaps hear if anyone in the village had need of such services as hers. Once she had been brought so low that she had had to accept a commission to rid a town of an infestation of wuzzles. Although the creatures were magical, they were so much like rats that Lythande had felt herself not much better than an exterminator.

For a time, Lythande was so cold that she only sat and warmed herself, paying little attention to the talk that ebbed and flowed around her. But as her body thawed, a conversation between two of the villagers worked its way into her consciousness. They spoke of a strange fire that had appeared at some distance in the woods.

"It's just burnin' away out there and no one can come near it. Every time I see it, it looks like it'll set the woods afire."

"My old man followed it for hours last week and ne'er came nary closer," another said. "If he wasn't such a good woodsman he'd a been lost an' ne'er found his way back at all."

Lythande pricked up her ears. This sounded as if some form of malevolent magic might be at work. And she knew from experience that where there was magic, there might be work for a mercenary magician—and where there was work there was pay. Perhaps the pockets of her mage-robe, now all but empty of coin, would soon be filled. Even the greatest of Adepts must eat, she thought, and surely something had led her here.

She said to the woman who feared for her husband, "Tell me, is this a magical fire?"

The woman looked at Lythande suspiciously at first, but the attraction of a new audience was overpowering. "It looks to be," she said, "an I wish it 'ud stop."

"Maybe no harm's bein' done just now," chimed in the first woman, "but how do we know it's not the gates of Hell?"

"And here to carry some of us down to Hell with it?" suggested another.

"It may be nothing but a harmless will-o-the wisp," Lythande said diffidently, though she knew she might talk herself out of a job. "Have you any evidence that it means ill to anyone?"

"No, an' I don't need no evidence," a man broke in. "I don't hold with no magic. We don't want no magic around this here place!"

"I truly advise you to let it alone," said Lythande "Most magic means no harm, and if you let it be it will do the same for you. But if you go seeking it, it may waken to your existence, and then it will be as if you had poked your fingers into a hornet's nest."

"But suppose 'tis really the gates of Hell?" asked one of the women. "How can we live knowin' *that's* right at our feet?"

"I cannot see how the gates of Hell right at your feet would make any difference, provided you do not go exploring them—nor let your children go poking sticks through the doors to see them burn," Lythande observed.

The woman bridled. "Seems to me, magician, it's everybody's duty to resist Hell any way we can. Anyway, that's what the Good Books say."

Lythande said smoothly, "I am not familiar with your Good Books, but I will grant that if Hell is a place of evil—of which I am not convinced—then it is a worthy duty to resist it."

"But you'll allow as there's Good and Evil," one asked belligerently.

"I do."

"Then you've got to believe in the Good Books."

Lythande considered a moment. "Is it permitted to ask why?"

"There's no other way to be righteous. It's written in the Good Books that no man is righteous of himself but only by the wisdom that is written in the Good Books." His voice had taken on the tone of recitation.

"Then we are to believe what is written in your Good Books because the Good Books say so? The logic fails somewhere." Lythande was coming to the opinion that if these people had no better occupation than this, then Hell was welcome to them. She wanted to rise and depart forthwith, shake the dust of the place off her boots and never enter it again. It hardly seemed likely that the inhabitants would thank her—or pay her—for dealing with their problem magically. But her oath did not recognize such considerations. Good Books or no—it required her to fight evil wherever she might encounter it, from now till the Last Day. Sighing, she bent again to her task.

"Why do you think it the gates of Hell?"

"It burns like no natural fire, and gives off the stink of brimstone," said one of the men. "The Good Books don't mention nothin' else like that. What else could it be?"

"Alas," said Lythande, "I can suggest nothing without seeing it. And I hesitate to condemn anything without first doing so. Nor have any of you seen it clearly, if I understand you correctly. So I ask again: how can you be sure it is the gates of Hell?"

That silenced them for a moment. Then one woman said, "Well, I ain't goin' near it. I've tried to live a righteous life and I ain't throwin' it away by chasin' after Hell!"

The muttered response of the crowd agreed that—given that the strange fire most likely was of Hellish origin—no one was particularly eager to make a personal confirmation.

One of the men stepped towards Lythande and said challengingly, "I don't suppose you'd be willing to take a look, seein' as you're not afraid of Hell."

She sat silently for a moment as if considering the idea. It seemed there might be a paying job here after all. "*Someone* should look at it, and try to determine what it is before deciding what to do about it," she said temperately.

"Would you be willin' to look at our curse?"

"I would," Lythande said. "I am curious to see this marvel—I would not at this point call it a curse."

"So what would you call it?" a woman in the crowd asked.

"I would call it mischance," Lythande said. "I think it a capital mistake to take anything in this universe as personally aimed at us. Whatever happens is probably no more than the gears of the universe grinding. So usually I mind my own business and do not seek to interfere."

"But it's up to us to right wrongs," a woman protested.

"I do not feel myself called to right all the wrongs of the world," Lythande said. "Surely some of them are none of my business." All too many of them, she thought, seemed to end up her business.

"I'd call that immoral," the woman said. "My old ma told me always that it was everybody's business to right any wrong she saw. Right's right, and wrong's wrong, no matter where you find 'em."

What a dreadful philosophy, Lythande thought. *That would make everybody a busybody.* But did not say it aloud; she still had hopes of finding work in this village and thought it better not to make too clear to these rigid people how different their notions of morality were. She simply murmured, "Certainly that is a philosophy many people hold," and left it at that.

One of the men seated by the fire asked, "So you'd be willin' to go out into the waste an' see if that there fire is really the gates of Hell?"

"I would—for a suitable fee," said Lythande. "But," she warned, "if it is really the gates of Hell, even with my magic I cannot promise to close them."

"We don't want nor need magic for that," said the man grimly. "If so be it's Hell, we can deal with it ourselves, like it says in the Good Book, with fastin's an' prayer."

Lythande fought the temptation to smile. *Will it then fall to me to protect the gates of Hell from an army of enraged villagers?* But aloud she only murmured "That must be a great comfort to the mothers of your children."

He looked at her sharply and said, "If you're goin' to go look at it, then don't just sit there."

Outside the inn, she was pointed in the direction of the woods. She saw at once what the villagers had meant, and wondered that she hadn't seen or sensed it on her approach. Far off the reddish glow of a column of fire could be seen, burning away by itself in the waste. At first glance—and maybe even on second or third—it did look rather like the gates of Hell: fierce, red, and glowing away behind the black bars of trees like the grate of a furnace.

As she walked toward it, she realized it was farther away than it looked. It seemed to slip through the trees as she approached, and even at Lythande's long striding walk, it took her the best part of two hours to come near to it. *Now whoever heard,* she thought to herself, *of Hell avoiding those who pursue it? And what will I do if I find it really is the gates of Hell? Why have I been led here anyhow, among these people who think they know the answers for everyone?* It all seemed absurd. Even if she believed in Hell, what would it be doing out here in the wilderness, burning all alone where there were unlikely to be any sinners for it to catch?

And yet the closer she approached, the more her senses—both ordinary and magical—told her that what the villagers feared might be correct. She caught up with the fire at last, examining the sultry glow which beat up as if from the very center of the world. Even as she looked over the edge, she knew it was not literally down under the earth. Here, she thought, among a people who consider themselves to be the most righteous on the face of the land, the gates which were only symbolic for others literally yawned down below. And then, after a long time, she began to understand why it was here, among these narrow people—so sure they knew what was best for everyone—that she should find the gates of Hell.

At last when she had figured out what she must do and say to them—and even perhaps, understood a little of why this task had been laid upon her—she turned about and went back toward the town.

When she left the fire it was chilly again, and she walked briskly to warm herself on the two hour journey back. She found herself again within the inn facing what looked like the same scant half-dozen glum-looking people, seated in the common-room awaiting her return.

"Well," they greeted her. "Did you find anything? Was the fire truly the gates of Hell?"

Lythande drew her face into a solemn expression. "I found it," she said, "and I am sorry to tell you that it is truly the gateway of Hell."

There was a confused outcry—a dozen people all talking at once—the gist of which seemed to be: "What ha' we done to deserve this?" One woman appealed directly to Lythande. "Alas! What evil have we done, that we should have the very gates of Hell at our doors?"

"Nothing," said Lythande. "Can you not see what a great honor it is to be trusted with keeping the very gates of Hell?" Which, of course, was one way of putting it, although not the one Lythande would ordinarily have chosen. But knowing these people it was impossible that anyone would stumble unwitting through those gates. The villagers would subject them to so many theological arguments that people would run away before coming into the slightest danger—and likely never return again.

Lythande pocketed her fee, which was not small, but the village was in so much pride of possession that no one protested. One would think, she mused, that Hell would be a popular attraction.

Well, she considered while going down the steps, maybe, in this town, it would.

HERE THERE BE DRAGONS
Marion Zimmer Bradley

When Lythande entered the town, it looked eerie. Pale light from a waning moon spread a thin cold radiance over the deserted streets of the town, In accord with her usual custom, Lythande first looked about for an inn or tavern, where she could for the price of a pot of beer, which she never drank, listen to all the gossip, and see if anyone in the village had need of the services of a mercenary magician.

There was but one inn, and it looked run down. A weak and yellowish lamplight spilled out the window in which Lythande looked. Inside a bare handful of men and women huddled around an ancient dark wooden bar; Lythande looked around to orient herself, and closed her eyes, not really believing what she saw. The population seemed all to have been taken from an ancient engraving in a text on witchcraft she had once seen. Men, women and even a few children all had about them some faint family likeness, something faintly deformed; yet, looking a little more closely, there was no physical deformity. She wondered then if they suffered some spiritual deformity—or if there really was such a thing as a spiritual deformity. It was at least possible that they all suffered some minor physical or other peculiarity too subtle to be identified by anyone unfamiliar with them and without special knowledge.

Oh, this was absurd; what was a spiritual deformity anyhow—or was there any such thing? And what gave her the idea that if there was, she could heal it?

Well, it would make more sense to go inside, rather than standing out here in the cold, gawking, and having neurotic notions about them.

Lythande hoisted her backpack and the embroidered case of light board covered in colored embroidered wools, which contained her harp. She shoved the door open. A blast of heat smote her in the face, smelling of burned meat and the acrid smell of stale beer. Lythande had been hungry; but on smelling the meat in this inn, she felt suddenly that the very thought of food was revolting.

She stepped up to the bar, and asked quietly for a pot of beer. The barman set a large mug before her. He was a an odd little gnome of a man with queerly pointed ears who looked, Lythande thought, more like the village idiot than a barkeeper of any sort.

"Come far today, stranger?" he asked her in a gritty voice.

"Far enough," Lythande answered politely.

"Stranger, be you a magician?" asked the queer little gnome of a man. "And do you take commissions at a reasonable price?"

"I do, then," Lythande observed, "But, forgive me if I sound crass— what would you consider a reasonable price? And how can I tell you unless I first know the scope of the job?"

He leaned over and drew a curtain which hung, she thought, over a gateway to the street outside. But as he drew it aside, Lythande stared—for it led, not to the outside, but to a view of a flight of steps which came out on a sunlit landscape out of doors; there were large expanses of sunlit summer trees and long green meadows where there should be nothing but snow.

"Just to go out yonder and see what's there. Le' me tell you another magician asked thirty silvers—and so I hung that curtain up—an' I can always just draw it closed. It won't bother us ifn's we don't bother it none."

Lythande felt like screaming with laughter. But she only asked soberly, "What would you consider a fair price?

"Mebbe three silvers, just to walk outside an' see something that probably ain't there?" he said sharply with an unpleasant smile.

"I see that there may be monsters or something worse at the top of those steps," Lythande said carefully. "What if I must come down even faster than I went up.? Will I have any time to come back here and collect enough silvers to do away with some mighty ogre?"

For, she thought the world behind those stairs might be anywhere—but the only place it was certainly *not* was outside in the street.

The little gnome behind the bar said "You can leave that there harp; I'll take care of it an' your pack too."

Lythande said "I never leave my harp. And what if I need something from the pack? I could as easily leave the Blue Star from my brow." She rummaged in the pack and took out her book of spells. "This at least I carry with me. The rest you may keep; if I do not return, some member of my Order will claim pack and harp."

"As you wish, sir sorcerer," Bat-ears conceded. "Is it likely that you will not return? Have you had any premonitions? Can you arrange to send me a message from the Other Side? Maybe what's good on the stock market?

"What kind of ghoul are you?" Lythande asked in disgust

"No offense meant," Bat-ears answered, "But you magicians—all that bosh about the afterlife, but nothing really useful, like never knowin' what's good on the stock market, or what will win at the racecourse—You magicians give me a pain."

I wonder if any of you know what you give me, Lythande thought, but aloud she only made a meaningless conciliatory murmur.

She thrust the spell book into the pocket of the breeches under her mage-robe, and went toward the window and heaved it open. It opened on a flight of stairs. Not really giving herself time to think, she set her foot upon the lowest step of the stairs and went up.

There were more stairs than there looked to be. Halfway along the flight of stairs, she felt a curious disorientation, no longer sure she was climbing; might she not, rather, have been descending? And from the sharp chill in the air, Lythande knew that at least they were no longer underground. Had they ever been?

Abruptly the stairs came to an end, and Lythande came to a stop with an unpleasant jolt. It was fully dark now, and Lythande could see only a little way through the thick darkness. She came to a stop, and looked around, wanting to assess this strange country somewhere above and behind the inn. Behind her, the stairs seemed to disappear into a thick mist.

If I turned around now and went down the stairs would I wind up in that same bar? she wondered, She would not bet on it; or even that she could, even now, return to the cozy fire-lit interior of the inn. At least not by simply turning round and heading back the way she had come, whether it might be up or down. Magic simply did not work that way; and by the prickling of the Blue Star on her forehead, she knew that powerful magic was somewhere in the darkness around her.

She felt within her pack; Her hand came out clutching a little carved-wood crucifix which she had been given a few years ago by a wandering priest. Now she began to worry whether this powerful talisman kept her from seeing something very evil. She cast away the cross, and all at once, as if a veil had been snatched from her eyes, a burning metallic sun turned the landscape an evil sulphurous yellow. She rubbed her eyes, wondering if indeed she were on the familiar earth at all or in one of the magical or demonic realms. And, if so, how had she come there, and why? And what were the magical realms doing that they should be at the head of a painted staircase—which oddly she had climbed—or descended—outside a window in an inn?

She thought she should return to the inn, now she saw what was here; go back and tell them what lay behind their curtain. But would they do anything, or would they simply thank her, draw the curtain and let it stay there, out of sight and out of mind? And if she did would she violate her Magician's oath to fight the forces of evil wherever they should be found? The prickling of her brow told her that this was a place of evil, and her oath bound her always to fight evil in any place whatever. Even, she wondered, outside the known world?

Yes, she thought, even there. She took a reef in her backbone, and stepped into the burning sunlight, which felt terribly hot on her face. She felt like turning about, and bolting back up—or was it down?—the stairs.

But she did not. She told herself that she had seen no evil yet, only guessed at an evil so great that while she carried such a symbol of good as her crucifix—never mind that to her, not being a Christian, the crucifix was essentially meaningless. This place was—must be—evil beyond guessing. And both her word to the innkeeper and her own vows bound her not to turn her back on such an evil without at least doing her uttermost to fight it.

Was she even equipped to fight it? She had left her harp with the barman and more than once the sound of her harp alone had been sufficient to drive some evil away. Well, it was no good thinking about it; for better or for worse, She had come into this place without her harp, essentially unarmed, and without any magical weapon she must face it.

Face what? So far she had only seen the wicked color of an alien sun. Maybe she would see nothing else.

Although that sun, she told herself instinctively was evil enough.

Then she recoiled within herself. Just what could be so evil about an alien sun and a sulphur-colored landscape? Was it only that they were different? In some ways it would almost be considered weirdly beautiful.

But that concept was too much for her. Her mind so revolted at the thought of calling that lurid landscape *beautiful* that she thought she would vomit. With a fierce effort she controlled herself, and brought her rebellious stomach to order. She drew herself fiercely upright and forced herself to take a few steps into the burning alien landscape.

After a few steps she turned about seeking the door where she had entered. There was no sign of any door or exit.

So, she told herself; there may be no return—no obvious return, at least not now.

No! Against that, her mind rebelled. She thought, I cannot stay here. There must be a way back; anything else was completely unthinkable. Yet she knew the unthinkable might well become fact and wanting it to be different would not make any difference at all. So she must put all her ingenuity to the business of return; She must above all remember where the doorway had been located, and hope that sooner or later she would have a chance to go through it again even if it must be at a dead run being pursued by whatever evil was there. And from hoping there was nothing there, she began to wish that she would discover something even those people would recognize at once as evil, if only to induce them to pay her. She guessed that the people at in this town would cheat a working woman out of her lawful due, even if they did not know she was a woman. Some folks would enjoy tricking any magician out of the lawful hire, and all the more so if the magician happened to be a woman. *Over my dead body*, she thought.

There was a sound in the darkness; it sounded like some beast, but no normal beast she could think of. If she had ever thought of what a

Tyrannosaurus rex sounded like, She might have expected it to be something like a dinosaur. But that was impossible—or was it? In a place like this, a dinosaur was no more unlikely than anything else. Maybe she had traveled not only in space but time. Or maybe—if this were a magical realm, a dinosaur was rather more likely than not. And she was no more unarmed against a dinosaur than she would have been against a dragon, or roc, or any other nonexistent but unpleasantly tangible creature.

And she had had no psychic warnings of any magical beast either. But were her sudden fears of a magical beast some form of warning? Magic sometimes worked that way. She had not let the possibility of dinosaurs cross her mind in years So why was she thinking of them now? Like an answer, somewhere in the burning glow came that same dreadful roaring. Lythande thought that if the doorway had still been there, she would have run up—or down—through it at once. Maybe that was why it was no longer there. Above all she must keep track of where it had been, in case there was really a dinosaur or a dragon somewhere here, and she could escape it only by taking to her heels.

That roaring might well have been a dinosaur or even a dragon, if she had had the faintest idea what a dragon or dinosaur might have sounded like; and the prickling of the Blue Star told her that it was no natural beast but something of magic. Well, for that she had a magical dagger; but she could have used a sword. She had never carried a sword in her life, and wondered why she was suddenly thinking of one.

The answer was not far to seek. A little path led through the trees, and at the very edge of the road stood a stone about waist high, on which was standing another round stone. It was engraved in low relief with a carving of a strange, long-necked. beast, And driven into the stone halfway to the hilt was a long sword.

She stared at it in disbelief. She knew of such things from old ballads, but that there might be such a creature or such a sword even in the magical realms strained her belief to the breaking point. Even to a magician, such things did not happen, and yet, unless she wished to deny the evidence of her own eyes, there it unmistakably was. If there was such an animal as a dinosaur on the face of this world, that was a dinosaur, and an extremely large and fierce one, at that. She had never seen anything like it, not even in a menagerie or an exhibit of exotic beasts, not even in such a display of magical beasts kept by a magician who had a roc and a camelopard. Yet the evidence of her own eyes was undeniable. And she had been thinking of a sword, but she had not expected to receive an answer so quickly.

At that very moment she heard through the bushes, a terrible roaring sound, and saw the bushes swaying and jerking as if something very loud were crashing through the plentiful underbrush. Galvanized, she jerked the sword free of the great stone, and ran. If she was to see a dinosaur—or a dragon—but she was in no hurry to validate her fears. Not even to reassure herself about her own sanity.

Now she caught a glimpse of a long snakelike neck, unusually high, of a curious leathery green. It had large reptilian eyes which looked almost as if they were on long insectoid stalks. The eyes swiveled and Lythande had the uncanny feeling that they were searching for her in the underbrush, She told herself not to be fanciful, but she could not help herself. She was not eager to try out her new sword against anything so large or fierce. But, it seemed, she was not to be given the choice. Well, she thought, I hoped there would be something fierce enough to justify my fears about evil. That will teach me to be careful what I wish for; like to the puppy who chases a wagon wheel. What would he do if he caught it? What will I do with this dinosaur?

And by what right do I assume I am meant to do anything about it? I came into its world, not he—or more likely it—into mine. It is big and terrifying; but if I let it alone it will let me alone. Nor did I ask for the sword. This is certainly not my fight.

They did not pay me to go up against a dragon.

Especially they did not pay me to kill or dispose of a dragon; they very specifically paid me to go into the world behind their window and see what was there. Just to see it, not to do anything about it. I made it clear that for what they paid I would but go and look if anything was there. They never expected anything would be there and spoke as if, the curtains drawn, they would be quite all right, So Lythande really should do nothing, but go back at once and tell her story. But in order to do that, she must remember where the door was located. Could she find it even now?

As she looked around the beast seemed to sigh, growl and breathe out fire. By the light of the burning forest, she turned about, and ran toward where she had seen the door to the stairs. Once inside, she almost tumbled down the stairs and with great relief through the door into the bar.

The little barkeep with bat-ears looked up, and said, "So, sir magician, back again? What did you find on the other side of those stairs?"

"A dragon, or perhaps a dinosaur, breathing fire. It was trying to set the woods on fire."

He looked perturbed. "And did you kill it?"

"No." said Lythande. "I did not; for three silvers I agreed to go into that wood and see what was there. For killing a dragon or dinosaur, my price is substantially higher. And for no reason at all, I got the notion that you grudged the price; you made it clear that you paid me only to look and find what was there.

"Oh," said Bat-ears, "I believed your Magician's Oath bound you to destroy evil wherever you found it."

"And so you believed you could get me to kill it for you without payment? By what right do you expect me to destroy an innocent beast blamelessly going about on its own affairs and harming no one? It is only doing what all creatures do. Looking for its food, and troubling no one."

"But it will burn the woods up, breathing fire!"

"That does not trouble me; if it bothers you, you can go and kill it yourself."

"But it will burn up the woods!"

"They are not my woods; if it wants to burn them, whoever owns the woods may go and kill it, or pay someone to do so. I am a magician, not an exterminator. The beast does not menace anything of mine."

She picked up the case with her harp and slung it over her shoulder. She went into the street. She would rather walk all night than stay anywhere near these people. Behind her she began to see through the door, a great fire breaking out. *It must have spread from the dragon in the woods*, she thought.

She turned back to look at the inn. Suddenly it buckled and with a great explosion, erupted skyward.

With all this, she thought, *they should not have grudged me a lawful fee*. She turned away from the inn, and began to walk. Maybe she could reach the next town before the moon set or it began raining.

NORTH TO NORTHWANDER
Marion Zimmer Bradley

It had been several years since the minstrel-magician Lythande had dared to go near Northwander at the height of summer, but this year she felt it should be safe enough to do so. Surely, she thought, the effects of the spell which had made her think it prudent to avoid the place had been nullified by now.

Not quite within reach of her destination, Lythande stopped in a small village, looking around the darkening streets. Not for the first time, she cursed to herself the *geas* which demanded she must forever travel in the guise of a man. Most of the time she simply lived with her fate and did not think about it much; it was simply the price of her magic, like the Blue Star tattooed between her brows, and she thought about it as little; but here in this town there was a cozy cafe filled with women, and hearing the sound of their voices, she felt a vague hunger, like the ache in a long-missing tooth, to join their company as one of them.

But, she asked herself forthrightly: would she sacrifice her magic? For a moment she entertained the idea; then brought herself back to sanity. For what else had she sought and suffered, if not to be free of this vast tedium? The life of a woman had wearied her before her breasts has fully grown. She would not have it again as a gift!

She had entered the cafe as she thought, and now the owner was looking inquiringly at her. She asked for a pound of raisins and two of prunes, with a single pound of dates, and obtained the loan of a mortar and pestle in which she pounded raisins and prunes into a single fragrant mass. Adding a few pitted dates for flavor, she spread them into sheets which dried quickly into leathery squares of a flavorful paste. She rolled each sheet into a tasty mouthful, to be stowed in the pockets of the mage robe and be eaten when she had no leisure for a meal unobserved.

Then she asked, "Am I right for the castle?"

One of the swaddled ladies, bearing themselves cozily upright like hens, almost clucked. "Right there. You can't get nowhere else from here, Lord Magician. An' may I ask why you're a-goin' there at this season?"

Not pleased—why in heaven's name had she been able to tolerate even the thought of living as a woman—she said calmly "I am a poor minstrel and magician; I must earn my bread by song or by magic; and often at festival, there are some who seek my arts or those who need my magic for hire."

"A magician for hire," said one of the women. "What an entertaining idea. Tell me, what sort of magic can you do for hire? Just for a f'rinstance, Sir Magician. What kind of magic can I hire you to do?"

Vastly entertained, Lythande prepared to give one of her sales pitches. "Oh, there are many things; once a township hired one of my kind to rid them of an infestation of magical beasts like rats—wuzzles—invisible creatures infesting the grain. And I do a nice business, of course, in love-charms; in fact one of my greatest businesses is in love charms. Could I work for you a love charm—find you a nice young cavalier, ma'am, madly in love wi' you?"

"Ai!" the woman giggled. "What would my ol' man say to that?"

"I know not, lady, but once I heard somewhere—though I have none—of such a potion which was strictly moral, having no effect whatever on faithful married persons."

The woman giggled again. "Could you make me up one of that kind? Strictly moral so me old husband wouldn't object?"

Good heavens, Lythande thought, *what madness prompted me to bring that up!*

"Oh, come on," giggled the woman, "I don't believe there ever was such a thing."

"Are you doubting my powers, Madame?"

Lythande knew she would be better off to say nothing—for she doubted it too—but some compulsion had prompted it—no doubt for its own reasons.

"Well, yes. Yes, I am," the woman replied, still giggling. "I don't believe anyone, however much a magician, can do such a thing. Nor I don't believe they ever could or would, so there! You're just bragging, like all those fellows call themselves magicians an' make up things they can't do."

Lythande told herself furiously that she should simply accept this, humiliating or not. What had prompted her to bring up the subject? And yet, as if compelled, she heard herself say, "Oh, I will take the challenge. But first, let us be clear about this: you wish for a lover who will be besotted with you and yet in no way endanger your marriage or your husband's feeling for you, or your own sense of morality."

"Yes, but it sounds pretty silly when you put it like that, don't it." The woman tittered.

Somehow, Lythande felt compelled by this challenge of her powers. She felt a sense of recklessness—and—perhaps too, at last, an element of caution.

She said calmly, "I will do even as I say," and looked straight at the old woman whose eyes fastened on her with a tardy half-horrified awareness.

"But I must first consult my books of magic," she said, thinking that at last this would give them a few sane minutes to reconsider. To reconsider what, she did not know or care.

Within her voluminous magician's robe she found her small condensed book of spells. A peculiarity of this book was that no particular spell was ever within this book until she had formulated a need for it. Now, suspecting that what she wanted did not exist, she searched only at random. What she sought could hardly be a love-charm; a romantic relationship for a married woman which could endanger neither health nor morals was almost by definition not a genuine love affair. What it was, she did not know; but by the end of this ill-fated experiment she might. This might be why she had agreed to it. Her inability to imagine such an affair might simply lie in the failure of her own imagination. And curiosity was a strong motivating force.

She arranged to sleep in one of the community barns, and before she slept, formulated in her mind all the qualities of the lover she sought. At least, she thought, if it met this standard it could not do her any great harm... explicitly no damage to her morals or her well-being. At last she drifted into a fitful sleep.

Outside the barn was a strange sound, a weird moaning. As Lythande slowly came up through the veils of sleep, she realized that what at first she had thought the mooing of a cow was the wailing sound of some great beast outside, wailing and moaning what appeared to be—of all things—her name.

"Lythande! Lythande!" and then a most frantic and desperate cry.

"Alas, Lythande my beloved! I cannot live without you."

Lythande drew the mage-robe about her body. What sort of great love had been attracted by her spell? Well, whatever it was, by the very precautions which had fenced it round, it would be incapable of doing her any harm; not to her health nor even to her morals, though she was quite sure that, by ordinary standards, she had no morals. She stepped out of the barn and under a great shadow darkening the early morning sun and closing off almost half the sky.

A creature of cloud? It was so vast that beneath the low-hanging sky she could hardly take it all in. Then it flapped its mighty wings, moaning out its call, blurred by the vibrations so near.

"Lythande! Oh, Lythande, come to me, my beloved! I have reconsidered, and of all I have known I love only you."

Lythande stood looking up at the sky. *Oh no!* she thought. It was the were-dragon Beauty! Beauty was the reason Lythande had been avoiding Northwander.

And Beauty knew her female identity.

"Beauty," she cried out. "Come down here at once. And please stop making that noise!" So this, she thought, was what her spell had brought.

Beauty's great shadow diminished somewhat as the were-dragon climbed down the sky and shrank into her human form, asking meekly, "Don't you like my song, Lythande?"

"I have no desire to criticize your musical talents," Lythande said quickly, "but it is still early in the day. I was experimenting with a spell, but it seems to have pulled you in, and you endanger my very existence, calling attention to me thus."

"Not for the world and everything in it would I cause you even a moment's pain or sorrow, Lythande. But I beg you, do not send me away from you so soon, Lythande. I live only to serve you."

Lythande felt just a little ashamed of herself—and very nervous. She wondered how she could have come to inspire the devotion of this powerful and capricious creature; apparently this spell was curious indeed.

"I think I owe you an apology, Beauty," she said. "Will you come into the inn, and have a drink or a morning bowl of coffee with me, and I will explain. But I am traveling incognito; you must say nothing of my true identity."

"I rather think you are always traveling incognito," said Beauty shrewdly. "But I would never endanger you, Lythande," she added in a soft and sincere voice.

"Come, then," Lythande said gently. "Share my breakfast and I will tell you what a foolish thing I have done." But, she wondered, had it been so foolish after all? She had been lamenting the secret of her womanhood—and this was what she had called to her? Was this not as good or maybe better than many lovers? What was better than a friend; a friend to whom her true identity was known, so that she could feel the freedom of her hidden womanhood. What was love but to have one who knew the truth of you and—spell or no spell—accepted you nonetheless?

Over a breakfast which she shared with Beauty, of bowls of milk and coffee for Beauty, she confided to the were-dragon what she had done and then released her from the spell. Fortunately Beauty chose to be amused, rather than annoyed.

And when Beauty had flown away again, still chuckling, Lythande awaited the woman who had demanded the spell which would never endanger her health nor morals nor the affections of her husband.

"Here it is," said Lythande, holding out her arms. In them, a small spaniel puppy wriggled. "Here is a love which will never endanger the love of your husband, perhaps the truest love of all."

The woman stared down. "A puppy dog," she said. "Now how, I wonder, did you happen to think of that?"

"Lythande smiled. "Because," she said, "If I gave you a dragon, she might step on you."

But, no matter how the woman begged, Lythande would not explain.

GOBLIN MARKET
Marion Zimmer Bradley

Lythande came into the village unseen by a back road; for since her last time in that town, she had been by strange roads, which probably no one in the village would have thought of as roads at all.

As was her usual custom when she came into a strange village, she sought out an inn and commanded a bowl of wine, which of course she could not drink, for no Adept of the Blue Star might eat or drink within sight of any man. But with a bowl of wine before her, safe in the man's dress she wore, she would have a reason to stay in the tavern's warmth. She was the only woman ever to infiltrate the Order of the Blue Star, and the price she had paid for her Adepthood was that she must wear forever the disguise which she had intended only as a brief temporary expediency.

She sat in the corner of the common room for a long time, half asleep— for she had been where there was little chance of sleep for many nights. After a time, an elderly villager who had just entered the tavern asked her, "Ho, master magician, be ye here for the Goblin Market?"

Lythande recalled her wandering attention and tried to rouse herself. "You still hold Goblin Markets in these parts?"

"Hey," said an old man, not too politely. "What kind of hedge wizard be ye if ye dunna' know about the Goblin Market? Dunna ye ha' goblin markets in your neck o' the woods? What sort o' Godforgotten country sha' it be, that dunna' trade wi' the goblin men for their steel knives an' swords?"

"Ho, is it so?" asked Lythande. "In my neck o' the country the goblins shew themselves only to innocent young maids and never to any man. There is even an ancient ballad about it, which I have sung all over this country—would it please your folk to hear it, lordlings and commons?"

"It would indeed," said one hearty old man with the well-fed look of a noble.

Thus encouraged, Lythande struck her harp and sang the ancient ballad. There were two sisters, one was a good maiden and minded her loom, and as reward the ballad had little to say of her save her name; but the other was naughty and given to daydreaming. She spied and peeped at the goblin folk, and finally ate of their sweet fruits and as reward pined almost to death. For the goblins never shewed themselves but once to any maiden; and so her good sister put a silver penny in her pocket and went forth to buy at the goblin market—and there she offered to buy. But the goblins mocked her and pressed her to eat, saying that they did not sell to fair maidens, but only gave. But she would not open her mouth, no matter how they pressed her to eat—and at last they clung round her, slapping and pinching her and thrusting their fruits upon her—but she kept her mouth tight shut, while they slapped and pinched her, attempting again and again to thrust their fruits on her physically—

"And so we have two sisters, and one was a good girl and minded her spinning wheel, and so of course the ballad—" and Lythande's bearing took on a cunning look. "I am a poor man, Excellency, and I must be out e'er it grows dark, to seek a well-sheltered haystack..."

"Innkeeper," the man interrupted, "at this hour it's unlikely you'll find a tenant for your rooms. Have you a spare chamber for this minstrel?"

"Ay', the li'l room where I ripens my winter apples. Let 'im sleep there; he's welcome to any of 'em apples. None on 'em'll be fit to eat for a month still; he's welcome, far as that goes, for them apples ain't ripe nohow, and he's welcome to any on 'em, if 'e dunna' fear the bellyache and gripes."

Lythande pricked up her ears. She had a ripening-spell at her command which would ripen, in the pockets of her mage-robe, as many apples as she could make away with. She wondered indeed if she should offer the spell to the innkeeper in exchange for a pocketful of apples, but held her peace. Most likely the innkeeper would offer her only one or two apples for her spell, and she would rather fill her pockets with the green fruit. With another small spell she could conceal her depredations however many she might take.

Bending her head to the harp Lythande sang her ballad to where one sister pined near to death for the goblin fruits; for the goblins never show themselves but once to any maid—and here Lythande paused again.

"I am but a poor man, Excellency, with little to sell but my ballads, and what small magic a mercenary may offer—but I offer you a spell which will keep your women and ladies and girls from the fruits of Goblin Market—"

"Na, na, na, we dunna want any o' your spells—as for the girls, their mothers ha' told them day and night to keep their eyes to themselves—ay, we lose a couple every year or so at Goblin Market, but we let them damn themselves as they will—what good is a girl who canna' mind her loom at Goblin Market? What our folk want from you, Sir Magician, is a spell for them as deals wi' the Goblin men—for they try allus to sell us not good goblin steel, but steel charmed to kill us—not our enemies."

Lythande, shocked, asked, "But what about the girls—don't even their mothers want them back?"

"Oh aye, but none on' us here has any brass for such foolery—what we want is a spell to make the goblins sell us good swords an' daggers—what good is a girl can't mind her loom an' goes about mooning after goblin lovers?"

So now Lythande knew why she had been sent here.

There was a force—Lythande knew it only as the Goddess—who would sometimes use her to right the wrongs of some woman or other, greatly to the destruction of Lythande's own will and plans.

This did not happen very often—it had last occurred in the episode where she had become entangled in somebody else's magic, where she had been forced to travel as a woman to return the sword of a priestess to her Goddess's shrine. But when it happened it over-rode any of Lythande's own magic. She was, to say the least, unhappy that it had happened again,

Still, she might as well get it over with. She said, "I do not know the customs of your village. At what hour do you hold your Goblin Market?"

"Oh. So, ye're going to the Goblin Market, Master Magician?" Curiosity grew in the old man's face, wrinkling it up till it looked like a withered pumpkin.

"If you will tell me at what hour it gathers." She had not been among goblin-folk for many years. "I have been travelling in far countries, and know none of your customs."

"Oh, is that so?" asked one of the men, glancing at his fellows, and Lythande wondered wearily if they would attempt to play a crude local joke on her. Well, there was nothing to do but get it over.

"They usually come in about moonrise; and it's held in that shed yonder. The goblins don't like strong sun or strong moonlight neither."

"True," Lythande murmured. She bid the tavern guests an indifferent good-evening, and wandered out, still burdened with her harp-case and travel pack, to stand in the empty cold square and watch the first goblins slipping into town. In the shelter of the huge barn, little booths and slender chairs were springing up like strange mushrooms.

Lythande had not been among goblin-folk for many years and she had forgotten much of what she knew about them. Yet she was honestly astonished to see a face she knew, belonging to a small squat goblin with bat-ears and a rounded, greying chin adorned with skimpy greying whiskers. After a time she realized that at least one of them knew her when he hailed her by name.

"Hullo, Lythande; I knew not that your kind were so long-lived! I thought that you had long-since gone to join your ancestors in whatever part of hell they inhabit!"

"Ah, Toad-kin!" replied Lythande. "I equally believed that your folk had long gone to stake out their own lands there. I had expected to find you reigning over their greatest boulevards."

"Will you take a cup of good goblin wine with me, Lythande?"

"I will," Lythande said, rejoicing that the goblin-folk were in no way men, and she could enjoy a cup of goblin wine (which she actually liked) in their company. "But none of your old tricks, Toad-kin, or I will cheerfully break every bone in your body. If you offer me anything unwholesome such as a cup of rat poison..."

The goblin's face twisted into drollness. "You have no sense of humor, Lythande?"

"About my own survival, none," Lythande answered, with cheerful brutality. A servant came bearing the goblin wine, which was delicately lemon-colored and looked delicious. Lythande picked it up and then, warned perhaps by some breath of humor in the eyes of her host, summoned power to her voice and asked, "Is this good wholesome wine?"

Held and transfixed by the magician's voice, the goblin muttered, "No."

"Which bone shall I break first, then?" Lythande asked grinning with the same cheerful brutality. The goblin winced.

"None, please," he asked in a small voice.

"Why, this is your own game, and I thought you willingly played it. Come now, let us begin," she said, "Perhaps a knee? An ankle?"

The goblin collapsed into loud blubbering wails. Horrified, Lythande regarded him in consternation.

"Why, what's this?" she asked. "Your brothers are singing—I hear them."

"You hear them? Under normal conditions, none but fair young maidens can hear them! Or is it magicians too?"

Caught right off-guard, Lythande snarled, "Ware, Toad-kin, or I begin with truth on the bone-breaking! Look I to you like a fair young maiden?"

"Not like any I have ever seen," he mumbled, "but what do I know of maidens?"

"I am as far from being a fair young maid as you are from being an honest young goblin!" Lythande grumbled and hoped that the goblin was not for once telling the truth. "Does it seem to you that I am a fair young maid?"

"Nay. All the world knows Lythande the greatest of magicians!" wept the goblin at her feet.

"From you I ask this in fee; if any maidens be ensnared by the goblin fruit, redeem them in my name," said Lythande at once in haste to be free of that village and the goblins. She threw down some bits of silver and departed immediately.

When Lythande passed next through the village there was no sign of any habitation: the great barn was locked and shuttered and falling down. And on the ancient wooden sign, faded and decrepit, were the words:

Goblin Market
CLOSED

THE GRATITUDE OF KINGS
Marion Zimmer Bradley & Elisabeth Waters

Lythande, Adept of the Blue Star, mercenary magician, and sometime minstrel, entered the inner courtyard of the royal castle of Tschardain still accompanied by four guards. Twelve more had split off from the traveling party in the outer courtyard. It had been quite an escort for one solitary magician, who needed no guards at all for safety, but Lythande knew that their master liked to make showy gestures, especially if other people were doing the work involved. No doubt he was thrilled to be able to send out such a large party of men to escort one magician. He was not motivated by chivalry; the fact that she was a woman was Lythande's deepest secret, the one that guarded her magical powers. Lythande had, on a few occasions, even killed to keep that secret. If she were proclaimed a woman in the hearing of any man, the Power of the Blue Star would be gone from her and she would die.

In truth, Lythande was not entirely sure that she wished to be here. The guard captain sent to summon her had informed her that his master would be most grateful if the magician would accept this invitation to his coronation, and Lythande, in her many centuries of life, was not without experience in the "gratitude" of kings. She had dealt briefly with Tashgan about ten years before, when his two elder brothers died and left him as his father's sole heir. Then he had been Prince Tashgan the wandering minstrel, who traveled each year from his father's court to Northwander and back, drinking and womanizing the entire way. His travels had not been entirely voluntary; his route and the duration of his stay in each place were enforced by a spell on his lute, set by the court magician at his brothers' request. They had made certain that he could not remain in one place long enough to gather allies who would plot against them, but when their deaths made him his father's heir the spell had been a real problem. Lythande had traded lutes with him, enabling him to go home to the kingdom he was to inherit; and, so far as she knew, he had been content with that solution.

Lythande was curious to see what settling down had done to Tashgan. The guards told her only that his father had died at long last and that Tashgan required her services. And it was certainly more pleasant to travel with other people who were doing the hard work at campsites and paying the reckoning at the inns.

The journey into the mountains of Tschardain was a surprisingly easy one. The biggest problem was that a couple of the guards seemed to be terrified of Lythande—or perhaps merely of magicians in general. The climate was mild for early winter, the inns were comfortable and close enough together for a leisurely journey, and the roads were well maintained. Nevertheless Lythande was surprised to see, as they approached the castle, what appeared to be a respectable-size trade fair being set up in a flat expanse of rock below the castle walls. She started to ask the guards about it, but the captain said hastily that it was just the trade fair, they did it every year, it wouldn't start until the morrow, it was nothing to concern the master magician, and Lord Tashgan was waiting, so if it would please the honorable magician to accompany them... Lythande suspected that the poor man would have dragged her into the castle by the hair, if he had only dared.

The inner courtyard was full of people hard at work, preparing for Tashgan's coronation as High King of Tschardain. The noise was incredible, the air was full of smoke and dust—and a sudden streak of cobalt-blue fire. The guard on Lythande's left, a young man who had been nervous the entire trip, gasped and ducked as the fire passed right over his head and straight toward Lythande's shoulder. Even though her cloak was fire-proof, Lythande disliked having to twist her head to speak to anything on her shoulder; it was such an awkward angle. Murmuring a spell to fireproof her skin, she calmly put up a hand and the salamander landed on her left wrist, enabling her to hold it in front of her. As she had suspected, she recognized the creature. While most people looking at it would see only a ball of flame, or, if they looked closely, a miniature dragon with flames licking about its form, Lythande had worked with elementals many times in her long career and could distinguish their differences as well as their similarities.

"Greetings, Essence of Fire," Lythande said gravely. The guards looked startled, and the nervous one shied away in fear, staring wide-eyed at Lythande. Lythande ignored them and lifted the salamander so that they were eye-to-eye. "Is Eirthe here, Alnath?" she asked.

The salamander streaked off through the air again, clearing a path behind it. Lythande followed, ignoring the pair of guards who hurried after her.

The flaming trail led to a roped-off work area at one side of the courtyard. Alnath dove into the fire beneath a large cauldron of wax. The dark-haired woman bending over it scarcely spared the salamander a glance as she carefully dipped a row of slender candles suspended from a wooden bar from the cauldron, lifted them out, and set them on the rack to wait for the latest coat of blue wax to dry. Then she looked up, met Lythande's eyes, and smiled. "Lythande. So they did find you."

"As you see," Lythande replied. Eirthe Candlemaker had been a friend of Lythande's for more than a decade. She was one of the few women now living who knew Lythande's secret. Although everyone who had known Lythande before she became an Adept was now long dead, from time to time a woman would discover what Lythande truly was. As long as Lythande could trust the woman not to betray her—and as long as none of Lythande's enemies suspected that the woman knew anything worth torturing her for—Lythande could have these women as friends. Such friendships were, necessarily, rare, and this was one Lythande particularly valued.

By now Eirthe must be in her mid-thirties, but she still looked like a girl of twenty, except for her hands, which were scarred and burned from years of handling hot wax, fire, and Alnath. "What brings you here, Eirthe?" Lythande asked. "You are far from home."

"The funeral, the coronation, the wedding, and the trade fair, not necessarily in that order," Eirthe answered briefly, picking up another row of candles and dipping them into the melted wax in their turn.

"I saw the fairgrounds on the way in," Lythande said, "but I still do not understand why. Is this not a rather out-of-the-way place for a trade fair?" Tschardain was tucked away in a mountainous region, well south of the more populated areas of the continent.

"It's Lord Tashgan's main contribution to the kingdom's economy," Eirthe explained. "He arranged the first one the year after he came back here, inviting many of us from Old Gandrin." She smiled fondly. "I think he missed us, once he no longer came to our fair each spring, so he brought us to him. Some of us remain through Yule-tide as well; Tashgan is a gracious host. I usually stay for a while—it's not as if I had any family left to spend the season with." For an instant Eirthe looked sad, then she pulled her thoughts back to business. "The fair is actually fairly profitable; he holds it the week before the Yule-feast, so everyone is shopping for gifts. There's also a pass through the eastern mountains between Tschardain and Valantia, which is the trade center for everything on their side of the mountains. That's where his bride comes from."

"So Tashgan is marrying. How interesting." Lythande forced her features into a suitably grave expression.

Eirthe didn't even try. She grinned openly. "Well, he does need an heir—he's the last of his family left. You should start thinking of suitable music for the wedding; it will be celebrated a week from today."

"Is *that* why he had me come all this way?" Few things in life truly surprised Lythande after the first few centuries, but it did seem that Tashgan could have found a musician closer to home. In fact, he fancied himself quite a musician—or had when Lythande had seen him last—so surely he must have at least one minstrel at his court. "I suppose I should go present myself to him," she added, "and leave you to your work."

"It is true that I still have a lot to do," Eirthe admitted. "I always come early for the fair, so I have plenty of time to make candles here instead of having to transport them, but I wasn't counting on the funeral and all the rest." She picked up another row of candles. "I'll see you later."

"You are well come to my court, Master Magician," Tashgan said, smiling broadly. From his voice one would have supposed Lythande to be his oldest and dearest friend. Tashgan sat in an elaborately carved wooden chair on a stone dais at the end of the great hall. A fire roared in the hearth behind him in addition to the large fires in the side hearths, so the room was comfortably warm—or at least as warm as any stone room in a castle could be.

Two women sat with him: the younger an absolutely gorgeous young woman who sat on a slightly less ornate chair next to his right. She had long midnight-black hair curling at the ends and sapphire-blue eyes which looked out of a face that could have been carved of marble or alabaster, except for the rose color in her cheeks. Her features were so perfectly symmetrical and regular that she could truthfully be called inhumanly beautiful. She looked a very well-made doll. A much older woman flowed over a stool on the girl's other side. Her heavy body was dressed in concealing dark clothing, and she had thin tight lips and a discontented expression.

Tashgan eyed the leather case on Lythande's back. "Is that a new lute? You must play for us after dinner," he continued, giving Lythande no chance to reply.

Lythande bowed silently in assent. She never minded playing; music had been her first love, before she came to know magic, and it was still an important part of her. Besides that, the practice of music held much less potential for disaster than that of magic.

"Certainly music is a much more appropriate profession for a man than magic is," snapped the elderly woman sitting on the dais.

Tashgan smiled again, but with the air of a man trying to be polite while listening once again to an argument he had heard too many times already. "I am sure that Lythande will change your mind about men and magic, Lady," he said. Then he turned to Lythande again. "Permit me to present you to my promised bride, Princess Velvet of Valantia," Lythande bowed to the Princess, who nodded a bit stiffly in return, "and this is her lady-in-waiting, Lady Mirwen."

Lythande bowed again, less deeply, but Lady Mirwen simply sniffed and turned away. *Apparently she does not wish the acquaintance*, Lythande thought. *Princess Velvet seems merely shy. How does she come to this marriage? Did Tashgan pick her for her name? He was ever fond of fine fabrics.*

Tashgan continued speaking, turning to Lady Mirwen. "Lythande will be my Champion in the Marriage Games."

This produced an outraged gasp. "That is completely impossible! A man cannot work magic—especially in such a delicate matter. Women are the only ones with the proper delicacy of touch and subtlety of feeling."

Subtlety of feeling? Lythande thought with a touch of amusement. *That woman would not know 'subtle' if it walked up and introduced itself to her.*

"Lady Mirwen," Tashgan said firmly. "This is my country, not yours. I am willing to conform to your customs so far as to include your rituals in my wedding, but the choice of Champion is mine, and I will not be bound by your customs there. I have dealt with female magicians—my father's Court Magician when I was young was a woman—and I have dealt with Lythande, and I choose Lythande."

"My lord?" Princess Velvet murmured softly at his side.

Tashgan turned to her with an indulgent smile. "Yes, my lady?"

"What happened to your father's Court Magician? Did you turn her away when you came to the throne?"

Tashgan shook his head. "No, indeed. Within her abilities, Ellifanwy was extremely skilled at her job. Unfortunately, she chose to venture outside her area of competence. She died in a were-dragon's lair years ago, before I ever came back to court."

"And what did *you* consider her area of competence to be?" Lady Mirwen asked. From her tone, she appeared to think there was no reason for her to be even polite to her charge's future husband. The Blue Star between Lythande's brows prickled. She had been aware ever since she entered the hall that there was magic at work here. This woman had magic, that much was sure; but something felt dreadfully wrong. This marriage was more—or maybe less—than it seemed. "Love spells?" Mirwen inquired scathingly.

Tashgan was momentarily speechless, which Lythande felt to be just as well—love spells were *exactly* what he had considered to be the pinnacle of Ellifanwy's work. But Lythande had known Ellifanwy as well, and while the woman had not been in Lythande's class—or anywhere near it—she had possessed strong skills in several areas. "Actually," Lythande said, before Tashgan could recover enough to open his mouth and blurt out anything unfortunate, "she was famous for her binding spells. Things she bound *stayed* bound." *Like that lute of Tashgan's.*

"Even beyond her death," Tashgan agreed. "Were she still with us, Lady Mirwen, perhaps I would chose her as your opponent, but, alas, she is no longer here. As you seem to doubt a man's abilities in this matter, surely you do not fear to match yourself against Lythande."

"Certainly not!" the woman snapped.

"Before I agree to this matter," Lythande said smoothly, "perhaps someone would care to explain just what it involves. 'Marriage Games' could be anything—from animated banquet sweets up to a magical duel to the death, although I should think anything that drastic would cast a damper on the festivities."

"Isn't that just like a man," Mirwen said, "always thinking of death."

You inspire such thoughts in me, Lady, Lythande thought wryly, but said nothing aloud.

Princess Velvet took a deep breath and replied, "They are a contest of skill, Master Magician. The two sorceresses—er, sorcerers—vie to see who can create the most fantastic and beautiful illusions." She looked nervously at Lythande and added, "In Valantia, it is generally women who practice this sort of sorcery, but I don't believe that there is anything which forbids a man to do so—if he wants to, I mean." She looked nervously at Lady Mirwen and then at Prince Tashgan. He smiled dotingly at her and reached over to take her hand.

"Have you seen many of these contests, Princess?" Lythande asked.

Velvet nodded. "I have nine older sisters, and I attended all their weddings."

"'Most fantastic and beautiful,'" Lythande mused aloud. "Who judges these contests?"

"The wedding guests do," Velvet replied. "Everyone except the bride and groom."

"The bride and groom presumably having other things on their minds?" Lythande asked smiling.

Velvet blushed and looked at her lap. Tashgan chuckled.

"Very well, Lord Tashgan," Lythande said. "I shall serve as your Champion in the Marriage Games."

"Excellent," Tashgan said enthusiastically. "I am most grateful to you. I know that you will make my wedding day a day that will be long remembered in my kingdom."

Somehow I feel certain it will be, Lythande thought, *although it may not be in the way any of us expects. I have an odd feeling about this...*

"I shall have my Chamberlain escort you to your suite," Tashgan continued, raising a hand to beckon the man forward. "We have put you next to Eirthe Candlemaker—as I recall, you and she are great friends."

From the smirk on his face, he had—and was giving everyone in the room—entirely the wrong idea of what kind of friends Lythande and Eirthe were, but Lythande did not doubt that Eirthe could take care of her own reputation. Besides, she suspected that this was his way of telling her that he knew she had stopped to talk to Eirthe in the courtyard on her way in. "As your Highness says," she replied, bowing, before she turned to follow the Chamberlain. She intended to have a long talk with Eirthe in any case; the younger woman could doubtless tell her a good deal about the current situation.

Lythande's suite was luxurious indeed; Tashgan was apparently displaying his gratitude to her with more than mere words. Eirthe's room was next to Lythande's but Eirthe was not there, even after dinner when it was dark outside. Lythande, forbidden by her vows to eat or drink in the sight of any man, had eaten alone in her suite, so she did not know whether Eirthe had been at dinner or not, and she had not seen the candlemaker among the people who gathered in the Hall after dinner to listen to her play her lute. She frowned thoughtfully and headed back to the inner courtyard.

Eirthe was still dipping candles, one rod after another, in a smooth unbroken rhythm. She had obviously melted a new pot of wax; this batch was golden instead of blue. She had plenty of light to work by; in a circle around her were eight of Cadmon's goblets, each with a ball of fire inside it.

Cadmon and Eirthe had been partners until Cadmon's death; they had been under curses which canceled each other. Until Eirthe, with some assistance from Lythande, had managed to free herself from her curse, nothing would burn near her, nor would any candles she made. Cadmon had been a glassblower, but anything flammable put in his glass burned up in an instant. Anything that was *not* usually flammable would burn at a normal speed as if it were flammable. Put together, his glassware and Eirthe's candles made excellent lamps; and in the fire pit he made for her one could burn even rocks.

Alnath's favorite resting place was a piece Cadmon had originally intended as a fishbowl. Any fish put in it would have been broiled to charcoal before it could be dumped out, but it was the perfect home for a salamander. At the minute, however, Alnath was in the fire under the cauldron, which, Lythande knew, was her normal place when Eirthe was working.

Lythande crossed between two of the goblets, frowning as she felt the faint flicker of a very simple warding spell. "Eirthe, what is going on here?" she demanded.

Eirthe looked up as she switched rods. "If you mean the warding spell, it's to keep people from getting burned. Between the salamanders, the fire, and the wax dripping, this is a dangerous area for the unwary. Tashgan *does* tend to choose his servants for their looks rather than their brains."

"That is true enough," Lythande agreed. Then Eirthe's earlier words registered. "Salamanders?" She took a closer look at the goblets around her. "Sweet Queen of Life, where did they all come from?"

"Alnath had babies last year," Eirthe informed her. "She comes into heat—no pun intended—every six years or so, but last year was the first time there was another salamander around when she did."

"How can you tell that a salamander is in heat?" Lythande was genuinely curious. Alnath was the only salamander she had ever spent much time with, and the only thing taught on the subject in the course of her magical studies was that salamanders were the elementals associated with fire and were considered capricious and dangerous. Of course, all elementals were considered capricious and dangerous—and so, frequently, were the elements they represented.

Eirthe laughed. "I can feel it through my link with her. It makes me restless and snappish; when she actually mated I didn't dare be around another human being for two weeks. And she must emit a scent or something like it, because Cadmon always used to sneeze when he was around and she was in heat. It was really awkward; it isn't regular enough to predict, and he couldn't blow glass while he was sneezing. After the first time, I took her off into the countryside to get both of us away from people, but it was still a real disruption to our business."

"I can see that it would be," Lythande agreed. "At the moment, however, they are certainly giving you enough light to work by. But why are you working so late?"

Eirthe sighed, and rubbed her middle back. "The trade fair starts at midday tomorrow; the funeral used up half of what I planned to sell there, and there's still the coronation and wedding."

"Can I help?" Lythande asked. She wanted to talk to Eirthe, and they were unlikely to be disturbed here.

"Have you ever dipped candles before?" Eirthe asked.

"Actually, I have," Lythande replied.

Eirthe's eyebrows rose skeptically. "Within the last century?"

"More like two," Lythande admitted. "But I think I can still manage to dip plain tapers."

Eirthe stood back and gestured to the next rod. "Very well, give it a try."

Lythande picked up the rod by the ends, positioned it over the cauldron, and smoothly dipped the candles into the wax until they were covered to same depth Eirthe had been using. Without pausing she pulled them straight up again, and held them over the pot as the new coat of wax ran down their sides and dripped off their bases. When the worst of the dripping stopped, she put the rod back on the rack, picked up the next rod, and repeated the process.

"Not bad," Eirthe said. "If you can finish this batch, it will let me get a start on the ornamental candles for the marriage feast." She grinned at Lythande, and added, "We can talk while we work. Despite the gossip from the Hall, I don't think you came looking for me for the sake of my beautiful brown eyes."

Lythande gave a mellow chuckle as she continued to dip the candles. The repetitive motion was soothing, rather like playing finger exercises on her lute. "You are correct, Eirthe. I find I am woefully behind on the gossip here. Tell me about this marriage and what you know of the people involved."

Eirthe pulled a stool next to the fire, carried over a small work table, and set it up next to Lythande. One side of the table held several blocks of pure white wax with wicks coming out of their tops and the other side had a narrow tray holding a number of thin silver tools that were obviously used to carve the wax. She picked up the first block and, with a few swift strokes, carved it into the shape of a man, robed and crowned.

"Prince Tashgan you know: third son of Idriash, King and High Lord of Tschardain, trained in minstrelry, self-trained in wenching and drinking. His father was ill for decades, and the Vizier ran the kingdom. He still does, although when Tashgan came home after his brothers' deaths he did take some slight interest in how his future kingdom was managed. Now that it *is* his, I expect he'll continue to let the Vizier do most of the work and make most of the decisions. The trade fair is a good example of how it works: Tashgan decided he wanted his own trade fair, he told the Vizier, and the Vizier made sure that all of the details were taken care of so that what Tashgan wanted happened. Of course, the kingdom makes a handsome profit off it as well, which makes the Vizier happy." She carved a good likeness of Tashgan's face into the wax she held, then placed it carefully in the exact center of the work table, setting her tools in a tray at the table's side.

Lythande, who had just finished dipping another rod of candles, froze in astonishment as Eirthe held her hands on either side of the candle figure and chanted softly. A glow radiated from her hands and surrounded the figure, and when she fell silent and dropped her hands, it was no longer white. Now it was a perfect likeness of Tashgan, from the color of his skin, hair, and eyes to the gold of his crown. "What are you doing?" she asked in astonishment, even as the prickling running through the blue star on her forehead answered her. "I did not know you could work magic!"

Eirthe shrugged, picking up the candle. "It seems I always had some natural aptitude for it—Alnath has been with me since I was a small child. After all the confusion with the volcano when we were getting rid of the curse on me, I decided that I should learn more about it before I killed myself or someone else. So I spent a couple of years at the College in Northwander. Now I can do a few simple spells, and I have a much better idea of what to avoid doing if I want to stay out of trouble."

"Very sensible of you," Lythande said approvingly, remembering the incident to which Eirthe referred. The 'confusion' with the volcano had occurred when the volcano demanded Lythande as a sacrifice to keep it from erupting. They had both had a narrow escape that time. "But making wax figures in the likeness of living people can be a dangerous thing."

"I know." Eirthe unlocked a metal trunk sitting in the far corner of her work area and took out a small wooden box lined with straw. She packed the Tashgan candle into it, closed it securely, and relocked the trunk. "I keep them locked up, with at least three salamanders guarding them at all times, and when they are burned at the feast, I'll be sitting near them. And these aren't magically similar representations of the people involved; they merely look like them. It's just a superficial likeness, not a true similarity. If it were not so, they could not be burned without harming the people they resemble."

"Are you sure?" Lythande asked. "Have you done this before?"

"Several times," Eirthe assured her. "I did one of Alnath first, and then several of myself, before I tried doing one of anyone else. I don't give them away still formed; they're always burned in my presence. Nobody has ever been harmed by these candles, and I intend to keep it that way." She spoke grimly, and Lythande remembered that it was Eirthe's refusal to make candles for a wizard who wanted to use them in an extortion scheme that had caused him to put his Cold Curse on her.

"I know you would never use them to harm someone," she assured the candle maker. "But if they aren't used for magic, why do people want them made?"

"Vanity," Eirthe said simply. "It's a bit like having a portrait painted, but it also shows that one is rich enough that one can afford to pay for the work and then have it destroyed."

Lythande laughed. "I know that sort of vanity well. It enriches the minstrel as well as the craftsman."

"That is truth," Eirthe agreed, picking up a second of the plain white blocks and beginning to carve the folds of a long dress. "Now Tashgan is King, and he needs a Queen. Or, rather, he needs heirs—legitimate ones—and he wants a useful alliance. So we have Princess Velvet of Valantia. She's the twelfth of thirteen children, eleven of them girls; and Valantia and Tschardain have trade interests in common. So her father gets rid of another daughter and can pay her dowry in trade concessions rather than hard cash."

"What does Tashgan get out of this?" Lythande asked. "Other than a beautiful princess, of course."

"Valantia's major product is their wines."

Lythande's lips twitched as she continued dipping candles in a steady rhythm. "I feel certain that was a major consideration."

"To Tashgan, at least," Eirthe agreed. "And the Vizier approves, so the marriage should do well enough..." her voice trailed off uncertainly. "Lythande?"

Lythande set down the last of the tapers she had been dipping and moved to Eirthe's side. While she had been working her way through the batch of tapers, Eirthe had finished another candle and set it in place for the spell to add its color. Lythande's frown as she studied it matched Eirthe's. "That is not Princess Velvet."

Eirthe chewed on her lip, picked up the candle and turned it over in her hands. "It's supposed to be," she said, "but it doesn't look quite like her. I've never had this happen before. Is there someone else's magic influencing me?"

Lythande took a deep breath, gripped the hilt of the magical dagger she wore under her robe, and cast her mind about the area. "There's quite a bit of magic in this castle," she said after a moment, "too much to identify it all without going into a full trance. But the simple answer is no. There is no magic influencing the work you are currently doing save your own."

"But that would mean that this is what Princess Velvet truly looks like—" Eirthe stared wide-eyed at Lythande. "Oh, Lord and Lady..."

"Finish the spell," Lythande ordered firmly. "Add the color."

Eirthe's hands trembled slightly as she put the figure down, and she stared at it in silence for a long moment. In the quiet, Lythande heard the voices of the guards exchanging greetings on the walls of the outer courtyard, and the soft whispers of salamanders basking in the faintly crackling fire. Then Eirthe placed her hands, now steady, about the figure and chanted the spell. When the glow died both women studied the figure intently.

"She's rather pretty," Eirthe ventured at last. "She has a kind face."

"And medium brown hair, pale grey eyes, and, I believe, freckles," Lythande sighed. "Can you imagine what Tashgan is going to say?"

"No," Eirthe said. "My imagination isn't that good."

"Why would anyone bespell her to change her appearance?" Lythande wondered. "Who would do such a thing? Who benefits by it?"

"Tashgan does," Eirthe said. "He likes beauty. And Velvet both benefits and is harmed by it."

"What do you mean?" Lythande asked.

"She probably wasn't given any choice about marrying him," Eirthe pointed out, "but her life will be vastly more pleasant if he likes her. He likes things which are beautiful, so he's disposed to like her now. But if she knows that her beauty is the result of a spell and not her true appearance, she knows that what he likes about her is an illusion, a lie." She shrugged. "I don't know Velvet well, but that would make *me* very unhappy."

Who here specializes in illusions? Lythande asked herself. "Lady Mirwen," Lythande said aloud. "Make a candle of her, and tell me about her."

"It would have to be magically similar to tell us much of anything," Eirthe pointed out. "And I don't do magically similar candles."

"You know how," Lythande said. "You can do it if you choose. I do not seek to harm the woman; I want only information. You may keep the candle and take what safeguards you wish."

"Very well," Eirthe said slowly. She opened the trunk again, packed the Velvet candle in a box, and buried it in the bottom layer before relocking the trunk. Then she picked up the next block of wax and began to carve it. Her brow furrowed in concentration, and she hummed something Lythande couldn't quite catch. Lythande stood watching intently, ignoring the prickling sensation of the blue star on her forehead.

When the spell was finished the candle was a chimera, the face of Lady Mirwen on the body of a very fat spider. Eirthe regarded it in dismay. "Oh, dear," she sighed.

"I think we have our spell-caster," Lythande said mildly. "Something about that woman has bothered me from the moment I met her, and you have captured what I feel about her most clearly."

"So what do we do now?" Eirthe said faintly. Lythande studied her. Her face was pale and her hands were trembling.

"You lock these candles up, and we put the trunk in my room," Lythande said, dropping her voice to a whisper to make very certain that no one would overhear them. "Then we both go to bed. Tomorrow, we talk to Princess Velvet."

"What about the tapers?" Eirthe looked at the drying rack. "Oh, you've finished them. Can you pour the wax remaining in the cauldron into that cube over there?" She pointed to one of the row of wooden cubes she used to store and transport solid wax.

Lythande nodded, carried the cube to sit next to the cauldron, and tipped the cauldron on its hook until the melted wax had all run into the cube. She was amused to notice that several of the baby salamanders came to help melt out the last drops. *Eirthe has quite a team working here.*

Eirthe relocked the trunk, and each of them took a handle. Escorted by a flight of salamanders they took the back stairs to their rooms, where Lythande set the trunk against the stone wall at the far side of her room and spelled it to stay locked, closed, and bound to the wall. "This will stay untouched unless the whole building comes down," she said reassuringly, "but if you want some of the salamanders to stay with it, I have no objection."

Eirthe, who had collapsed in the nearest chair as soon as she set down her side of the trunk, nodded wearily. Alnath and two smaller balls of flame settled down on top of the trunk.

Lythande, seeing that Eirthe had clearly reached the end of her resources for one day, marched the woman next door to her assigned room, stripped the swaying body down to her shift, and tucked her into bed. As she closed Eirthe's door behind her and returned to her own room, two guardsmen passed by at the end of the hallway. They eyed Lythande curiously, saying nothing as they tried unsuccessfully to keep speculative grins from showing.

Eirthe recovered quickly; the knock on Lythande's door the next morning came at what Lythande considered an indecently early hour. Rolling out of bed and throwing on the concealing mage-robe, she went to let the candlemaker in. Three salamanders flew from the trunk to mingle with the group accompanying Eirthe.

"They say that all was quiet last night," Eirthe said. "I am glad." Then she looked more closely at Lythande. "Did I wake you? The sun has been up for almost an hour."

"How nice for the sun," Lythande growled.

Eirthe's lips twitched. "Shall I order breakfast? You will probably feel better once you have eaten."

"Only if you want your reputation to be completely ruined," Lythande replied. "A couple of guards were in the corridor when I left your room last night."

Eirthe chuckled. "We can order breakfast from here and confuse them all. You need not worry about my reputation; Tashgan values me for my craft, not my virtue or lack thereof." She crossed the room to tug on the bell-pull. "Besides," she added, "most of the people here already think I'm Tashgan's discarded mistress. Why else would I be housed in the castle at all—much less in such luxury?"

"I wondered about that myself," Lythande admitted. "Why are you housed in the castle?"

Eirthe laughed. "The first year the fair was held—before the Vizier had the roads fixed—the weather was bad and my wagon got stuck in the mud a few miles away. There weren't very many people here then, so Tashgan allowed me to stay in the castle. The next year my room was ready for me when I arrived, and by the third year, of course, it had become a tradition for me to stay in the castle. I have no idea what, if anything, Tashgan was thinking, but I admit it's very nice to be indoors with servants to look after me."

"Perhaps you remind him of a time when he was young and carefree," Lythande suggested, "before he had to stay in one place and settle down."

"Probably," Eirthe agreed, going to the door to admit the servant she had summoned.

Lythande sank into a chair and pulled her hood to shadow her face while Eirthe dealt with the girl. She didn't move until Eirthe bolted the door behind the servant who had brought their food and handed the magician a full plate.

"The salamanders are all female," Eirthe said, "in case that matters to the rules you follow."

"It matters not," Lythande said, beginning to eat. Eirthe was right; food did make her feel at least a bit better. "It is only in the company of men that I am forbidden to eat or drink. If my companions are not human, their gender is not important."

After breakfast they set off in search of Princess Velvet. "We need not worry about encountering Tashgan," Eirthe explained. "He sleeps most of the morning."

"And Lady Mirwen?" Lythande asked skeptically.

"I sent Alnath to look. Mirwen is in the courtyard with the Vizier, and the Princess is in the solar."

"Not much of a chaperone, is she?" the magician commented.

"Just as well for us," Eirthe pointed out. "Alnath will keep watch and warn us if Lady Mirwen is coming."

"Very well," Lythande said. "Follow me and do not speak until we reach the solar." She led the way across the Great Hall and up the stairs to the solar, casting a minor glamour to keep anyone from seeing them. Princess Velvet was indeed in the solar, curled up on a cushioned window ledge intent on the book she was reading. Lythande dropped the spell and cleared her throat. The Princess squeaked in surprise and shoved the book under the cushion before looking up to see who had entered.

Eirthe laughed softly. "You need not hide the book on our account, Highness. I was here when you arrived; I know that half your baggage was books."

"Oh." Velvet looked at her with interest. "Do you like books?"

"Oh, yes," Eirthe responded. "Half my things are books, too—they are much more interesting than clothes or jewels."

Velvet looked down at her dress, which was twisted around her legs and showing both her ankles. Blushing, she stood up and straightened her skirts. "I beg your pardon, Lord Magician," she said to Lythande.

"No need for that," Lythande said dryly. "I am not young enough to be inflamed to madness by the sight of a woman's ankles." She realized belatedly that this was not reassuring; the Princess looked as if she wished to sink through the floor.

Eirthe glared at Lythande. To the girl she said, "Lythande is several centuries old and no longer remembers how it feels to be young and easily embarrassed. Pay him no heed."

Velvet looked shocked at this lack of respect for a great magician. "Did you wish to speak to me, Lord Magician?" she asked Lythande.

"As it happens," Lythande replied, "I do. First, where is your lady-in-waiting?"

Velvet's bland mask dropped and her face suddenly wore an astonishing look of cynicism. "Off chasing after the Vizier. She will probably be gone for at least another hour—she has spent each morning since our arrival with him."

"Wants to be the power behind the throne, does she?" Lythande's centuries of experience were suddenly quite apparent.

Velvet shrugged. The blank-faced innocent look was completely gone now. "Why else would she leave home and come to a foreign land? I assure you that it was not for love of me."

"Has she cast any spells on you that you know of?" Lythande inquired.

Velvet's eyes rounded in surprise. "Not that I know of," she said uneasily. "You think I am bespelled." It was not a question.

"Eirthe." At Lythande's command Eirthe put the candle figure of Princess Velvet on the table in the center of the room. The sun, streaming in through the eastern window cast a glow around it. Lythande turned to Velvet. "Can you tell us what this is, Princess?"

Velvet picked it up and turned it over in her hands. Then she smiled at Eirthe. "Did you make this?" Eirthe nodded. "It is an excellent likeness," the princess said. "You have a great gift."

"This looks like you?" Lythande asked.

Velvet looked at Lythande as if doubting the magician's sanity. "Yes, Lord Magician."

"Have you seen a mirror since you arrived here?" Lythande demanded.

"No." Velvet looked uneasy. "I never paid much attention to my looks. I have so many sisters that I never expected to marry, and in an arranged marriage, a princess's looks are much less important than her dowry. I do not even own a mirror—I'm the twelfth child, and mirrors are very expensive."

"True," Lythande agreed, "but they are useful in certain spells, so I always carry one." She pulled a small mirror from her belt pouch and handed it to the princess. "Look at yourself now."

Velvet stared into the mirror, gasped, and ran her hand over her lips as if to be certain that it was her own reflection in the mirror. "I look like one of my father's mistresses," she exclaimed in horror. "They're the only women I know of who use face paint. Is this some sorcery of yours, Lord Magician?"

"Sorcery, yes," Lythande replied, "but not mine."

Velvet thrust the mirror back at Lythande, who took it and put it back into her belt pouch. "Can you remove this spell?" she asked anxiously. "I do not wish to go through the rest of my life looking like this! I look like a doll!"

"I could remove the spell quite easily," Lythande said, "but consider: this is how Lord Tashgan thinks you look." Velvet sank back onto the window ledge with a soft moan and buried her face in her hands. Lythande hoped the girl would not start crying. "And your lady-in-waiting doubtless had her reasons for changing your appearance," the mage added. That brought Velvet's face out of her hands, her expression a thoughtful frown as she stared at Lythande and Eirthe.

"How did you find out that it was not my true appearance?" Velvet asked.

"Lord Tashgan asked me to make candles of both of you for the wedding feast," Eirthe explained. "And although I saw the illusion when I looked at you with my eyes, when I made the candle, it came out as you see." She gestured to the candle, which Velvet had put back on the table. "So I asked Lythande why what I made did not match what I had seen."

Velvet rose and walked around the table, studying the candle. "Could you make a candle of Lady Mirwen?" she asked. "I would like to know what *she* would look like."

"I did," Eirthe said soberly. "It came out with her head on the body of a giant spider."

Velvet giggled. "You do indeed have a gift." Then she sobered. "But this isn't funny. She must be plotting something even more devious than her usual schemes." She frowned. "We have not been here long, but even I can tell that the Vizier is the one who truly runs the kingdom. And Lady Mirwen has always regarded people as expendable tools. My father does not like her; that is why she was able to gain his consent to accompany me to my new home. But he is a man—" she broke off, looking quickly at Lythande. "I mean to say that he does not see the side of her that she shows only in the women's quarters."

"You do not seem a stranger to palace intrigue yourself, Princess," Lythande said smoothly.

"But I am," Velvet said, twisting her hands nervously in front of her, "especially compared to Lady Mirwen. She has practiced it as long as I can remember, while I have done nothing but observe from the sidelines. I wasn't expected to marry, and I'm not a particular favorite of my father's, so I was not important enough to bother with."

"Interesting as all this is," Eirthe said. "I have candles to finish before the fair starts, and I need to get back to work. Are we certain that it was Lady Mirwen who changed your appearance?"

"I am certain," Velvet said grimly. "She made me wear a veil from the moment we approached the border until we arrived here, and while we were traveling she came to my room each night to brush my hair and help me prepare for bed—which she never bothered to do before." The princess frowned. "She still comes each night, but I doubt she will once I marry Tashgan." She looked up at Lythande. "Could she be using this illusion to distract him, to keep him from noticing her and wondering what she is doing?"

Eirthe picked up the candle and packed it back into its small straw-lined box. "If I wanted to distract Lord Tashgan, a beautiful girl is one of the surest methods I know of."

Alnath returned, streaking through the open window and landing on the wrist Eirthe held up for her. Eirthe had no difficulty interpreting the salamander's message. "Lady Mirwen is on her way here," she informed Lythande.

"We must go." Lythande bowed to the princess. "Highness, if you think of anything more I should know, you may tell Eirthe. She has worked with me before and is to be trusted. And it would be better if your lady-in-waiting did not know that you and I have spoken together."

"Of course, Lord Magician," Velvet nodded regally, then added anxiously, "but you will remove this spell, will you not?"

Lythande smiled at the girl. "If you truly wish it, it will be my wedding gift to you."

"Start thinking of a way to explain it to Tashgan," Eirthe advised as Lythande pulled her toward the door. "Good luck!"

Eirthe spent the rest of the morning making candles and moving her stock around until she was satisfied that it was displayed to the best advantage, while Lythande prowled the castle, the outbuildings, and the fairgrounds, stopping occasionally to sing a few songs where people were gathered, and always listening to whatever was being said around her. Unfortunately, while some of it was mildly interesting, none of it was any particular help.

The fair opened formally at noon, with a speech of welcome from the Vizier. After the formalities were over Lythande followed him as he went through the fair, speaking to each merchant and checking for any last minute problems. She was pleased to observe that he appeared to be well-liked and competent.

Not that Tashgan isn't well-liked, Lythande thought to herself, *but his areas of competence are rather limited. He needs a good Vizier, and he's very lucky to have this one.*

Lythande spent the next three days wandering around the fairground, looking at all the different merchandise, thinking of possible illusions for the Marriage Games, and pausing frequently to play for the fairgoers. She stopped by at least once each day to see Eirthe, who was selling her stock almost as fast as she could make it. It seemed to Lythande that Eirthe was selling enough candles to light every home in the kingdom at least through the winter, if not until next Yule.

On the fourth day, Prince Tashgan's old lute arrived. Lythande, who was standing a short distance Eirthe's booth, was surprised to see a woman, past her first youth but still very beautiful, approach the candlemaker's stall. The hood of her cloak was thrown back, revealing braided loops of long golden hair and the cloak hung open in the front, showing off a dress of green silk with gold dragons embroidered on it. The woman certainly did not appear feel the cold. Lythande, recognizing her at once even after ten years and many adventures, *knew* she didn't feel the cold. Then again, she wasn't really a woman.

"Mistress Candlemaker," the woman greeted Eirthe. "I see you have been blessed." A wave of her hand indicated the salamanders.

"Lady Beauty," Eirthe smiled. "How good to see you again. Yes, Alnath had babies last summer. Aren't they wonderful?"

"They're lovely," Beauty said with unmistakable sincerity. "Speaking of children, I hear that dear Lord Tashgan is finally going to marry. Have you seen his bride? What is she like?"

"Very young," Eirthe replied, "but she seems like a nice girl." She shrugged. "It's a political arrangement, of course."

"Of course." The lady in green smiled, showing rather a lot of teeth. "I must go up to the castle and congratulate the dear boy." She turned away and walked off, giving Lythande an excellent view of Tashgan's lute case slung across her back.

Lythande gave Beauty plenty of time to get beyond earshot before approaching Eirthe. "What do you know of that creature?" she inquired, careful to keep her voice low.

"Lady Beauty?" Eirthe asked, looking at Lythande in surprise. "She's an old friend of Tashgan's; she comes here every year at this time. She's an excellent musician—perhaps you saw the lute?"

"Eirthe," Lythande said urgently. "How long does she stay here when she comes?"

"Five days," Eirthe said. "Why? Do you need to avoid her?"

"Where else have you seen her?"

"She comes to the Fair at Old Gandrin each year," Eirthe replied promptly, "and she was in Northwander at mid-summer both the years I was there." She frowned. "Lythande, what's wrong? You called her a creature—is she not human?"

"Does she seem so to you?"

"Not a normal human, certainly," Eirthe said softly. "I've known her for years now and she hasn't aged. And her clothes never get dirty—most people don't travel dressed as she does—and she's quite fond of Alnath, which is unusual. I thought she must be some kind of mage—she *does* have magic, I know that." She lowered her voice even more. "If she's not human, what is she?"

"A were-dragon," Lythande replied grimly.

"Oh, dear." Eirthe looked wide-eyed along the path Beauty had taken. "That would explain why she and Alnath get along so well." She frowned in concern. "Is she an enemy of yours, Lythande?"

"I don't know," Lythande admitted. "I gave her the lute, but I thought she'd be able to remove the binding spell easily... certainly after all these years..."

"What binding spell?" Eirthe demanded.

"When Tashgan's brothers were still alive and he was not the heir," Lythande explained, "they had Ellifanwy, the Court Magician here, put a binding spell on his lute. It governed both his route and the amount of time he spent in each place. He came here for five days at Yule-tide each year, passed through the Fair at Old Gandrin each spring, spent mid-summer in Northwander, and then made his way back here, only to start the same route anew."

Eirthe's eyes went even wider. "And Beauty is following that route, as she has done every year since—" she chewed on her lower lip, obviously trying to reckon the years.

"—since the year Prince Tashgan came to me at Old Gandrin and asked me to take the binding spell off his lute," Lythande finished the sentence. "Ellifanwy was dead by then—she died in a were-dragon's lair, oddly enough—and he was in a hurry because his brothers had just died. I traded lutes with him, intending to remove the spell at my leisure. Of course, I was following his route in the meantime—"

"I'll be *that* was interesting," Eirthe said with a grin.

"Very," Lythande said dryly. "In any event, I still had not removed the spell when the lute led me to a house in the middle of a swamp. Beauty lived there. Apparently she was quite fond of Tashgan—"

"She still is," Eirthe interjected.

"—and she was not at all pleased to see me in his place," Lythande continued, "although she did calm down somewhat once I convinced her I had not killed him."

Eirthe snickered.

Lythande glared at her. "Tashgan had mentioned her when he gave me the lute—not that he told me anything useful about her, of course; he just said 'Give my love to Beauty.' So I made up a grand tale about his sacrificing his love for her to his duty as his father's heir, and I gave her the lute to remember him by. I really didn't think it would bind her—certainly not for almost ten years!"

"She's been coming here every year," Eirthe said, "but that doesn't *prove* she's bound. She could be doing it of her own free will."

"I hope you're right," Lythande said. "I had best go up to the castle and find out. If she's angry with me, things could get very awkward."

"Wait until the Fair ends," Eirthe said. "It's only another hour, and I want to go with you. I wouldn't miss this for the world!"

By the time the Fair ended and Eirthe had inventoried and packed up her stock, it was rather more than an hour. Lythande, however, was in no particular hurry to confront Beauty, so she waited until Eirthe and the salamanders were ready to accompany her.

They entered the back of the great hall quietly. Tashgan and Velvet still sat side by side at the high table, with Lady Mirwen on Velvet's right. The green cloak draped over the back of the empty chair at Tashgan's left hand indicated where Beauty had sat at dinner, but now she sat on a stool at the front of the dais, playing an intricate melody on her lute.

Lythande was immediately impressed by two things: the fingering required was difficult enough to challenge any musician, and every single person in the hall was listening with rapt attention. No one was fidgeting, or looking bored, or whispering to a neighbor, and no one had so much as turned a head when Lythande and Eirthe entered. Lythande clasped the two daggers concealed beneath her cloak and checked for the presence of magic—long years of being a traveling minstrel had taught her that this sort of music was most definitely *not* the way to enthrall an audience—but the only active spell was the one Lady Mirwen was using to change Velvet's appearance. Even a more thorough check for the presence of potential magic picked up only what Lythande already knew: the salamanders, Eirthe's talent, Lady Mirwen, and the magic that Beauty had by virtue of being a were-dragon.

The song died away into silence and everyone applauded, even the armsmen and the servants. Lythande, joining in the applause, whispered to Eirthe, "Is her playing always so well appreciated?"

"Invariably," Eirthe murmured back, still clapping along with the rest of the hall's occupants. "Lady Beauty *likes* to be appreciated, and she is known to have quite a temper."

"Ah, there you are, Lythande!" Lord Tashgan had just looked up and spotted them. "What do you think of Lady Beauty's playing?"

"Most impressive." Lythande strode boldly forward and bowed to Tashgan and Velvet, then bent over the hand that Beauty extended. "My compliments, Lady Beauty. I applaud both your skill and your courage; I would not dare to undertake such a sophisticated piece in general company."

Beauty smiled blandly at Lythande. "Thank you, Lord Magician." Her fingers squeezed Lythande's briefly before she released them. "I come here each year to celebrate the Yule feast, and I flatter myself that the audience improves in its ability to appreciate good music each year."

"That requires no flattery, Lady," Lythande said, inclining her head respectfully. "The response of your audience is proof of the correctness of your opinion."

"Perhaps you would consent to play a duet with me," Beauty said, smiling sweetly. Lythande could almost hear her thinking: *I know your secret, and you know I know, and you wonder what I shall do with the knowledge. How amusing.*

"It would be my honor," Lythande said, bowing again.

"Excellent!" Tashgan said. "You there," he pointed at the nearest page. "A stool for Lythande."

The boy ran to do as he was told, and a few minutes later Lythande was sitting knee-to-knee with Beauty, tuning her lute to match the were-dragon's.

"Now what shall we play?" Beauty mused aloud. She played a few bars of music, her fingers flying over the strings. "Do you know this one? I believe that your voice is high enough to manage it."

Lythande, joining obediently in the introduction, did indeed recognize the piece, and she very much hoped that no one else did. It was an old song of a love between two women that endured even when both of them fell in love with the same man. Beauty was teasing her, but at least she was being subtle about it. Lythande could only pray that the point was too subtle for their audience to grasp.

The song was followed by enthusiastic applause, and Beauty followed it up with a piece often used as a showpiece by competing musicians. The first player would lay down a complicated melody and the second would improvise and elaborate upon it, then the first would play an even more complicated version of what the second had just done, and so forth. Lythande was prepared to let Beauty win the duel if she could so do without being obvious and was slightly chagrined to discover that it was not necessary. Beauty was good enough to outplay Lythande, though it did take her the better part of an hour to do so.

"We must do this again, dear boy," Beauty said to Lythande as they rose to their feet and bowed together to Lord Tashgan and graciously accepted his praise. "It is not often that I have the pleasure of playing with someone who comes so close to keeping up with me."

Lythande, still buoyed up in the exaltation of playing really good music, grinned happily. "It would be my pleasure, Lady Beauty." She gave the were-dragon a courtly bow.

"Indeed." Beauty looked around the hall and chuckled softly. "I think perhaps we were all caught up in the music's spell," she said. "Look, the candles have burned low, and," she added lowering her voice to reach only to Lythande's ears, "Tashgan's little bride looks ready to fall asleep where she sits."

"It can't possibly have been the music," Lythande whispered back.

"I suspect it's more the strangeness of being in a new land for the first time," Beauty said softly, "and, of course, the spell on her saps her energies somewhat."

The two magicians' eyes met. "Which do you see?" Lythande inquired.

"Her true face, or the illusion?"

Beauty's laugh rivaled the wind-chimes that were sold at the Fair. "Why, both, of course." She turned away to pack up her lute, and Lythande followed her example.

By the time Lythande reached her room the energy from the music was wearing off and she felt ready to fall asleep in the doorway. But first she checked to make certain that no one had tried to disturb the box with Eirthe's spelled candles. To her relief, things were just as she had left them that morning.

Eirthe tapped on her door and came in with a tray of bread, cheese, and dried fruit. "Try to eat something before you fall asleep," she said. "You look even more tired than I feel—and I'd like to sleep for a week! At least we have one day to rest before the wedding."

"It's a good thing we do," Lythande said. "I'm going to need it."

The day of the wedding was beautiful and unseasonably warm. By the time Lythande woke, the sun was halfway up the cloudless bright blue sky, and the air had only enough chill in it to be refreshing. The wind was the gentlest of breezes. Lythande sat on the windowsill, basking in the sun, ignoring the salamander who left the group guarding the trunk with the wedding candles and streaked past her into the open air.

A short time later there was a tap on Lythande's door. Lythande opened it to find Eirthe had brought breakfast.

"Thank you, Eirthe," she said. "Please join me—or have you eaten already?"

"Hours ago," Eirthe replied with a smile, "but I wouldn't mind a bit more fruit. I've just finished setting out all the tapers in the great hall. It's going to be the best-lit room you have ever seen."

"Are the wedding preparations completed then?" Lythande had spent the previous day in her room, resting and practicing illusions. Eirthe had brought her food at regular intervals, but had left her alone otherwise, so Lythande didn't know the current state of the castle. She knew Eirthe would have informed her of anything obviously crucial, so she assumed that things had been quiet—at least magically.

"Very nearly," Eirthe replied, smothering a yawn. "You did well to stay out of the mess yesterday—between the tear-down of the Fair and the preparations for the wedding, it was the most chaotic mess I've ever seen. Most of the Fair folk are pretty efficient, but the castle staff doesn't put on a wedding every year. And from all the fuss and bother, I think some of them deliberately left things until the last moment so they could run around and yell at other people and seem busy and important."

"Does that include the Vizier?" Lythande asked curiously.

"Fortunately he had delegated the wedding preparations to the Head

Steward," Eirthe said, "because Lady Mirwen kept running to him all day with crisis after crisis, and he didn't have had time to do anything yesterday except deal with her."

"Interesting," Lythande mused. "I should think that sort of behavior would be likely to give him a dislike for her."

"Perhaps not," Eirthe said. "She certainly didn't miss a single opportunity to tell him how wonderful he was and how she just didn't know how she could have managed to cope without him."

"What did you do, follow her around all day?"

"Of course not," Eirthe smiled innocently. "I was dipping candles in the courtyard almost the entire day. Ask anyone." She grinned. "I had the salamanders keep watch. We've been here long enough now that no one pays much heed to them as long as they don't get too close—and have you ever noticed how seldom people look *up*? And no one looks closely at the wall sconces; one of the babies has spent several days in Velvet's room impersonating a candle flame. He's still there, in fact; I think he likes her." She looked thoughtful. "I wonder how Tashgan would react if I gave his bride a salamander for a wedding gift?"

Lythande chuckled. "I suspect that would depend on where it wanted to sleep at night."

Eirthe popped the last piece of fruit into her mouth, swallowed it, and licked her fingers. "I'll think about it." She rose to her feet. "I had better go and dress for the ceremony. Have you decided what illusions you'll use for the Games?"

"I have a number of possibilities," Lythande said, "but I expect to do a lot of improvisation once the duel gets started."

"I expect it will be very interesting," Eirthe said. "I'll see you at the ceremony."

The ceremony was held at the entrance to the castle, so as many people as wanted to could witness their lord's wedding. Tashgan was resplendent in a long cloth-of-gold tunic, while Velvet wore a dress of deep sapphire velvet with a matching headdress that completely covered her hair. A pale blue silk veil attached to the crown of the headdress covered her face. The wedding party: the priest, the bride and groom, and their chief witnesses stood on the steps, and the courtyard was crowded with spectators. The Vizier was the witness for Tashgan, as Lythande had expected, but she was surprised to see Lady Beauty standing with Velvet. She looked around the courtyard, but did not see Lady Mirwen anywhere.

"Do you know where Mirwen is?" she whispered to Eirthe, who was standing next to her.

"Still in the great hall, I guess," Eirthe replied. "That's where she was when I came out, but I thought she'd be out for the ceremony."

"It would appear that she has better things to do than to watch her charge get married," Lythande said dryly.

"Several of the salamanders are in there," Eirthe said reassuringly. "I'll find out what she was doing as soon as the ceremony is over."

But as soon as the ceremony ended the marriage-feast started, and Lythande's status meant that she was stuck at the high table with Tashgan and the Vizier. Fortunately it appeared to be the custom to separate, by the full length of the table, the Champions of the Marriage Games, so the Vizier sat to Lady Mirwen's left, with Velvet on his left, followed by Tashgan, Beauty, and Lythande.

This left Lythande with Lady Beauty as a dinner companion, but at least she was spared having to make conversation to both sides. She applied herself to her food while Beauty complimented Tashgan on his bride's beauty—as if he had anything to do with that—and joked about how eager he must be to begin his duties as a husband. Tashgan laughed, agreed with everything she said, and drank his wine. Beauty reminded him to eat "—you'll need your strength, dear boy, and 'tis well known that too much wine dulls the performance..."

As Tashgan obediently began to eat, Beauty turned her attention to Lythande. "I hear that you, dear boy, are to be Tashgan's Champion in a contest of magic after dinner."

Was there a twinge of jealousy in her voice? Lythande wasn't sure. At least she seemed willing to keep Lythande's secret. "That is true," Lythande admitted, then succumbed to curiosity. "Tell me, Lady Beauty; do you call everyone 'dear boy'?"

"Frequently," Beauty said with a smile. "It's so much easier than remembering names; people come and go so quickly, don't you think? It also reduces the chance of my miscalling someone—by the wrong name, I mean," she said, looking deliberately bland.

"Quite." Lythande kept her voice and face equally bland.

"I do believe that your little friend is looking for you," Beauty added, indicating a salamander hovering in the doorway.

"So it would seem," Lythande murmured. "If you would excuse me for a moment, my lady?"

Beauty smiled and bent closer, obviously willing to enter into the conspiracy. "If anyone asks, you've gone to the privy."

Lythande nodded assent and slipped from the room as quietly as possible.

In fact the salamander did lead her in the direction of the privies, where she met Eirthe, apparently returning from there to the hall.

"She was casting some sort of spell on the contest area," Eirthe said quickly, smiling as if they were exchanging greetings. "Something fairly elaborate, but the salamanders couldn't give me any details—aside from the fact that she used her own candles and not any of mine! *That* they noticed."

"Well, I'm sure we'll find out the details soon," Lythande said with resignation. *I was afraid this day was going to be interesting.*

"No doubt," Eirthe agreed, continuing back to the hall. Lythande went to the privies before going back herself; the easiest way to carry off deception was to make as much of it as possible the truth.

The feast continued for several hours. Lythande ate sparingly and drank little, knowing that she would need to be alert for the work to come. Finally Tashgan stood up to announce the contest.

"It is the custom of my bride's people," he began, "to have a contest of magical illusions to celebrate a wedding. The two Champions will vie with each other to create the most fantastic and beautiful illusion, and you, my friends, will be the judges." Waiting for the applause to die down, he continued, "The Champions will be Lady Mirwen for Valantia, and Lythande for Tschardain. Let the Games begin!"

As Lythande stood, Lady Mirwen strode quickly to the area cleared for the contest and faced Tashgan. "Lord Tashgan, as I told you when you first proposed this sacrilege, these Games are for women. No man may be a Champion in the Marriage Games. I have, therefore, bespelled this area so that only a woman can work magic in it." Lythande froze in place, but kept her face impassive as Mirwen gloated. "Unless your 'Champion' can prove himself a woman, you will have to concede the Games—or find a *suitable* Champion."

"Lythande?" Tashgan turned to look at his Champion. "Can you remove her spell?"

Lythande hoped her laugh did not sound as forced as it felt. "Easily, Lord Tashgan. But I'm sorry to have to inform you that the quickest way to do so is to undo *all* her spells, which will, of course, make her unable to compete in the Games." *And will, of course, remove the illusion from Velvet as well. I'm not certain that Lady Mirwen wants that to happen just yet.*

It seemed that Lythande was correct on that point, for Lady Mirwen looked distinctly nervous. She had just opened her mouth, presumably to offer to cancel the spell herself, when Beauty intervened.

"Lord Tashgan," she said, rising to her feet. "I ask a boon. Let *me* be your Champion!"

Tashgan looked at Lythande, who could appreciate his dilemma. He certainly must know enough about Beauty that he would never wish to offend her, but he wasn't certain just how powerful—and likely to take offense—Lythande might be. But Lythande had excellent reasons for wishing to keep Beauty happy as well.

"If Lady Beauty wishes it," Lythande said promptly, "I would be well content to relinquish my place to her. I have the greatest respect for her magical abilities."

"And Lady Mirwen would have no cause to complain of 'sacrilege,'" Beauty pointed out.

"Very well," Tashgan said. "Lady Beauty shall be my Champion. Lythande shall act as referee." Lythande gallantly pulled Beauty's chair back and escorted her from the dais before returning to her own place at the head table.

Lady Mirwen faced Beauty with the self-satisfied look of a spoiled child who had gotten her own way once again. "This is much better, don't you think? Men shouldn't try to play at magic; it finds its highest and truest expression in the human female. No one can deny that."

"I wouldn't stake *my* life on that," Beauty said, smiling enigmatically.

Mirwen obviously didn't understand that statement, so she ignored it. She waved her hands in an elaborate showy pattern, and chanted something that was clearly intended to be a spell. Lythande, from her long life and extensive musical background, recognized it as a very old students' drinking song, old enough that the language was no longer spoken in that form. From the twitching of Beauty's lips, Lythande was sure that she was not alone in identifying the "spell." But Beauty stood quietly, allowing her opponent to create the first illusion.

It was quite pretty; Lythande was willing to admit that. A line of trees made a backdrop for the scene and concealed Mirwen, which Lythande thought improved the esthetic appeal considerably. A meadow with bright green grass dotted with brilliantly colored flowers hid the floor, and a crystal blue pond filled the foreground. Beside the pond sat two figures: Velvet—a copy of the illusion, which was still on the real princess—and a younger-looking idealized form of Tashgan.

And that's probably exactly what he thinks he does look like, Lythande thought. *Clever move. Not brilliant, but clever. Not bad for an opening illusion, and quite suitable for a wedding.*

The murmurs of appreciation in the hall died away as everyone waited to see what Beauty would do to answer this. When the hall was completely silent, Beauty began.

A glittering silvery mist rose up from the pond, hiding the figures and the landscape. Lights flickered within the mist for several minutes, and then a breeze came out of nowhere and blew the mist away. Gasps of astonishment and pleasure swept through the hall as the scene was revealed. Beauty had made the illusion larger, so that everyone could see it, and she had added a castle of glistening white marble, carved into fantastic shapes and ornamentation. As the spectators oohed and aahed, the illusory "sky" changed from blue into a beautiful multicolored sunset, followed by darkness, broken by lights shining from the castle and reflecting off the water of the pond. The entire banquet hall darkened as well, enabling the audience to see the illusion better and without distraction. Then dawn came, with more colors, soft pastels deepening as "day" dawned. As the light brightened around the figures of Tashgan and Velvet, Lythande gave an appreciative chuckle. The figure of Velvet was pregnant.

"Fast work," a man's voice called from somewhere in the hall. That got a round of laughter from nearly everyone, including Tashgan.

Lythande thought that she heard Lady Mirwen hissing through her teeth, but she couldn't be sure because the castle blocked her view of the woman.

Beauty stepped back and allowed Mirwen to take her next turn. A sudden darkness hid the scene, and when it lifted, just as suddenly—nowhere near as artistically as Beauty's idealized sunset and sunrise—Velvet and Tashgan had two children: a sturdy boy toddling around at the edge of the pond and a baby in Velvet's arms. Both children had the same perfect beauty as the illusion Velvet wore.

Not the best move, Lythande thought, listening to mutters from the hall. *Children who favor their mother so completely could be fathered by anyone. It would be more politic to have at least one of them resemble Tashgan.*

Beauty seemed to share Lythande's opinion. She gave an audible sniff of disdain as she moved forward to take her next turn. The boy grew from a toddler into a young boy and, as he grew, his form changed so that he looked very much like Tashgan. The baby wriggled out of its mother's lap, crawled to the edge of the pond and surveyed its reflection in the water, tilting its little head to one side as if in thought. Then it reached forward with a chubby little hand and splashed water on its face. The coloring and features changed as if a layer of paint had been washed away. The little girl who sat up and began to gather flowers for a chain had brown hair, grey eyes, and freckles. She was cute, and she looked very much the way Velvet must have looked at that age.

Lythande looked around. At the high table Velvet was laughing, and Tashgan was smiling. Mirwen became visible through the towers of the castle as she moved from behind it to stand just behind the trees on her side of the illusion. She looked furious. Obviously she had not expected anyone even to see through the illusion she had placed on Velvet, much less to let her know that they had done so. "How dare you!" she snarled softly.

But Beauty wasn't done yet. From the edge of the patch of illusion, animals began to appear. At first they were fairly ordinary: a sapphire blue bird flew to perch on the illusory Velvet's shoulder, picking up the color of her eyes; an elegant sleek golden hound came to sit at Tashgan's side. The complexity of the illusion increased: a group of deer in all the colors of the rainbow came to drink from the pool, blue and green ducks and silver swans floated across its surface, and a pure white unicorn with a silver horn spiraling outward from the center of its forehead walked up to the little girl, dipping its head so that she could put her flower chain around its neck.

Mirwen raised her arms dramatically and snapped out a few words in a language Lythande didn't recognize. It still sounded like a curse. *Oh oh,* Lythande thought, *this is getting ugly.*

A pack of black wolves came out of the pond and rushed to surround the unicorn and the girl. The girl backed up against the unicorn's side, and the unicorn defended itself as best it could with kicks at any wolf who got too close, but they were badly outnumbered. A couple of wolves darted in to attack, and the unicorn was bleeding by the time it beat the back.

This is too much. Lythande rose to her feet and shouted "Hold!"

All action in the scene froze as Mirwen turned to Lythande and snarled, "What is your problem?"

"The game being played here, Lady Mirwen, is *not* 'My illusion can kill your illusion,'" Lythande said sternly. "This is not a magical duel. You appear to be forgetting that."

"It is not your place to interfere," Lady Mirwen snapped. "I was weaving illusions before you were born!"

"I very much doubt that," Lythande said calmly. "Lord Tashgan named me referee for these games. You are supposed to be making something beautiful, not causing bloodshed—even if it is illusory." She turned to Beauty. "Lady Beauty, I believe it is your turn now."

"Of course, dear boy," Beauty said, smiling. She stepped forward and began to work. First she dissolved a section of trees, revealing Lady Mirwen to the audience, and cast the illusion of a tree over the rival sorceress. It wasn't a beautiful tree; it was gnarled and twisted and actually quite ugly— and very clearly what Mirwen *would* look like if she were a tree. Laughter echoed around the hall as people caught the joke. The Mirwen tree twisted, trying to glare at the people who were laughing, but Beauty waved a slender hand, and water fell from above, covering the tree completely. Beauty looked at it and inhaled sharply, and the water froze, coating the tree with ice, which caught the light from Eirthe's candles and glittered in a flickering pattern.

That's as close to beautiful as Mirwen is ever likely to get, Lythande thought.

Beauty turned her attention to the wolves surrounding the unicorn and smiled again. She waved her hand, and the wolves were transformed into cuddly black puppies. They frolicked around, emitting enthusiastic little yelps, and butting at the girl's ankles before darting off to play with the boy.

The unicorn, with the girl still at its side, walked forward to dip its horn in the pool. The pool spread toward Lady Beauty until it touched the hem of her skirt, and she began to transform as well. Her arms dropped to touch her sides briefly before sweeping upward and back, and as they moved, her green and gold sleeves changed to wings with scales so bright they seemed made of gold and emeralds. Her body grew, her face elongated, and before anyone could so much as blink, a dragon stood in her place, towering over the pool and dominating the scene.

The soft gasps and hushed attention of the spectators were more of an accolade than any applause. The audience waited in fascination to see what would happen next. Even Lythande sat transfixed, and Tashgan was scarcely breathing.

The dragon puffed out its cheeks and blew out a soft pale flame which melted the ice covering the tree. Lady Mirwen snapped out of the illusion and stalked through the line of trees to confront her adversary.

"The Champions are *not* supposed to be part of the illusions!" she snapped. "And I don't know what you think you've turned yourself into, but I assure you that it's *ugly*! Didn't anyone tell you that these illusions are supposed to be beautiful?"

"I am a dragon," Beauty replied calmly, "and I *am* beautiful. If beauty is the main criterion of this contest, however, I can readily see why you disqualify yourself—although as an ice-covered tree you had a certain charm."

"While you are hideous, scaly, and altogether loathsome!" Mirwen snarled. "You call yourself a sorceress? A simple hedge-witch has better taste!"

"I really couldn't say," Beauty mused aloud. "It's been so long since I've eaten a hedge-witch that I'm afraid I've forgotten the precise taste of one. Anyway, once they are properly broiled, most humans taste pretty much alike."

"You're not funny!" Mirwen was almost screaming by now. "I won't let you make a fool out of me!"

"My dear girl," Beauty replied, obviously quite amused, "I don't have to. You do it so well yourself."

Even Lythande chuckled at that, though she doubted that she could be heard above the roar of laughter coming from the rest of the hall. Tashgan was almost doubled over, and now Lythande could see Velvet beyond him. The girl was well-trained, one had to admit that; she was still sitting upright with a reasonably composed face. Having a side view, Lythande could see clearly where Velvet was biting the inside of her cheek so she wouldn't laugh aloud at her lady-in-waiting. Too bad that Tashgan didn't have the same restraint.

Unfortunately, being laughed at was something Mirwen obviously didn't tolerate. She drew a dagger from her sleeve and rushed at Beauty. Lythande moved to intercept her, just in time to catch the edge of the blast of flame that incinerated Lady Mirwen. The flames, however, were carefully angled to avoid the high table, so they missed Lythande's face and struck the side of her cloak. Since it was fire-proof, there was no damage, except to Lady

Mirwen—and to Velvet.

In the instant that Mirwen turned to a pile of ash, the illusion spell on Velvet vanished. Lythande and Velvet were face to face, and as soon as Velvet saw Lythande's expression, she realized what had happened. Demonstrating the quick intelligence Lythande had always suspected she possessed, the girl gasped and did an excellent simulation of a faint, landing in a graceful sprawl on the floor with one of her long trailing sleeves completely hiding her face. Eirthe's salamanders promptly clustered around the princess, making it even harder to see her clearly.

Beauty returned to human form, without even a hair out of place. Ignoring the total confusion in her audience, she banished the illusion with a negligent wave of her hand, and rushed to join Lythande on the dais. Eirthe came around from the other end of the dais to join her salamanders in hovering over Velvet's supine body.

"What happened?" Tashgan asked, looking down at Velvet. "Is she all right?"

"She just saw her governess die, my Lord," the Vizier said, looking down at Velvet. "It is bound to have been a shock." He frowned at the confusion. "Can someone get those salamanders out of the way?"

"They like the princess," Eirthe explained. "They are simply trying to protect her."

"And quite successfully, too," Lythande remarked. "While they're there, nobody is going to step on the poor girl. "By your leave, Lord," she bowed to Tashgan, "Eirthe and I will take your wife to her room. She's just seen her only companion from home incinerated right before her; she will need time to compose herself."

"Yes, of course," Tashgan said distractedly.

"It's a bit much for him to take in all at once," Beauty said, pouring a goblet of wine. "Drink this, dear boy, and just sit quietly while they tend to your wife." She shot a sharp look at Lythande, who obediently moved to pick up Velvet, thankful that the girl was slender and easy to carry. As she followed Eirthe towards Velvet's room, she could hear Beauty demanding that someone fetch her lute. *Good*, Lythande thought. *By the time she's done playing, this crowd won't know—or care—what they just saw.*

When they reached Velvet's room, Lythande dropped the girl unceremoniously on her bed. The salamanders moved off to one side. "All right, Princess, you can wake up now."

Velvet's eyes snapped open instantly, but when she tried to sit up she began to sway, and Lythande had to steady her.

"Not so fast," Eirthe said, handing Velvet a goblet of watered wine. "It has been a rather eventful day for you."

"I'm all right," Velvet insisted. "I didn't really faint."

"You didn't?" Eirthe asked, startled.

Lythande chuckled. "If she ever tires of being Lady of Tschardain, she can go on the stage. That was as neatly acted as anything I've ever seen. Excellent timing, too."

"But why—" Eirthe started to say, and then realized. "Of course! The spell was broken when Mirwen died."

"It was, wasn't it?" Velvet asked. "I thought it must be when I saw the way Lythande was looking at me—am I back to normal?"

"Oh, yes," Eirthe assured her. "You look just like the first candle I made of you."

"The first candle?" Lythande asked.

"I made a second one to match the illusion," Eirthe explained. "I wasn't sure what she'd look like by the time it came to display them."

"What about the candle of Mirwen?" Lythande asked.

"I still have that one," Eirthe replied. "I'll burn it down tonight. I didn't want to do it while she was alive because that one *is* magically similar."

"Could I have it?" Velvet asked. "I'd like to burn it myself."

Eirthe looked at Lythande, who nodded. "Of course, princess, if it will make you feel better."

"I'm sure it will," Velvet said grimly. "Now, about my appearance—"

She broke off as Tashgan walked in, followed by Beauty and the Vizier.

"Princess," the Vizier began formally, "I hope that you are recovered."

Velvet opened her mouth to reply, but before she could say a single word, Tashgan gasped.

"What happened to you?" he asked in horror.

"What?" The Vizier looked at Tashgan in bewilderment.

"Look at her face!" Tashgan burst out.

The Vizier, obviously puzzled, looked at Velvet, squinting in an effort to see her more clearly. "What's wrong with it?" he said. "It looks fine to me."

He's short-sighted, Lythande realized. *To him she still looks the same. Too bad Tashgan isn't.* "Lady Mirwen cast a spell on her," Lythande explained quickly.

"You can reverse it, can't you?" Tashgan asked urgently. "You said you could undo all that woman's magic."

"Yes," Lythande said carefully, "I can change her back to the way she was this morning, if she wishes it. But the spell only alters her outward appearance. She's not ill or injured, and she's still exactly the same person she was before. Do her looks matter that much?"

"Yes, of course they do!" Tashgan snapped. Velvet looked down at her lap. "I can't have people saying that marrying me turned her into a hag."

Eirthe drew her breath in an outraged gasp and moved to stand nose to nose with Tashgan. "She is *not* a hag, and that is a stupid and cruel thing to say!"

"I see nothing wrong with your wife's appearance," Beauty said calmly.

"Lythande." Tashgan was obviously trying for a man-to-man rapport.

"You understand. You know how important beautiful surroundings are to me."

Lythande sighed and looked at Velvet. The girl looked up, blinking back tears, and nodded. "Yes, Tashgan," Lythande said with another sigh, "I do understand. I can change her face back—but keeping her beautiful depends on you."

"What do you mean?" Tashgan asked.

"The thing most important to the beauty of a married woman is her husband's love," Lythande explained. "You have to treat her with love and respect—and you have to keep doing so, or her beauty will not last."

"Lord Tashgan, surely there are more important things to worry about. Does it really matter what she looks like?" the Vizier asked impatiently.

"Yes, it does," Tashgan said promptly. He looked appealingly at Lythande. "Change her back, please, and I shall do whatever I have to in order for the spell to hold."

"If your wife is willing," Lythande said.

"As my husband desires," Velvet replied promptly. "It might be best, however, if all of you returned to the feast. I feel sure that there has been enough disruption for one day."

"Quite right, your highness." The Vizier nodded and left the room.

"She's right, dear boy," Beauty said, taking Tashgan's arm. "Let us go back to the feast, and your bride can join us as soon as she is able."

Tashgan nodded wearily. "Fix her face before she comes down again," he ordered Lythande. Beauty dragged him out of the room, and Velvet sagged back down onto the bed.

"I see what you meant, Eirthe," she sighed, "when you told me to think of a way to explain the change in my appearance to him and wished me luck. There's isn't a way, is there?"

"I've known him for over ten years and I can't think of one," Eirthe admitted. "Lythande?"

"I'm afraid his view of other people does tend to be superficial," Lythande agreed.

"That's a no, isn't it?" Velvet's smile was weak. "Well, if it's what my husband wants, I'll have to do it—especially since he can still set aside the marriage if he decides to."

"What?" Eirthe said.

"A marriage has to be consummated to be valid," Lythande explained. "Until that happens, it can be annulled quite easily."

"Especially after your lady-in-waiting tried to kill his Champion," Velvet said wryly. "Today has been quite a day, and I still have tonight to endure."

"Tashgan did say that his wedding day would be long remembered," Lythande remarked.

"I don't think *I'll* ever forget it," Velvet agreed. "I've never seen an illusion contest like that. I'm still trying to figure out how Lady Beauty managed to kill Mirwen—not that I'm complaining. But surely Mirwen knew that the illusion of fire can't kill, so why did it kill her?"

"Because it wasn't an illusion," Lythande said.

"Of course it was an illusion," Velvet said, puzzled. "That's the whole point of the contest. You're not trying to tell me that Tashgan and I were in two places at the same time and that the unicorn and all the other animals were real."

"*They* were illusions," Lythande agreed. "The dragon was real. Is real. Beauty is a were-dragon."

"Beauty is a were-dragon." Velvet was moving past shock into numb acceptance.

"Yes, but don't let on that you know," Eirthe said. "Just be very polite to her and make certain that you always listen to her music with proper appreciation."

"She is a wonderful musician," Velvet said.

"A few extra centuries of practice don't hurt," Lythande agreed.

"A were-dragon," Velvet repeated, shaking her head. "In a way that's a relief. I was afraid that Tashgan preferred her to me and was going to have the marriage annulled so he could marry her. But I guess that's silly."

"I think he wants human heirs," Lythande pointed out. "And besides, I don't think Beauty would agree to marry him. He's just a temporary diversion to her. She remarked to me at dinner that people come and go quickly, and from her viewpoint, they do."

"Yes," Velvet said, considering that matter. "After a few centuries, I guess we all look alike to her..." Her voice trailed off and she looked up at Lythande. "What she said about not having eaten any hearth-witches lately—she wasn't joking, was she?"

"I'm sure she hasn't eaten any lately," Lythande said, "but I do think she was joking. She has quite a sense of humor, and it's rather peculiar. But she's certainly pragmatic enough to realize that Tashgan needs a human wife, so as long as you don't antagonize her, you don't need to worry about her. She'll probably play the part of a doting aunt to your children."

"My children," Velvet sighed. "The point of this whole marriage. But I had hope that, if I had to marry, I would get a husband who could at least learn to like me as a person."

"Give Tashgan some time," Eirthe said consolingly. "He's not always as bad as he was today."

"But first we need to change her appearance so that he'll look at her long enough to get a chance to know her," Lythande pointed out. "Go get the figure candles you made, please."

Eirthe nodded and hurried from the room.

"Maybe he'll get to like me in time," Velvet said wistfully. "He seemed to think the little girl was cute, and she took after me."

"I think he will," Lythande said reassuringly. "He's a bit on the shallow side, but he has a good heart."

"I hope you are right."

"So, Princess," Lythande asked, "is it your wish that I restore your appearance to what it was under Mirwen's spell?"

"Yes," Velvet said with resignation. "At least I don't have to look at myself. I only have to remember that what people see when they look at me isn't real and that their opinions of me are false."

"Only their initial impressions," Lythande reminded her. "You *are* still the same person, and once they have known you for even a short while, that will still be what counts."

"Now that I'm married, what I look like doesn't matter much—as long as my husband likes the way I look. It's just too bad that he prefers the illusion."

"Your job is to consummate the marriage, be crowned beside him in three day's time, and bear children," Lythande pointed out. "The illusion spell is only a means to that end. And remember, Tashgan thinks the illusion is real."

"He does?"

"He doesn't know much about magic," Lythande explained, "and he thinks of beauty as a natural state. He thinks that Lady Mirwen cast a spell to change your appearance as she died."

"She died almost instantly, and she didn't see it coming," Velvet pointed out. "And she was thinking of something else at the time."

"Tashgan is not a deep thinker."

"Or even a shallow one," Eirthe said, returning with the candles. "Here you are, Lythande. I wasn't sure which you needed, and I wanted to keep them under my eyes, so I brought them all." She opened the boxes and set them out on the table.

"Set Tashgan aside for the minute," Lythande said. "We don't need him."

Eirthe carefully reboxed the Tashgan candle. "We'll need it for the feast. But we don't need Mirwen," Eirthe shoved the spider candle back into its box and handed it to Velvet. "Here you are. Do what you like with it."

The two versions of Velvet sat side-by-side on the table facing Lythande. Lythande dragged a chair behind them and waved Velvet into it. The salamanders arrayed themselves behind Velvet, near the ceiling, except for Alnath, who went to join Eirthe at the side of the room.

"Eirthe, Alnath, would you guard the door, please," Lythande requested. "I don't want to be disturbed while I'm working."

Eirthe nodded, and she and Alnath left the room, closing the door behind them.

Lythande looked at the pale and nervous princess. "Try to relax, Velvet. This isn't going to hurt, and if you don't look in a mirror, you'll never know the difference." She kindled mage fire to light the candle that showed Velvet's true appearance.

Velvet started crying as the wax began to melt. "I'll know," she sobbed. "Even without a mirror, I'll remember every time I look into my husband's eyes."

"Try not to remember," Lythande advised, watching wax tears run down the face of the candle and slide down the folds of its dress. "You are the only one who will be hurt by remembering."

She heard the echo of Eirthe's voice: *Velvet both benefits and is harmed by it.*

Velvet cried the entire time it took the candle to burn down, but stopped as soon as it was consumed. Now all that remained was the candle of the Velvet Tashgan preferred, and the living princess to match it.

"Will I always look like that now?" Velvet asked.

"Yes," Lythande replied. "Try to think of this as a wedding gift, and make the most of it."

"It's funny," Velvet mused. "I never wanted beauty—I always thought brains were more important."

"I think so, too," Lythande agreed, "but now you have both."

Velvet smiled weakly. On her new face, even this faint smile looked radiant. "Thank you, Lord Magician."

Eirthe and Alnath came back into the room. "All done?" Eirthe asked brightly.

"You know perfectly well we are," Lythande said, "or you wouldn't have come in." She glanced up. "I supposed the salamanders told you."

"Of course," Eirthe nodded to the salamanders near the ceiling. One of them detached itself from the group and moved to hover beside Velvet's right shoulder. "This is Caldon," Eirthe said. "He wants to stay with you, Princess. Will you accept him as a wedding gift?"

Velvet turned her head and smiled at the salamander. "Greetings, Caldon. I'm glad of your company." She turned back to the candlemaker. "Thank you, Eirthe. Now I won't feel quite so alone here."

Eirthe packed up the remaining candle. "I'm glad you like him. Not everyone deals well with salamanders."

Lythande quietly added an extra degree of resistance to burns to the spells on Velvet's skin as Velvet reached out to stroke Caldon with a tentative finger. Then she turned her hand over, and he hovered in the palm of her hand.

Velvet stood, moving Caldon to a position beside her right shoulder. "It's time to go back to the wedding-feast," she said resolutely. "I have a husband to charm."

Two nights later Lythande and Beauty were together in the hall packing up their lutes after another evening of musical duels. "I shall miss this," Lythande admitted. "I truly enjoy playing with you." She took a deep breath and asked the question which had been with her ever since Beauty's arrival. "Are you leaving tomorrow?"

Beauty raised her eyebrows. "And miss dear Tashgan's coronation?" Once again Lythande saw the were-dragon's 'I know what you're thinking' smile. "Dear boy, I plan to stay at *least* another week."

THE CHILDREN OF CATS
Marion Zimmer Bradley & Elisabeth Waters

"The children of cats can catch mice."
Old Gandrin proverb

Lythande, mercenary magician and minstrel, dodged quickly out of the way of the rapidly-approaching, loudly-screaming man. The people in the village just outside of this forest had warned of bandits. They had not mentioned that the bandits were likely to be on fire. Fortunately it was springtime and it had just stopped raining a quarter-hour since, so he wasn't setting the trees alight. Lythande quickly called up a water-spell, just in case, and held it ready.

The bandit's screams turned quickly to choking sounds and then silence as he collapsed. Lythande turned to check that the corpse wasn't starting a fire, but a roar from the direction he had come made it a very quick check. The magician turned to see what new menace was approaching. Judging from the crashing noises as it passed through the trees, it was big.

Lythande gripped the twin daggers hidden beneath the mage robe: the left-hand one for dealing with magical perils and the right-hand one for fighting non-magical attackers. Although the size of the thing which now burst into the clearing implied that it was magical, Lythande was taking no chances. As the giant cat rose over her, Lythande thrust both daggers through its ribcage. It popped like a soap bubble and disappeared.

"Ki-ki-kitty!" The figure that rushed into the clearing appeared to be a small child, a girl of perhaps eight or nine. Lythande, who had seen sea monsters in the form of beautiful maidens—not to mention a lady who not only changed her apparent age but also turned into a dragon—reserved judgment. When the girl threw a fireball, Lythande struck back with the already-formed water-spell.

The suddenly-soaked child sputtered with fury and lifted her left hand, which held a mage's wand.

Not a small child, then. Lythande sheathed the daggers to have both hands free for what seemed to be shaping up to be a full-fledged magical duel—albeit one lacking both formal challenge and proper protocol.

"Hold!" A middle-aged woman halted, gasping and clutching a tree trunk for support, at the edge of the clearing behind the girl. Half-a-dozen balls of flame surrounded her, and one streaked forward toward Lythande. Lythande caught the salamander on an upraised hand, and looked at the woman.

"Eirthe, what in the name of all the gods..." A levin-bolt from the wand the child was holding knocked Lythande backwards. Feeling somewhat breathless, the magician watched the hovering salamander move to block the child.

Eirthe, who had either caught her breath or pulled more energy from somewhere, dove forward and hooked an elbow around the child's neck in a very efficient choke-hold. The girl went down so fast that Lythande wasn't sure whether she had time to hear Eirthe snarl, "I meant *both* of you, dammit!"

Lythande sat up, shaking off the effects of the levin-bolt. Fortunately there hadn't been much power behind it, and Lythande had not been entirely unshielded when it hit. Being a minstrel as well as a musician, Lythande turned quickly to check on the condition of her lute, which had flown free when the bolt hit. Fortunately it was in a sturdy case and was less damaged than the mage. The salamander darted anxiously back and forth between the Lythande and Eirthe, who was now kneeling over the girl—or whatever the thing was.

"What is that?" Lythande asked.

"It's a little girl, Lythande," Eirthe replied. "Surely you have some familiarity with the species." She did not add "you were one once." Eirthe Candlemaker was one of the very few people who knew that Lythande was a woman and not the man she appeared to be, but she also knew that Lythande's power—and her life—depended on keeping that fact a secret. Every Adept of the Blue Star had a secret which was the key to his powers, and if the secret became known, the powers would be lost and the magician could be killed with impunity. As long as the secret remained unknown, the Adept lived and did as he pleased until the time when he would be summoned to fight on the side of Law in the Last Battle between Law and Chaos. In the meantime, however...

"Lythande, could I hire you to help me?"

"Help you do what?"

"I'm not a great magician, and I don't have enough power to deal with her. She has power and no idea how to use it. I want to take her to the college at Northwander so she can be trained."

"So you want me to help you get her to Northwander without her killing somebody on the way?"

"Basically, yes. It would also be nice if she didn't maim or injure anyone."

"Very well," Lythande agreed. Centuries of roaming while awaiting the Last Battle necessitated taking the odd job here and there. "I hope you don't mind if I put a restraining spell on her before she wakes up."

"Please do," Eirthe said fervently.

The girl's eyelids were already starting to flicker as Lythande stood over her and cast the spell. It wouldn't prevent her from moving, but it would slow her down considerably, probably enough so that even Eirthe could handle her. For good measure, Lythande picked up the wand. She curled her nose in disgust at the phallic carvings and shape of the wand—why would a girl-child carry such a thing? Lythande opened her pack and removed a large square of silk to wrap the wand in; the silk would serve as an insulator and make it more difficult for the child to access the wand's power, even if she were holding it. As she wrapped the wand and thrust it under the folds of the mage-robe, a memory teased at her brain. *I have done this before; I have wrapped this wand in silk and carried it thus. When and where? And whose was the wand then?*

The child sat up, slowly, looking dazed. "Ki-ki-kitty?" She looked around anxiously, and then her gaze fell on Lythande. "Eirthe," she wailed, "the bad man ki-killed Ki-ki-kitty!"

"Lythande is not a bad man, Raella," Eirthe said firmly. "He is going to help us get to Northwander."

"I want Ki-ki-kitty!"

"Would that be the cat-form that attacked me?" Lythande inquired wryly.

Eirthe sighed. "Big enough to put its front paws on your head? The color of carven oak?"

"Sounds familiar."

"How dead did you kill it?"

"Stabbed with both daggers. It popped like a soap bubble."

"Oh dear," Eirthe said. "Alnath, would you mind?"

The salamander, still hovering in the middle of the clearing, dropped to hover a hand-span above the ground, and the other salamanders hanging back at the edge of the clearing moved to join in the search. After a moment, they all clustered in one spot, then shot upwards as Eirthe reached into the low-growing plants and pulled out a small piece of oak crudely carved in the shape of a cat. It didn't even fill her palm as she brought it to her face to examine it.

"The basic form is intact, Raella; your father can probably fix it."

"He is *not* my father!"

"We are going back to the wagon now." Eirthe tucked the carving into her belt pouch and hauled the child up with a firm grip on the back of her tunic.

Lythande fell in behind them as they left the clearing, accompanied by the salamanders.

Eirthe's wagon wasn't far. It was stopped next to a stream, where she had obviously begun to set up camp. The donkey had been unhitched and was eating the plants at the edge of the stream, there was a fire in the portable fire pit that Eirthe carried with her, and a pot of soup hung over it. And sitting on the bench that folded out of the wagon when it was set up as a display booth, was... well, the man was clearly dead, but he turned his head. As his eyes met Lythande's, she remembered where she had seen that wretched wand before.

"Rastafyre the Incomparable." *Also known as Rastafyre the Incompetent. The last time I saw this wand was when he hired me to return it to him after it was stolen from him.*

"Health and prosperity to you, O Lythande," the corpse replied carefully.

Eirthe dropped the carving into his lap. "Can you fix this, please?" she asked.

Rastafyre ran a pallid hand over the wood. "I need my wand," he said. "Have you seen it?" He looked around vaguely.

Lythande pulled the wand out of the mage-robe and handed it to him, being careful to keep her hand on the silk and not touch either him or the wand itself.

Rastafyre took it without comment and waved it over the cat, muttering something under his breath. After several minutes of obvious effort he looked up and extended it to Raclla. "Here you are, child."

Raella grabbed it out of his hand, clutched it to her chest, and rapidly retreated several steps.

"What do you say?" Eirthe prompted her.

"Thank you." It was a sulky mumble, but at least the words were correct.

"Would you please stir the soup so that it doesn't scorch?" Eirthe asked her.

"Wait," Rastafyre said suddenly. "Co-come here, child." Raella moved to stand before him, eyeing him warily.

"Lythande," Rastafyre said urgently. "You were right."

"About what?" Lythande asked.

"Other men's wives." Rastafyre held out the wand to Lythande. She reached for it with the silk, but Rastafyre dipped it so that it touched the back of her hand. It stuck there. "I gi-give you my wand, Lythande, and my magic, and," he took Raella's hand and placed it on the wand between himself and Lythande, "my daughter. May you be a better father to her than I was." His eyes closed and his body dropped to the ground, every remnant of life gone from it.

"He is *not* my father!" Raella said angrily. "He killed my father!"

"Stir the soup, please," Eirthe reminded her. "We'll be back soon, and the salamanders will watch over you."

She pulled a length of canvas out of the wagon, and wrapped Rastafyre's body in it. Lythande helped her secure the wrappings, and then lifted the body into her arms while Eirthe took two shovels from the wagon. Lythande waited until they were out of Raella's sight before shifting the body to hang over her shoulder for easier carrying. They moved far enough away from the stream so that they could bury the body without its contaminating the water.

"Would you care to tell me what's going on here?" Lythande asked. "Obviously your job offer was missing a few details."

"After supper," Eirthe sighed. "I'll give her a sleeping potion—she's had too many shocks to cope with in the last couple of days—and we can talk then."

Lythande nodded, and they finished burying Rastafyre's body in silence. Eirthe said a short prayer for the repose of his soul as they filled the grave. Lythande really couldn't think of anything to say that seemed appropriate.

The soup was a bit on the salty side; Lythande suspected a few extra tears had gone into the flavoring, but it was good to be able to eat without having to worry about another of her troublesome vows. In addition to keeping her sex a secret, she was also forbidden to eat or drink in the sight of any man. But Rastafyre was dead and buried, his child was a girl, and the salamanders were patrolling the surrounding area to make certain no bandits remained in this part of the forest.

Raella ate her soup, drank the herb tea Eirthe gave her, and went to bed in the wagon, sinking so deeply into sleep that Lythande suspected she would have slept even without the potion.

"All right, now," she said to Eirthe. "Let's have the whole story. Am I correct in thinking that Rastafyre was her natural father and that her mother is another man's wife?"

"That's the start of it," Eirthe said. "Rastafyre wanders—wandered through this area every three years or so, while I come here twice a year to sell candles. This year I met up with the Lord of Sathorn on the road as I came in. He was returning from a trip to court a day sooner than he was expected, and we passed a charcoal burner's hut, which should have been empty this time of year. There was smoke coming from the chimney, so the lord and his men went to check it out. Unfortunately, he had taken Raella to court with him, so she saw the whole mess."

"Rastafyre and his wife?"

"Yes, and with the number of men with him, he couldn't ignore the situation. His wife seemed to think he'd forgive her anything, but he said that he'd forgiven her when Raella was born and she had obviously failed to amend her behavior." Eirthe sighed. "He ran her through with his sword. It was quick, and I don't think he realized that Raella was right behind him. She screamed, he was distracted, and Rastafyre managed to knife him in the ribs. He returned the favor before he died, but Rastafyre had some sort spell set up. The men went to get carts for the bodies while I tried to get Raella calmed down, and while they were gone Rastafyre got up and—I think it must have been a *geas*—the next thing I knew I was traveling away with an animated corpse and a hysterical child with out-of-control magic. She'd met Rastafyre a few times—he gave her Ki-ki-kitty when she was two—but she had no idea that he was her father, or that the Lord of Sathorn wasn't. Apparently she adored him, and seeing him kill her mother and then be killed, followed by being forced to travel with his murderer..."

"Latent magic awakened by severe trauma."

"Now you know why I need you. And why she needs both of us."

"And a safe haven and a lot of training," Lythande added. "She'll get it."

"Did he put a *geas* on you as well?" Eirthe asked. "At the end?"

"More than a *geas*, I suspect," Lythande admitted. "Probably a full binding. And unbinding spells are not my specialty."

"Raella really needs you, binding or no."

"True enough. And I need sleep. Can you take the first watch?"

"The salamanders will wake us if need be," Eirthe yawned. "They haven't been carrying bodies and digging graves. And tomorrow's likely to bring still more problems."

They bedded down in the wagon, with Eirthe sharing one bunk with Raella while Lythande took the other one.

As her eyes opened the next morning Lythande realized what the next problem was. And even if she hadn't, Raella's first words would have been a clue. "I want to go home!" She rolled out of bed and eyed the adults defiantly.

"Of course," Lythande said promptly. "We'll take you home. How far is it?"

Eirthe sat up and stared at both of them as if she thought them deranged. "Half-a-day's travel, but we can't take her home! We have to take her to Northwander for training!"

Lythande frowned at her. "Is the *geas* that Rastafyre put on you still in effect?"

"What's a *geas*?" Raella asked.

"It's a spell that makes a person do something she doesn't want to do—like kidnapping you."

Eirthe looked at her in horror and sagged back against the wall, closing her eyes. Obviously this view of her actions had not occurred to her.

Raella looked at her curiously. "Didn't you mean to kidnap me?"

Eirthe shook her head. "I don't even remember much of anything from the time Rastafyre got up off the floor until we met Lythande yesterday."

Raella frowned. "I don't remember much either. Everything's all mixed up in my head."

"We'll stick to the simple version, then," Lythande said. "There was a fight, your parents were killed, and Rastafyre was mortally wounded. Before he died he put a spell on you and Eirthe and made her take him and you away in her wagon. He died of the wound your father gave him late yesterday, we buried his body, and now that you and Eirthe are free of his spell, we're taking you home. What family do you have left?"

"My brother and sister," Raella said.

"Is your brother of age?"

"He's twenty-two and Suella is nineteen. I guess he's my guardian now—if he still wants me." Raella's voice trailed off uncertainly.

Eirthe got up and hugged the child. "None of what happened is your fault."

Lythande nodded confirmation. "And in the unlikely event that your family doesn't want you, I'll take care of you."

Raella eyed her suspiciously. "Did he put a spell on you, too?"

Lythande shrugged. "He might have, at the end. Sometimes you don't notice a spell on you until it makes you do something you wouldn't normally do. I am sworn to uphold Law, and I protect the innocent, so I don't need a spell to make me do that." She decided a few words on Eirthe's behalf would be a good idea. "And Eirthe, of her own free will, would protect you from enemies and make sure you got the best magical training she could get you, so Rastafyre didn't have to work hard to get her to start to Northwander with you—all he had to do was get her to believe that you were in danger where you were."

"Did you believe that?" Raella looked up at Eirthe.

Eirthe nodded. "You actually *are* in danger; an untrained magician is a danger to herself and everyone around her. That's why I went to study at Northwander. I don't have nearly as much magic as you do, but I have enough that I almost got someone I cared about killed."

Raella looked wide-eyed at her. "You did?"

Lythande chuckled suddenly, remembering an incident in which she had come unpleasantly close to being sacrificed to a volcano—not that it had been amusing at the time. "She certainly did."

"Am I evil, the way *he* was?"

"No," Lythande said positively. "You are not evil."

"But you are rather grubby," Eirthe said calmly. "Let's go down to the stream and get cleaned up, and then we can take you home."

Once they got out of the forest and back onto the main road they soon met up with a party of Lord Sathorn's vassals, coming to attend his funeral and swear fealty to his son, so they entered the castle courtyard as part of a large party. Eirthe went off to park the wagon in its usual place, while Lythande took Raella by the hand and headed for the main hall. They had barely crossed the threshold when a beautiful dark-haired girl in a black velvet gown ran the length of the hall and grabbed Raella into a hug tight enough to make the child gasp for breath.

"You're safe," she sobbed. "We were so afraid when the men found you missing!" Raella started to cry as well.

Lythande pulled two handkerchiefs from under her robe and handed them to the girls. "Lady Suella," she said with a bow, "I am sorry for your loss."

Suella looked up uncertainly. "Thank you," she cast around for a polite form of address to one to whom she had not been formally introduced, then spotted the lute case hanging from Lythande's shoulder, "Lord Minstrel."

"He's not a minstrel; he's a magician," Raella said. "Like—is it true that Rastafyre was my father?" The last came out as a wail and several nearby heads turned in their direction.

"Let's continue this discussion in the solar," Suella said hastily, dragging Raella towards the stairs. Lythande followed.

"I was a minstrel before I was a magician," she said, making calm conversation for the sake of their audience. "Now I am both. I am called Lythande."

"I am honored to make your acquaintance," Suella said politely. "How did you meet my sister?"

Lythande's reply was cut off by their arrival in the solar and Suella's sending the maids off in search of water for a bath and clean clothing for Raella. Moments later the three of them were alone in the room, but the pounding of boots on the stairs heralded another arrival. There was barely a token tap on the door before a young man, tall, blond, and also garbed in black velvet, burst into the room. He knelt and grabbed Raella into a hug, and she promptly started sobbing again.

He glared up at Lythande. "What did you do to my sister?"

"I brought her home to you," Lythande said calmly.

"And he rescued me from the evil magician!" Raella added.

"Rastafyre?" Lord Sathorn asked.

"Theo?" Raella said. "He said he was my father? And Mother and Father—" her voice broke and she started crying again.

Lythande, figuring that tears would damage her clothing less than the formal velvet the other two wore, picked up Raella and let her sob into the shoulder of the mage robe.

Theo looked at Suella, who squared her shoulders. "Mother was buried quietly yesterday," she said. "There will be gossip about her, of course, but there always was. Father was our father by choice; only Theo is his natural child. My natural father was a traveling musician."

Raella raised tear-filled eyes and looked suspiciously at Lythande's face. Suella managed a shaky laugh. "No. If Lythande had been my father, mother would have named me Lyella. I don't believe I ever met my father; Mother told me that I got my musical talent from him, but that's all I know."

"You didn't get it from Father," Theo said. "He couldn't carry a tune if you gave him a bucket to put it in, and I'm no better."

"Father knew that Suella and I weren't really his daughters?" Raella asked uncertainly.

"We *are* really his daughters," Suella said firmly. "We're not his get, but we are his daughters and he loved us."

"Why did he kill Mother?"

Theo frowned. "Are you sure?"

Raella nodded, chewing on her bottom lip. "He said he forgave her when I was born, but she hadn't mended her behavior—and he stabbed her with his sword. Then Rastafyre stabbed him, and he stabbed Rastafyre, and—" she laid her head on Lythande's shoulder and sobbed. Lythande ran a hand over the child's hair and added a whisper of a calming spell.

"I think it may have been because his men were there to see," Theo said.

"And because she was still dallying with Rastafyre so many years after the first time," Suella added. "A casual affair, even if it produces a daughter, is one thing, but a relationship that goes on for years makes it appear that she loved him more than she did Father—though I don't see how she could have been such a fool!"

"She may not have been," Lythande said. "I encountered Rastafyre before, many years ago, and he seemed to consider," she paused to find the most delicate possible way of saying this, "satisfying his desires for other men's wives to be a legitimate use of his magic."

Suella glared. "I trust you don't agree with that."

"Not at all," Lythande said. "Love is worthless unless it is freely given, and no one should be deprived of their rightful choices by magic."

"He made Eirthe kidnap me, too," Raella added.

"Eirthe Candlemaker?" Suella and Theo both stared at her incredulously, and Theo added, "That must have been quite a spell; she's one of the most honorable people I know."

"At the time," Lythande pointed out, "Eirthe was holding a hysterical child who had just seen her parents murdered—and Eirthe had seen the same thing. She was distracted, her concentration was on caring for Raella, and Rastafyre simply built on that, convincing her to take Raella to the magical college at Northwander for training."

"Magical training?" Theo asked. "Does Raella have magic?"

"She used to," Suella said. "She used to move the candle flames around in the nursery until the maids slapped it out of her."

"That's not a long-term solution," Lythande said. "In the first half-hour of our acquaintance yesterday, she attacked me with a magical beast, threw a fire-ball at me, and hit me with a levin-bolt from Rastafyre's wand. Any control she had over her magic is gone now; she needs training."

"She's not doing magic now," Theo pointed out.

"I put a restraining spell on her right after the levin-bolt," Lythande said, "but that's a temporary solution. I promised Eirthe I'd escort them to Northwander; Eirthe's magic isn't strong enough to handle Raella."

"So why are you here, instead of on the road north?" Theo asked.

Lythande raised her brows. "I said I'd escort them to Northwander; I didn't say I'd do it with a child screaming to go home, while her kin—quite justly—pursued us for kidnapping. I'm also not minded to deliver her as a student to the college at Northwander with only the clothes she stands in after weeks on the road."

Suella nodded. "The men brought her baggage home. We can pack what she'll need for school."

Theo turned to Suella in astonishment. "Are you daft? We are not sending our little sister away! Her place is here, with us!"

"But she needs training..." Suella started to protest.

"She can go away to school when she's older. If we send her away now," Theo pointed out, "especially in front of all Father's—my—vassals, nobody will ever believe that we accept her as family. The gossip will be horrific. And I have problems enough already. The news from court isn't good—it seems I'll be calling our men up for the king's service within the year—and our people don't know and trust me the way they did Father."

"And Mother's continued affair with Rastafyre makes Father appear weak." Suella grimaced. "If you think the gossip among the *men* is bad, you should hear the women!"

"The women don't have to follow me into battle."

"Their husbands do," Suella pointed out, "and their fathers and their brothers."

"Do they listen to their women?" Theo asked.

Suella rolled her eyes. "You're listening to me right now."

Theo pinched the bridge of his nose as if his head ached. Lythande had no doubt that it did. He turned to look at his little sister. "Raella, do you understand what's happening here?"

Raella shook her head, looking unhappy.

Theo tried again. "Do you want to go to school at Northwander?"

Another headshake.

"Then you will have to be a good girl and not use magic. Can you do that?"

Raella nodded.

"Very well. Go with Suella and get cleaned up. You'll sit with us at dinner today and at the funeral tomorrow, and we won't say anything more about Rastafyre."

The girls left the room, and Lythande looked at Theo. "While I sympathize with your political problems and your desire to avoid scandal, this is not a solution. Raella may think she can control her magic, but I assure you that she can't."

"How long will your restraining spell hold?"

"Probably through dinner, but definitely not through the night."

"Can you—I don't know—renew it? Without anyone's noticing?"

"After a fashion, I can. The problem is that it's a simple spell, and she's both strong and very upset. The spell will become less and less effective, even if I keep recasting it—and I suspect she'll figure out how to nullify it entirely within a week."

"I thought you said she needed training—how can she nullify a spell if she doesn't know how to cast one?"

"The point of training is to give her *control*, not power. She already has power, and magic isn't just chanting spells and making gestures. Power can be raised by any strong emotion. She doesn't need to understand the spell; all she needs is to be unhappy enough to lash out at the world around her or anyone standing in front of her." Lythande meet Lord Theo's eyes squarely. "In her current state, she is capable of killing—probably not deliberately, but the corpse would be no less dead for that."

Theo sighed. "Can you at least keep her under control for a few days? I really *cannot* send her away immediately."

Lythande bowed. "I shall do my best. I think it will be better, however, if your guests think me merely a minstrel."

Theo shook his head in bewilderment, a perfect portrait of a man who has sustained too many shocks in too short a period of time. "Whatever you wish."

Lythande sat unobtrusively in a corner near the hearth during dinner and played calm, soothing music on her lute. The night before a funeral was no time for dance music, and under the circumstances most of her vocal repertoire would not do at all. She put a subtle spell in the music, just enough to keep quarrels from starting and to make everyone seek their beds at an early hour.

As soon as the trestles were laid away from the great hall and the pallets laid down for sleeping, Lythande left Raella in Suella's care. While they went to sleep in the solar, Lythande went to Eirthe's wagon.

"Here," Eirthe shoved a bowl of stew into Lythande's hands as she tied the wagon's shutters firmly into place. "You must be starved after all those hours in the hall."

"You're a good friend, Eirthe," Lythande remarked, sitting on the bunk she had slept on the previous night and spooning in the stew. "And you even kept it warm, bless you."

"Not hard to do when you've got a handful of salamanders around," Eirthe pointed out.

"Speaking of salamanders, can you set a few of them to watch Raella tonight? I can hardly stay in the bower with her."

"Already done." Eirthe and Lythande had worked together before. "One's in the flame on the night candle and a couple are in the fire in the solar. Alnath will let me know if anything happens."

"Something probably will," Lythande said resignedly. "I warned Lord Sathorn that the restraining spell probably wouldn't last much past tonight—if that long, but he's afraid to let his vassals see him send her away."

"With luck," Eirthe said hopefully, "he'll be much more reasonable about it as soon as they've cleared his gates." She grinned wickedly. "Don't stifle the poor child *too* much."

Lythande handed back the empty stew bowl and raised an eyebrow. "Did you think I was planning to?"

Eirthe refilled the bowl and passed it back. "Eat some more and then get some sleep. You're going to need it."

Lythande slept, but not well. She strongly suspected that nobody in the neighborhood was sleeping well that night. The wind whirled around the walls, making a sound somewhere between whistling and shrieking, apparently searching for a way in. Even inside Eirthe's snug little wagon, Lythande would not have been surprised to see spectral fingers with long claws digging their way inside, and she suspected that for the ladies sleeping in the tower the noise was even more unnerving. And then the rain started.

By the time she and Eirthe got up the next morning, reheated and ate the remaining stew, and prepared to go to the great hall, the rain wasn't just falling, but whipping in every direction, carried by the winds. Lythande tucked both Eirthe and the lute under her mage robe for the dash to the hall.

Suella met them inside, with Raella tucked protectively at her side. "Can you do *anything* about this weather?" she whispered. In spite of the black velvet and a large black shawl tucked over both of them, she was shivering, and Raella looked stiff and frozen.

"It's really something, isn't it?" Eirthe agreed. "Do we have to go outside for the funeral?"

"No, thank all the gods," Suella replied. "The chapel's attached to the main tower, and the crypt is under it."

Lythande sketched a bow to the ladies which put her face close enough to Raella's to whisper. "How are you feeling this morning?"

"I had nightmares," the child whispered back, "and I don't like having all these people here. They keep staring at me."

"As long as it stays stormy like this, they're stuck here," Lythande pointed out quietly. "But if the weather clears and the roads are dry enough, they could start leaving late today or early tomorrow—as soon as the funeral and the oath-taking are over."

Raella blinked at her. "Oh."

Lythande said nothing more as they moved to join the ladies around one of the fireplaces, though she did expend just a bit of power to make sure that the fires burned cleanly, undisturbed by the turbulent winds.

The funeral was somber and dignified, and the priest took as his theme for the homily the brevity and uncertainty of life, rather than referring to any particulars of the life or death of the deceased, which Lythande considered a wise choice under the circumstances. Raella clung to her sister throughout the service and the interment, but never made a sound, although tears dripped down her face. But Suella was also crying silently, so it would be hard to fault the child for that.

When they returned to the hall after the service, Lythande noticed that the howling winds had stopped. Eirthe, who had also noticed, communed briefly with Alnath and then remarked softly, "The rain's changed to light drizzle, falling straight down. What did you do?"

"About the weather?" Lythande murmured softly. "I pointed out to Raella that as long as the storm continues all the people she complained were staring at her are stuck here."

Eirthe quickly turned her chuckle into a cough. "Better than having to fix the weather yourself, fighting her all the way."

"I certainly thought so," Lythande agreed blandly, as they took places at the side of the hall where they would be out of the way but still be able to see and hear.

The ceremony began with the reading of the late Lord Sathorn's will by the priest.

"To Theo, firstborn son of my body—"

"—born exactly nine months after the wedding night, and at least she was a virgin before *that*," one of the servants near Lythande muttered.

"... I leave my entire estate, with the following exceptions..." the priest continued to read. The list that followed included bequests to various servants and household officials, along with respectable dowries for "my daughters Suella and Raella, provided that their marriages be in accordance with his prior approval." Theo was also named guardian of both girls. If one didn't know differently, Lythande reflected, there was nothing in the will to suggest that Lord Sathorn had any doubt of the girls paternity. *Well, apparently he didn't have any doubt. He simply chose not to hold it against them.*

There was some quiet muttering about the size of the girls' dowries when the reading ended. "Good thing he put in the part about Theo's having to approve their marriages beforehand," Eirthe said. "Cuts down on the temptation to kidnap and marry by force."

"He seems to have been a remarkable man," Lythande remarked. "I'm sorry I never got to meet him."

"You've met Theo," Eirthe pointed out. "They're a lot alike."

The priest then formally presented Theo to the assembly and asked if anyone challenged his right to inherit. After a few seconds of dead silence—apparently nobody doubted *his* paternity—Theo sat in a chair on the dais to receive the oaths. As he sat down, the sun suddenly shone through one of the small windows high on the wall behind his right shoulder, making a golden halo of his blond hair.

Each vassal came forward in turn to kneel before him, place their palms between his, repeat the oath of fealty and receive Theo's oath of protection and justice in return. Suella and Raella stood quietly behind and to the left of their brother and looked solemn. Lythande thought it well-nigh miraculous that Raella didn't fidget during the long ceremony.

She has strength, and she has enough control of her body to get through this ceremony at her age—she's probably going to be quite a good mage when she's trained.

Finally it was over, and people cleared the hall long enough for the tables to be set up for the funeral feast. During this interlude, quite a few people made their way outside and returned to comment on the wondrous improvement in the weather. Even in the corner where she was quietly playing her lute, Lythande overheard several people making plans to leave as soon as the feast was over.

After the feast, while Theo and Suella bade farewell to the departing guests, Lythande and Eirthe took Raella for a walk in the kitchen garden.

"That was a very nice touch with the sunbeam during the oath-taking," Eirthe remarked. "Did you do that on purpose, Raella?"

The girl looked startled, then frowned. "No," she said slowly, "I don't think so. I was wishing it would be sunny so that the roads would dry and they'd all go away... and I was thinking that Theo's really a terrific brother... and it just happened."

"Well, it looked good, whether you did it on purpose or not," Eirthe said consolingly.

"Could *you* have done it on purpose?" Raella asked her.

"Certainly," Eirthe said. "It's not terribly difficult." She grinned at Lythande. "Stand over against that wall and put your hood down, would you, Lythande?"

Lythande placed herself as directed and watched calmly as Eirthe made a swooping motion, as if gathering a handful of sunlight, and tossed it at her head. She could feel the glow of the halo Eirthe had cast around her head as a pleasant warmth against the skin of her cheeks and scalp.

Unfortunately Raella tried to copy Eirthe, and Lythande barely had time to get her shields in place before the fireball hit. She dodged quickly away from the wall and pinned Raella's arms at her sides.

"I'm sorry," Raella said quickly. "I didn't mean to hurt you."

"You didn't hurt me," Lythande said dryly, "but you didn't do the wall any good, and you really frightened Eirthe." She frowned at her friend. "Eirthe, breathe—preferably before you pass out!"

Eirthe, still staring in horror at the charred spot on the wall where Lythande's head had been, sat down rather quickly on one of the low stone walls that separated the herb beds from the path.

"However," Lythande continued, looking Raella straight in the eyes, "if you had done what you just did to anyone here *but* me—to Eirthe, or to Theo or Suella—that person would be either dead, or horribly burned and scarred for the rest of his or her life."

"But Eirthe has magic!" Raella protested.

"I'm not as strong as Lythande," Eirthe said shakily, "or as fast, and my shields aren't nearly as good. I'd have been badly burned at the very least."

"And Theo and Suella don't have magic at all," Raella said, her lip beginning to quiver. "I could kill somebody by mistake, the way Eirthe almost did, couldn't I?" She started to cry. "I don't want anybody else to die!"

"Of course you don't." Eirthe's color was coming back and her voice had stopped shaking. "That's what the college in Northwander is for. They can teach you not to hurt anyone by mistake. That's why I went there."

"Did you go there, too?" Raella asked Lythande.

Lythande shook her head. "I'm a lot older than I look, child. I learned magic in a faraway land before the school at Northwander was built. But I think it would be a very good place for you to go." Raella didn't reply, but she was obviously giving the matter serious thought.

"Right now, with your permission," *or without it, if necessary*, "I'm going to put a spell on you that will stop you from doing magic for a day or two."

Raella looked down at the grip Lythande still maintained on her arms and nodded. "Please," she said. "I don't want to hurt anybody."

Lythande released her and Raella stood absolutely motionless until the spell was finished. Then she looked at them. "Will you please tell my brother he has to send me to that school?"

Lythande said, "You're going to have to tell him that you want to go. The last time he asked you, you said you didn't."

Raella nodded. "All right. I'll tell him. But will you help me explain why it's important?"

"Of course we will," Eirthe said, standing up and moving to put and arm around Raella's shoulders. "But let's wait until tomorrow after the guests leave, all right?"

"All right," Raella said.

In the end it was two more days before the last of the vassals left and they could talk to Theo. Lythande sat in the solar with Eirthe, Raella, Theo, and Suella and explained, again, why it was important that Raella be properly trained immediately. Raella poured out a semi-coherent account of how she didn't want to kill anyone—the way she almost had in the garden the other day, and Eirthe gave a much more coherent account of what had happened.

"I wondered where those burn marks on the wall came from," Suella said. "Theo, if you have any doubts that they're right about Raella, go and look! A couple of the stones even melted together."

"She has enough power to melt stones?" Theo asked incredulously.

"I didn't mean to," Raella said timidly.

"Lots of power, very little control," Lythande said. "She did hit the area she was aiming at—my head!"

"And that would have killed anybody but a really powerful wizard," Raella said quickly, stumbling over the words. "So I want to go to that school where they won't let me hurt anyone and can teach me how to control my magic." She looked anxiously at Theo. "I know I said when I came home that I didn't want to go, but I was wrong." She gulped. "I need to go, before I hurt you or Suella or anyone else."

Theo looked gravely at her. "Are you absolutely sure?"

Raella nodded. So did Eirthe and Lythande.

Theo frowned. "I don't want to send you away, little sister, but if it's that important, you can go." He turned to Lythande. "What about school fees?"

"The school would teach her for nothing if they had to; an untrained mage is too dangerous to everyone. But I intend to give Rastafyre's wand to the school to be studied; they'll train her in exchange for that. He gave it to me as he died, and I can think of no better use for it." *Except as kindling, and that's too dangerous.*

Theo sighed. "Very well. I consent to your taking her to Northwander for training, but I want her to come home for any school holidays and after her training is done."

"Home?" Raella lifted her head and looked at him through her tears.

"Home," Theo repeated firmly. "This is your home and you are my sister. Nothing changes that."

Raella hugged him tightly around the waist. "Thank you, Theo? Can I travel with Eirthe? Can she help me pack?"

"We'll both help you pack," Suella said, taking Raella's hand. Eirthe followed them towards the next room.

Just as they reached the door, however, Suella turned her head back. "Lord Lythande?" she asked. "I'll be playing my lute after dinner today. Could I persuade you to join me?"

Lythande bowed. "I would be honored, Lady Suella."

As she accompanied Lord Theo down the stairs to the hall, Lythande asked, "How good a musician is she?" *I wouldn't want to outshine her too much.*

"She's very good," Theo said. "It appears that both my sisters prove the old saying: 'The children of cats can catch mice.'"

AFTERWORD
Elisabeth Waters

Lythande's development began on June 3, 1930, a few seconds after the birth of Marion Eleanor Zimmer, when Marion's mother discovered—to her horror and astonishment—that she had given birth to a daughter instead of the son she had expected and wanted. Evelyn Zimmer spent a large part of Marion's childhood telling her that boys were more important than girls. Marion spent her life proving her mother wrong.

Lythande is both musician and magician. The musician was influenced by the aunt for whom Marion was named, a composer, and by Aunt Marion's husband, first a church organist and later an Episcopal priest. Marion lived with them for a time during her teens. She was baptized in the Episcopal Church then, at the age of fifteen, strengthening both her love of Church music and her familiarity with ritual magic. (Anyone who thinks Christians don't use ritual magic should spend some time with High-Church Anglicans.)

Another musical influence was the Metropolitan Opera. As a young girl Marion made sure to do the family ironing at two o'clock on Saturday afternoons, when "Live from the Met" broadcast that week's opera. In addition to her life-long appreciation for music, it also gave her some skill in foreign languages, although she admitted that her German was better suited to asking if there was a dragon in the vicinity or when the next swan boat was expected than mundane questions such as "where is the train station?"

Opera also helped train the magician. Dragons and enchanted swan boats may not help you with everyday travel in Germany, but they do stretch your mind, introduce you to the strange and fantastic (and to the rules that limit even the most powerful types of magic), and accustom you to being in a different world every week.

Marion wrote the first Lythande story for a shared-world anthology called THIEVES' WORLD. (It's a true challenge to write a story without revealing the gender of the main character. Marion left the manuscript with me to be sent in—she was staying at my parents' house on her way to England—and I found two places where I needed to change pronouns into nouns before I mailed it.) Unfortunately, neither Marion nor Lythande found that world to be a particularly congenial place, so Lythande left, never to return. (Given the nature of a shared world, other authors could include Lythande in their stories, but Marion never wrote another story set there.) By the time she wrote the second Lythande story ("The Incompetent Magician") for her anthology GREYHAVEN in 1982, Lythande had moved to the city of Old Gandrin, on a world called "the world of the Twin Suns." She remained there for the next two stories ("Somebody Else's Magic" and "Sea Wrack"), which were published in *The Magazine of Fantasy and Science Fiction*. Then she started to jump worlds again.

I had written a story for the first volume of another shared-world anthology: MAGIC IN ITHKAR, edited by Andre Norton, and published in 1985. I was working as Marion's secretary at the time, so she heard all about it. Marion was interested in doing a story for that world, so she wrote "The Wandering Lute" using my character Eirthe the candle maker at the beginning of the story. The story immediately moved away from the trade fair where it started, and Andre rejected it on the grounds that it wasn't set firmly enough in Ithkar. Given that a global search and replace to change "Ithkar" to "Old Gandrin" was all it took to make it a non-Ithkar story, nobody disputes that Andre was absolutely right. But when Marion's agent sold the story to *Fantasy & Science Fiction*, somehow the wrong version got printed, so Lythande was—very briefly, and after a fashion—on Ithkar.

Marion continued to write Lythande stories for various projects, and she even let me use Lythande, along with my character Eirthe from the Ithkar anthology, for my story "Out of the Frying Pan" in SWORD & SORCERESS in 1991. That story was, of course, from Eirthe's viewpoint. Lythande's version of it appears in this volume as "The Virgin and the Volcano."

"The Gratitude of Kings"—a Lythande novella—was first published by Roc as a Christmas gift book in 1997, and went on to be reprinted in France, Germany, Italy, and Portugal.

At the time of her death in 1999, Marion was working on "The Children of Cats," having coined a proverb "The children of cats can catch mice." The "cat" in question was the magician from her second story, thus bringing the cycle pretty much full circle.

For all of Marion's accomplishments, however, she and Lythande had one thing in common. Both of them started their careers with people believing they were men. Unlike Lythande, who *had* to be male in order to get what she most wanted in life, Marion didn't deliberately set out to hide her gender. But she had a the masculine spelling of her first name, she was active in the science-fiction community, and she typed her correspondence, so there was no handwriting to give clues. She lived in small towns, first in upstate New York and then in Texas, so she didn't meet other fans and professionals in person before she started attending conventions.

She said frequently in later years that she never met an editor who cared if she was male, female, or a monkey hitting the keyboard as long as she produced saleable stories. While this is probably correct (although it might be difficult to get a Social Security Number for a monkey), I think it's possible that her earliest sales may have been made to editors who truly didn't know she was female. Also, at the time she started selling, female authors had names like Leigh Brackett, and C.L. Moore (and few people knew that C.L. stood for Catherine Lucille). Women could write science fiction, but they couldn't have it published under an obviously female name. That, fortunately, is one of the many things that changed during Marion's lifetime. It's also one of the things she was proud to have helped to change.

ORIGINAL PUBLICATION

The Secret of the Blue Star, THIEVES' WORLD, 1979
The Incompetent Magician, GREYHAVEN, 1983
Somebody Else's Magic, *Fantasy & Science Fiction*, 1984
Sea Wrack, MOONSINGERS'S FRIENDS, 1985
The Wandering Lute, *Fantasy & Science Fiction*, 1986
Bitch, *Fantasy & Science Fiction*, 1987
The Walker Behind, *Fantasy & Science Fiction*, 1987
The Malice of the Demon, *Fantasy & Science Fiction*, 1988
The Footsteps of Retribution, *MZB's FANTASY Magazine # 11*, 1991
The Wuzzles, *MZB's FANTASY Magazine # 14*, 1991
The Virgin and the Volcano, SWORD & SORCERESS VIII, 1991 (rewritten)
Chalice of Tears, GRAILS, 1992
To Kill the Undead, *MZB's FANTASY Magazine # 23*, 1994
To Drive the Cold Winter Away, SPACE OPERA, 1995
Fool's Fire, *MZB's FANTASY Magazine # 26*, 1995
Here There Be Dragons, EXCALIBUR, 1995
North to Northwander, *MZB's FANTASY Magazine # 36*, 1997
Goblin Market, *MZB's FANTASY Magazine # 44*, 1999
The Gratitude of Kings, Wildside Press, 1997
The Children of Cats, not previously published

ABOUT THE AUTHOR

Marion Zimmer was born in Albany, New York, on June 3, 1930, and married Robert Alden Bradley in 1949. Mrs. Bradley received her B.A. in 1964 from Hardin Simmons University in Abilene, Texas, then did graduate work at the University of California, Berkeley, from 1965-1967.

She was a science fiction/fantasy fan from her teens and made her first professional sale to *Vortex Science Fiction* in 1952. She wrote everything from science fiction to Gothics, but is probably best known for her Darkover novels. In addition to her novels, Mrs. Bradley edited many magazines, amateur and professional, including *Marion Zimmer Bradley's FANTASY Magazine*, which she started in 1988. She also edited an annual anthology called SWORD AND SORCERESS for DAW Books.

Over the years she turned more to fantasy. She wrote a novel of the women in the Arthurian legends—Morgan Le Fay, the Lady of the Lake, and others—entitled THE MISTS OF AVALON, which made the *New York Times* bestseller list both in hardcover and trade paperback, and she also wrote THE FIREBRAND, a novel about the women of the Trojan War.

She died in Berkeley, California on September 25, 1999, four days after suffering a major heart attack. For more information, see her website: www.mzbworks.com.

CPSIA information can be obtained
at www.ICGtesting.com
Printed in the USA
LVOW04s1630250416

485219LV00021B/997/P